THOSE *Scandalous* RAVENHURSTS

VOLUME 3

2 2 4 20

THOSE *Scandalous* RAVENHURSTS
COLLECTION

February 2016

May 2016

March 2017

THOSE *Scandalous* RAVENHURSTS

— VOLUME 3 —

LOUISE ALLEN

Published in Great Britain 2017
By Mills & Boon, an imprint of HarperCollins*Publishers*
1 London Bridge Street, London, SE1 9GF

THOSE SCANDALOUS RAVENHURSTS VOLUME THREE
© 2017 Harlequin Books S.A.

The Notorious Mr Hurst © 2000 Melanie Hilton
Disrobed and Dishonored © 2009 Melanie Hilton
The Piratical Miss Ravenhurst © 2009 Melanie Hilton

ISBN: 978-0-263-92794-8

09-0317

Printed and bound
by CPI Group (UK) Ltd, Croydon, CRO 4YY

THE NOTORIOUS MR HURST

LOUISE ALLEN

Louise Allen loves immersing herself in history. She finds landscapes and places evoke the past powerfully. Venice, Burgundy and the Greek islands are favourite destinations. Louise lives on the Norfolk coast and spends her spare time gardening, researching family history or travelling in search of inspiration. Visit her at louiseallenregency.co.uk, @LouiseRegency and janeaustenslondon.com

Author Note

Lady Maude Templeton believes in love, as I discovered during the course of THE SHOCKING LORD STANDON, when she refused to marry the hero on the grounds that she just knew the right man was out there waiting for her somewhere.

And then she found him and fell in love instantly with Mr Eden Hurst, who is not only resoundingly ineligible for the daughter of an earl, but as a man who most definitely does not believe in love.

Maude sets out to convince Eden not only that love exists but that she is the woman he needs in his life. It seems a hopeless task, but Maude can be quite as shocking as any of her Ravenhurst friends when she puts her mind to it and Eden Hurst soon finds that doing the right thing is harder than he can ever have imagined. If only he can work out what the right thing is. . .

Chapter One

February 1817

'And so, my false love—I die!' The maiden sank to the ground, a dagger in her bosom, her white arm outflung.

The audience went wild. They applauded, whistled, stamped and, those members of it who were not weeping into their handkerchiefs, leapt to their feet with cries of 'More! More!'

The dark-haired lady in the expensive box close to the stage gripped the velvet-upholstered rim and held her breath. For the audience who had flocked to see the final performance of *The Sicilian Seducer, or Innocence Betrayed*, the tension was over and they could relax into their appreciation of the melodrama. For Lady Maude Templeton, the climax of the evening was about to occur and, she was determined, it would change her life for ever.

'You would never guess it, but she must be forty if she's a day,' Lady Standon remarked, lowering her opera glass from a careful study of the corpse who was just being helped to her feet by her leading man.

'One is given to understand that La Belle Marguerite never

mentions anything so sordid as age, Jessica.' Her husband turned from making an observation to Lord Pangbourne.

'Fine figure of a woman,' the earl grunted. He was still applauding enthusiastically. 'Not surprising that she was such a sensation on the Continent.'

'And so much of that figure on display,' Jessica murmured to Maude, who broke her concentration on the shadowy wings long enough to smile at her friend's sly remark. The loss of focus lasted only a moment. Tonight was the night, she knew it. With the excitement that surrounded a last night at the Unicorn she had her best opportunity to slip backstage. And once she was there, to make what she could of the situation.

Then her breath caught in her throat and her heart beat harder, just as it always did when she glimpsed him. Eden Hurst, proprietor of the Unicorn theatre, strode on to the stage and held up both hands for silence. And by some miracle—or sheer charisma—he got it, the tumult subsiding enough that his powerful voice could be heard.

'My lords, ladies, gentlemen. We thank you. On behalf of Madame Marguerite and the Company of the Unicorn, I thank you. Tonight was the last performance of *The Sicilian Seducer* for this, our first full Season.' He paused while exaggerated groans and shouts of 'shame!' resounded through the stalls and up into the gods. 'But we are already looking forward to *Her Precious Honour* to open in six weeks' time and I can assure her many admirers that Madame Marguerite will take the leading role in this dramatic tale of love triumphant over adversity. Good night to you all and I hope to welcome you next week for our revival of that old favourite, *How to Tease and How to Please*, with the celebrated Mrs Furlow in the leading role.'

'Damn good comedy that,' Lord Pangbourne pronounced, getting to his feet. 'I recall it when it first came out. In '09, was it? Or the year after?'

Maude did not hear her father. Down below in the glare of the new gas lights stood the man she desired, the man she knew she could love, the man she had wanted ever since she had first seen him a year before.

Since then she had existed on the glimpses she had caught of him. In his theatre she sat imprisoned, in a box so close she could have almost reached down and touched him. On the rare occasions he had attended a social function where she had been present he had been frustratingly aloof from the unmarried ladies, disappearing into the card rooms to talk to male acquaintances or flirting with the fast young widows and matrons. And even she, bold as she was, could not hunt down a man to whom she had not been introduced and accost him. Not in the midst of a society ball and not a man of shady origins who had arrived in England trailing a tantalising reputation for ruthless business dealing and shocking *amours*.

And last Season he had closed the Unicorn for renovations and returned to the Continent for a tour with his leading lady only months after they had arrived in England.

Standing there, he dominated the stage by sheer presence. Tall, broad-shouldered, with an intense masculine elegance in his dark coat and tight pantaloons, yet somehow flamboyant and dramatic. Maude caught the sharp glitter of diamonds at his throat and from the heavy ring on his left hand and recognised that his clothes had been cut with an edge of exaggeration that would be out of place in a polite drawing room. He was a showman, demanding and receiving attention just as much as the most histrionic actor.

'Maude.' Jessica nudged her. 'One of these evenings your papa is going to notice that you dream through the performances and only wake up when Mr Hurst is on stage.'

'I don't dream,' she contradicted, finally getting to her feet as Eden Hurst walked off stage to loud applause. 'I am watching and I am listening. I have to learn how this place works.'

She had never managed to speak to him. The only words he had spoken in her presence had been to a shopkeeper while she, the bright, lively, witty Lady Maude had stood in Mr Todmorton's perfume shop, struck dumb by the sheer beauty of the man. But three days ago, thanks to an overheard conversation at Lady Robert's otherwise dull reception, she had discovered that Mr Hurst had been making discreet approaches to potential investors. And that, she realised, gave her the perfect excuse.

Now she must have her wits about her as she followed her father and the Standons down to the main lobby of the Unicorn. Parties were gathering and chattering beneath the famous clock that hung from the neck of the one-horned beast charging out of the wall like a ship's figurehead. As she had hoped, Jessica stopped to speak to a friend. Gareth, her husband, waited patiently beside her while Maude slid through the crowd to her father's side.

'Papa, Jessica invited me to drive home with her and to spend the night,' she said as he clicked his fingers at the attendant for their cloaks. It was quite true, Jessica had done just that and Maude had thanked her nicely and explained that she thought her papa would expect her home tonight.

Which was also true, so very gratifyingly she had told no actual untruths. And she was, after all, a lady of resource with money in her reticule who was perfectly capable of finding herself a hackney carriage. Eventually.

'Very well, my dear.' Lord Pangbourne craned to see the Standons in the crush. 'I'll see you at dinner tomorrow. Say all that is right to Lady Standon for me, won't you? I can't fight my way through this like you slender young things.'

'Yes, Papa.' Maude watched until he was outside and then slipped through the door to one side of the entrance. She was not certain where it went, other than backstage. But that was enough for her purposes.

'Can I help you, miss?' She was in a passageway, as brown and dingy as the lobby was brilliant and gilded. Maude dragged in a deep breath compounded of oil and dust, gas fumes, overcrowded hot people and greasepaint, and smiled brilliantly at the youth who had paused in front of her. His arms were full of hothouse flowers, an incongruous contrast to his shirtsleeves and baize apron.

'Mr Hurst's office, if you please.'

'The Guv'nor, miss?'

'Yes,' Maude said firmly. 'The Guv'nor. I have a proposition for him.'

Eden Hurst tugged his neckcloth loose from amidst the heavy ruffles of his shirt, flung himself into his great carved chair and put his feet up on his desk. Ten minutes of peace and quiet, he promised himself. Then back down the corridor to Madame's room to flatter and reassure in the midst of enough blooms to fill a conservatory.

Why she needed reassurance after a reception like tonight, Heaven only knew, but he had sensed a petulance that must be soothed. Ever since she had reluctantly agreed to return to England after years on the Continent she had been on edge, more demanding, more insecure, and the return tour while the renovations were carried out had only made things worse.

Perhaps the light of the new gas lamps was unkind when her dresser finally creamed away the greasepaint. He would have the oil lamps on their stands brought back into her dressing room. Anything to keep the star of the Unicorn happy.

Feet still on the desk, he leaned forward and reached for his notebook to add *oil lamps* to the never-ending list of things to be done. His groping fingers nudged a pile of stiff cards, sending them to the floor. They lay face up, yesterday's social obligations.

Eden dropped his head back and stared at the ceiling, oblivious to the cracks that created fantasy maps over its grey surface. Was it worth it, allowing himself to be lionised by Corwin and his vulgar wife? He shut his eyes, annoyed with himself for revisiting a decision that had already been made. He needed an investor if he was to continue to make the improvements the Unicorn needed to keep it in the forefront of London's smaller theatres, and he needed a damned sight more cash than the gas lights had cost him if he were to finally persuade the owner to sell it to him.

Through his agents he had bought several small theatres around the country over the past two years as investments, leaving them in the hands of managers while he continued to tour Europe with Madame. Then had come word of the kind of theatre he had been dreaming of ever since he had stepped on to a stage, and he sold them all to raise the money to restore the Unicorn. It had meant coming to England and it had meant risking everything on a building that was not his own, but Eden Hurst had learned to trust his gut instincts in business and was prepared to be ruthless with himself, and with Madame, if necessary.

He could stomach Corwin, even Mrs Corwin in her purple toque, at a pinch. What was tightening his gut was the thought of the simpering Misses Corwin: Miss Calliope, Miss Calenthe and Miss Coraline. One of them was the price Corwin was going to ask for his investment, Eden was sure. He'd marry a Corwin daughter over his dead body and he'd been certain of managing the thing tactfully in the end. Certain— until he'd heard the girls giggling and plotting together in the overheated conservatory.

No time to think about that now. He lowered his feet back to the threadbare Turkey carpet, twitched his neckcloth into order and ran his hands through his over-long hair. Outside his office the corridor was deserted, with all the noise and the activity coming from the stage where they were striking the sets in one direction, and the Green Room where the actors were entertaining their friends and admirers in the other.

Eden took a deep breath and stopped. Gardenia was not a familiar scent in the utilitarian passage outside his office door. Nor was the rustle of silk skirts from the shadows expected. As he realised it, he saw her, an indistinct form in the alcove opposite. Young, slender—he could tell that from the way she moved, the glimpse of white skin at neck and breast.

Those accursed girls. He had thought himself safe for a day or two while they perfected their scheme to ensure that one of them was comprehensively compromised by him. But, no, here was the first of them, it was irrelevant which. If he pretended not to have seen her and went to the Green Room, she would be into his office, probably prepared to strip off for maximum effect when he returned, with or without a witness. And he was damned if he was going to stand here and shout for help in his own theatre, which seemed the only other option.

Or was it? Perhaps he could scare the living daylights out of her. Eden smiled grimly, took a long step forward and caught the half-seen figure by the shoulders. She came easily, with a little gasp, like a maid into her lover's arms, he thought with habitual cynicism, just before he took her mouth. Hard.

She had been kissed before. At the age of twenty-five, and after several Seasons energetically avoiding becoming betrothed, Maude had flirted with sufficient young gentlemen and had dallied in enough drawing rooms to have experienced everything from gauche wet ineptitude, to boldly snatched kisses, to shyly gentle caresses.

But she had never been kissed by a man who knew what

he was doing and had no inhibitions about doing it thoroughly. How he managed it she had no idea, but one minute she was hiding in a dark alcove, poised to step forward and introduce herself, and the next she was moulded against the long hard body of a male who was quite frankly and obviously aroused, whose lips were crushed to hers and whose tongue was taking full possession of her mouth.

For a moment she froze, passive with shock in his grip. Then her mind began to work and caught up with her body, already pliant in his arms. It was Eden Hurst who was kissing her. She had dreamt of this for months and now it was happening. Hazily she acknowledged that he had no clue who she was and that he also appeared to be thoroughly out of temper, but just now that did not matter.

Maude found her fingers were laced in his hair, that romantic mane of black that gave him such an exotic appearance. Her breasts were pressed to his chest so that the swell of her bosom was chaffed by the brocade weave of his waistcoat and against hers his heart was beating, disconcertingly out of stroke with her pulse. But she was only peripherally aware of those tantalising discomforts. Her entire world was focused on what he was doing to her mouth and the devilish skill with which he was doing it.

Should a kiss make the soft flesh of her inner thighs quiver and ache? Should the insolent thrust of his tongue send shafts of desire deep into her belly, setting going an intimate pulse that made her want to twine her legs around his and press herself hard against him?

He growled, a warning she did not heed, was incapable of taking, then his hands slid to cup her buttocks and he pulled her up against him so that the ridge of his erection pressed into the delta of her thighs. Now she knew what her body was searching for. Roughly he pushed her back to the hard wall, letting the movement rock them intimately until she was moaning in total surrender against his mouth.

And then, just when she would have gone to the floor with him, done anything if only his mouth had stayed on hers, he released her, all but one hand, and stepped back. He reached behind him to fling open the office door and the light spilled out across her face when he tugged her into its path.

'Now let that be a lesson—hell and damnation,' Eden Hurst said quietly, loosing her wrist. 'You aren't one of the Corwin girls.'

'No, I am not.' *Thank God, I can still articulate.* She reached out one hand to the wall beside her, unsure whether her legs would be as obedient as her voice. 'I am Lady Maude Templeton, Mr Hurst.'

'Then why the hell did you let me kiss you?' he demanded with what she could only characterise as a total lack of reasonableness.

'One, you took me by surprise; two, you are somewhat stronger than I am; three, you are very good at it,' she said coolly. This was not the moment to cast herself into his arms and declare her undying love. Besotted she might be, but she had her pride. One of these days he was going to tell her he loved her, but he needed to find that out for himself.

'Well, I thank you for that last,' he said on a disconcerting choke of laughter. 'You are not inclined to slap my face?'

Maude very much doubted that her legs would allow her to take the two steps necessary to achieve that. 'No, I do not think so.' It was so long since she had been close to him that now it did not seem there was enough air to breathe. Or else that kiss had dragged the air from her lungs. 'Perhaps I should explain why I am here?'

'You want a job, my lady? I need a costume mistress and a scene painter. Oh, yes, and a couple of handmaidens for the farce.'

He kept his face so straight that she could not decide whether he was totally literal or had a nasty sense of humour. 'I doubt whether I would be suitable for any of those positions,' she responded, deliberately matching his tone. 'My sewing is poor, my painting worse and I would make a thoroughly heedless handmaiden. I have come to congratulate Madame Marguerite on her performance and to broach a matter of business with you, sir.'

'Business?' He studied her, expressionless. Maude was used to male admiration; this indifference piqued her, not unpleasantly. Her Mr Hurst was not in the common run of men. 'Well, shall we start with Madame and then we can agree a more suitable time for a meeting tomorrow?'

Maude would have thought him quite unmoved by what had just happened if it were not for the tension that seemed to flow from him, fretting her aroused nerves as though he had dragged a fingernail along her skin.

'You are without an escort, Lady Maude?'

'Yes,' she said, daring him with her eyes to make something of it. 'Perhaps you would be good enough to find me a cab later, Mr Hurst?'

'You are a practical woman it would appear, ma'am. And one with strong nerves as well as—' He broke off. Maude turned her head to follow his gaze. From the direction she had come there were soft footsteps and the sound of nervous giggling. 'Hell.' He caught her hand again and pulled her into the office, closing the door behind them.

'Mr Hurst, I declare you appear quite hunted.' Now she could see him clearly. The golden skin that always seemed lightly tanned, the dark brown eyes, the sensuous, sensual, mouth and the elegant, straight nose. She had been correct— those were diamonds in the pin at his throat and one old-fashioned cabochon stone in the barbarically heavy ring on his hand. And as he turned to face her, she saw another glinting in the lobe of his right ear. It should have looked effeminate, but it simply gave him the air of a pirate and she guessed that was quite deliberate.

'Truer than you know, Lady Maude. Perhaps you would care to sit? I fear you are about to be the audience for a private performance of a farce.' He gestured to a chair on one side of the desk and went to take the other, a great carved monstrosity of a throne with eagles on the back and lions' heads on the arms

The door inched open. More giggles, muffled, then a girl came in, her head turned to speak to someone outside. 'Oh Calenthe, I am so nervous!'

'But why should you be, Miss Corwin?' Hurst enquired in a voice like sugar soaked in aloes. 'You are amongst friends here.'

The girl gave a shriek and dragged at the door to reveal her companion just behind it. Maude blinked at the sight of two thoroughly overdressed young women clinging together on the threshold.

'Lady Maude, may I introduce Miss Corwin and Miss Calenthe Corwin to your notice? Ladies, this is Lady Maude Templeton. I fear I cannot offer you refreshment as Lady Maude and I are discussing business.'

Maude, who was beginning to get some idea what was going on, enquired, 'No doubt your mama is waiting for you close by?' Their faces were so easy to read it was almost laughable. 'No? Well, in that case I will take you home in my hackney, for you most certainly should not be out alone at this hour. Perhaps you would be so kind as to obtain one, Mr Hurst. I am afraid I must forgo the meeting with Madame this evening, but I do feel that seeing these misguided young ladies safe home must take priority. Shall we say eleven tomorrow to continue our discussion?' She knew she sounded about fifty, but her tone was certainly having a dampening effect on the girls.

'Certainly, ma'am.' He might not be a professional actor, but the manager of the Unicorn could dissimulate like a master. His face showed nothing but a slightly obsequious attention to Maude and a faint irritation directed at the two younger women, as though at the antics of a pair of badly trained puppies.

Maude swept out into the corridor, amazed to find her legs steady again. Who these two girls were she had no idea, other than that they were certainly not of the *ton*, but she had no way of knowing if they would gossip about her. It was imperative that she kept them on the defensive, more worried about their own position than speculating about what the daughter of an earl was doing unchaperoned in Mr Hurst's office at eleven in the evening.

He led them through a maze of corridors and out into the night. Maude drew her veil down over her face and raised the hood of her cloak to shield her face from the crowd of gentlemen who were milling around the stage door, inside and out, while the stage door-keeper produced a hackney with a blast on his whistle. She allowed Mr Hurst to seat her in the vehicle before he stood back to allow the Misses Corwin to scramble in unaided. 'Thank you, sir.'

'Thank you, ma'am. Until eleven, then.' He stopped to give the driver an address in the city, then turned away as the carriage rattled out into the late evening bustle of Long Acre.

Maude waited with interest to see what her two companions would say now they were alone with her. In the gloom of the carriage they fidgeted, whispered and eventually one of them blurted out, 'You won't tell anyone, will you, Lady Maude?'

'What exactly do you not wish me to reveal?' she enquired

coolly, finding herself irrationally annoyed with the pair of them. Why she should feel so protective of Eden Hurst she had no idea. He was more than capable of looking after himself, if their encounter in the corridor was anything to go by. If he had pounced on one of these girls in that manner, she would have fled screaming, just as he intended, no doubt. They quite obviously had not got a *tendre* for him, either of them, so what on earth were they about, risking ruin like this?

'That we were trying to…um, encourage Mr Hurst into making an offer,' the shorter one ventured.

'For which of you?' Maude enquired, intrigued. Yes, he had known about this plot and had mistaken her in the gloom for one of these silly girls.

'With any of us. Mama thinks he will, because he wants Papa to invest in his theatre, but we aren't sure because he never takes any notice of us. We don't understand it,' she added naïvely, 'because we are ever so well dowered.'

'Perhaps Mr Hurst already has an attachment?' Maude ventured, finding her irritation turning into something more like amusement until she realised that might very well be the case. She had no idea—Eden Hurst was a very private man.

'Well, if he has, it isn't anyone from amongst the merchant families. Papa would know,' the taller sister offered confidently. 'And he can't marry anyone in society, because of being a bastard.'

That was a relief. Then Miss Corwin's words sank in. 'A…a what?'

'Bastard. Although Mama says not to use that word and say *love begotten*, instead. But it doesn't matter really, because his father was an Italian prince or something equally grand.'

That would explain his colouring, Maude thought hazily. *Was* Eden Hurst illegitimate? She had never heard a whisper, although it was not the sort of thing mentioned in front of unmarried ladies. Oh, Lord, if he was, that would be another obstacle to overcome. Trade was bad enough, the scandalous world of theatre even worse. Being the love child of an Italian prince was hardly going to make it any better. Papa was going to have palpitations, poor man, when he was finally presented with Eden Hurst as a son-in-law.

The hackney cab stopped. 'We're home.'

'And how do you propose to get in?' Maude enquired. They did not appear to be too worried by the prospect.

'Through the service area.' The girl hesitated on the carriage step. 'Thank you, Lady Maude.'

'Well, don't do anything like this again. If I were you, I would not talk about this little adventure to anyone,' she added repressively. 'And please tell the driver to take me to Berkeley Square.'

Maude was deep in thought when the hackney came to a halt again. The door was stiff and the light from the flambeaux either side of the Standons' house flickered wildly in the stiff breeze. She almost tripped getting down, then stood shivering while she fumbled in her reticule.

'All right, m'lady, Mr Hurst paid,' the man said, leaning round to slam the door shut.

'Oh. How kind of him.' Maude felt very tired all of a sudden. The shallow steps up to the front door seemed endless as she looked at them. Her hopes for the evening had been vague, beyond making contact with Eden Hurst, but she had not expected to be ruthlessly kissed and then find herself chaperoning two girls.

'He's come along to see you home,' the man added over his shoulder as the horse moved off.

As she stared across the corner of the square she saw another hackney drawn up, a tall figure standing by its open door. He raised a hand in acknowledgement as he saw her looking at him, then climbed back in. Maude drew her cloak around her and ran up the steps to Jessica's house, no longer tired.

Chapter Two

'Lady Maude, your ladyship.' Jordan, the Standon's butler, managed not to appear shocked by her unannounced arrival on the doorstep at almost midnight without so much as a valise about her person.

'Maude darling, I thought you said you couldn't come tonight.' Jessica put down her book, removed her stockinged feet from the fender and regarded her with mild surprise.

'I was trying not to tell an untruth to anyone,' Maude explained. 'Thank you, Jordan, a cup of tea would be perfect. And one of the special ginger biscuits if Cook has made any,' she added hopefully.

'You intrigue me vastly.' Jessica curled up in her chair and waved Maude towards the one opposite. 'You have been exploring at the Unicorn, I surmise?'

'How did you guess?' Maude kicked off her slippers and tucked herself up in the depths of the chair.

'Where else would you have slipped off to? Reveal all,' she commanded, reminding Maude that her friend had once been a governess.

'I told Papa that you had invited me and let him think I was coming back here with you directly after the performance.

And I told you he was expecting me to go home with him, without actually saying that I did not intend to.'

'There is a word for that sort of thing. Devious.'

'I prefer to think of it as considerate. No one was worried.'

'Go on—' Jessica broke off as Jordan entered with a tray loaded with tea things, bread and butter, some tiny cakes and the famous ginger biscuits. 'Thank you, Jordan, that will be all for tonight. His lordship will let himself in.'

Maude waited patiently while Jessica poured two cups of tea and then pounced on a biscuit. 'I'm famished. Well, my intention was to visit Madame Marguerite in her dressing room and congratulate her upon her performance and while I was at it, just happen to encounter Mr Hurst and make an appointment to discuss a business matter.'

'And?' Jessica nibbled a triangle of bread and butter.

'I, er…encountered Mr Hurst first.'

'And he threw you out? You do look somewhat flustered.'

'He kissed me. Ruthlessly, indecently. Without mercy. Until I almost lost the use of my legs. The man is a complete rake.'

'Oh, my dear! How frightful, you must be devastated—' Her face full of concern, Jessica put down her cup and began to scramble to her feet.

'It was wonderful,' Maude finished. It was beginning to feel unreal, like an incredible dream. Only, her mouth still felt swollen and all those alarmingly wonderful sensations kept rippling through her whenever she thought about Eden's body pressed intimately to hers.

Jessica sat down again with a thump. 'Is that all he did?' she demanded. 'Kiss you?'

'Yes, although I don't think *all* is quite the word. But he thought I was someone else. He was extremely courteous afterwards and sent me home in a hackney. He followed in another one to see I arrived safely,' she added in an effort to reassure.

That a number of questions were fighting for priority in Jessica's head was obvious from her expression. 'Who did he think you were?' she asked eventually.

'One of the Misses Corwin, apparently. I've never heard of them, but their father is a merchant and he is about to invest in the Unicorn. The daughters are determined that one of them is going to marry Mr Hurst. Two of them arrived moments after he let me go, apparently hell-bent on getting the elder one compromised. I was able to foil that and escort them home, adding a warning about their behaviour while I was about it.'

'The pot calling the kettle black?' Jessica enquired.

'Not at all.' Maude frowned. She had been worrying about that as she drove back. 'I have no intention of entrapping Eden Hurst,' she reassured Jessica, and herself into the bargain. 'Only of giving him every opportunity to fall in love with me.'

'How can he resist?' teased Jessica, relaxing somewhat.

'Well, your darling Gareth could, very easily,' Maude pointed out.

'It was mutual, was it not? And I won't lecture you, I promise. How can I, given what I got up to disentangling you and Gareth?'

'You made a perfectly captivating loose woman,' Maude said, deciding she could, after all her adventures, manage a third ginger biscuit. 'Whereas I have no intention of doing anything more forward than making sure I am very much in Mr Hurst's life from now on. Sooner or later he will come to realise he cannot exist without me.'

'It did not strike him like a thunderbolt at your first encounter,' Jessica pointed out. 'I might have been heavily veiled at the time, but I could see quite clearly and I have never observed a less struck man in my life. I described him to Gareth as an icicle, but an iceberg would have been more accurate. And he appears to have survived kissing you without falling at your feet either,' she added cruelly.

'He is probably racked with desire, the more he thinks about it,' Maude asserted. 'Another cup of tea?'

They drank in silence, the plate of biscuits mysteriously diminishing until Jessica said, 'You are sure, aren't you, that it isn't just his looks? I know I described him as an icicle, but he is also the most exotically beautiful man I have ever seen. It would not be at all surprising if you fell for that.'

'You mean, am I being extremely superficial?' Unoffended by the question, Maude brushed crumbs off her skirt and got up to place some more coals on the fire. 'You forget, I have grown up surrounded by men of character. Dearest Papa, Gareth, to name but two. I could not possibly love or marry a man without intelligence, drive, fine qualities. Yes, I was attracted to Eden Hurst because of his looks. But it was also his presence, his strength.

'And then the more I found out about him, the more I admired him. He has revived the Unicorn's fortunes in mere months in the face of the Patent theatres' opposition, created a vehicle in England for Madame Marguerite when she was known only by reputation. And everyone says he managed one of the most successful theatre companies on the Continent—and that cannot have been easy under the circumstances of the past years.'

'How old is he?' Jessica asked. 'Thirty, at least, I would have thought.'

'I do not know.' Maude frowned into the hot centre of the fire. 'I can't find out anything like that about him, who his parents are, where he was born, when.' She was not going to mention the rumour about his father. Time enough to cross that bridge when she had to.

'You don't think he and Madame are, er, involved…?' Jessica asked tentatively.

'Surely not?' Maude stared back, aghast. That had never occurred to her. 'She's *years* older than he is, surely?'

'Well, I have no doubt she's a creature of unrestrained passions, if her acting is anything to go by, and he is a very handsome man. Tell me…' Jessica leaned forward '…what was it like?'

Maude felt herself colouring up. 'Amazing,' she said finally. 'I have been kissed before, but this was quite unlike anything else. Is it *supposed* to make you feel odd all over?'

'The odder the better,' her friend said with a grin, uncurling from the depths of the chair. 'Time for bed, although I doubt you are going to get a wink of sleep after that.'

'Don't you think so?' Maude took the proffered candle. 'I was rather hoping I was going to dream.'

Eden waved the tired dresser out of the door and closed it behind him. 'I have called your carriage, Madame.'

'Call me Marguerite, darling. How many times do I have to ask you?' The actress fluffed at her hair petulantly.

'It does not feel right. Here, let me help you with your cloak.' He settled it around her shoulders as she stood, enveloping them both in a cloud of Attar of Roses, drowning the faint remembered fragrance of gardenias in his nostrils.

'Foolish boy.' She twisted round, her head on one side, and smiled. Always the coquette, always practising her charms. 'Are they all gone?'

She meant the swarm of admirers who had infested the Green Room and queued, petulant if they were not given instant admission, at the stage door. 'All gone. I got rid of them at last.'

'They adore me.' It was a statement, but underneath he

heard the need for reassurance. Always the need for reassurance.

'They worship you,' Eden agreed with a smile, his watchful dark eyes cataloguing the faint betraying lines beside her eyes, the slackening of the skin over the exquisite jaw line, the harshness of the dark hair tint. He knew he must begin to edge her towards the more mature roles. And how was that to be achieved without her throwing a tantrum to rival Mount Etna? He had witnessed the eruption in 1810, and the fiery image came to mind with increasing frequency whenever Madame was thwarted.

There had been a time, when she had first taken him from the palazzo, before he had learned to harness his emotions and not to entertain foolish fantasies about love, when he had hated her. Now, he thought he understood her, had come to accept her total lack of empathy for anyone else and to admire her talent, her sheer determination. But when he was tired it was still an act of conscious will to humour her.

'You must be exhausted after that performance,' he suggested, edging her towards the door. 'So much emotion.'

She lifted a daintily manicured hand and patted his cheek. 'Darling, you are cold.'

'I have been out, a small matter of business to take care of.' And if Lady Maude had not been there he would still have been dealing with it. The consequences of Corwin discovering that two of his daughters had been found, unchaperoned, in his office late at night would be the most almighty row and the loss of his most promising investor.

Eden smiled grimly, then caught sight of his saturnine expression in the big glass. Why the devil would a woman want to marry him in any case? Used to scrutinising the faces of actors at close quarters, all he could read in his own features was cold, hard ruthlessness wedded to the theatrical tricks of a mountebank—the earring, the hair. His profession and his birth made him ineligible to all but the merchant classes and below, and his character was surely something a woman would take on only in return for his money.

Which brought him back neatly to Corwin. 'What are you scowling about, darling?' Marguerite allowed herself to be guided out and towards the Green Room. The square chamber with its green velvet curtains, Turkey rug and motley collection of chairs, sofas and side tables was both the common room for the company and the reception salon after a performance.

Now, in the wake of Marguerite's admirers' departure, the room resembled the aftermath of a drunken party. Bottles were upended into ice buckets, flowers were strewn everywhere, empty glasses stood around and most of the company were sitting or reclining in various combinations of stage costume, street clothes and undress.

They struggled to their feet, or, in the case of George Peterson, the heavy who was already well in his cups, vaguely upright, as their leading lady swept through. 'Good night, darlings,' she trilled, blowing a kiss to the three walking gentlemen, the bit-part players, who swept her bows as she went.

Eden noted in passing that Miss Harriet Golding, the ingénue, was sitting almost on the lap of Will Merrick, the juvenile lead. That could spell trouble—Merrick was living with Miss Susan Poole, the lively soubrette who had apparently already left. He could well do without a love triangle in the middle of the cast, especially with a visiting leading lady next week. Madame would sail blithely through any amount of emotional turmoil provided it was not her own emotions at stake. Mrs Furlow could well find it most disagreeable. He dug out the notebook and added *Merrick/Golding/Poole* below the note on oil lamps. If this was serious, then Miss Golding would have to go; ingénues were two a penny.

'I am utterly drained,' Marguerite announced, draping

herself across the gold plush of her carriage seats. '*Drained*. I have given my all for a month.'

'Well, you have two weeks when you need only rest and get up your lines for the next part, then rehearsals,' Eden soothed, the words forming themselves without any conscious work on his part. Then some demon prompted him to add, 'And I have an idea for the piece after that.'

'And what is that to be?' she demanded.

Eden knew he had been hedging round breaking this to her, seeking the right moment. Oh well, now, with no audience of dresser and sycophants to fan her tantrums, might be as good a time as any. 'Lady Macbeth.'

'Lady Macbeth? *Lady Macbeth?*' Her voice rose alarmingly. 'That Scottish hag? A mad woman? A *tragedy*? Are you insane?' She subsided. Eden braced himself; she was not finished yet. 'In any case, we cannot perform it. The Patent theatres have the monopoly on *legitimate drama*.' Her voice dripped scorn.

'Not if we introduce music, have a ballet in the background in some of the scenes. I have been working on it and we can scrape past the licence issues.'

'Why should we want to?' she demanded. Even in the dim light he could see the alarming rise and fall of her bosom.

'You do not want to do it?' Eden injected amazement into his voice. 'One of the great Shakespearian roles? The woman who is so seductive, so powerful that she can drive a great king to murder? Imagine the dagger scene. Every man in the theatre would take the knife from your hands and do the act if *you* commanded it. The sleepwalking scene—you, magnificent yet so feminine in your night rail...' He fell silent. She was already rapt, eyes closed, lost in her imagination.

Eden offered up silent thanks to whichever minor deity looked after theatre managers and sat back against the soft squabs. Finally, he could contemplate those hectic few moments in the corridor with Maude Templeton in his arms.

Thinking about it had the inevitable physical effect. He crossed his legs and tried to pin down the nagging feeling he had seen her somewhere before. It would not come and concentrating was virtually impossible while the memory of the feel and the scent and the yielding of her filled his brain and agitated his body.

What business had she with him? he wondered. She was quick witted as well as beautiful, with a sense of humour that matched his own, he rather suspected, recalling her stated reasons for allowing him to kiss her. He did not believe for a moment that she had been subdued by his superior strength. Which left the flattering probability that she had enjoyed the experience.

And the not very flattering recollection that a second later she had been all business. Not that there was any legitimate business an unmarried *lady*, with the emphasis on lady, could possibly be transacting with him, which was puzzling. Eden found himself intrigued, aroused and curious, a combination of emotions that he could not recall experiencing before.

He indulged himself with the memory of her slender waist, spanned by his hands, of the slither of silk under his palms, the erotic hint of tight corseting as his thumbs had brushed the underside of her breast...

'I need a new carriage.'

Back to reality. 'This one is only eighteen months old, Madame. I bought it in Paris, you recall. I cannot afford a new one.'

'Why not? You are a rich man, Eden.'

'Yes. And very little of that is liquid just now. I invested heavily in the gas lights, as you know, to say nothing of all the rest of the renovations, the costumes, the props. Then the foreign tour while the work was being done was not all profit.' And just maintaining Madame Marguerite in gowns and millinery was a serious drain. His investments stayed where they were until the time was ripe for each to be liquidated. The bedrock of his hard-won fortune was not to be frittered to sate Madame's urge for novelty.

'Oh, fiddle! Cash some gilts or whatever those things are called. Or sell out of those tiresome Funds or something.' He could hear the pout in her voice. 'My public image is important, darling. I need to cut a dash.'

'You would do that from the back of a coal-heaver's cart,' he said drily. 'I am not touching the investments until I can get the owner of the Unicorn to talk to me about selling it. I need to invest in the place, but I am not spending any more now until it is mine.'

'Darling, I thought you were getting money from that vulgar little cit.'

'Corwin? Yes, I hope to. I just have to be sure I can keep him from interfering in the running as part of the deal.' Never mind the detail that Corwin would insist on making Eden his son-in-law.

'You are so stuffy, Eden.' She subsided into a sulk, leaving him once more free to contemplate Lady Maude and the inconvenient fact that, if he was going to have any hope of sleep tonight, a visit to Mrs Cornwallis's hospitable establishment was probably the simplest way of achieving it. Surely all he needed was the scent of another woman's skin, the heat of another smiling mouth under his, the skills of a professional, to rout the memory of innocently sensual beauty.

'Are you coming in?' They were already at the Henrietta Street house, pretty as a jewel box with the white porcelain flowers filling the window boxes and the shiny green front door flanked by clipped evergreens.

'No, Madame.' Despite the footman, he helped her down himself, up the steps to the front door, dropping a dutiful salute on her cheek. 'Sleep well.'

'Blackstone Mews,' he said to the coachman, climbing back in. Mrs Cornwallis would have some new girls by now. It was six weeks since he had last called.

Two hours later Eden lay back on the purple silk covers, his eyes closed. If he kept them closed, the girl probably wouldn't talk until he was ready to get up and go. He had already forgotten her name.

A fingertip trailed down his chest, circled his navel, drifted hopefully lower. His imagination made it Lady Maude's finger, with predictable results.

'Ooh!' she said with admiration that was not all professional. 'Why not stay all night?'

'I never sleep here.' Her voice chased away the image in his mind. Eyes open, Eden rolled off the bed and reached for his breeches.

'Oh.' Another woman who could manage an audible pout. 'But you'll ask for me next time?'

'No. I never ask for the same girl twice.' No entanglements, no expectations. No messy emotions on her part. Certainly no night spent with her in his arms, waking up off guard and vulnerable.

'But I thought you liked me...' And she had that wheedling tone off to perfection too. He kept his back to the bed as he fastened his shirt. Madame, cajoling over her millinery bill, actresses fluttering their eyelashes as they tried to persuade him to give them a role, those simpering Corwin girls in pursuit of a husband. Did every female in existence, he thought irritably, have to coax like that? It occurred to him that Lady Maude had been admirably direct. No simpering, pouting or wheedling from her. What, he wondered, did *she* want from him?

'Good night.' Eden did not look back as he went out of the door.

Chapter Three

Eden Hurst was pacing like one of the caged lions at the Tower. *No*, Maude silently corrected herself. Those animals were confined behind bars. However menacing they looked, with the muscles bunching under their sleek hides and the flash of white fangs, they were impotent.

This man was free. This man made things happen, just as she had sensed he would. He turned from checking a ledger someone had handed him and Maude moved back between the flats, stumbling slightly over the grooves they ran in. The paperwork dismissed, Hurst strode to the front of the stage and began a highly technical discussion with someone invisible in the pit about the placing of the instrumental players to achieve a certain required effect.

He had discarded his coat and rolled up his sleeves. There was no sign of last night's exaggerated tailoring, unless one counted the very whiteness of the linen shirt that made his skin even more golden in contrast and the expensive cut of his pantaloons and waistcoat. There were no diamonds in his ear today, just the ring to give emphasis when he swept a hand down in a gesture to reinforce his orders.

Maude found her eyes fixed on the point where his waistcoat had been laced at the small of his back, emphasising the balance between broad shoulders and narrow waist, slim hips and long legs.

Now he put his fists on his hips and leaned back to stare up into the gods to where a hand was shouting a query. The line of his throat was that of a Greek statue, she thought.

'Extraordinarily beautiful animal, isn't he?' a dispassionate male voice asked, just by her ear.

Maude felt herself colouring: she could hardly deny to herself how she had been looking at him. 'Mr Hurst appears very fit,' she said repressively, turning to find one of the walking gentlemen at her elbow.

'I'm not interested in him *that* way, you understand,' the man continued, still watching his employer through narrowed eyes. Maude tried to appear sophisticated and unshocked at the suggestion he might be *interested*. 'I just wish I could move like that. I watch and watch, but I'm damned if I can get it. New, are you? Nice gown, by the way. My name's Tom Gates, walking gentleman and hopeful juvenile lead if that clot Merrick upsets the apple cart.'

Maude regarded him with some interest. He looked about twenty-one, but from a distance, with make-up, she could see he could easily pass for a lad of seventeen. 'Thank you, it is one of my favourite gowns. I'm sure you'd make a very good juvenile lead. Is Mr Merrick prone to trouble, then?'

'He will be if he doesn't stop lifting La Golding's skirts,' Tom confided frankly. 'Either Susan Poole will run him through with a hat pin or the guv'nor will have his balls for making trouble in the cast. What's your line, then? Too classy to be a walking lady, I'd have said.'

'I am not an actress, I'm an investor,' Maude explained, watching the blood drain from the young man's face as he realised his *faux pas*. 'I am early for a business meeting with Mr Hurst.'

'Oh. My. God.' He smote his forehead dramatically. 'Should I go and pack my bags now, do you think? Let me see, have I remembered everything I said that you'll be complaining about?'

'Lady Maude. Gates? Be so good as to explain what will cause her ladyship to complain to me.' Eden Hurst was standing right behind them, his expression one of polite interest. Maude thought that it was just how a shark would look before sampling one's leg.

'Good morning, Mr Hurst. There is absolutely nothing to be concerned over. I arrived somewhat early and Mr Gates has been so helpful in explaining things, but he seems conscience-stricken because he forgot to address me by my title. I do not regard it at all.' She shared a sweet smile between both men. Gates shot her a look of adoring thanks, Mr Hurst merely raised one eyebrow in a manner calculated to infuriate anyone else who could not manage the same trick.

'I'll get your coat, Guv'nor.' Gates shot across the stage like a retriever and returned with the garment, brushing it assiduously. His complexion had returned to normal.

'Thank you. Have refreshments sent to my office.' Hurst took her arm. 'Alone again, Lady Maude?'

'My maid is waiting in the Green Room.' Maude had left Anna there, wide-eyed in anticipation of witnessing some of the scandalous behaviour she was convinced must go on in such a wicked place. So far, Maude imagined she had been seriously disappointed. The language might be colourful, but everyone was focused totally on their work. Mr Hurst ran a tight ship.

'I will leave the door open, then.' He showed her in, gesturing to the chair she had sat in the night before.

'Why? Do you fear you may be unable to restrain your animal impulses again, Mr Hurst?' Maude sat and placed a folder of papers on the desk.

Behind her the door shut with a sharp click. She pursed her lips to restrain the smile; it was part of her strategy to keep Eden Hurst on edge and she did appear to be undermining that control, just a little. 'I was not failing, Lady Maude, and I was not acting upon impulse. I fully intended to do what I did. I always do.'

'Excellent. So do I. And I prefer to keep my personal business confidential, so do, please, leave the door shut.'

She waited, hands folded demurely in her lap while he circled the desk and sat down on his sorcerer's throne. He steepled his fingers, elbows on the carved arms, and regarded her in silence. The light from the window was behind him, no doubt intentionally. Maude, who had trained in the hard school of the Almack's patronesses, waited, outwardly unruffled. Inwardly her stomach was executing acrobatics that would have impressed at Astley's Amphitheatre.

'In what way may I help you, Lady Maude?'

She felt she had scored a point by not babbling to fill the silence. She wanted to babble. She wanted him to kiss her again. She wanted to climb into that big chair and curl up against him. 'By moving my chair to the side of your desk, Mr Hurst. I dislike holding a conversation with someone whose face I cannot see.'

Without a word he got to his feet, came round the desk again, waited for her to rise and then moved the chair. 'Here?' How many people challenged him on his own ground? Would it impress him or merely irritate?

'Excellent, thank you.' Unasked, he moved her papers too, then shifted his chair so he could face her.

'I wish to invest in the Unicorn, Mr Hurst.'

'Indeed.' *Damn him, he might at least look faintly surprised.* How many unmarried ladies did he have coming in offering him money? 'And what makes you think I require investors, ma'am?'

'I have heard some gossip to that effect and I should imagine all theatres need funds. And Miss Corwin tells me her father is thinking of investing with you.' His mouth twisted wryly for a second, whether at the thought of Miss Corwin or of her father, Maude was not certain.

'And what does *your* father think of this, might I ask?'

'I have not discussed it with him as yet. Mr Hurst, I am five and twenty and I have had control of my own money for some time.' An exaggeration—it was only since last year, in fact, when Papa had recognised that withholding control of it was not going to force her into the marriage with Gareth Morant, Lord Standon.

A gallant man would have exclaimed in surprise at her claiming such advanced years. It surprised Maude herself sometimes to realise how old she was and to acknowledge that most people would consider her almost on the shelf. Eden Hurst made no reference to her age at all. Now, was that galling or refreshing?

'I have always been interested in the theatre, so this seemed an obvious thing to do. I am not intending to over-commit myself, I realise this is a risky business, however well run.' That earned her an inclination of his head. Still no smile. The shark appeared to be circling, perhaps puzzled about what kind of prey had swum into its territory.

'You have been a leading light in country-house amateur theatricals, no doubt, Lady Maude?' The way he said her name made her swallow hard, every time. It was difficult to define just why. Something about the deep voice, perhaps, the touch of mockery she sensed behind the respectful address. Or was it just that she was so close and they were, at long last, talking?

'I cannot act for toffee,' she admitted with a smile. 'As my family and friends always point out to me. No, my strengths lie in writing and producing dramas.'

'Well, you are not writing or producing any in my theatre, let us be quite clear about that.' So, the first sign of hackles rising. She was reminded of prints she had seen of Italian Renaissance princes, hard, handsome, elegant men staring out at the watcher in their pride and their power. Or perhaps, as those dark eyes narrowed and the sensual line of his mouth thinned, he was not an earthly prince, but one of the Devil's henchmen.

Yes, the Unicorn was very much Eden Hurst's theatre. 'I do not wish to, not here—I am quite clear about the differences between amateur and professional theatre. I propose investing a sum of money. Our respective men of business can assess it as a percentage of the value of the business and I will thereafter take the appropriate share of the profits.'

'Or losses.'

'Or losses,' she agreed equably. He had lowered his hands and now each curved over the lion masks at the end of the chair arms. He had big hands, she noticed, with long, elegant fingers. The well-kept nails contrasted with bruises and cuts on the backs of his hands, presumably from handling scenery. The contrast between strength and sensitivity was somehow arousing. Those were the fingers that had held her helpless with such negligent ease. Maude dragged her eyes away.

'So you do allow a man of business to act for you?'

'Of course. I believe in employing experts as I need them. Well? Does my proposal interest you?'

He did not answer her question directly. 'And what involvement will you require?'

'To see the books. To visit behind the scenes and watch rehearsals. To discuss policy and to put forward my ideas. But hardly to direct policy—you are the owner of the Unicorn, after all.'

There was a tap at the door and it swung open to reveal a large tea tray dwarfing the young woman who carried it.

'I've raided Madame's best tea, Guv'nor. Tom Gates said to make an effort.'

'Thank you, Millie. I am sure you have.' He waited until the door closed again. 'Perhaps you would care to pour, Lady Maude.'

He waited while Maude busied herself with the tea things, then settled back, his cup unregarded on the desk. 'How much, exactly, are you proposing to invest?'

She had given it a great deal of thought. Enough to make him take her seriously and to give her an entrée to the theatre and its management. Enough to give her every excuse to enter into his professional life on a regular basis. But not so much she would seem foolish or rash. Maude flipped open her folder and slid a paper across the table. 'That much.'

There was silence for a long moment. Eden Hurst picked up the sheet and tapped it thoughtfully on the desk. 'A not insignificant sum.'

'I am a wealthy woman, Mr Hurst. That is the maximum that will be available. I do not regard this as a frivolous amusement to be pouring money into, you understand.'

'I do. And you calculated your investment on your understanding of the value of a theatre I own.'

'Yes.'

'Then I am afraid your research was not thorough enough, Lady Maude. I am not the owner of the Unicorn.'

'You are not?' He watched with interest the effect surprise had upon her. Those delicately arched brows shot up, a faint groove appeared between them. Then he saw her begin to think and speculate, the big brown eyes alive with intelligence. 'It belongs to Madame Marguerite?'

'No. I have to confess I have no idea who owns it. I deal with their agents, I pay the rent, I observe the lease conditions and I am met with a very polite refusal when I ask to meet their principal.'

'How very mysterious.' Another expression, one of lively curiosity, flitted across her face. That lovely visage was as easy to read as a book, but only, he suspected, when she wanted it to be. He was convinced that last night, after he had kissed her, her feelings were far from being reflected in her expression. In fact, he was beginning to wonder if she used that openness as a weapon to make him underestimate her.

Her dazzling smile took him by surprise. 'Well, then, Mr Hurst, we must buy it.'

'What? The Unicorn? *We* must?'

'Can you afford it alone?' This was frank speaking indeed. Eden contemplated snubbing her by loftily remarking that he had no intention of discussing his financial position with her, then caught himself. He was enjoying this meeting. There was no one he could discuss business with, not on equal terms. Madame merely wanted to know if there was sufficient money to maintain her lifestyle; his banker and his solicitor expected only to take orders and to offer advice when asked.

The small circle of men he admitted to anything approaching friendship were either too interested in his business for comfort if they were from the merchant class or completely uninterested if they were gentlemen. He had become used to taking all decisions alone, arguing problems out with himself.

And now here was, of all things, a young lady. Bright-eyed, confident, interested and quite unabashed at being alone with a man, speaking of things ladies were simply not expected to understand. And, miracle of miracles, she did not simper, she did not wheedle and she most certainly did not try to cajole.

Eden smiled. Lady Maude blushed, which was unexpected. Hastily he resumed a straight face. The last thing he wanted was for her to think he was flirting with her. Not after last night. 'No,' he responded frankly. 'I cannot afford to buy it alone just now. At least, not without committing myself more than is prudent.'

'And are you always prudent, Mr Hurst?' There was a laugh lurking in her eyes. Was she thinking about last night? He wished he was not, it was too damn uncomfortable.

'With money, yes,' he admitted and the answering smile made the corner of her eyes crinkle. Yes, she had been thinking about last night. So why had she blushed earlier?

Eden was used, without vanity, to women reacting strongly to his looks, although he saw to it that they never got close enough to him emotionally to react to the man behind that handsome face. His appearance was nothing to be proud of, in his opinion. He owed his looks to the father who had refused to have anything to do with him. As for the rest, he took care of his body, exercised hard and spent more than he needed on his clothes.

But Lady Maude was not flirting. She had reacted to his kiss with a mixture of innocence and appreciation that was arousing, yet her response afterwards had been that of an assured young matron and now... Now he had no idea how to read her. Which ought to be infuriating, not intriguing.

He realised that he must have been silent, thinking, for over a minute. Unperturbed, Lady Maude had opened her portfolio and was scribbling energetically. When she saw he was back with her she smiled, the uncomplicated smile of a friend. 'I will need to rework these figures, for I am sure my banker will tell me I should not invest so much if you do not own the Unicorn. It is very vexing—you must press for information about the owner.'

'I have tried; it is not going to be forthcoming.'

She sent him a look that said clearly that he had not exerted himself sufficiently in the matter. She was wrong. Ever since he was fourteen he had wanted his own theatre. Not a little provincial playhouse, but a significant, fashionable, demanding theatre to satisfy the longing that had entered him the first time he had set foot on a stage, the sense that he had come home. He had found the Unicorn and had known that this was love and that this was the only passion he could, or would, ever trust. But he could not speak of that to a near-stranger, or try and justify an emotion he only half-understood himself.

'Lady Maude, have you considered what Lord Pangbourne is going to say when he knows what you are doing?'

'Of course. He said I was old enough to make my own mistakes with my own money.' She hesitated, her eyes sliding away from his. 'Some time ago…he wanted me to marry someone; he had wanted it for years, in fact. Neither the gentleman nor I wished for it and things became—' she broke off, searching for a word '—*complicated*, before Papa understood how things were. He has always been somewhat unconventional in his attitude to women's education and freedoms. What happened has made him somewhat indulgent in many ways.'

So, not only was she intelligent, but she was also strong enough to stand up to parental pressure over her marriage. And now, at twenty-five, the Marriage Mart would consider her on the shelf, or almost so. Or was the daughter of an earl, wealthy in her own right, ever on the shelf? Perhaps she had grounds for her confidence.

'He may be indulgent about how you invest your money, but he is not going to be so if he knows you are alone with me in my office, is he?'

That appeared to amuse her. 'Do you imagine he will call you out, Mr Hurst?'

'I imagine he will want to horsewhip me. I am not, after all, a gentleman, and therefore would not merit a challenge.'

Maude looked at him, her eyes wide and steady. 'Yes, you are, in every way that counts. Or I would not be here.'

Her certainty knocked the breath out of him. He was accepted, to a point, in society as an intelligent, personable exotic. He could imagine the reaction if he so much as flirted with one of the young ladies on the Marriage Mart. And they, he was quite certain, would have had him pointed out by their mamas as completely ineligible, if not dangerous. Yet Lady Maude appeared to have no such scruples.

'I will speak to my man of business tomorrow and amend my figures,' she continued. 'Would it be convenient to call in a few days' time?'

'I should not—' He meant to say, *I should not be doing business with you*, but it came out differently. 'I should not expect you to come here. Could I not meet you at his office? It would be safer, surely?'

'For whom?' she enquired, suddenly very much Lady Maude and not the unconventional young woman conducting her own negotiations. 'I feel quite safe. Are *you* frightened of something?'

Eden drew in a deep breath, ignored the interestingly unsafe suggestions his body was making. 'For myself, I fear nothing and nobody, Lady Maude.' He let a chill harden his voice. He could not act, had never wanted to, but he had grown up surrounded by good actors and learned a trick or two. When he wanted to, he could intimidate and he found that useful.

Her lashes swept down to hide her thoughts, and he thought he had shaken her. Then she lifted her eyes and murmured, 'Good. I will hold you to that.' She closed her portfolio and got to her feet, smiling with ladylike composure as he rose to open the door. 'I will send a note and come back here next week to discuss how to proceed.'

'You will attend the first night of our new play?'

'On Monday? I am looking forward to it. You will be putting on a ballet and a farce for the intervening nights, I assume?'

'Yes. Trifling things, but I do not care to have the theatre dark.' He looked down at her and knew he had to take control of this situation, whatever it was. 'Lady Maude. Unless you tell Lord Pangbourne of your intentions, I must decline to discuss this matter further with you.'

For a moment he thought she would admit defeat and did not know whether to be relieved or disappointed. 'You make terms, Mr Hurst?' she asked, her face unreadable.

'That is what businessmen do.'

She stood there, one hand in its tight kid glove resting on the door frame, quite clearly thinking. 'Mr Hurst, do you want me to take my money and go away?'

'It would be safer for your reputation and it would certainly make life simpler,' he said honestly.

'That is not what I asked you,' she said, managing to look down her nose at him, a considerable feat considering their respective heights.

'No,' Eden said, surprising himself. 'No, I do not want you to go away. After all, I have so little in my life to worry about as it is. You will doubtless be the grit in my oyster.' She glared in response to his sarcasm. To his horror he found himself thinking about kissing her face back into smiles. 'But I mean it. Tell Lord Pangbourne before this goes any further. I want your word on it.'

'My word, Mr Hurst?' Her chin came up as she gathered her skirts in one hand. 'You have it, sir. Good day to you.'

Chapter Four

Maude cupped her chin in her palm and regarded her father thoughtfully. For once they were both at the breakfast table at the same time, he having declared that he was not going to the House that day and she deciding it would be good tactics to forgo her usual early morning ride in Hyde Park in order to speak to him about the Unicorn.

She had spent an uncomfortable night fearing Eden's scruples had overturned all her plans right at the outset.

'Papa?' He seemed to be in a good mood. His perusal of the *Morning Post* and *The Times* had provoked only half a dozen exclamations of wrath and he had not yet screwed up any of his morning correspondence and lobbed it at the fireplace.

'Yes, my dear?' He folded his paper and laid it beside the plate. 'When your mother addressed me in that tone, she usually had some fixed purpose in mind.'

'Well, and so I have. You recall saying I might have the control of my money unless I wanted to do something foolish with it and you would rely on Mr Benson to warn you if I did appear to be doing just that?'

'I believe I said something of that nature,' he responded, wary. 'Rainbow, that will be all. I will ring if I need anything.'

The butler bowed, nodded at his subordinates to follow him and left them alone.

'Tell me. I am braced for the worst.' Lord Pangbourne folded his hands over his stomach.

'You know the Unicorn theatre?'

'I should do, since you rent a box there and we have visited regularly since it reopened.'

'You will have noticed that it is one of the best of the non-Patent theatres and that the manager, Mr Hurst, has been improving it.'

'The gas lighting, yes.'

'I wish to invest in it.' She sat back and tried to look calm, as though she had asked if she should buy government bonds, or some rental property in a good area. Her fingers hurt; she found they were knotted into her napkin. Maude frowned at them and made herself relax.

'In gas lighting? I believe that could well be the coming thing.' He lifted the newspaper. 'There are some companies advertising here, in fact—'

'In the Unicorn, Papa.' Time for complete frankness. Almost. 'I wish to invest a sum in the theatre and to take an interest in its overall policy. I find it most interesting.'

'The theatre? But, Maude, that is not at all a respectable world, not on that side of the curtain. It is inhabited by the demi-monde and frequented by gentlemen who are not there because of their interest in the dramatic arts—I am sure I need not say more. For a woman to be connected with the stage is to court ruin. It is quite out of the question.'

'I do not want to appear *on* the stage, Papa,' Maude said. 'That *would* be a scandal indeed—think how bad my acting is! And I most certainly do not want to be behind the scenes when the gentlemen come calling in the evening. I can quite see what a risk that would be.'

He was frowning at her, bless him. He did try so hard to let her be herself. Maude knew she was indulged, far beyond what most single young women of her background were. And she knew too that her position meant that what would be condemned as outrageously fast if done by, say, the daughter of an obscure baronet, could be carried off with dash by the daughter of an earl.

'What about your charity work?' Lord Pangbourne asked. 'Are Lady Belinda's wounded soldiers no longer absorbing your time?'

'Of course, I have a committee meeting this afternoon. But it is hardly a full-time occupation, Papa.'

'And the Season will soon be in full swing,' he pointed out.

'Yes. And neither is that all consuming, at least, not during the day. I like to be busy, Papa, and to use my brain.'

'I would like it if you just stood still long enough for a nice young man to catch you,' Lord Pangbourne said with a sigh. 'I suppose you want me to say that Benson should call on this manager chap—Hurst, is it?—and suggest a basis for your investment.'

'Yes, Mr Hurst. But I have already called upon him and proposed my scheme.'

His lordship choked on his coffee and put his cup down with enough force to rattle the saucer. 'Called on him? My God, Maude, of all the shocking—'

'I took my maid, Papa, and called at the theatre in the morning, not at his home, naturally.' Maude knew she couldn't act, but she felt fairly confident in her expression of outrage.

'It is still most unwise. The man is not a gentleman. And the theatre of all places!'

'Well, his behaviour was most gentleman-like,' she asserted. 'I felt quite comfortable. I was served tea and waited upon by a maid.' That was doubtless stretching the description of the lass who was probably the general dogsbody. 'And everyone there was behaving most decorously.' If one disregarded Mr Gates's indiscretions, of course. 'Would you meet Mr Hurst and judge for yourself? I thought perhaps we could invite him to our box in the interval on Monday. You do want to see the revival of *How to Tease and How to Please*, don't you, Papa?'

It would allow Papa to judge Eden face to face and it would reassure Eden that she had spoken to her father. He would not take kindly to being summoned to the house to be inspected, she was sure of that, but on his home ground he might be less prickly. She would order champagne with the refreshments and think carefully about who to invite to join the party for the evening. No one who would be shocked by a man wearing a diamond ear stud, that was for sure.

The committee for Lady Dereham's Charity for the Employment of Soldiers Disabled by the Late War—or Bel's Battalion, as her husband irreverently referred to it—was somewhat diminished in numbers that afternoon. Bel's cousin Elinor was on the Continent with Theo Ravenhurst, her new husband; Elinor's mother Lady James Ravenhurst was studying Romanesque churches and the Grand Duchess Eva de Maubourg, a cousin by marriage, was at home in Maubourg and not expected in London until early March.

Jessica had been welcomed into the committee on her marriage. It was a positive coven of Ravenhurst cousins, her husband Gareth Morant, Earl of Standon—himself a cousin—had joked. Maude would have become a Ravenhurst if her father's intention to marry her to Gareth had come to pass and she had known most of the family since she was a child.

The Reverend Mr Makepeace, Treasurer, was already seated in Bel's dining room, fussily arranging his papers on the long mahogany table while assuring Lady Wallace, a lady of a certain age and indefatigable energies, that the money she had extracted from her long-suffering husband had been safely banked. Mr Climpson, Lady Wallace's solicitor, and legal adviser to the charity, bowed punctiliously to Maude and pulled out a chair for her while Jessica waved gaily from the other side of the room where she was talking to Bel.

The minutes read, and matters arising dealt with, they sat through Mr Makepeace's interminable report. Maude surfaced from a daydream involving Eden Hurst and herself alone in her box at the Unicorn to discover that the charity was in excellent financial health.

'In fact, our only problem at the moment appears to be finding other sources of employment for the men on our books,' Jessica remarked. 'We have bought three inns now, which employ all those suited for the various roles those offer.' She scanned the lists in front of her. 'We have placed sixteen men with various craftsmen and a further twelve in domestic service or stables, but there are still fifteen unsuited and, as you know, more come to us every week, despite the war being over now for almost two years.'

'What about theatres?' Maude asked, the idea coming straight out of her daydream. 'Stage-hands, door-keepers, scene painters, carpenters—there must be many types of work the men would be suitable for.'

'Excellent,' Lady Wallace applauded, shushing Mr Makepeace, who started to say something about immorality. 'What a clever idea, Lady Maude.'

'But however will we find out what is available?' Jessica asked, all wide-eyed innocence. 'Who can we *possibly* ask?'

'It just so happens,' Maude said, attempting to kick her

friend under the table and painfully finding the table leg instead, 'I know someone who might be able to help.'

'I was going to ask you and Gareth to join me in my box on Monday,' she said to Jessica as the others departed. 'And then you could have met Mr Hurst because he is taking champagne with Papa and me during the interval.' At least, she hoped he was; she hadn't written to him yet. 'But if you are going to be so unkind as to tease me, I will ask Bel and Ashe instead.'

'Ask us what?' Bel came back into the room and eased herself down on a chair. 'Oh, my feet! I have been playing with Annabelle all morning and I am quite worn out with that meeting on top of it.'

'How exhausting can playing with a baby be?' Maude demanded. 'She's tiny.' A doting expression came over Bel's face, so she added hastily, 'Anyway, will you and Ashe be able to come to the theatre with us on Monday?'

'We'd love to. Your box at the Unicorn? Do you mind if we bring another gentleman with us? Ashe has a navy friend coming to spend a few nights.' She looked up, obviously making connections. 'Is that where you think you may be able to find employment for some of the men?'

'Possibly. I am intending to invest in the theatre and Papa wishes to meet the manager before he will support me.'

'I should think he does.' Bel narrowed her eyes. 'You are up to something, Maude Templeton.'

'As I said, investing. Of course, it *is* somewhat unconventional,' Maude said airily.

'And of course Mr Hurst of the Unicorn is very good looking,' Jessica added slyly. 'Gareth and I are definitely coming on Monday. I'm not missing this for anything.'

'No!' Bel sat up straighter, weariness forgotten. 'Hurst? But surely I have heard of him.' She bit the tip of her finger in thought. '*Eden* Hurst? But he is notorious for his *affaires* with married ladies! Ashe warned me about him, although I gather he is hardly predatory; he just stands around looking handsome and they throw themselves at him as they did at Byron. But Maude, even if he is a lay preacher in his spare time, he still has to be utterly ineligible, you wicked woman. Darling, I don't think this is sensible; he's received, but that doesn't mean you can't be ruined by associating with him.'

'I wish to invest in his company,' Maude protested, flustered that Bel had immediately leapt to the conclusion that she wanted Eden Hurst. As for his reputation—well, she refused to think about that just now.

But Bel had seen Jessica's face and Jessica knew only too well what she wanted. 'Oh, very well, Jessica will tease until you know it all anyway. I intend making Eden Hurst fall in love with me. He is intelligent, charismatic, dynamic and beautiful. When I talk to him it is not like any other conversation I have with anyone. I was right when I sensed he was meant for me; when I am with him I feel more alive than you can imagine. There is so much passion in him, so tightly controlled. Passion for the theatre, I mean,' she clarified as Jessica rolled her eyes.

'He just doesn't know yet that I am the woman for him. I intend to give him every opportunity to realise it.'

'Goodness,' Bel said weakly. 'And then what? You cannot *possibly* marry him. Think of his reputation.'

'If he marries me, he will not be having *affaires*. And why should he not marry me?' Maude demanded. 'He is very well off. And his father, I believe, was an Italian prince.'

'But was he married to Mr Hurst's mother? That's the point,' Jessica queried. 'Hurst is not exactly a Italian name, now is it?'

'Er...no.' She turned in a swirl of skirts and plumped down in a chair. 'It is no use the pair of you looking at me like that. You don't have to tell me it is going to be difficult. I want to marry an illegitimate, half-Italian theatre owner with a reputation. He is quite a *rich* illegitimate theatre owner,' she added hopefully.

'Maude,' Bel said gently. 'Money is not going to be the issue. Breeding is.'

'I have enough breeding for both of us, and he is a gentleman, even if society won't see it,' Maude declared, beginning to be alarmed despite herself. She had expected Jessica and Bel to support her.

'Yes, but what does he think about this?'

'Nothing at all, as yet, other than I am very unconventionally intending to invest with him. I have been cool and businesslike. I intend to grow upon him.'

Jessica snorted inelegantly. 'Maude, I am your friend, so I can say frankly that you are a very beautiful woman. The man has kissed you—passionately, by all accounts. And you are waiting to grow on him? I should imagine your financial assets are the last thing on his mind at the moment.'

'He has done what?' Bel's face was a picture.

'Kissed me. By accident. He thought I was someone else,' Maude explained patiently. 'It was wonderful, but he appears more than capable of restraining his animal passions when I am alone with him, believe me.'

'Oh. That's not very encouraging,' Bel said, then caught herself. 'I mean, what a good thing. To be fair, according to his reputation he does not appear to be dangerous to virgins.'

Maude determinedly ignored contemplating who else Eden Hurst might be dangerous to. 'Well, I am not concerned. I want him to fall in love with me, gradually. Not lust after me. That, too, of course, in time, but I am sure desire clouds men's brains. Love first, then lust.'

'It doesn't work that way round,' Bel observed, smiling. Jessica nodded in agreement as she continued, 'I'm afraid the poor weak things work on the basis that anything female between the ages of sixteen and sixty is looked at with the eye of lust. One's finer features, such as your mind or your skill at the harp, or your lovely nature, have to grow upon them.'

'Oh.' Somewhat daunted, Maude regarded her two friends. 'I wanted him to be so passionately in love with me that he would disregard the difference in our positions.'

'Not if he has the gentlemanly instincts you say he has,' Jessica pointed out with depressing logic. 'If he loved you, then he would sacrifice himself by refusing to see you any more. As Bel said, he does seem to restrict himself to married women, so he has some scruples.'

'And anyway,' Bel added, 'it isn't what *he* thinks about your respective positions, it is what society thinks.'

Maude fell silent, wrestling with the conundrum. The only possible solution appeared to be to become his lover, then hope he fell in love and realised that, having hopelessly compromised her, he must marry her. But what if he did not fall in love and felt he had to offer anyway?

'This is 1817,' she said, raising her chin and meeting their sympathetic looks with determination. 'Things are changing, men with wealth and intelligence are breaking into society.'

'Merchant bankers and nabobs, maybe,' Jessica said doubtfully. 'But the theatre is simply not respectable. Not for marriage.'

'In that case,' Maude declared, getting to her feet, 'the Unicorn is going to become the first respectable theatre in the country.'

'The evening post, sir.' Eden's butler proffered the laden salver. 'Dinner will be served in thirty minutes, sir.'

'Thank you.' Eden took the pile of letters and began to flick through them. He was dining at home, alone, for the first time in weeks and finding it hard to relax. His brain was still working on too many levels. There were the remaining issues with the staging for *How to Tease*, there were the tactics to persuade Madame to take the role of Lady Macbeth and, if she did, the problem of producing a version that would not bring down the wrath of the Patent theatres and the Lord Chamberlain for performing 'legitimate' drama without a licence.

Ways of improving the scene shifting were beginning to form at the back of his mind, there was the situation between Golding, Merrick and Poole to resolve and decisions about investments to make.

Investments. He tossed the letters down on to his desk unopened. They were not normally a problem. His instructions to his broker were straightforward enough, he simply had to decide on one or two points and send a letter to the man. No, it was Lady Maude Templeton and her hare-brained desire to invest in the Unicorn that was baffling him. And Eden Hurst did not like being baffled. Challenged, yes—he enjoyed a good fight. But not baffled by a brown-eyed lady with a pointed chin, a cool manner and a staggering disregard for convention.

He wanted to make love to her. Oh, yes, he most definitely wanted that. His imagination had no trouble conjuring up the image of her naked on his big bed upstairs, that thick hair tumbling around her shoulders, her hands gripping his shoulders as he sank into the tight wet heat of her. But he also, oddly, wanted to get to know her. Understand her, not simply discover why she had come up with this madcap scheme. And why should he want to do that?

Eden gave himself a brisk mental shake and returned to his post. Bills, letters from aspiring players, the opening scenes of a play written in odd green ink… He really should get a secretary for all this.

One plain white wrapper of fine quality paper, sealed with

a crest pressed into the dark blue wax; that looked more interesting. He cracked the seal and spread out the single sheet.

Lord Pangbourne requests the pleasure of Mr Hurst's company for refreshments during the second interval at the Unicorn on Monday next.

'My God, she *has* told him.' Eden stared at the invitation, reluctant admiration stirring. No sign of a horsewhip, not yet at any rate. Perhaps the earl was as unconventional as his daughter, or perhaps he thought to show her just how unsuitable a person Eden was for her to associate with by putting him into a social situation.

That was the logical answer. And in order to remove the puzzle of Lady Maude from his life, all he had to do was to turn up and act as Lord Pangbourne would expect. Eden toyed with the combination of clothing and manner that would make him appear louche, dangerous and entirely impossible.

His on-stage style was already established; he just needed to develop that to the point of caricature. He had seen enough old-school actor-managers to be able to assemble the worst characteristics of all of them. And then even the most indulgent father would take fright and bundle his daughter off out of harm's way, leaving Eden to manage his theatre in tranquillity.

He picked up the paper and as he did so the faint scent of gardenias wafted to his nostrils. So, this firm black hand was not that of the earl or his secretary. Lady Maude herself had penned it. Eden smiled thinly. Was her father even aware he was going to have a visitor to his box on Monday night?

Chapter Five

'It is fortunate that the private boxes at the Unicorn are spacious, for this one seems very full of large men tonight,' Jessica remarked to Maude on Monday evening as the Derehams entered with their guest. Lord Pangbourne, with Gareth at his side, was greeting them, giving the friends the opportunity to study Ashe's naval acquaintance.

'Why not fall for *him*?' Jessica whispered. 'He looks so distinguished in that uniform and he is very good looking and not too old either. Not more than thirty, do you think? A younger son, of course, but excellent connections. Your father would be delighted.'

'I have no interest in other men, as you very well know,' Maude hissed back, too tense to enjoy being teased. The officer was tall and rangy in his dark blue uniform, his hair close cropped, his eyes, as he turned to be introduced to the two young women, a deep and attractive blue against weather-tanned skin.

'Lady Standon, Maude, this is Captain Warnham. My lord—Lady Standon, my daughter Lady Maude.'

Greetings exchanged, the captain settled his long frame between Maude and Jessica. 'It is a long time since I have been inside an English theatre,' he commented, looking around with interest. From the boxes opposite came the flash of light on lenses as opera glasses were raised to scrutinise comings and goings. It would be all round the *ton* before long that a handsome naval officer was newly in town.

'You have been at sea for many months?' Maude enquired, fanning herself. The theatre was crowded and the heat rising from the gas lamps added to that generated by the crowd and her own anxiety.

'Three months in the South Atlantic, ma'am. I am back for some weeks before sailing for Jamaica on another mission.'

'The West Indies? How fascinating, I have always wanted to go to those islands.' Maude, her twitching nerves over Eden momentarily forgotten, leaned closer. 'They always sound so romantic and exotic.'

Captain Warnham smiled. 'They have their charms, I am sure, but they also have slavery, hurricanes, tropical disease and pirates.'

'And sunshine and blue seas and parrots and waving palm trees,' Maude said wistfully, thinking of the drizzle that affected London.

'My husband and Lady Belinda have a cousin in Jamaica, do you not, Bel?' Jessica raised her voice to catch Bel's attention.

'Jamaica? Yes, Clemence Ravenhurst. We are expecting her father to bring her over to England this summer to stay so she can have an English come-out next Season. I expect your ships will pass in mid-Atlantic, Captain.'

They began to chat, Bel and Gareth explaining what they knew about their youngest uncle, a highly successful West Indies merchant.

Now he *is in trade*, Maude thought resentfully. *The youngest son of a duke and no one thinks the worse of him for it.* But, of course, Lord Clement Ravenhurst was a very successful man and did not soil his own hands with the details of his luxury goods business. Presumably wealth and birth wiped out the stain of trade, if you had sufficient of both.

'What a pity he will not be at home when you are there, Captain Warnham,' Bel concluded. 'We would have given you letters of introduction.'

The orchestra began to file into the pit and tune up, earning catcalls and jeers for the cacophony from the common folk up in the one-shilling gallery. The noise gradually subsided back to the usual hubbub and then the lights were dimmed and the curtain rose on the first piece of the evening, a short farcical item featuring the company heavy as a strict father, thwarted at every turn by the ingenious antics of his daughter's suitors.

'I have every sympathy with the fellow,' Lord Pangbourne remarked as the furious father chased a young man over a balcony while, behind his back, another rake took advantage and snatched a kiss from the daughter. Maude recognised Tom Gates, the ambitious walking man, who whisked out of sight behind a convenient curtain in the nick of time.

'It is an ingenious piece,' Captain Warnham agreed, laughing at the business between the cast, the maid changing clothes with her mistress, while the two young men dressed as footmen and the baffled father searched frantically for his daughter. In a few minutes the happy couple escaped down a rope ladder, the remaining suitor consoled himself with the maid and the curtain came down on appreciative applause.

There was a short interval before the next piece, a ballet. Maude reviewed her preparations for the main interval: canapés, champagne, two small tables to be brought in and the seats rearranged. But who to place where?

She wanted her father to appreciate Eden's strong points, not be distracted by long hair or diamond ear studs or over-emphatic tailoring. Perhaps best not to place him next to the clean-cut Lord Warnham in his dress uniform. Between Bel and Jessica then…

'You are muttering,' Jessica said.

'I want you and Bel to sit either side of Mr Hurst,' Maude whispered back. 'I don't want him sitting next to Captain Warnham and making Papa think of haircuts.'

'I think the length of his hair is the least of your problems.'

One step at a time, Maude told herself, sitting through the ballet in such a state of abstraction that she would have been hard pressed to say whether there had been dancers or circus horses on stage if questioned afterwards.

Eden's note in response to the invitation had arrived, punctiliously prompt and formal. But would he really come?

The waiter came in with the refreshments and, on his heels, a tall figure, dark against the brightness of the open doorway.

'Standon, my dear fellow, would you—?' Lord Pangbourne broke off in confusion, realising that the man he thought he was addressing was still seated to his left. The figure moved, the light fell across his face and Maude let out a long, inaudible sigh. Eden.

Her father got to his feet, ponderous and, for all his formal good manners, wary. 'Mr Hurst?'

'My lord.' He came in, as the waiter closed the door behind him, and inclined his head to his host.

'Allow me to make you known to Lady Dereham, Lady Standon, my daughter Lady Maude—'

Papa is pretending we have not met, Maude realised, returning the bow with slight curtsy, while her father completed the introductions and waved Eden to the chair by his side.

And then she realised what was different about him. Gone was the exotic theatre manager, gone too was the working man in his shirtsleeves, and in their place was a perfectly con-

ventional gentleman in well-cut evening formality, a modest
ruffle on his white shirt, the dull sheen of garnet satin on his
waistcoat and just a hint of sparkle in the strange old ring,
his only piece of jewellery. Even his hair had been ruthlessly
pomaded and brushed into a fashionable style that distracted
the eye from its length.

He is making an effort, she thought, astonished. It had
never occurred to her that Eden Hurst might go out of his way
to impress her father. Was it because he needed the money, or
because he did not want to lose her as...as what? An investor? That was all she could be to him at the moment, surely?

Lord Pangbourne, nobody's fool, even though he cultivated an appearance of bluff and bluster, had apparently realised that he could hardly explain to a boxful of guests, one
of whom was a virtual stranger, that he had invited Mr Hurst
there to interview him as a potential business partner for his
daughter. He had also, while introductions had been made,
managed things so that the men were all sitting to one side
of the box and Maude was safely trapped between the other
two ladies.

She realised, with sinking heart, that Bel and Jessica had
not exaggerated the unconventionality of what she was doing.
Gareth and Ashe were regarding Eden with expressions of
politely neutrality, but she knew them both too well to be deceived. They were watchful and suspicious and, she feared,
disapproving.

'Good of you to join us,' her father remarked, pouring
champagne. 'I'm very interested in this new gas lighting
you have here. Thinking of installing it myself. What do
you think?'

'I would not put it in my own home, not just yet.' Eden
took the glass, but did not drink. Close to the naval officer's
tanned skin his colouring seemed less exotic. He looked and
sounded just like the rest of them, yet he was the focus of

more than polite attention. 'There is an odour, and it is dangerous without proper ventilation. But, in a year or two, I think it will replace oil everywhere.'

Captain Warnham, for whom this was apparently the first sight of gas used inside, joined in the conversation with a remark about the gas lights installed on Westminster Bridge in 1813 and all four men were soon deep into the technicalities.

Maude rolled her eyes at her friends, but Bel smiled and nodded encouragement. And, yes, superficially it was a success. They could have been any group of gentlemen engrossed in discussion, but she sensed relief all round at such a neutral topic that could distance the men from the ladies.

Eden, she realised, had muted his forceful character. He deferred to the older man, held his own with the others, yet it was as though he had turned down the wick on the lamp of his personality.

Clever, Maude thought. He is adapting himself to his company, blending in. She met his eyes across the table. His expression hardly changed, yet she sensed rueful amusement. He knew exactly what he was doing, but he did not seem entirely happy that he was doing it. And he sensed the raised hackles of the other men.

'We are neglecting the ladies,' he remarked, bringing all eyes to where his gaze was resting, her face.

'But I am *fascinated* by gas lighting,' she said sweetly, all wide-eyed feminine attentiveness. His lips were definitely quirking now. It was infectious. She bit the inside of her lip to stop herself smiling back. 'Still, we do not have that much time before the curtain rises again. Will you not tell us about the next piece? My father saw it the last time it was produced in London.'

'In 1810 at Covent Garden, my lord? We have had to adapt it here, of course, because of the licence, add a short ballet, and some songs, hence our choice of Mrs Furlow in the lead;

she has just the voice for it. Still, it is very much the same comedy you will recall from before.' He uses his voice like an actor, Nell thought, listening to how he spoke, not what he said. It was a deep and flexible voice, shaded with colour. He seemed to have it as much under his control as his face, betraying only what he wanted to show.

Her father was relaxing now; she saw his shoulders shake as he recounted some piece of amusing business from the production he remembered.

The conversation moved on while she was brooding. Gareth must have asked Captain Warnham about his new ship. 'Do you welcome another commission so far from home?'

'I am a career officer, I go where I am ordered and may do most good, but in any case I could not turn down the opportunity to make war on pirates. They are everything I loathe.'

'But are there any left?' Maude asked. 'Enough to be a problem?'

'Not so many now, we have them under control in many areas. But those that remain are the worst of them. And like rats they know we almost have them cornered and that makes them the more vicious. They used to take prisoners for ransom; now they cut their throats and throw them overboard.'

The party fell silent, chilled, Maude sensed, not so much by the horror of what he was describing, but the controlled anger with which he said it.

Bel, the more experienced hostess, picked up the thread of the conversation after a heartbeat had passed and moved them on to safer ground. 'I love to read the shipping news in the daily papers,' she remarked. 'It is so fascinating to see where they have come from to reach us, bearing our luxuries all that way.'

All those luxuries, Maude thought, unfurling her Chinese fan and looking at it with new eyes, brought over huge distances at such risk. She looked up and found Eden was still watching her and was visited by the odd idea that he knew what she was thinking. Then the imagined look of understanding was gone and he rose to his feet.

'You will excuse me, my lords, ladies. The curtain rises soon.' He bowed and was gone, his champagne untouched, leaving the crowded box feeling somehow empty.

'What a pleasant man,' Bel remarked, carefully not looking in Maude's direction. 'Not at all what I would have expected of a theatre proprietor.'

'Indeed not,' Jessica added. 'One can only think that the theatre is becoming so much more respectable these days.'

'Superficially, perhaps. But it is scarcely eight years since the riots over the changes at Covent Garden,' Gareth countered. 'Nor can one call that sort of thing *respectable*.' He nodded towards the box opposite where a party of bucks were becoming very familiar indeed with three young women whose manners and clothing clearly proclaimed them to be of the *demi-monde*. Gareth appeared quite unconscious of the dagger-looks his wife was darting in his direction.

'And matters will be laxer on the Continent, I have no doubt,' Ashe added, his eyes resting on the door as though he could still see Eden.

'Oh, look,' said Maude with bright desperation, 'Here come the string players.' Across from her, Lord Pangbourne appeared sunk in thought.

'What did you think, Papa?' Maude ventured as the carriage clattered over the wet cobbles on its way back to Mount Street.

'Excellent production. In my opinion, adding the songs helped it. It was a lot livelier than I remembered.'

'Not the play, Papa, although I am pleased you enjoyed it. Mr Hurst.'

'Surprising chap. Not what I expected.' Lord Pangbourne fell silent.

'And?'

'And I need to sleep on it.' He sighed gustily. 'Confound it, Maude, I know I promised you more freedom, but I don't know what your mother would say if she were here.'

'*Yes*, probably,' Maude ventured. 'She was very unconventional, was she not, Papa?'

'Very fast, you mean,' he said, but she could hear he was smiling. 'Your mama, my dear, was a handful. And so are you. I don't like refusing you anything, Maude; I promised your mother I would never make you feel as she did as a girl—caged. But I don't want to see you hurt too.'

'Hurt?' She swallowed hard. He realised her feelings were involved?

'By any kind of scandal. You can ride out a lot in your position, but that's an uncommon man you'd be dealing with.' *He certainly is…* 'I'll sleep on it,' he pronounced. And with that she knew she would have to be satisfied.

It was not until she was sitting up in bed an hour later that what he had said about her mother sank in. *I don't want to see you hurt too.* Mama had been hurt? But by what? Or whom?

Breakfast was not a good time to ask questions about the past, Maude decided, pouring coffee and schooling herself to patience. It would take three cups and the first scan of *The Times* before she could expect anything from her father.

'Well,' he said, pushing back his chair at length and fixing her with a disconcertingly direct look. 'I was impressed by that Hurst fellow, despite myself. You may invest in that theatre, to the limit that Benson advises, and not a penny more. You will not go backstage after four in the afternoon and you will always, *always*, go there with a chaperon. He might be a good imitation of a gentleman, but he's young, he's ruthless and he's unconventional. A chaperon at all times—is that clear, Maude? I see no reason to be telling all and sundry about this involvement of yours either.'

'Yes, Papa.' *Oh, yes, Papa!* 'Thank you. I do believe this will be a worthwhile investment.'

'It will be if it makes you happy, my dear. Just be prudent, that is all I ask.'

Prudent. That was what Eden declared himself to be, with money at least. Men seemed to set great store by prudence. Maude's lips curved. Now she had to teach him to be imprudent with his heart. This morning she would write and tell him she had her father's approval, make an appointment to call with Mr Benson.

Chapter Six

Papa had not been speaking lightly when he had insisted upon a chaperon, Maude thought, torn between amusement and annoyance. Anna, her Sunday best hat squarely on top of her curly mop of hair, was seated in one corner of Eden Hurst's office, an expression of painful intensity on her face.

As they had alighted from the closed carriage—the one without the crest on the door, Maude had noticed—the maid had assured her, 'I'll stick like glue, never you fear, my lady.'

'Like glue?' Maude paused on the step up to the stage door and stared at the girl.

'His lordship said so. He told me he was relying upon me to maintain the proprieties.' Anna nodded earnestly, her face pink with combined delight at having been spoken to so and alarm at her responsibilities.

'Indeed.' Thoughtful, Maude walked in and smiled at the door-keeper. 'Mr Hurst is expecting me. There will be a gentleman as well.'

The man consulted his ledger. 'Mr Benson, ma'am? Came in five minutes ago. I'll take you through, ma'am, if you'll just wait a minute while I get the boy to watch the door.' Maude shook her head.

'No, it is quite all right, I know the way, Mr—?'

'Doggett, ma'am.'

'Mr Doggett. This is my maid, Anna—you will probably be seeing quite a lot of us from now on.' The man knuckled his forehead and grinned, revealing several gaps in his teeth, as they walked past.

'The stage door-keeper is an important man backstage,' Maude explained as they walked along the corridor to the Green Room. This passageway had been painted green up to the dado rail, then cream above with prints of theatrical subjects hung on the walls, no doubt in acknowledgement of the class of visitors to the Green Room. 'You will need to speak to Doggett when you want to call the carriage, or if you need to go out on an errand for me. He keeps an eye on things and makes sure no riffraff come in.'

'Yes, my lady.' Anna nodded solemnly. Maude hoped she was absorbing the idea that it would be all right to leave Maude from time to time. It was going to be impossible to establish any sort of relationship with Eden Hurst with the maid always at her side.

'You'll be able to reassure his lordship about how well run and respectable things are here,' Maude continued chattily.

'Oh, yes, my lady. I'll do that.' So, she was expecting to report back.

Bless him, Papa was no fool, however indulgent he might be, Maude thought, half her mind on the proposals Mr Benson was outlining, half on her tactics for dealing with Anna.

Eden Hurst was silent, listening. His head was bent over his hands clasped on the desk, his eyes apparently fixed on the gold tooling around the edge of the green leather top.

Benson put down his pen and sat back, too experienced to prolong his presentation.

'Reduce the return by one percent and I will consider it,'

Eden said at last, looking up, his eyes clashing with hers, not the attorney's.

'By one quarter of one percent,' Maude said promptly.

The dark eyes looked black; there was no softening tilt of the lips or warmth in his voice as he responded, 'Three quarters of one percent.'

'Half.' She felt as though she had been running, the breath was tight in her chest and it was an effort to keep her voice cool and steady. This was, somehow, not about the money.

She was meticulous in keeping all hint of feminine charm out of her voice, her expression. When she was buying supplies for the charity or coaxing donations from patrons she would use whatever pretty wiles worked—wide-eyed admiration, a hint of chagrin, a touch of flirtation. But with this man she sensed they would not impress and he would think less of her for it.

'I will meet you halfway,' she added.

'Will you indeed, Lady Maude?'

'But no further.' Beside her Benson shifted, uneasy. She did not turn her eyes from Eden Hurst's face. It was like trying to outstare ice. Then slowly, subtly, she was aware of heat and realised she was blushing and that those cold, dark eyes were warming, smiling, although the rest of his face was impassive. There was no air left in her lungs now, but she was not going to give in, she was not...

Anna coughed, Benson put his pen down and the spell was broken. Which of them looked away, Maude had no idea, but Eden was on his feet, his hand extended across the wide desk. 'Come, then,' he said. 'Halfway.'

No man had ever offered her his hand to seal an agreement before. It was not done. A gentleman told her what he would do and she took his word for it. A tradesman agreed a price and bowed her from his premises. Men shook hands on deals with other men. Some instinct made her pull off her glove as she stood and took his hand. It was warm and dry and she could feel calluses on the palm as it closed around her fingers, firm, positive, but careful not to squeeze hard as it enveloped them.

A lady allowed her gloved hand to remain passive in a man's for a few seconds while he bowed respectfully and then released her, or placed her fingertips on his forearm so he could escort her. A lady did not grasp a man's hand in hers and return pressure with her naked fingers as she was doing now. He must be able to feel her pulse thudding, she was certain.

Mr Benson cleared his throat, her hand was released and they sat down as though nothing had happened. She had finalised a business arrangement—why did she feel almost as disorientated as she had when he kissed her?

'I will amend the documents now.' The attorney produced a travelling inkwell and pen and began to alter the documents before him. Maude sat silent while the nib scratched over the paper, occupying herself with removing her other glove and tucking them both into her reticule.

'There.' Mr Benson finished, pushed one set across the desk to each of them and handed his own pen to Maude. 'If you will read them through and sign, then exchange copies.'

Maude Augusta Edith Templeton, Maude wrote in her strong flowing hand. It was not a ladylike signature, her governess had complained, trying vainly to make her produce something smaller and altogether less assertive. She initialled the other pages as she had been taught and handed them to Eden, taking his in return.

Eden Francesco Tancredi Hurst, it said in writing equally as black and considerably more forceful. Maude signed below it, the sudden image of a marriage register flashing through her mind. 'Francesco Tancredi?' she said before she remembered the rumour about his father. It must be true.

'Augusta Edith?' he retorted.

'Great-aunts.' He did not respond with any explanation of his two very Italian names.

'I will call at the bank and arrange for the transfer of funds.' Mr Benson was on his feet, pushing his papers together. 'May I take you up, Lady Maude?'

'Thank you, no. I have my carriage.'

He bowed over her hand before clapping on his hat. 'My lady. Mr Hurst, I bid you good day.'

Eden stood while she sat down again. 'Would you like to see around behind the scenes now?'

'Yes, please. But first—' But first she wanted to speak to him alone and there was the small matter of one attentive lady's maid sitting like a watchdog in the corner. 'I would love a cup of tea.' Eden reached for the bell. 'Anna can go and find that little maid—Millie, wasn't it? Run along and ask Doggett at the stage door where to find her, Anna—and no gossiping with anyone else, mind.'

Trained obedience had the maid on her feet and halfway out of the door before she realised the conflict in her orders. 'But, my lady, Lord Pangbourne said—'

'And you are doing very well, Anna,' Maude praised. 'I will be sure to tell him so.'

'Yes, my lady.' Beaming, she hurried out, closing the door behind her.

'So, your father has set a watchdog to guard you? Not a very fierce one.' He strolled round the desk and hitched one hip on the edge, looking down at her.

'No, she is not, although she is very serious about it. I wanted to say thank you for Monday night.'

He did not pretend to misunderstand her. 'The counterfeit English gentleman?'

'The perfectly genuine one,' she retorted.

'Oh, yes?' He smiled down at her, the first time she had

seen him really smile. His teeth were very white, very even and, like the rest of him, looked as though they would bite. Hard. 'You expected the earring, or worse, didn't you?'

'Yes,' Maude admitted. 'Actually, I rather like it, but it might have raised eyebrows.'

'I will confess I was very tempted to go completely to the other extreme and give you my version of the old-school actor-manager.'

'Why didn't you?' she asked, intrigued.

'Because, upon reflection, I found I did not want to scandalise your father to the point where he forbade you to interfere with my theatre. You are my grit, remember? I expect us to produce pearls.'

He was being deliberately provocative. Interfere, indeed! She refused to rise to it, let alone react to being compared to a piece of grit. 'Describe how you would have turned into the old-school actor-manager,' she said instead.

'A shirt with enough ruffles to make you a ballgown, very tight evening breeches and a wasp-waisted tail coat with exaggerated satin lapels.' He sketched the clothes over his body with his hands. 'I would have raided Madame's dressing room for a large diamond ear drop and her curling tongs.' He twirled a lock of shoulder-length hair between his fingers. 'A touch of lamp black to line my eyes and the oil, of course.'

'The oil?'

'Olive oil. I would have oiled my hair and my skin. Your father would have thrown you over his shoulder and swept out of the theatre, believe me.'

'I believe you,' Maude said appreciatively. 'I would like to see that look, one day. But oil?'

'I will give you some. I import it for my own use. It hardly gets used for cooking here in England, although it should be—for both cooking and salads. But Madame bathes with it, treats her hair with it. It is excellent for dry skin in winter weather.'

'But doesn't it smell horrible?' Maude wrinkled her nose, imagining all the sorts of cooking oil she had come across. The image of Eden, his naked body glistening, kept sliding into her imagination. Much better to think of nasty, smelly grease.

'Here.' He reached down into a wooden crate standing by his desk and produced a bottle full of greenish-golden liquid. 'A consignment has just come in.' The cork popped. 'Hold out your hand.'

As Maude hesitated he reached out and lifted her hand. The oil was cool as it trickled into her palm, forming a tiny pool no more than a gold sovereign's width across. 'Smell.' He set the bottle down, glimmering in the light from the window like a bottled lake of enchantment.

Her hand still cupped in Eden's, Maude dipped her head and sniffed. 'Earth and fruit and...green.'

'Taste it.'

'No.' She shook her head as though he had asked her to drink an enchanter's potion.

In response he bent and licked the little pool of oil straight from her hand. His tongue sweeping across her palm was hot, strong and utterly shocking. Maude gave a little gasp and tried to pull away, only to be held firmly. 'Careful, you will mark your gown.' He pulled a handkerchief from his pocket and wiped her palm clean. 'Are you sure you do not want to taste it?' His mouth was so close to hers, his lips slicked with the golden oil. Of course, he *could* mean he would pour her a little more.

And, yes, she wanted to taste it, warm on his lips. Summoning up reserves of willpower she had no idea she possessed, Maude said calmly, 'This is why Papa insists upon a chaperon, Mr Hurst.' He was looking deep into her eyes, his own amused, mocking. Hot.

'Wise man, Maude.'

She had dreamed of hearing her given name on his lips. Caution, tactics, pride made her stare at him haughtily. 'I have not allowed you to address me so familiarly, Mr Hurst.' She spoiled the effect somewhat by tugging at his restraining hand. 'Will you please let me go!'

He released her and went back to his own side of the desk. 'But we are partners, Maude.'

'Business partners,' she said reprovingly as the door opened to admit Anna and the maid Millie with her huge tea tray. 'Thank you, Anna. Why do you not go with Millie and find some refreshments of your own?'

The girls had placed the tea tray in front of her, so she began to pour, trying to think of some topic of conversation that would neither be stilted nor provocative.

'Your cook uses the olive oil, then?'

'My cook regards it as a foreign frippery, not to be compared to good English lard.' He took the cup and saucer, shaking his head at the proffered cream jug. 'If I want Italian food, I must cook it myself.'

'You cook?' It was unheard of.

'Country food,' Eden said with a shrug, but he was smiling with remembered pleasure, not defensively.

'*Italian* country food?' How much could she ask without revealing she had heard the rumour about his parentage? 'How very unusual.'

'I lived in an Italian palazzo until I was fourteen,' Eden said. 'In the kitchens and the stables, I should say, because that was where I was consigned. Both my cooking and my Italian are on the coarse side.'

He had grown up in his father's house, then? But with the servants? The use of the word *consigned* was both unusual and bitter. But she could risk asking no more. His face as he drank the cooling tea had become shuttered.

'May I take that tour behind the scenes now?' Maude asked. 'Or have you other business to take care of?'

'I always have business.' But Eden's grimace as he extended a long finger to ruffle the pages of the notebook that lay on the desk was amused. This was far more than an occupation for him, she realised. He loved the work, the theatre. 'And some of it can be done while we go round.'

Maude set down her cup and saucer and stood up, aware of his eyes on the sweep of her almond-green skirts. This was going so much better than she had dared hope. This was the man Jessica had described as an icicle, and yet he had let her into his theatre, allowed her a glimpse of his early life and surely, unless he was a complete rake and licked olive oil from the palm of every lady he met—surely a flirtation way out of the ordinary?—he was attracted to her. Yes, he was admiring the hemline, or perhaps it was the glimpse of ankle...

'I would suggest something less suitable for morning calls the next time you visit,' Eden remarked, holding the door for her. 'That pale colour is highly impractical here.'

So much for him admiring the gown she had selected with such pains! But then she had somehow known it would be an uphill struggle, breaking through to the real Eden Hurst she sensed behind the façade.

Maude followed through a maze of passageways, up and down steps, trying to keep her sense of direction.

'The dressing room for the chorus.' Eden opened a door on to a deserted rectangular room, a long bench running down the middle. It had stools on either side, a row of mirrors and everywhere there was a feminine litter of pots and jars, brushes, lopsided bunches of flowers in chipped vases, stockings hanging over looking-glass frames, pairs of slippers, scraps of paper, prints and letters stuck to the walls or

under the pots. It reeked of cheap perfume and the gas lighting, greasepaint and sweat. 'It is organised chaos an hour before curtain up,' he commented, closing the door again. 'The
other dressing rooms are further along.

'Mrs Furlow is in here,' he added as he opened the door
into the room. 'The room used by visiting leads. Madame's
dressing room is just beyond.'

Maude realised there was something amiss the moment she
stepped into the dressing room in front of Eden and heard the
sounds. It was gloomy, with the shade drawn over the high
window. In the half-light the gasps were even plainer, more
disturbing than if it had been broad daylight.

Confused, Maude peered at the far side where bodies were
tangled on what seemed to be a makeshift bed. Someone
was being strangled—she started forward to go to their aid,
then she realised that it was a couple making love, that the
choking cries were a woman in the throes of ecstasy and
the curved shape she could see were the naked buttocks of
the man between her spread thighs.

'Out!' Eden seized her around the waist, lifted and dumped
her bodily into the corridor before stalking back into the
room. 'Merrick!' There was a feminine scream, a thump.
Shaken but shamelessly curious, Maude applied her eye to
the crack of the half-open door—then closed it hastily. A
young man was pulling on his breeches. He was also gabbling
something she could not catch. Cautiously Maude opened
her eyes again.

'Be quiet.' That was Eden. 'I will see you in my office in
half an hour.' Maude glimpsed him as he turned to face the
bed, his face hard. 'Miss Golding, you will pack your bags
and be out of here at once. I will have your wages made up
to yesterday and sent to your lodgings.' There was a gasp, a
girl's voice protesting. 'You, Miss Golding, are easy enough
to replace, Merrick less so. Oh, for pity's sake, stop cower-

ing under that sheet, girl, and get some clothes on. I am quite unmoved by your charms, believe me.'

He stepped back out into the passage, shutting the door behind him with a control that was as chilling as the look on his face. 'I am sorry you had to witness that.'

'So am I, but not half so sorry as I was to hear what you have just said,' Maude snapped. 'That poor girl you have callously dismissed—what is going to become of her now?'

Eden's dark eyes rested on her face with indifference. 'She will find a place in the chorus somewhere. Or a position on her back if that fails.'

'On her—' The crudity took Maude's breath away. Behind Eden's back the door opened and Merrick eased out, his coat bundled in his arms, and hurried away. From the room came violent sobbing. 'Poor thing, let me go and speak to her. He is just as much to blame as she—why does the woman have to take the blame?'

'No.' Eden reached out and shut the door, cutting off the sounds of distress. 'Come, back to my office; it is better if you leave before I have my interview with Merrick.'

Yes, the middle of the passageway was not the place for this conversation. Maude gathered up her skirts and stalked ahead of him in the direction he indicated. Eden Hurst was going to have an interview with her before he got anywhere near the delinquent juvenile lead.

Chapter Seven

'That was cruel and unfair.' Maude stood with her back to the desk, her fingertips pressed to its surface behind her. It was easier to confront him standing up, with some support. 'That young man probably coerced her.'

Eden came in and stood in front of her, close enough to touch, close enough for her to see the coldness that turned his eyes almost black. 'Fairness has nothing to do with it. I am running a business here. If Merrick goes, I will probably lose Susan Poole, his mistress, who is our soubrette. I can ill afford her loss at this stage in the Season, but ingénues like Harriet Golding are two a penny.' He shrugged as though that settled the matter.

'But Miss Golding is just a girl, alone. Don't you care that she might become a prostitute as a result of this?' She admired this man, was convinced she loved him. Surely he could not be this cruel? Could she have so misjudged him?

'Her choice. Merrick was not forcing her, nor has he seduced her. I have been watching them for a few days now.'

'Then you should have done something before now, she was your responsibility.' He was close, too close. Maude resisted the instinct to bend back, put one hand firmly in the middle of his chest and pushed. 'And don't crowd me, you bully.'

It was like pushing the wall. Apparently oblivious to Maude's hand planted on his chest, Eden dug into his pocket and produced his notebook, flipped it open and turned it so she could read what was written on the page.

Under *oil lamps* the definite black letters said *Merrick/ Golding/Poole*. 'Oh. Well, you should have done something sooner. Will you *please* move!'

'If I wanted to crowd you, Maude, I would get a great deal closer than this.' Eden tossed the notebook on to the table, seized her wrist and removed her hand from his waistcoat without any apparent effort. He then took one step forward. Maude tried to retreat, came up hard against the edge of the desk and swayed back. Both big hands came down on the leather, bracketing her hips, a knee forced hers apart and then he was standing between her thighs, leaning over her. 'Now *this* is crowding you.'

Maude struggled for balance, gripped his shoulders and stared, furious, up into his face. 'Let me go.'

'When you admit you were exaggerating,' he said calmly.

Maude, braced to fight, blinked. *'What?'*

'You accused me of crowding you, bullying you. This, I agree, is both. But before, no. You accuse me of unfairness and yet you spent an hour this morning with your attorney making certain this theatre was run as a business.

'I am not running the Unicorn as a recreation, Maude. I am not a gentleman, although you appear to be having trouble grasping that. This is my life and my business and I will not be indulgent with *anything* that threatens it. Harriet Golding is not some little innocent I am tossing out into the cold— she knew exactly what she was doing when she spread her legs for Merrick.'

The fact that he was standing between her own parted

thighs was not lost on Maude. Nothing was, not the heat of him, the smell of him, the tightly contained anger nor the discomfort in her back, bowed over the desk. And most of all, more mortifying than all the rest, the knowledge that she wanted to pull him down to cover her body and make love to her here and now and as wantonly as those two actors.

'Very well.' She swallowed. 'I may have been a trifle... emotional about the situation, I admit. Will you please let me up now?'

Eden stepped back and she came with him, pulled by her grip on his shoulders. When she found her feet Maude let go, brushed down her skirt and walked, as steadily as her aching, shaking, legs would allow her, to pick up her hat, gloves and reticule. She had something more to say to him, but she did not know how she was going to find the courage; it was far too close to her own feelings. Yet, how could she not do her best for the girl?

She set the hat on her head, tied the ribbons beneath her chin and then drew on her gloves as she walked back to where Eden Hurst stood in front of the desk, watching her from under lowered brows.

Maude found her mouth was dry and her throat tight. She made herself look up into his face. 'Mr Hurst, have you considered that she may be in love with him?'

'No.' There was a flicker of surprise at the question, that was all. 'There is no such thing as love, Maude. There is lust, there is sentimentality, there is neediness, there are the transactions people make for all kinds of reasons. But there is not love. It does not exist, it is merely a romantic fantasy.'

'Of course love exists.' She stared back, aghast. 'Even if you do not believe in love between adult men and women, surely you acknowledge family love? Parents love their children, children love their parents—I know, I love my father and he loves me.'

'Society and convention makes family units,' he observed. 'Nature influences mothers to tend to helpless infants. And some of them,' he added with chilling flippancy, 'even heed that influence. Familiarity, dependence, desire—you can call it love if you want to.'

'Oh.' *Poor little boy.* He had betrayed so much hurt in those cynical words. She stood there feeling the tears start at the back of her eyes. But this was not a damaged, abandoned child in front of her. Not any more. This was a grown man with scars to cover those wounds. Scars that so obviously hurt. 'You poor man,' she murmured. Then she turned and walked out, knowing that if she stayed she would take his face between her palms and try to kiss away all the years of neglect and loneliness those words betrayed. Would this man ever allow her to try to do that?

Eden stood looking at the door Maude had closed so gently behind her. She pitied him because he denied the existence of love? What sort of foolish feminine fancy was that? He had so much—his independence, work he lived for, wealth, achievement and the sense not to give up his heart and his soul to be toyed with and then discarded by some damn woman. He had made all this out of the stony soil of a mother who had left him for years until it suited her to *find* him again, an uncaring father who refused to acknowledge his son and fourteen years of neglect in the servants' quarters of an Italian palazzo.

It was not even as though Prince Tancredi had maltreated him physically. He could have endured that, for at least that would have been a recognition of sorts. No, the magnificent father who dazzled him with the longing for a look, a word, had simply refused to acknowledge that he was anything but a liability, like a feeble old servant that duty did not allow you to cast out. If a man who had everything—wealth, title, position, looks—could not spare a kind word for his own son, then that son had to learn a hard lesson and open his eyes to the realities of the sentimental nonsense people spoke about love.

And Lady Maude Templeton had the effrontery to pity him? Not apparently for being outside the *ton* or for having no family he could acknowledge, but because he did not believe in the mind-sapping dependency of a foolish emotion. *Dio!* What had he tied himself to? This was as bad as fighting off Corwin's daughters. Worse.

The tap on the door sent him back to his chair behind the desk. 'Come! Ah, Mr Merrick.'

'Sir.' The young actor had tidied his clothing and brushed his hair and now stood bashfully, giving a very acceptable performance of troubled penitence. Yes, he was a good actor, even if Eden would never gratify him by saying so. All the more reason to keep him. 'I'm very sorry, sir, it won't happen again.'

'No, it will not because Miss Golding will be leaving us. Is Miss Poole aware of what has been going on?'

'No, sir.'

'You are lodging with her still?'

'Sir.'

'Then you had better think up an explanation for why you are not getting paid this week, Merrick.' The young man looked up sharply, the boyish charm slipping. 'I will add your wages to what I owe Miss Golding.' That, at least, ought to please his sentimental new partner. If she ever came back.

'Be very clear about this, Merrick. I am keeping you only because of Miss Poole. She's a better actor than you'll ever be and I doubt she'd have the lack of judgement to expose her spotty buttocks to my guests either.' That produced a furious blush, but Merrick held his tongue.

'Nothing to say? I need hardly add that if I find you involved with any other female in this company I will ensure that Miss Poole is fully aware of it. I'll even hand her the blunt carving knife. Now get out of my sight.'

Methodically Eden opened his notebook, crossed out the line about the three actors and added a note about Merrick and Golding's wages and the need to cast another ingénue, then went to open the door. 'Millie!'

'Yes, Guv'nor?' She appeared round the corner, her face screwed up in her usual earnest scowl. 'Post, Guv'nor.' She thrust several envelopes into his hand.

'Thank you. Go and make sure Mrs Furlow's dressing room is in good order.' The maid scurried off and Eden leaned back against the doorjamb, his eyes unseeing on the deserted passageway, wondering if he was coming down with something. He felt decidedly odd. After a minute he scrubbed his hair back with both hands, rubbing his eyes until he saw stars.

There was no time to be ill and no excuse for indulging himself by looking for symptoms either. Eden went back into his office and glanced at the clock. An hour to the afternoon rehearsal. Time to read his post, send Millie out for some food and decide what to do about finding a replacement for Harriet Golding.

There was, almost inevitably, an invitation from the Corwin household. This time it was for a soirée, two evenings hence. Having survived one of Mrs Corwin's soirées before, he was not over-eager to repeat the experience. Did he still need Corwin's money? He was reluctant, but the man had not asked for any involvement with the theatre, not like Lady Maude, and money, wherever it came from, was money.

The other invitation emerging from the pile was unexpected. Lady Standon requested the pleasure of his company, again for a soirée, again in two evenings' time.

It had not been uncommon for him to receive invitations from members of society since his arrival in London, espe-

cially those of the faster set. His wealth, and the rapidly growing popularity of his theatre, accounted for it, he supposed,
in the same way as prominent bankers or merchants would
receive invitations if their manners were sufficiently refined.
Such outsiders showed a hostess was daring and completely
secure in her own position.

Occasionally he accepted when one of his particular
friends pressed the point or when an evening's entertainment included a celebrity singer or writer he was interested
in. But he was wary, for he realised that, for some of the female guests—and on one occasion, not just the females—his
person was the attraction. As a decorative exotic it seemed
he was a desirable accessory on a lady's arm and in her bed.
He was not averse to a brief dalliance with charming ladies
whose husbands were either tolerant or neglectful, but he
liked to make his own choices. He was aware it had given
him a certain reputation.

But Lady Standon did not appear to be the kind of lady
who thought that slumming it with men from beyond her
social circle would be amusing; in fact, he rather suspected
she was unfashionably attached to her husband, a man who
looked as though he would kill anyone who so much as laid
a finger on his wife. Maude would doubtless say they were
in love. So there was a strong possibility that, after meeting
him in Maude's box, she had simply included him on her
guest list with no ulterior motives.

Eden pulled the notepaper towards him and began to write,
one letter an acceptance, the other a regretful refusal due to
a prior engagement. As he sealed them he smiled, amused
at his own choices.

Millie poked her head round the door. 'I've done the room,
Guv'nor. You want me to take your letters?'

'Yes, send one of the lads to deliver them now.'

* * *

Eden was not surprised to find Corwin waiting in the office when he came back after rehearsal. Millie had provided the merchant with tea and he sat in front of the desk, seeming, to Eden's resentful eye, to occupy more than his reasonable share of the space.

'Well, my boy,' he began. Eden showed his teeth in what might be construed as a smile and sat. 'As you can't come to Mrs C.'s soirée, there's a little chat I think we should have.'

'Indeed?' Eden injected polite boredom into his voice.

'Mrs C. is that disappointed, I can't tell you,' Corwin remarked, stirring a heaped spoon of sugar into his cup. 'Bessie, I said to her, it's about time I settled matters right and tight with Mr Hurst, then we'll all know where we are and he won't be bashful about accepting invitations. Why, I said, he won't need them!'

Eden raised an eyebrow. 'I would regret causing Mrs Corwin disappointment, but I am afraid my refusal is due to the fact I will be at the Standons' soirée that evening, not to any bashfulness.'

'Lord Standon? Well, that just goes to show what I said to my Bessie was right—you're just the man we need, sir.'

'For what, exactly?' Eden asked, knowing all too well what the answer would be.

'Why, for our girls!' Corwin took a swig of tea.

'All of them? I fear that is illegal in this country.'

'Ha! You'll have your joke, sir.' The merchant did not look as though he found it funny. 'No, whichever of them you choose, although Calliope is the eldest. Once one of them's wed to you, the others will get off soon enough, I make no doubt of it, especially with the fine friends you've got, my boy.'

Eden toyed with the options before him, of which physically ejecting Corwin was the most tempting. *Uno, due, tre,* he counted silently, then smiled. 'You flatter me with your proposal, sir, but I must decline.'

He expected anger, but Corwin's face merely displayed indulgent understanding. 'I know what it is, and it does you honour, my boy, but we don't take any account of the circumstances of your birth. Why, Mrs C. herself never knew her father, let alone him being an Italian prince.'

'You would oblige me by ceasing to discuss my parentage, Corwin. What you think of the circumstances does not interest me. I have no intention of marrying one of your daughters and that is the end of it.'

The other man's face darkened and he set his cup down sharply. 'Then you'll not get a penny piece of my money for your damned theatre.'

Eden shrugged. 'Your decision, sir.'

'So you do not intend doing the honourable thing, despite compromising my Calliope?' the other man blustered.

'Ah, so you did know about that very unwise visit, did you?' Eden relaxed against the high-carved back of his chair, aware that when he did so the soaring eagle at the top seemed to rise from his shoulders, claws outspread, threatening. A theatrical effect, but it amused him.

'Corwin, I may be a bastard, in all the ways that word can be defined, but I am not able to compromise one young lady while she is chaperoned by her sister and, happily, by a respectable third party who happened to be having a business meeting with me at the time.' The merchant's face fell, ludicrously. 'I suggest you go home, tear up whatever draft contract you have been working on and go and seek your sons-in-law elsewhere. You'll not find one at the Unicorn.'

'He doesn't believe in love,' Maude stated baldly. With complete disregard for the skirts of her evening gown she was curled up at the end of Jessica's bed, her back against the bedpost, her eyes meeting her friend's in the looking glass.

Jessica swivelled round on the dressing-table stool, her diamond ear drops dangling from her fingers. 'You told him you loved him? Maude, of all the—'

'No, of course I did no such thing. He sacked one of the actresses for having an affair with the juvenile lead actor and I said, what if they are in love? And he said, there is no such thing. He is so bitter, Jessica, no wonder he seems like an icicle. I think it all goes back to his childhood, because he seems to regard even maternal love as something nature imposes just to make sure children don't starve. Like birds knowing they have to build nests. Although I don't think he got much paternal love either,' she added with a sigh.

'He's a grown man,' her friend said robustly, hooking one earring into her lobe. 'Ouch, oh, bother this thing. Ring for Mary, will you?'

'No, I'll do it.' Maude slid off the bed and went to help. 'You've got your hair tangled in it. There. Yes, I know he's a grown man,' she said, reverting to her preoccupation with Eden. 'But how we are brought up affects who we are when we grow up, don't you think?'

'Yes, although some people rise above early hardship and others fall into despair or bad ways, even though they had the happiest of childhoods. If the man is bitter and cold, Maude, are you so sure you love him? I don't know how you can really, you hardly know him.'

Troubled, Maude perched on the edge of the bed again, absently smoothing out the creases in her skirts. 'It isn't logical, is it? I ask myself, I truly do, whether it is just because of the way he looks. But even when he upsets me, even when I see all that bitterness, I still *feel* for him. And there is something, even when I disagree with him quite violently, that makes me sense our minds are linked.'

'Just so long as he does nothing to hurt you,' Jessica said, rising and reaching for her reticule. 'I was in half a mind whether to invite him this evening—Gareth won't be best pleased when he finds out—and then I thought, he won't accept anyway...'

'He's coming to the soirée? Eden?' Jerked out of her brown study, Maude scrambled to her feet and seized the hand mirror off the dressing table. 'I knew I should have worn the pearls. I look a fright, I—'

'You look lovely.' Jessica removed the mirror and took Maude by the shoulders. 'Maude, I do think there's some hope for the two of you if Mr Hurst becomes known in respectable society more.' She frowned as though she was trying to convince herself. 'If we can play down the theatre and play up his wealth... And it helps that you are now so firmly on the shelf.' She laughed at the expression on Maude's face. 'Only teasing, but it does make a difference that you've been out for so long. People might just accept a love match that seems...eccentric. Your papa is being extremely tolerant, you know.'

'He doesn't know I have any feelings for Eden, he just thinks I am interesting myself in the theatre,' Maude said, leaning forward to drop a kiss on her friend's cheek. 'Thank you for helping.'

'Bel will, too, and Eva when she arrives. Eva can make *anyone* acceptable.'

'Even an Italian prince's bastard son?' Maude asked.

Jessica slipped her arm through her friend's. 'Come on, time to go down. I'll have to think about this. But I warn you, Maude, if I find he has hurt you, I'll set Gareth on him.' She paused at the top of the stairs. 'After I have operated upon Eden Hurst's manhood with my embroidery scissors.'

Chapter Eight

'He is not going to come,' Maude said to Jessica as they met at one end of the long reception room. The party had been in full swing for over an hour, the rooms were full of people, all talking at the top of their voices and drowning out the string quartet that was playing valiantly on a dais half-way down the room.

Young ladies just making their come-out were giggling together or blushing up to their hairlines if addressed by a young man, groups of middle-aged gentlemen stood around discussing politics and sport, the chaperons were exchanging politely barbed compliments on each other's charges and in one of the side rooms some of the older guests were playing cards.

Gareth, who took the view that there was no point in entertaining if you did not do it properly, had ordered only the best wines to be served and the guests were already anticipating one of the Standons' famous buffet suppers.

'Don't give up on him,' Jessica urged, 'It isn't late yet.'

Maude was already shaking her head. Then instinct sent a shiver down her spine as tangible as the trail of a cold finger running slowly over every vertebra. 'Eden is here.' She scanned the room, searching for his arrogant carriage and dark head. 'There. By the door.'

He was causing a small stir, heads turned. It was not exactly disapproval, Maude realised, more surprise at his presence at such a very respectable soirée. She remembered what the others had told her about his reputation, the fact that he had been seen at some of the more dashing gatherings, the way he attracted not a little attention from the more adventurous ladies. Whether he really fell for their lures she had no idea; people did not mention such things within the hearing of unmarried girls.

Probably, for the man was hardly a saint. Bel was no doubt right. But she was curiously unmoved by the thought of Eden's past *amours*. It was his future fidelity she was interested in.

'Seeing him like this,' Jessica murmured in her ear, 'you can understand the rumours about his father. He's a Renaissance portrait come to life.' Then she added, her tone puzzled, 'And yet, there is something about him that is familiar.'

But Maude hardly heard her. She was already moving, drifting nonchalantly down the room on the opposite side to Eden, wafting her fan, smiling at acquaintances. She stopped opposite where he was standing, deep in conversation with a group of men she recognised. They were all in their thirties, titled, fashionable, known for their sporting pursuits. And Eden, she realised with interest, was already familiar with them. The way they were together spoke of easy acquaintance. But she had dined at their tables, attended the parties their wives gave, and had never met Eden there.

Yet here he was, obviously comfortable in their company and dressed, just as they were, in the height of elegant male fashion, as he had been the other evening in their box at the theatre. So, he was admitted more comfortably into male society, was he?

'We must hold another charity ball, Lady Maude.' Maude focused her attention on Lady Wallace who had appeared at her side, the aigrette of feathers in her coiffure a danger to everyone within three feet of her. 'Or some other fund-raising event, don't you think so?'

'For the soldiers? Yes, indeed. Last year's ball and the picnic were very profitable, were they not? I was wondering whether we should not try for something a little different this year, but I confess, I have had no ideas yet.'

She had lost Lady Wallace's attention. 'My goodness, there's that Mr Hurst, such a surprise to see him here. So decorative, don't you think? And such lovely long legs. Not that I should be saying so,' she chuckled richly, 'Seeing that he must be young enough to be my son. And of course, there's no *family*, so he's not exactly one of us. To say nothing of that reputation.'

'Really?' Maude held her breath, praying that Lady Wallace would not suddenly recall that she was speaking to an unmarried woman. 'Do tell.'

'He is notorious for bedding married ladies.' The aigrette dipped so low that it almost put Maude's eye out as her companion leaned closer to whisper.

'That is hardly unique,' Maude commented drily, glancing around the room. She could see any number of young matrons with a certain reputation. Once they had provided their spouses with the obligatory 'heir and a spare' they had no shame in engaging in heavy flirtation, or worse, with attractive gentlemen. Anything was possible, provided they were discreet.

'But they do say that he never returns to the same one twice,' Lady Wallace confided, startling Maude. She had assumed that Eden would indulge in an *affaire* with the same lady for some time. 'He invariably loves them and leaves them after the one night, despite their pleas for him to return. And given that, by all accounts, his performance in bed is quite spectacular—oh my goodness, I quite forgot you are not married, my dear. You must forget I said anything about—' She broke off, her pale blue eyes opened wide in alarm. 'Mr Hurst!'

'Lady Wallace.' Maude turned to find he was standing just behind them, looking quite unmoved at being confronted by two ladies, one of whom was goggling at him as though he was a pantomime demon emerging from a trapdoor, the other, Maude was only too aware, who was blushing like a peony. 'Lady Maude.'

'Sir.' It was as much as she could manage to articulate. *Quite spectacular performance? In bed?* She had desired him all year, she still tingled all over when she thought of his kiss, but somehow she had never let herself imagine in detail what it would be like to be taken to bed by Eden Hurst. She knew, in theory, what happened, but it had all seemed a rather hazy concept. Rather daunting, if truth be told, and something she put off quizzing Jessica about. Now, so close to the long frame she knew was hard, muscled...

'Maude?' Lady Wallace nudged her foot with one pointed shoe. She appeared to be more than a little flustered to find herself actually in conversation with such a notorious character. 'I was just saying to Mr Hurst how much I enjoyed the new production of *How to Tease and How to Please*. You have seen it, have you not?'

'Yes, of course. So amusing, and Mrs Furlow was in fine voice. Papa invited Mr Hurst to our box during the interval.' Best to establish early on that they had met in innocuous circumstances.

'Oh, so that is what you meant when you mentioned the theatre at our meeting the other day.' Lady Wallace smiled nervously at Eden, who was looking politely mystified. 'Excellent.' She rallied and tapped him firmly on the arm with her fan. 'You can do so much good, young man.'

'I haven't asked Mr Hurst yet, Lady Wallace,' Maude said, smiling through gritted teeth.

'I've let the cat out of the bag, haven't I? I had better take myself off and let you work on him.' She gave a little gasp at her own choice of words and scurried off in a flurry of feathers like an affronted hen.

'So, Lady Maude, you have something to ask me, have you?' He was smiling in that disconcerting way he had, which always gave her the sensation that there was a lot more than mere amusement going on inside his head. 'Am I going to regret accepting Lady Standon's invitation when I hear what I am to do for you?'

'What I would chiefly like you to do for me, at this very minute, is to procure me something to drink,' Maude declared, 'and find me somewhere to sit down. This is the most incredible crush.'

'The mark of success, surely?' Eden steered her through the crowd to an empty alcove, reaching it just ahead of another couple. Maude recognised Lord Witchell and his latest flirt, Mrs Bailey. There was an interesting moment while the two men eyed one another, then Lord Witchell bowed sharply and walked off. It did not escape her that, far from seeming put out, Mrs Bailey directed a lingering look back over one white shoulder at Eden. A look that said, as clearly as words, that she knew him. Very well indeed.

'I will not be a minute.' Maude fanned herself and studied the room while she recovered her composure somewhat. She refused to contemplate whether Mrs Bailey knew Eden in the Biblical sense or not. It was more to the point to worry about whether he had heard what, or who, Lady Wallace had been talking about.

'Lady Maude.' He was back, a bottle of champagne in one

hand, glasses in the other. 'I thought it likely I would need fortifying.' He seemed either unaware, or uncaring, that it was more than a little fast for an unmarried lady to be drinking champagne like this, especially with him. Maude could only be grateful for the wine—the combination of embarrassment, heat and the close proximity of Eden Hurst were a dizzying combination.

'That is not very gallant, Mr Hurst,' she said lightly. 'It sounds as though you would be unwilling to help me.'

'A few days' acquaintance with you, Maude, has taught me caution,' he observed, pouring the wine and handing her a glass. He lifted his in a salute. 'Here's to our partnership.'

With any other gentleman Maude would be flirting lightly, and unexceptionably, by now. Fluttering her eyelashes at being toasted, teasing him charmingly as a reward for fetching her refreshment. But she could not, without jeopardising her business partnership with Eden, flirt with him. It was too soon.

She contented herself with raising her own glass slightly and smiling at him before sipping. 'Lady Wallace, Lady Standon and I are on the committee of a charity founded by Lady Dereham to find employment for soldiers disabled by the war.'

She glanced at him, hoping for a nod of encouragement at least, but he was regarding her steadily, his eyes serious. Why she had the impression that he was thinking about something entirely other than the charity, she had no idea. 'We have bought several inns that are run and staffed by our men, placed others in trades or service, but we are always looking for new opportunities. It occurred to me that you might have some vacancies at the Unicorn.'

The dark brown eyes focused on her; he was back from wherever his mind had been wandering. 'I don't suppose you have an ingénue amongst them?'

'No. Do not be frivolous, if you please, Mr Hurst; this is serious. Surely you can use carpenters and scene painters, doormen and so forth?'

'I am rebuked, Maude. I presume I am still not forgiven for that particular decision?'

'Not unless you have changed your mind.' She should back down on the subject of Miss Golding, she knew. It was unbecoming to argue with a gentleman and, besides, there was nothing in their agreement to allow her rights of veto over Eden's employment decisions. But the cold practicality of his action still chilled her.

'No, I have not. But I expect I can employ one or two men, if they can pull their weight. I am not carrying passengers.'

Maude nodded. 'They will. Our concern is to restore their independence and self-respect by placing them where they can do a fair day's work, not rely on charity. It is finding those positions that is the challenge.'

'Good, I would support that. On one condition.' He had captured her fan, a piece of spangled nonsense that looked ridiculous in his large hand, and was gently wafting it for her.

'What is it?' she asked, wary of both his easy acceptance of her proposal and of what his condition might be. He was sitting back at his ease on the spindly gilt chair, legs crossed, expression relaxed. Why then did he give her the impression of being poised to spring?

'That you call me Eden.'

'I cannot!' Maude glanced around, concerned he might have been overheard. The sight of one of the ladies on Bel's committee ruthlessly cornering gentlemen and lecturing them until they opened their pocket books for the charity was so familiar that no one, so far, showed that they thought the *tête à tête* in any way out of the ordinary, even if they had realised with whom she was conversing, but for her to address a gentleman by his first name was simply not done.

'Not where we may be overheard, of course. But when we are…negotiating?' He furled her fan and handed it back while he refilled their glasses.

'Negotiating?' There was a caress in the way he said the word, as though they were coming to terms about something far more intimate. Maude swallowed wine without noticing, then started as Eden took the fan again, his fingertips brushing the lemon kid glove that sheathed her hand so tightly.

'But yes. We have, after all, a business relationship, do we not?'

'Of course.' She smiled brightly, refusing to let him see how he was disturbing her. But of course, how could he guess how deep her feelings ran? 'If we are negotiating, then I must state my terms. You may call me Maude and I will call you Eden, in private, if you both take some of the men *and* join our committee.'

'Very well. You do not ask me to take Harriet Golding back?'

'I assumed that to ask you to help her would be a lost cause.' Vaguely she was aware that the noise level in the room had dropped—people must be moving off towards the buffet.

'Not necessarily. I will not take her back, but I could probably get her employment at one of the other theatres.' Eden's attention was on the fan, holding it on his knee while he untangled the ornamental cord, which had twisted around his wrist. Maude found herself studying his face, the thick lashes hiding his eyes, the fine modelling of his cheekbones under the olive skin, the strong line of his jaw, the mobile mouth that looked as though it should betray so much and yet hid its secrets so well.

'Then why don't you?'

He did not look up. 'That would mean asking a favour, putting myself in someone's debt. It would need to be worth my while.'

'What would make it worth your while?' she asked. And then he did look up, straight into her eyes and she could not look away, nor, strangely, did she blush. The look went too deep for that.

'Do you know what decided me to play the English gentleman for your father the other night?' he asked.

'No.' The glass was in her hand and Maude drank as though thirsty, her eyes not leaving his. She had asked herself over and over again why he had accepted her money, accepted her interference in his theatre, troubled to soothe her father's concerns. 'Tell me.'

'Because when you want something, you say so. And if you do not get it, then you put forward reasons, you negotiate. You do not wheedle or whine or pout or flutter your eyelashes. You have no idea how refreshing that is.'

'Oh,' Maude said. 'Thank you.' *I think*. It appeared to be a compliment. He liked her intelligence enough to take her investment. So to continue to influence him, to insinuate herself deeper into his life, she had to ensure she did not deploy any of the feminine armoury of flirtation or persuasion. *Not that I have ever whined in my life*, she added to herself. 'What would make it worth your while to help Miss Golding?' she asked briskly.

'Dine with me after the performance on Tuesday.'

After a second Maude became aware that her mouth was open and shut it. Then she reached out, took the fan from him and began it ply it vigorously. How much champagne had she drunk? Two glasses? Or three? Because she was surely hearing things. '*What* did you say?'

'Dine with me.'

'Impossible.'

'You have a prior engagement?'

'No.' Her appointments book was so full for the next month that she had deliberately kept this next Tuesday night free. Papa would be out so she would have the evening to herself to curl up with a frivolous novel.

'You see, Maude? How refreshingly unusual for a young lady to admit she is not engaged every night of the week. Well?'

'I promised Papa I would not go behind the scenes at the theatre in the evening and you are not, I hope, suggesting I dine at your house?' She felt her voice rising slightly and swallowed. Was she wrong about him after all? Was he simply a heartless rake who would try and seduce her?

'I am not suggesting that, no. I am intent upon getting to know you, Maude,' Eden said, 'not ravishing you.' He grinned, the look of genuine amusement transforming his face, taking at least five years off her estimate of his age.

'How old are you?' she blurted out.

'Twenty-seven,' he admitted.

'I thought you older,' Maude said. 'But that is irrelevant.' *Probably.* 'Where are you proposing we dine?'

'Somewhere private that is not my house and will not cause you to break any promise to your father.' He smiled, tempting her.

'If I agree, it will be because I wish to know you better as a business partner and because I desire to help Miss Golding. You should not conclude anything else about my motives,' she stated, trying to look businesslike and not as though Lady Wallace's words were dazzling her brain like exploding sky rockets: *spectacular in bed...*

'You think I might jump to conclusions?'

'I have heard about your reputation, Eden.' There, she had said his name aloud. 'You are notorious for your liaisons with married women, so I hear.' She could feel the heat in her face, just speaking of such things.

'But you are not married, Maude. Say yes.' There had been a shadow behind his eyes when she spoke of his *affaires,* a fleeting darkness, gone so rapidly she thought she had imagined it.

Distracted, she spoke before she had time to consider properly. 'Yes, Eden. I will dine with you on Tuesday.' It must be the wine, otherwise why had she agreed? *So fast, so much faster than I thought. All my plans scattering like dust. How did I ever think I could make him fall in love with me according to a design? How could I not realise that he would set the agenda for whatever he is involved in?*

'Thank you. And will you be my partner for supper now?' He glanced across the room and Maude followed his gaze. The crush had diminished greatly and the sound of the string quartet was once again clearly audible. 'If there is any left, that is.'

'You have obviously never been to one of the Standons' soirées before.' Maude stood up, still holding her glass. Eden lifted his and the champagne bottle in one hand and offered her his arm. She took it, smiling up at him. 'They are famous both for quality and quantity—you need not fear going hungry.'

The queue into the refreshment room was not great and footmen were hurrying back and forth replenishing the long tables. Eden stretched up, looking over the sea of heads. 'I can see a table for two over there in the far corner. If you trust me to choose for you, you could take it now.'

'Anything except crab,' Maude told him, gathering her skirts ready to slip through in the direction he was looking. 'And lots of marchpane sweets, please. Give me the bottle and glasses.'

A young lady should pretend to have the appetite of a bird, of course, she acknowledged ruefully as she found the table and set out the wine. And, given that she wanted Eden to fall in love with her, she supposed she ought to be employing all the ruses at her disposal to make him see her as attractive.

'Why are you frowning?' Eden enquired, placing a platter laden with what must be a selection of every savoury on the buffet in the middle of the table. He was followed by a footman with two plates, forks and a dish brimming with marchpane sweetmeats. 'Enough?'

'A feast! Thank you, but I couldn't eat a tenth of it.'

'I will help.' He poured more wine. 'Now, why the frown?'

'I was thinking—' Could she tell him? Oh, why not? He professed to like her lack of feminine tricks. 'Any lady will tell you that it is most unbecoming to display any appetite at all. I should be nibbling on one patty, perhaps, and you could then, with much persuasion, tempt me to sample a sweetmeat.'

'I see.' Eden's lips quirked into a smile. 'And you have just given yourself away? I have often wondered—and seeing that we are being so frank, perhaps I may ask—are all young ladies, except yourself, possessed of incredible will-power or are your stays laced so tight there is no room to eat?'

Chapter Nine

Maude burst into laughter. Not a giggle, not a titter, but genuine, uninhibited laughter. Heads turned, one or two grey heads were shaken, but no one seemed too shocked. This was, after all, Lady Maude Templeton and much would be forgiven to the Earl of Pangbourne's charming daughter. Even, apparently, taking supper with him.

Eden watched her, his own amusement fading away to be replaced by something quite unfamiliar: affection and a kind of warmth. Maude, he realised, made him feel good inside. He gave himself a little shake, wondering if he was sickening for something, as he had suspected the other day. But it was a very strange fever that seemed to come and go like this.

'Oh, dear.' She struggled with her reticule and produced a handkerchief, which she used to dab at her eyes. The tears of laughter made them sparkle as she looked at him. 'Stays indeed! No, and it is not will-power either—we are expected to eat a large supper before we come out. Didn't you realise?'

'How should I?' he countered. 'I have no sisters.'

'And little to do with unmarried girls in the Marriage Mart,

I would assume.' Maude studied the platter and pounced on a salmon tartlet.

'Are we back to the married ladies again?' he enquired, wary.

'No.' She shook her head, making the loose curls that spilled from the combs set high on her crown tremble. 'That's just your guilty conscience.'

'I doubt I have one,' Eden admitted, biting into a savoury puff and wondering how far Maude's hair would tumble down her straight white back and gracefully sloping shoulders if he pulled out those jewelled combs. Slowly, one by one.

'Then how do you know what is right?' she asked, puzzled.

'I don't know. Judgement, experience, assessment of the alternatives, I suppose.' It was not something he ever thought about. 'There is no good business sense in being capricious or dishonest. You keep your word because otherwise no one trusts you; you deal honestly, or they don't come back a second time.'

'But in your personal affairs?' Maude pressed, choosing a cheese patty.

Eden shrugged. 'The same thing. One does not get involved with anyone who does not understand the rules, then no one gets hurt.'

'Your rules,' she said, raising one eyebrow.

'Yes, my rules, in everything, business and pleasure.' To have the power to make your own rules and live your life by them, not to be dependent on cold, grudging duty. Yes, that was freedom. 'Except with you, Maude—you set your own rules.' She looked at him, faintly troubled, it seemed, then the long lashes swept down to hide her wide brown eyes and she smiled.

Damn it, there was that sensation of…dislocation again, of things shifting. It wasn't dizziness exactly. Like many very fit men Eden found the prospect of being ill not just worrying, but irritating too. He'd go and get a check-up. He couldn't afford to be unwell.

'Would you like me to let you know when I audition for the ingénue part?' he asked abruptly. 'It will be next week, the advertisements have gone out.'

'Thank you, yes, I would be most interested.' She sipped some wine, then began to study the sweetmeats with close attention. 'I must only have three, you understand, more would be greedy, so I have to choose carefully. Do you have your notebook, Eden? I imagine you never move without it.' Maude popped a strawberry-shaped morsel into her mouth and regarded him limpidly.

'Yes, I have my notebook.' Was he that predictable? He dug in his breast pocket and produced it.

'Then please make a note to help Miss Golding find another position.'

'You, Lady Maude, are a very managing woman.' He made a note and pushed the book across to show her.

'And you, Mr Hurst, never do anything you do not want to,' she retorted, closing the notebook and handing it back.

'No,' Eden said slowly, feeling the light brush of her fingers as he took it, inhaling the heady scent of gardenia and warm woman. 'Not always.'

The sudden jolt of physical desire took him aback. She was single, unobtainable, quite out of his reach in *that* way and he had thought, now he knew her, his own self-control would have ensured he was safe from the heat that licked like flame across his loins. He had learned the hard way not to yearn for what his birth debarred him from, to take his pleasures where he was in control without the inconvenience of either attachment or snubs.

When he glanced at her, Maude was cheerfully waving at an acquaintance across the room. Hell, she'd flee screaming if she had any idea what he was thinking about. Then he recalled their very first encounter. She had not fled then; instead, she had dealt with the situation calmly and with humour. Which, Eden decided, resolutely ignoring the rising tension in his groin, meant she did not consider him a threat in that way, any more than she would fear that any of the professional men in her life—her doctor, her attorney, her banker—would press their amorous desires upon her. That was, he had to believe, a very fortunate circumstance.

'He has agreed to join the committee.' Maude swept into Bel's drawing room, cast her bonnet and gloves on to the side table and bent to kiss Bel and Jessica, who were seated side by side on the sofa studying a pile of silk brocade samples.

'Who?' Bel enquired, with a wicked twinkle.

Maude wrinkled her nose at her. 'Eden, of course. And he will take some of the men.'

'Excellent,' Bel smiled. 'Another really forceful man on the committee besides Ashe and Gareth will be so useful. And we can set him on all the rich widows to seduce money out of them.'

Jessica raised an eyebrow. 'Eden? Are you on first-name terms now, then?'

'I agreed to call him Eden, and to allow him to call me Maude—in private, of course—in exchange for him agreeing about the charity,' Maude informed them smugly.

'So he is moving the relationship on to more intimate ground, is he? Oh dear, Maude.'

'I thought it was a step forward,' she protested. 'But I have discovered what he likes about me, and it is hardly particularly flattering.'

'What?' They both regarded her with gratifying interest.

'He likes my lack of feminine wiles. Apparently I do not wheedle or pout when I want something.'

'Perhaps surrounded by thespian temperaments he appreciates something less dramatic and easy to deal with,' Jessica suggested. 'It is encouraging, I suppose—if you are really set on this. So, what is the next step?'

Maude had been agonising over whether to confide in her friends about the dinner. It would be the sensible thing to do. The prudent thing. But they would doubtless try to talk her out of it. 'I am to attend the auditions for a replacement in-génue for the company.'

'Fascinating,' Bel drawled. 'Of course you'll *love* that. Who in their right mind would want to go shopping, or driving or making calls when they can sit in a dusty theatre watching auditions?'

'Me,' Maude stated. And realised it was not just the prospect of Eden's company that made her so eager—she was looking forward to watching him at work. Would he listen to her opinions or would he tolerate only her presence? 'I enjoy shopping too,' she added, in case they thought she had undergone a complete change of personality. 'What do you think of this hat?'

'Delicious,' Jessica pronounced, leaning over to pick up the black straw bonnet with its high poke, tall crown and row after row of looped and ruched green ribbon. 'You don't wear this sort of thing to go behind the scenes at the Unicorn, do you?'

'No, there's dust everywhere and people rushing about with pots of paint, or gesticulating with a handful of grease-paint sticks.' And she did not want to look too obvious. Eden was going to wonder at it if she turned up in the latest fashions. 'I'm wearing last year's walking and carriage outfits mainly.'

'Oh, *those* old things,' Jessica teased. 'You won't catch a man by wearing last year's fashions.'

'You caught one dressed like a governess,' Bel pointed out.

'And I changed into garments fit only for a courtesan very

soon after we met. I have a strong suspicion that Gareth rather preferred the latter.'

'I am not sure Eden notices what I wear,' Maude said, anxious. 'He seems not to be interested in unmarried ladies.'

'Really?' Both Bel and Jessica looked relieved.

'No, nor actresses, as far as I can see. But according to Lady Wallace he goes through married ladies like a knife through butter, just as you said.'

Her friends regarded her with wide-eyed interest. 'I *knew* I was right about his reputation,' Bel said. 'What else does Lady W. say?'

'That he only stays with them the once, however much they plead. And that he is...um, spectacular.'

'Spectacular?'

'In bed,' Maude mumbled, wondering just what *spectacular* involved in practice.

'*Really?* Rich, handsome and a spectacular lover—you certainly have good judgement, Maude,' Bel remarked.

'He is also in business and illegitimate,' Jessica reminded her tartly. 'And the last thing we want is for Maude to be seduced—however wonderful the experience—and then abandoned after one night. Do we?'

'Well, no, of course not. But Maude is very levelheaded...'

Jessica snorted. 'Not about this man, she isn't. You forget, I was there when she first saw him. We were standing in Mr Todmorton's shop and in he walks, looking like a dark angel from the chillier regions of Hell, and Maude just stood there gawking.'

'I *am* here, you know,' Maude interjected, annoyed. 'You do not have to speak about me as though I was somewhere else. And I didn't gawk, I was merely struck dumb with desire. Dark angel, my foot!' The fact that it perfectly described Eden when he was in one of his frostier moods was neither here nor there; she refused to believe that was the real person. Behind that façade was someone much warmer, someone who needed her love as much as she needed his.

'Yes, exactly: desire,' Bel said seriously. 'You do know what happens when a man makes love to you, don't you, Maude, because we don't want you being swept out of your depth through ignorance.'

Maude retreated into one corner of the sofa, clutching a cushion against her stomach defensively. 'Of course I understand what's involved. And I have been kissed and—'

'I mean the bit between him kissing you and the point of no return.'

'Not *precisely*.' Maude rather suspected that the point of no return would be reached rather rapidly if—*when*—Eden kissed her again, but she was not going to say so or her two friends would probably insist on chaperoning her everywhere.

'Are you going to talk to her about it, or shall I?' Jessica asked Bel. 'Someone ought to, she doesn't have a mother—'

'I am going,' Maude declared, leaping to her feet and snatching up her bonnet. 'You are talking about me in the third person again and I have no intention of sitting through a hideously embarrassing lecture on lovemaking. I will work it out as I go along.' Bel moaned faintly. 'I am serious, you know,' Maude said, halfway to the door. 'I love him. I always knew there was someone, somewhere, who was right for me; that's why I wouldn't marry Gareth, even though I love him dearly. It isn't the right sort of love. I know I might not ever be happy with Eden, I know what the obstacles are, but I am not going to give up without even trying.'

Her friends were on their feet, hurrying across the room to embrace her and reassure her. Maude let them fuss, allowed herself to be drawn back into the room to be seated on the sofa and apologised to, and all the time a little voice was nagging in her mind. *What if he does not learn to love you? What if he never does?*

* * *

Tuesday night approached with the speed of a runaway horse when Maude was worrying about it, and like treacle when she talked herself out of the megrims and started to look forward to it. There was no excuse to go to the Unicorn before Tuesday, try as she might to think of one, and no word came from Eden to tell her where they would dine together.

Maude drove Anna distracted on Monday by having all her evening clothes out, trying on one gown after another, and then declaring that she had not got a thing to wear.

'For what engagement, my lady?' the maid asked after an hour.

'A dinner party,' Maude said fretfully, staring down at the heaps of gauze, tulle and flounces. She wanted to look wonderful for Eden, but she did not want to look as though she was trying too hard and she did not want to stand out, wherever they were going.

'There's the dark blue watered silk,' Anna suggested, lifting it out of the back of the press. 'Only you don't like the under-sleeves.'

They spread the gown on the bed and studied it. It fell into full folds from a high waist, the skirt ornamented by swags and bows in a matching tulle. The neckline was boat-shaped, front and back, with cream lace peeping out to add a little modesty, and full white silk under-sleeves reaching to the wrist from beneath the short puffed sleeves.

'Can you cut them off? They make me feel like a bishop.' Then it would be perfect, Maude mused. Elegant and charming, it would show off her bosom and the whiteness of her arms while at the same time it was dark and simple enough for discretion. 'I will need it for tomorrow night,' she added, hoping Eden had not changed his mind.

The note came that afternoon. *I would appreciate your opinion on some changes we have made to* To Tease, Eden had written. *I trust it is not too late for you to find suitable companions to accompany you tomorrow evening. I would, of course, be more than happy to arrange for them to be escorted home afterwards so your carriage would not have to make any detours.*

So, they were to go on after the play. Maude frowned in thought. Who to invite? She could hardly sit in the box alone and Jessica or Bel would be impossible to shake off. Of course, Miss Parrish! Maude took her old governess out every month, but she had not invited her to the theatre for some time. This would be perfect, if she could just manage to work out how to get them both there, and Miss Parrish home again afterwards, without worrying Paul the coachman.

In the event everything worked so smoothly that Maude had an uneasy twinge of conscience. The primrose path was certainly straight and even...

Miss Parrish was delighted at the thought of the play, Paul Coachman quite reassured by Maude's explanation that he should take the governess back to Somers Town afterwards while she went on to supper with friends who would send her home in their own carriage, and Papa departed for his own meeting at his club with jovial good wishes to pass on to Miss Parrish.

Her old governess, now employed from her own home teaching young ladies French and Italian, was pleased, as always, with the luxury of the box and the refreshments Maude had ordered. Her enjoyment of the entertainment was so great, her affectionate thanks for the treat so fulsome, that Maude was positively wincing with guilt by the time she had seen her off and slipped back up to the box.

It was strange, watching the theatre change after the audience had gone. The boxes emptied, as did the stalls and galleries, the noise ebbing away until only the murmur of it from the entrance reached her. Maude sat in the shadows and watched while the curtain was hauled up and stagehands began to restore the set to order for the morrow. The cleaners, she knew, came in first thing; soon she was going to be alone in this echoing space.

One by one the gas lights dimmed and went out, leaving only a few. Where was Eden? The tap on the door behind her brought her to her feet, unsure whether to shrink back into the hangings or call *Come in!* As she hesitated, the door opened and a complete stranger walked in.

'Good evening, ma'am. I'll just sort the furniture out if that's all right with you.' Without waiting for her response he gathered up all but two of the chairs and walked out, to be replaced by two men struggling with a small table and a third laden with a pile of linen and a basket of flatware, porcelain and glasses.

They were going to dine in the box? Maude felt the delighted laughter bubbling up and bit her lip to contain it. How clever of Eden—she was not breaking her promise to Papa not to go behind the scenes at night and she was somewhere private where they could dine with discretion.

And still the men hurried in and out, now with flowers, wine bucket on a stand, bottles, candles… And were as suddenly gone. Now what? Where was the food going to come from?

The door opened and there was Eden, regarding her in the soft glow of the dimmed lamps and the flicker of the candlelight. He was still in his dramatic black evening clothes with the theatrical ruffles and the watery glint of diamonds at ear and throat. Maude realised, with a sickening jolt in her stomach, just how nervous she was and then, just how happy she was also. The laugh escaped as a half-suppressed gurgle and he smiled, and everything was all right.

'What amuses you?'

'You really should have a drum roll to announce you, you look so dramatic in that costume.'

'And you look—' He broke off, frowning, then came fully into the box and closed the door behind him. 'You look quite lovely.'

'Why, thank you, sir.' He held the chair for her and she sat, studying him candidly as he took the place opposite. 'This is a very clever solution to the problem of where to dine.'

'I enjoy problems.' He seemed content to sit and watch her, his long fingers interlaced on the white table cloth, his relaxed body elegant in the dark clothes.

'But I was wondering where the food was going to come from.'

'You are hungry? You have not already eaten one supper so you may pick daintily at what I provide?' he enquired, mock-serious.

'No, I have not. Do not tease me, Eden, I am positively ravenous. You have no idea what an effect nerves have on my appetite. I know they should put me off my food, but I seem to react quite differently. If I am subjected to much more stress, I will end up as round as Prinny.'

Eden smiled and shook his head at her exaggeration. 'Are you nervous, Maude?' He seemed not displeased that she should be, which puzzled her for a moment until she realised that he saw it as a purely feminine response to being alone with him. And that, she thought, aroused and flattered him. Not that there were any overt clues to that. It was more something she sensed, something just glimpsed in the dark intensity of his eyes as he watched her, the deep purr of his voice.

'Of course,' she said lightly, smiling to hide the effect the thought of his arousal had on her. 'It was not easy to arrange to be here like this.'

'You may relax now, then, and eat. My cook is ferrying an

entire dinner from my house and, provided there has been no accident to the carriage, we may expect it at any moment.'

'Eden, that is—ridiculous! You cannot expect the poor man to cook dinner and then deliver it hot and in one piece after driving halfway across London.'

'How do you know where I live?' He seemed interested.

'A figure of speech,' Maude said repressively. She knew exactly where he lived, had caused her carriage to be driven past his home, now and again, but she was certainly not going to admit it to him.

'And the *poor man* is highly paid to produce my dinner when and where I want it, so you may save your sympathy. Ah, here we are.'

The door opened to admit two footmen bearing a tureen, small dishes and a basket of rolls, which they deposited and bowed themselves out.

Eden lifted the lid of the tureen. 'See? Steaming. All done with hay boxes.'

Maude sipped and exclaimed, 'This is delicious!'

'I am glad it meets with your approval. Maude, may I ask you something?'

'Of course.' She put down her spoon, happy with any excuse for looking openly at him, and found his eyes dark and thoughtful on her face.

'You are very frank with me. You let me into the secret of young ladies' lack of appetite, you share your opinions about matters that I know full well we should not be discussing. Are you as frank with any man?'

Chapter Ten

'I am not sure I quite understand.' Maude's heart sank. He thought her unattractively fast? She had thought him amused, if anything, by her unconventional attitude. But perhaps he merely found her eccentric.

'I have heard that ladies are extremely indiscreet with their hairdressers. Are you simply refreshingly free from silly notions about what is proper, or do you regard me in the light of your hairdresser?' *He is smiling, thank goodness. In fact, he is teasing me...*

'I can assure you, Eden, I most certainly do not regard you in the same light as Monsieur Maurice, as I hope you would realise if you ever met him. Unless...' she frowned thoughtfully at the crow-black wing of hair he was pushing back from his forehead '...unless you too wear a toupee?' His snort of laughter answered that. 'When I am with young men at balls and dinners I act as they expect, because they do not have the flexibility of mind to cope with anything else.'

'And I do?'

'I hope so.' She added more seriously, 'I hope you realise that I am not dining with you alone like this because it seems amusing to be scandalous, or because I am fast and would do so with any man who asked me. It is simply that, with you, I find I can be myself.'

Another man would have been taken aback by that comment, or teased her. Eden merely looked thoughtful. 'Why is that, do you think?' he asked, the piece of bread in his fingers crumbling, uneaten, as he studied her face.

'Because I enjoy your company and I feel quite safe with you.' *And I wish I did not...*

'Despite the fact I kissed you the way I did, nearly took you in the corridor on our first encounter?' he asked outright, almost making her choke on the spoonful of soup she had just lifted to her lips. And the reminiscent gleam in his eyes made her reconsider exactly how safe she felt.

'It was an error,' Maude managed to say calmly. 'And if I had been someone you intended to kiss for the usual reasons...' his lips twitched at her choice of phrase, but she pushed on, managing not to stare at them '...I imagine matters would have concluded in your office and not in the corridor. That was most excellent soup.' She had not seen the little bell until Eden lifted it and rang. The footmen came in, cleared and replaced the tureen with more dishes.

'Lobster, a fricassee of chicken, various vegetables. May I serve you?' Maude nodded and waited while the plates were filled and white wine was poured. 'So, you like my flexible mind, you admire my chef's cooking, you covet my theatre and you are able to disregard my reputation. Is that all that brings you here?'

'Are you fishing for compliments, Eden?' Maude enquired, lingering a moment to savour the meltingly tender chicken. 'You are also aware that you are considered a very handsome man. Perhaps that is why I am here.'

'Thank you.' He smiled as she shook her head reprovingly at him for assuming it was her opinion also. 'I have looks that appear to strike some women as attractive. For which

I must thank my father—it is hardly an attribute for which I can claim any merit. But you, I think, are not looking for something so superficial, or a trophy to shock your friends.'

'Exactly. So you are quite safe,' Maude said prosaically. 'We may discuss matters of mutual interest and you need not worry that I am about to fling myself into your arms or tear off my clothing.'

'I am sure I ought to say that is a relief,' Eden said, cutting into his lobster. 'But you must be aware that any man who is conscious and under the age of ninety would wish to find you in his arms, so you must give me full credit for my restrained behaviour.'

It was the nearest he had come to open flirtation. Maude lowered her eyes to her glass to keep her expression hidden while she controlled the impulse to beam at him. 'I do,' she said after the merest pause. 'You mentioned your father just then. Are you very like him in character as well as looks?'

For a moment she thought he would not answer her. 'I hope not.'

'You did not get on well together?'

'He never spoke to me. If it was necessary to decide something, he would speak of me in the third person to one of the servants.'

'Perhaps he wasn't very good with children,' she suggested, chilled. 'Some people aren't.' Eden merely looked at her, but the expression in his eyes said everything. 'Oh.' She swallowed. 'Have you ever gone back, since you became a man?'

'You are wondering if I created an ogre in my mind and it would do me good to confront him? Yes, I went back, once. I suppose I thought it would be amusing to see what he made of the scrawny little kitchen rat now I'd grown up to look like him, with good clothes and money in my pocket.'

Maude flinched. 'And?'

'And I found it…interesting to see what I would look like in thirty years time, although I wondered if I would ever learn the self-control to stay that calm, that distant, in the face of an arrogant twenty-year-old. Or that contemptuous,' he added, his lips thinning. 'It was a lesson in the perils of sentimentality. I had thought, perhaps, to have made him proud of me; I learned that the only person whose opinion matters is my own.'

'You have found no one else whose opinion matters?' she asked, unable to find anything to say about the rest of that speech. Not and keep from weeping.

'I had thought not,' Eden said. 'Now, let me tell you about the auditions.' His explanations took them through the main course and into dessert. Maude listened and nodded, all the time conscious of the long fingers gesturing to mark a point, the intensity in his eyes when he was serious about something. She did not dare venture into anything more personal again. 'There has been a considerable response to my advertisements, so I expect it to take all day,' he concluded.

'When will you start? I want to make sure I am here to see everything,' Maude said, spooning a syllabub as light and rich as spun silk. 'Mmm. This is *heaven*.'

'You will be bored to death, Maude. I will be starting at nine, but you will hardly want to do more than drop in for half an hour or so, surely?' He reached over and dipped an almond biscuit into the dish in front of her, licking syllabub off the *tuile* with sensual enjoyment.

'You said you didn't want any!' Maude raised her spoon in mock aggression. 'This is all mine and I will defend it to the death.'

'But that was before I tasted it.' Eden feinted with another little biscuit and Maude rapped him over the knuckles and they both laughed. Then their gazes locked and Maude found she was staring, the laughter dying on her lips as something happened, deep in the dark eyes fixed on hers. 'Perhaps I am not as good with temptation as I thought,' he said slowly. There was a long, breathless moment before he broke the gaze with an almost physical abruptness and reached for the platter of cheese.

Maude got her breathing back under control. 'I will be here for the auditions at nine, then,' she said. 'I would like to give you my opinions and I cannot compare one actress with another if I do not see them all.'

Eden put down his knife, his face showing no signs of amusement or flirtation now. 'The decision is mine. We made no agreement about casting or employment.'

'Yes, of course. I am not claiming any privilege in the matter.' What was it Jessica had called him? *A dark angel from the chillier regions of Hell*—yes, that was it. Well, he was not apparently angry, so Hell was presumably on hold, but his severe masculine beauty and the implacable expression certainly fitted the first part.

She shivered, more unnerved than she liked to admit to herself at his rapid change from amused teasing to icy assertion of his rights. 'I thought I would sit up here and watch, as though I was a member of the audience. My opinion may be of value to you, and if not, you will ignore it.' She did her best to sound neither defensive, nor shaken by his territorial reaction.

'Very well.' Eden could not be said to have relaxed again, for his body had not noticeably stiffened in the first place, yet Maude sensed the moment of tension had passed. *Don't touch my theatre!* He should have a sign hung up, she told herself, striving to find a lighter note. 'Yes, that will be interesting,' he added, 'to see what you think of each from this vantage point.'

'It is agreed, then.' She risked further provocation. 'And Miss Golding? What news of her?'

'She has found a place at the Sans Pareil in the Strand. They specialise in burlettas; it will suit her well enough.'

'Thank you,' Maude said, warmly. 'I am so happy that you did that.'

'You are happier than Mr Merrick in that case, for he is short one week's wages that I added to what was owing to Miss Golding.'

'So you are not completely heartless, then?' Maude watched his face from beneath her lashes, caught the wry twist of his mouth. 'You did not tell me before that you had done so.'

'It was no loss to me and it served as a lesson for Mr Merrick,' Eden said coolly, disowning any motive of kindness. He must, surely, have a softer side?

'You left me to think you were cruel enough to simply cast her out,' Maude observed, 'and you were not.' Instinctively she reached out, laid her own hand palm down over his. 'It isn't a crime to admit to compassion, Eden.'

He sat looking down at her hand, then turned his under it and lifted until her fingertips were an inch from his lips. *He is going to kiss them...* She could feel his breath, hot on the sensitive skin. Then he raised his eyes, watching her under the thick black lashes as he lowered her hand to the table and released it.

'It is probably as well if you have no illusions about my character, Maude. I am not one of your society gentlemen, running tame in ballroom and parlour. I grew up differently and I know weakness is not gentility, it is danger.' He did not appear to expect an answer to that, instead picking up a knife and looking at her questioningly. 'May I tempt you to some cheese? A glass of port?'

'No, thank you.' Maude shook her head, distracted by wondering how she was ever going to crack Eden's defences.

'Shall I see you to the carriage, then?' She nodded, still

not concentrating completely. 'I would like to prolong the evening, but I have no desire to cause Lord Pangbourne any anxiety.'

'Thank you. But he is engaged with friends until the early hours,' Maude said vaguely. 'Still, I should not keep my maid waiting up for me.' Eden came and pulled out her chair for her to rise and she smiled her thanks over her shoulder as she did so.

It happened so fast, came out of nowhere—there was no time to think. At one moment they were formal, she rising gracefully from her seat, he placing the chair to one side so her full skirts were unimpeded, the next she stumbled, her low French heel catching in the carpet rucked by the table, and she was in his arms.

Instinctively her hands went up for balance, fastening on his lapels, and his arms were around her, swinging her away from the low edge of the balcony, folding her against his chest. Her overwhelming sensation was of the scent of him: clean, warm male with a hint of an exotic spice mingling with starched linen and that green earth smell of olive oil.

'You've been oiling your hair,' she said, such a foolish thing to be talking of when she was strained against his body and he was looking down at her as though he was still ravenously hungry.

'Yes,' he said, half-laughing at her, half-serious, with a kind of confusion that seemed alien to him. 'Maude?'

A question, a statement? A plea? She couldn't tell. Nor, she realised with something like despair, could she pull away. He was going to kiss her. *Too soon...*

Eden felt the sensations wash through him, searching with his mind for his self-control like a man who has dropped something precious into a fast-flowing stream. He was going to have to do this, *he* was going to have to be the strong one, the responsible one. Maude was simply too innocent to re-alise what was happening here. She probably thought he was going to kiss her, a light good-night kiss, perhaps.

And instead she was a finger's breadth away from being pulled down to the upholstered bench that ran around the box and ravished. He tried not to hold her so tightly, ach-ingly aware of the force of his arousal, aware of the soft skin, the fragrance that rose from it, the primitive need to strip the silks and lawns from her body. What was it about this woman? He had never so much as flirted with a respectable single woman. She was a *virgin,* for God's sake!

Under his hands she quivered and he realised his big hands were gripping her shoulders, the fragile bones trapped under his palms. But she made no sound and the pansy-dark eyes were watching him with something he was quite unable to read.

What had happened? He had thought after that first mis-taken kiss that he was simply enjoying her company, the intel-ligent, amused comments, the sweet femininity surrounding him without any games being played, without any demands being made. Maude was a novelty, a woman he thought might actually become a friend and now—this.

This overwhelming desire came out of nowhere, over-setting him just where he thought he was strongest. He had believed that his will was firm, that his self-control was abso-lute, that his life was ordered, controlled, planned. And now here was this society chit reducing him to a mass of scream-ing, mindless need without so much as a flirtatious glance.

And this was not need he could take to some whore to slake. Oh, no, this was need for *her,* for Lady Maude Tem-pleton, and he might as well desire the moon.

He had done harder things than this, Eden told himself, gritting his teeth and forcing his hands apart. Harder things, more painful things, although just at the moment, in the grip of this madness, he could not recall what they were.

Where had this come from? He was a sensual man, he knew that, knew he would never be celibate. But this lust for an innocent young woman he hardly knew? But he did know her, he realised, with the part of his brain that was functioning clearly. He knew her better already than any woman in his life, other than Madame Marguerite.

He managed to let Maude go, then caught her elbow as she staggered slightly, as though her knees were shaking. How long had he been standing there, holding her, drowning in those lovely, wondering eyes? 'I'm sorry, did you hurt yourself when you tripped?'

'No. No, not at all. So clumsy of me.' She stepped away, apparently steady on her feet now, which was more than he felt. That damned dizziness again. 'That will teach me to drink two glasses of wine,' she added, sounding ruefully amused.

Did she not realise what had almost happened just then? Had she not seen how much danger she had been in? It seemed not. And he—what peril was he risking? He could not afford to find himself obsessed with the daughter of a peer, he could not afford the lack of focus that unrequited desire would bring. Or the retribution Lord Pangbourne would bring down on his head if his self-control slipped and he debauched the earl's daughter.

'Time to go home,' Eden said, finding his voice emerged quite normally, not with the huskiness of the desperation he was feeling.

'Yes, of course. My cloak…' Maude gestured towards the shadows, then stood while he swung the heavy velvet around her shoulders. 'Thank you. Now, where did I put my reticule? Ah, here it is.' She seemed to Eden's bemused eye to be quite calm, which could only mean she was very innocent, despite her assured air and her age, or completely impervious to whatever dubious attraction he had for other women, or both.

He held the door for her, then followed her out into the wide passageway, resisting the urge to take her arm, knowing he could not trust himself to touch her. She did, however, seem unusually quiet. Perhaps some sixth sense was making her uneasy. Eden walked beside her, racking his brains for conversation and finding none. And finding no possible excuse for not sending her away, breaking their contract, never seeing her again.

Eden seemed unusually silent, Maude thought as they made their way along the wide, deserted corridors and down the sweep of the stairs to the front lobby.

She looked up, seeing the hard line of his jaw, the dark shadow of his beard just beginning to show. Beyond she could see the head of the unicorn, thrusting out of the wall, its horn lowered, its nostrils wide. It had never seemed fierce to her before, or threatening, but now it did.

Someone materialised from the shadows, opened the door and whistled. Eden stepped out into the night, still not taking her arm, and the cold air struck her skin, making her realise just how heated she was. There were the sound of hooves on the cobbles and a carriage drew up.

Eden snapped his fingers at the groom, who jumped down and hurried to let down the steps and help her enter. 'Eden?' she queried.

'I will ride on the box.' He shut the door and she was alone. Shivering slightly, Maude fidgeted with her cloak and tied the cord at her neck. There were gloves in the pocket and she pulled them on, feeling the need to cover as much skin as possible, as though that flimsy warmth would stop the fine tremor running through her.

Now she was alone she could think about those few

crowded moments after she had stumbled and he had caught her in his arms. What had happened? She was not sure. She was not certain even how long he had held her, his strong fingers locked around her shoulders. She had stumbled, Eden had caught her—and for her the world had stopped on its axis.

But for him? He had been so still, his eyes so intent, his breathing hard. Had he felt the sensual shock that had gone through her? Or was it simply that he had found himself, late at night, with his arms full of young woman and it had taken a moment for him to control a man's natural reactions?

But she did not want him to feel only desire, flattering though that was. She wanted his emotions involved, not his instincts. When they made love—she closed her eyes and shivered—she wanted it to be because he loved her. But Jessica and Bel had warned her that was not how men thought. And it seemed they were right.

Maude was still wrestling with her desires and her ignorance as the carriage slowed and stopped. When the door opened Eden was standing there, his hand held out to help her down. It seemed he was prepared to touch her now. The groom was already climbing the front steps to knock.

She made herself hold Eden's gaze for a long moment, then pulled up her hood and put her hand in his. 'Thank you.'

'Thank you, I enjoyed your company very much.' He kept his voice low, conscious, as she was, of the driver up on the box.

'And I, yours. It was a delicious meal; please thank your chef for me,' she responded, as though they were parting after a normal society dinner party. 'I look forward to the auditions.'

One of the footmen had come to open the door. Maude inclined her head to Eden with a smile and walked with perfect poise across the pavement, up the steps and into the hall.

'Thank you, James. You may lock up now. His lordship will be very late and he has his keys.'

She kept her back straight all the way up the stairs, along the landing and into her room, even though there was no one to see her. Anna came in answer to the bell and chatted cheerfully as she unlaced Maude's gown, put away her jewels, unpinned and brushed her hair, unperturbed by her mistress's silence.

When she had gone Maude sat up in bed and watched the dying fire and contemplated, for the first time in her life, a problem she did not know how to solve.

Chapter Eleven

Maude was up there, in her box, although it was scarcely half past eight. He could sense her as clearly as if the scent of gardenias had wafted down to the bare stage and driven away the stink of gas, greasepaint and dust. Eden took the list of hopefuls for the audition from the stage manager and scanned it, although he already had it clear in his mind.

'Who have you got to play opposite them?'

'Tom Gates.' Howard, the stage manager, ran his hands through his grizzled brown curls and frowned at the stage. 'What props do you want, Guv'nor?'

'Table, chair. Throw a shawl over the chair, put something on the table—give them something to use.' He could feel himself turning to look up at the box and swivelled back, despising himself. He had dealt with his frustration, but he had not been able to force himself to think of just any woman. Instead, his mind had been filled with the image of Maude, her supple body, her soft, warm mouth, and he had groaned aloud, the sweat standing out on his brow. 'Here.' He thumbed through the pages of the play in his hand. 'Give them all this scene.'

'Right you are, Guv'nor.' Howard turned back to take the

pages. 'Her ladyship's here.' The man lowered his voice and jerked his head towards the tier of boxes up on the right. 'Been here since eight. Said not to disturb you.' Eden allowed himself a grunt of acknowledgment. 'I sent Millie up with some coffee and sweet rolls.'

'Good.' At least he wasn't fantasising, Maude really was up there. Perhaps there was nothing wrong with him at all, except lust, and slender brunettes with heart-shaped faces and haughty little noses were what it took to reduce him to this state of distraction.

His doctor had patiently examined him, peered into his eyes, listened to his heart, performed whatever mysteries medics did over a urine sample and pronounced him as fit as a racehorse. The man had offered to bleed him should the strange dizzy spells recur, advised laying off the port and drinking more Burgundy instead and recommended a few early nights. 'Not that there's a damn thing wrong with you, Hurst,' he'd added. 'Still, I expect you want some advice for your money.'

Eden stalked off to straddle a chair set stage right, his back to Maude's box, without acknowledging that he was aware she was there. It was ungracious, he knew. He dumped the papers on the small table set beside it, pulled a pencil out of his pocket and tried to make his mind go blank. And failed.

And it wasn't just the physical attraction, it was the way she looked into his eyes as though she wanted to touch his soul and asked him questions and he found he was betraying his innermost thoughts, his weaknesses, the sore areas he tried to ignore.

Try common sense... The more you avoid thinking about her, the more obsessed you will become. There are two options—make love to her or get used to her. The first was patently impossible, which left the second.

Eden stood up, moved centre stage and shaded his eyes to look up at the boxes. 'Lady Maude?'

'Mr Hurst.' He could see her easily now. Maude had taken off her bonnet and she was resting her elbows on the velvet padded rim of the box, a coffee cup cradled in her hands. 'Thank you for my breakfast.' She could pitch her voice to reach him without shouting, he realised, professionally impressed at the clarity.

He should, of course, acknowledge that it had been Howard's idea to send up the refreshments. 'My pleasure.' He wrestled with the conscience that he had assured her he did not possess. 'But you must thank Mr Howard, our stage manager, for that.'

'Thank you, Mr Howard,' she called, waving, and the man produced a rare smile and raised a hand in acknowledgment. *Now she is going to charm the entire company*, Eden thought, resigned to hearing Maude's praises sung by all and sundry.

'Right.' He looked at his pocket watch before laying it beside the script. 'Let's get on with this.'

Maude bit the end of her pencil and concentrated. Mr Howard had given her a list of the hopeful ingénues and she was making careful notes against each. Not very clear… Moves awkwardly… Over-dramatic… Too old… Moves beautifully, but couldn't hear her…

When Eden stood up and announced a break for luncheon, she had come to the conclusion that there were only three so far who seemed right. 'Mr Hurst!'

Eden turned, looking up, and she was almost tempted to launch into the balcony scene from Romeo and Juliet. She repressed the urge; her acting would reduce the audience to fits of laughter. 'Would you care to take luncheon up here?'

She had managed, with some success during the day at least, not to think too much about those moments in Eden's arms that night. Now he seemed to hesitate and she felt her poise slipping.

'Thank you, but, no, Lady Maude. Perhaps you would join Howard, Gates and me down here?' He must have thought her silence meant she was doubtful, for he added, 'With your maid, of course.'

'Thank you, we will be right down.' It was not doubt, Maude thought, managing to keep the smile off her face with difficulty, it was delight. For if he was inviting her to join them, then it meant he was prepared to listen to her ideas.

With Anna at her heels she made her way on to the stage to find hands were transforming the make-shift set into a dining room and putting chairs around the table. Millie bustled on with a tray and began to lay out plates of cold meat, a raised pie, bread and cheese.

'Have you ever been on stage before?' Eden asked her as she stopped, centre front of the fore-stage, and looked out over the ranks of seats.

'Only in small private theatres in country houses. This is breathtaking. It feels so much bigger than it looks from the box.' She glanced at him and saw he was standing, studying the view from the stage with the same look on his face as she sometimes saw on her father's countenance when he came home to Knight's Fee, their Hampshire estate. This was not just Eden's work, not just a tool of his trade—this theatre belonged to him in a way that went far beyond deeds of ownership. What she could see was passion and possession and pride.

'You have good projection and pitch,' he remarked, turning back to the table and taking the jug of ale from Millie. 'Are you sure you cannot act? Think what the appearance of Lady Maude Templeton on the stage would do for the box office.'

'Empty it,' she said, laughing, and took the chair he held

for her. Anna, looking alarmed, was seated next to Tom Gates and Howard took the foot of the table.

'Help yourselves.' Eden waved at the spread before flattening his notes next to his plate and pouring ale. 'Can you drink this, Lady Maude?'

'I expect so,' she said, cutting the pie and serving it out. 'It is thirsty work, listening.'

'Right, then. The first one.'

It took about three minutes for the men to forget who she was and to absorb her into the discussion. Elbows appeared on the table, notes were scribbled with one hand while the other waved a slice of bread to make a point, slices of meat and cheese were heaped on her plate without ceremony and Gates clinked his mug against hers. 'Cheers.'

Anna sat, quiet as a mouse, eating steadily, while Maude listened. So far, everyone was agreeing with her impressions, although their analysis of faults and talents were far more detailed and technical than her own.

'Number ten,' Eden said, spearing an apple with his knife. 'No projection. No presence.' The others nodded. Maude looked at her notes.

'I don't agree.'

The three men reacted as though the loaf of bread had addressed them, she thought, amused. 'I beg your pardon, Lady Maude.' Howard stopped gaping at her. 'She wasn't good technically.'

'She looked charming, she is graceful and she reacted well to Mr Gates's lead,' Maude stated. 'Can't you teach her to project her voice better?'

'She should know how,' Eden said.

'But she's young, she cannot have much experience. Won't you call her back?'

Gates looked at Howard. Howard looked at Eden. Eden poured more ale. Maude could almost hear their thoughts. His theatre, his company, his decision—and if he let her override him, would it diminish his authority?

'Why didn't you say anything about the others?' he asked.

'Because I agreed with you about them.'

'Ah. Well, Lady Maude, you are our expert in the audience. Howard, put number ten down to call back.' Face studiously blank, the stage manager made a note. 'Number eleven?'

By mid-afternoon Anna had fallen asleep on the padded bench and was snoring softly, but Maude was still engrossed. She had three more possibles on her list and was finding her judgements easier now she had heard the men's opinions over luncheon. Finally, at half past five, Eden called a halt and she went back down to the stage, leaving Anna sound asleep in the box.

'Well,' Eden said. 'Show me your lists. Lady Maude, gentlemen.' He spread them out on the table side by side. 'It would appear we are unanimous. There's six for you to call back tomorrow, Howard.'

'You mean I got them right?' Delighted, Maude bent over the table, tracing the notes with her finger.

'I'm impressed.' Eden was standing close beside her, the others had walked off; in the distance she could hear Howard calling the names of the afternoon's selection. 'Are you tired?'

'No,' Maude said, then found she could not stifle a most unladylike yawn. 'But I do have a thick head. All that concentrating, I suppose.'

'And no fresh air. These gas lights are all very well, but it is not a good atmosphere to be in all day.'

'We could go for a walk,' Maude suggested, watching as Eden stretched like a big cat, all supple muscle and long limbs.

'It will be dark. This is February, remember.' He stood,

turning his head as if to ease his neck, then sat to gather up the papers.

'Is your neck stiff?' she asked as he rotated his shoulders. His attention was on the sheets in his hand; she doubted he was even aware that he was doing it.

'My neck? Yes, a little. I am usually on my feet more.'

'Let me.' Maude moved behind him, put her hands on his shoulders and dug her thumbs into the hard muscle. 'I do this for Papa when he's been in the House all day.' Under her hands Eden's shoulders stiffened. 'Am I hurting you?'

'No.' She wasn't sure if she believed him; his voice sounded more than a little constrained. But it was such a delight to find a perfectly innocuous excuse to touch him. No one could object to having their shoulders massaged, surely?

'Thank you. That is much better.' He moved restlessly and she lifted her hands away. 'I will call your carriage.'

'I love the streets after dark. Walk me home, Eden?'

Eden had been turned away from her, now he swung round. 'It is too far.'

'To Mount Street? Half an hour, I should think. But I will send Anna home in the carriage, she is tired.'

'You cannot walk through the streets with a man and no chaperon,' Eden said firmly.

'I have a veil on my bonnet and they are all perfectly respectable streets.' Maude contemplated him, wondering what argument would work. 'I have a headache. It will be much better for me to cure it with fresh air and exercise than having to dose myself with something when I get home.'

'Is it a thick veil?' Eden asked. She could almost hear the sigh.

'Very,' Maude assured him. 'Will you ask Mr Howard to send Anna home in the carriage when she wakes up?'

'Yes.' Eden looked resigned more than cheerful at the thought of the walk. 'Come along, then.'

'I will meet you in the front lobby,' Maude said. 'It is after four, so I cannot go back stage, remember?'

'I assume your father was attempting to safeguard your reputation when he imposed that condition.' Eden regarded her with a jaundiced eye. 'No doubt it never occurred to the poor man that you might want to take to the streets with me, unchaperoned?' As he strode off stage without waiting for her answer, it appeared to be a rhetorical question.

The evening was cold but dry; the air, even full of the smell of horse manure and smoke, was refreshing after the close atmosphere inside. Maude slipped her hand through the crook of Eden's left arm and breathed deeply as they made their way along Long Acre towards Leicester Square.

The streets were crowded, bustling and, in this part of town, thoroughly vulgar. 'I love this,' she confided. 'Look at how much *life* there is going on here.'

'Indeed.' Eden sounded less enchanted by the sight of barrow boys, ladies of dubious virtue on street corners and groups of working men noisily making their way to the nearest tavern. 'And a couple of streets further north and we're into the St Giles rookery, so hold on to me and don't go wandering off or you'll experience more life than you've ever dreamt of.'

'As if I would,' Maude said demurely. 'Oh, look, Eden, hot chestnuts. May I have some?'

Eden bought a cone of old newspaper, filled with blackened, fragrant nuts and began to peel them as they walked, hampered a little by Maude on his arm, although he gave her his gloves to hold. She laughed at his muttered comments as he struggled. 'You'd curse if it were your fingers being burned,' he grumbled at her when he finally freed the hot kernel. 'I suppose you want the first one too, don't you?'

'It would be the gentlemanly thing to offer it to me,' Maude observed, amused by the glimpse of Eden fumbling with the nut like any schoolboy. 'And don't tell me you aren't one,' she added as he opened his mouth. 'But *I* am definitely a lady, so I think you deserve the first fruit of your labours.'

'Thank you.' He popped it into his mouth, then mumbled, 'I'dths too hot!'

'I know,' she said, laughing. 'Why do you think I let you have the first one?'

He grinned back at her teasing and began to extract another. 'Here, open your mouth, it will mark your gloves otherwise.'

Eating in the street, let alone having a man popping food into her mouth, was thoroughly unladylike behaviour, Maude knew, lifting the edge of her veil just enough for Eden to deliver the chestnut between her parted lips. But as they walked down Cranburn Street into Leicester Square the people they were passing weren't ladies and gentlemen, but people with far fewer inhibitions about enjoying themselves, and their chestnuts were not the only things being consumed. Regaining proper speech again, Eden tossed the rest of the parcel to an urchin. 'Here, catch.'

'Oh, look, Stagg and Mantle's are still open,' Maude said, veering sharply off to the left as soon as they got into the square, only to be brought up short by Eden digging in his heels.

'Over my dead body are you dragging me into a linen draper's,' he stated, with more firmness than gallantry. 'And,' he added as Maude studied his face for any signs of yielding, 'if you so much as flutter an eyelash at me, I will call a cab and that's the end of our walk.'

'All right.' She tucked her hand more firmly into the crook of his elbow. 'It is your turn anyway.'

'For what? Mind that coal cart!'

'For a treat.' Maude looked up at his austere face. 'I had the chestnuts, now it is your turn.'

'I wasn't aware that walks involved treats.' Eden sounded amused—or was he simply bemused?

'My governess started it, and then my girlfriends picked it up and it has become a tradition. So—your turn to choose.'

'I can't think of anything I want. Nothing, that is, that it is reasonable to want on a crowded street,' he added as they walked down Coventry Street towards the bustle of Piccadilly.

'Hatchard's?' Maude enquired hopefully. Once she had lured him into a bookshop, there was the prospect of browsing together companionably, finding out what kind of books he liked, edging him towards the poetry...

'I have far too much reading waiting for me, without adding any more. Aren't you tired yet?'

'Certainly not, this is a mere stroll. At home in Hampshire I walk miles. Oh my, look at that quiz of a hat.'

'It probably cost twenty guineas. The family estate in Hampshire, no doubt?'

'Yes, Knight's Fee. I love it. So does Papa—bone deep. You know, this afternoon, when I saw you looking out from the stage at the theatre, you had just the sort of expression he does when he looks out at the land.'

'Bone-deep love? Yes, I suppose that is what it is. The first time I stepped into a theatre I was fourteen years old and the magic got hold of me and has never let me go. I had never possessed anything before that was my own creation. The theatre let me create and then I was able to buy one, and another, to put on plays. But none of them were right—but I knew I would know when I found it. And in the Unicorn, I have.'

She held her breath, willing him to go on, to let her see more, to understand more. But he had caught himself up, she could sense it.

'And you, Maude—you couldn't live without your country estate and your town house, your balls and your charities, could you?'

'I could if I still had my friends and I could still visit Knight's Fee. Women have to get used to the knowledge they must leave their childhood home, at least, unless we give up all idea of marriage.' It made her slightly breathless, actually speaking of marriage to Eden.

'And you haven't given up, despite your advanced years?' He sounded serious, despite his joke about her age.

'No, of course not. I have always said that there was the right man out there for me and I would know him when I saw him. Just like you and your theatre. I will remain a spinster all my life, rather than compromise on that. That's what gave me the strength to stand up to Papa when he wanted me to marry Gareth.'

'Standon?' He sounded surprised. 'So that is who you were telling me about. But you are good friends, are you not?'

'Excellent friends and we have been for years. It would have been like marrying my brother. Oh, look—' Maude pointed up Dover Street '—that's where we first met.' *Oh, Lord! I blurted that out without thinking...*

'What, you and Standon?'

'No.' Nothing for it. 'You and I. In Todmorton's perfumery shop. I was with Jessica—Lady Standon—you had come in to collect something.'

Eden stopped, ignoring the pedestrians who bumped against him, then began to flow round them as though they were a rock in a river. 'I knew I had seen you before.' He frowned in concentration. 'Sponges. Why do I think of sponges?'

'Because Jessica and I were tossing little ones to and fro and you walked in and had to catch them. We were being foolish and you were looking exceptionally severe.'

Eden ignored that. 'You were wearing green. Moss green and a bonnet with a big satin ribbon and ruching all under the brim.'

He remembered her! And Jessica had said he hadn't noticed them at all. 'That's right,' Maude confirmed happily until she realised with a jolt that she should have pretended not to recall any detail at all. 'It was brand-new. I remember Jessica commenting on it as we went into the shop.'

'And there I was, thinking every detail of the day was burned on your memory because that was the day we met,' Eden said, creating an inner turmoil that made her feel light-headed. If he only knew!

'Well, it was not burned on yours,' she retorted as her scrambled wits reasserted themselves. 'I had to remind you.'

'I could hardly stare at a beautiful young woman, chance met in a shop, now could I?' he asked reasonably, beginning to walk again. 'I saw the gown, the bonnet, a glimpse of your face. I knew you were familiar when I saw you at the theatre.'

Maude could have told him every detail about what he had been wearing: the highly polished Hessians, the buff pantaloons, the dark blue coat, the cane with the silver head, the high-crowned hat in his gloved hands. She could have described in minute detail how his hair had curled over his collar, his words to the shop assistant, the almost physical blow to her senses that seeing him had been.

'Nearly there now.' They were turning into Berkeley Street, up the side of Devonshire House. 'It seems we were fated to meet again,' he added, almost to himself.

'Yes,' Maude agreed, striving for a tone of bright amusement at the coincidence.

'One could almost say that passing the shop again this evening was an omen,' Eden mused. They had reached the narrow alleyway that ran between the end of the Devonshire House garden boundary and the length of Lansdown House's high wall. The lighting was poor there, contrasting to the open space of Berkeley Square a few yards ahead. 'Do you know, I think I know what I want for my treat.' He stopped and stepped into the mouth of the alley, almost too narrow for them to stand side by side.

'You do?' He was drawing her into his arms, bending his head until his mouth was just above hers.

'I left that shop wishing I could kiss you.'

'You have. Outside your office.' It was an inelegant squeak, but the best she could manage.

'It was hardly my best effort,' Eden said thoughtfully. He lifted her veil back, then his hands bracketed her face, his thumbs caressing lightly against her cheeks.

'Eden—we are on the street!' Her breathing was all over the place and her hands, without any conscious volition, had come up to rest against his lapels.

'Safest place,' he said, sounding rather grim for a man about to kiss a woman. And then he kissed her and Maude stopped thinking about his tone of voice at all.

Chapter Twelve

The pressure of Eden's mouth on hers was light—a caress, not a demand. He did not draw her closer, or try to master her, he simply let his lips stray over hers, tasting, caressing, until finally his tongue-tip slipped between her lips and she could taste in her turn.

His gentleness made her shyer than his force had done; his restraint ensured that every move she made would be very plain to both of them. Maude's fingers closed around his lapels, rather than slide into his hair, which was what she wanted; she stood still rather than pressed herself against him, which was what her body wanted.

The kiss was over almost before it had begun, before her legs could begin to tremble, before her mind became completely blurred with sensation. Eden released her, dropped a kiss on to her forehead, adjusted her veil, then drew her out into the open, her hand once again tucked chastely into his elbow.

'Thank you,' he said seriously. 'That won't happen again.'

'It won't? I mean, why did it happen at all?' Maude asked, flustered and not at all certain she was not angry with him. That brief caress had agitated more than it had satisfied, confused her more than answered any of her doubts and questions.

'It happened because I needed to get that out of my mind,' Eden said. 'I needed to be sure I would not reach out for you when we were alone together. Shall we just say, I was satisfying my curiosity?'

'You may if you like,' Maude retorted. Yes, she was angry. 'Why here, now, in the street?'

'Because it is a very safe place. Even I am not going to go any further than that out here.'

'Even you?' she demanded, coming to an abrupt halt on the corner. 'What do you mean by that?'

'I have a certain reputation,' Eden said, looking down at her. It was hard to see in the poor light, but she thought he looked as grim as he had sounded just before he kissed her.

'For liaisons with married ladies. Very short-lived liaisons,' Maude retorted. 'I hadn't heard that you went about debauching virgins.'

'And I do not intend to start.' Eden strode along the short end of the square, forcing Maude to do a hop and a skip to keep up.

'Excellent. Because I have no intention of being debauched. It sounds horrible. Seduction sounds much better. With the right man, of course.' And if Eden had kissed her like that, that night in the box after dinner, then she could not fool herself—he could have seduced her with no difficulty whatsoever.

He stopped again on the corner of Curzon Street and looked down at her. The sound he made might have been a huff of laughter. 'Hold on to that thought, Maude. Am I forgiven?'

'Of course. It was very pleasant, and instructive, if brief. I could have told you to stop, could I not? And,' she added, risking a smile, 'I did not limit what your treat could be.'

'No, you didn't.' Eden's smile was genuine, if fleeting. Then he was serious again. Maude wondered if she was imagining the look of bleakness in his eyes, then decided it must be a trick of the torchlight flickering from the flambeaux outside the houses on the corner.

She was making progress with Eden, Maude decided, pouring the earl's morning coffee as a dutiful daughter should, and closing her ears to his robust, if muttered, comments on the government's taxation policy.

Eden was obviously attracted to her, or he would not want to kiss her. And it must be something more than mere desire, because he was so gentle with her. And he had remembered what she had been wearing in the shop that day. And he had listened to her views at the audition. It was slower progress, though, than she had daydreamed of. Foolishly she had expected him to take one look and fall in love with her—or at least manage to do so after a short acquaintance.

And just as obviously the fact that she had fallen in love at first sight did not mean it must be mutual. She sighed, remembering the gentleness of his kiss, the total control. He was very obviously *not* out of control with desire for her.

'You are up very early, my dear.' The sigh had obviously penetrated the barrier of the *Morning Post,* which lowered to reveal her father's face. He frowned, causing his bushy eyebrows to waggle. 'Bad night?'

'Mmm. I couldn't sleep.' Mysteriously, light and gentle kisses appeared to wreak the same havoc on her internal organs and her nerves as passionate, forceful ones. Maude's sleep had consisted of feverish dreams interspersed with long periods tossing and turning and thinking—fruitlessly—of tactics to make Eden fall in love.

'Well, rest today in that case. I don't want you burning the candle at both ends with all those parties and that committee of yours. How's your theatre doing?'

'My theatre? It is very much Mr Hurst's theatre, Papa, even though he does not own it. I am reminded of a big dog with a juicy marrow bone—no one may have so much as a nibble without express permission.'

'He is insolent?' The earl folded his paper and slapped it down beside his plate. 'I'll not have that.'

'No, Papa. Not at all. It is simply that…' She groped for the words to explain. 'It is like you and Knight's Fee. You tolerate the advice of your bailiff and steward and Mr Lambert at Home Farm—but it is you, and you alone, who makes the decisions. Only you inherited the estate; he has created everything himself and I think he can never shake off the fear that he could lose it too.'

The eyebrows rose. 'Territorial, is he? A fine thing for a theatre manager, I must say.'

'He is a powerful and intelligent man, Papa.' He narrowed his eyes at her, suspicious, as she hastened to add, 'You need have no fear my investment is at risk.'

'Humph. Glad to hear it. Ah, now here's the post. Thank you, Rainbow. Good gad, what have we here?' He poked a long finger at the pile.

'Invitations for Lady Maude, my lord.'

'Yours, yours…' Maude scooped up the pile her father extracted and began to slit seals. She was going to have to get her diary out and study it. It was already full, and some of these were events she wanted to attend.

'Papa?' The earl was staring at the sheet of paper in his hand, an odd expression on his face. 'Is anything wrong?'

'Someone your mother and I knew a long time ago is very ill.'

'I'm so sorry. Will you visit?' Maude got up and went to take the chair next to him.

'Visit? No, she lives in Scotland. By the time I got there…
Anyway, she was more a friend of your mother's than mine.
Almost became your godmother, in fact.' His gaze was un-
focused, as though he looked back down the years.

'Really? Why, almost?'

'The old earl, your grandfather, did not feel she was…suit-
able. And in those days,' he added with a mock-scowl at her,
'one did what one's parents advised.'

'Would I have ever met her?' Maude asked.

'No. Never. Pity she's going.' He sighed. 'Lovely woman.
Very talented. Ah well, I must be off to the House.'

Papa's obvious sadness at the news of his long-ago acquaintance subdued Maude's mood and left her the subject
of a not-unpleasant melancholy by the time she settled herself in her box again. Anna appeared to have decided that it
was quite safe to leave her mistress after yesterday's long,
and as far as she was concerned, highly tedious, proceedings.

'May I go down and see Millie, my lady? Only she said
she'd show me the costumes and it's ever so interesting.'

'Yes, of course.' Maude waved her away with a vague hand
and settled back to brooding on hopeless love, the futility of
pleasure, the fleeting nature of existence…

'And lo! What light…'

Maude jerked upright and peered over the edge of the box
to find Eden looking up at her. 'Hello. I was indulging in a
comfortable fit of melancholy.' Seeing him again after last
night should have been awkward, but he appeared his normal, rather cool self, despite the joking quote from *Romeo
and Juliet*. Maude reminded herself that they were supposed
to be working. 'Sorry, I am paying attention now.'

'In that case, your ladyship, we will begin.' He stalked
back to his chair and sat, his back to her. Was he cross with
her? Did he expect her to be looking out for him, eager to

see him after last night? Or was he angry with himself? Or merely impatient to get on with the job in hand?

Maude cupped her chin in her palm and indulged herself by studying Eden's back. He had discarded his coat and was in shirtsleeves, waistcoat and breeches, an outfit which made him look even more powerfully masculine than usual.

'Miss Jones, hurry up, if you please!'

The first actress hurried on stage, Tom Gates at her heels, and proceeded to say her lines. Maude saw Mr Howard prowling about in the stalls, listening from various positions. She scribbled notes.

Eden called the girl over and began to speak to her, apparently taking details of her past experience. With nothing to do, Maude watched Tom picking up small objects from the table and beginning to juggle. In contrast to his acting, his juggling was positively amateur, she thought, watching him fumble a small jar.

Then it hit her, her wonderful idea for the charity event. Maude scrabbled amongst her papers, found a clean sheet and began to write.

'Next!' Bother. She found the name of the second candidate and made herself concentrate.

By the time all six had been seen it was almost one o'clock and Millie was setting the table again with, Maude was amused to see, Anna helping her. She sorted her notes and went down onto the stage.

Eden and Howard were pacing up and down arguing, Gates at their heels trying to get a word in edgeways.

'Jones or Thomson,' Howard was saying.

'Thomson, possibly, but Miss Lewis was far and away better overall,' Eden asserted.

'Miss Jones picked up cues...' Tom started and was ignored. He saw Maude and grimaced comically.

'I like Miss Jones too,' she offered, but went unheard as the two men began flourishing sheets of notes at each other. Maude marched up, ducked under the stage manager's arm and bobbed up between them. *'Gentlemen.'* They fell silent. 'I liked Miss Jones best.'

'That's three of us then, Guv'nor,' Howard was unwise enough to say.

Eden eyed him coldly. 'Have I said or done anything to give you the impression that this theatre was run as a democracy, Mr Howard?' he enquired.

'No, sir.'

'Lady Maude?'

'No, Mr Hurst.' She smiled sweetly at him. 'But you did say we would discuss this. And I would like my luncheon.'

Eden pulled out a chair for Maude. 'Let us eat, then. And discuss.'

She smiled again as she sat and he had to fight not to smile back. As if he needed any other cue than the gathering heaviness in his groin when he had seen her that morning, her face solemn and a little sad, her chin propped on one cupped hand. Kissing her again had not done a damn thing to stop him wanting her. It had been a thoroughly bad idea, one he had justified to himself at the time and which he now saw as simple self-indulgence. In fact, to call it an idea was crediting himself with an illusion of decision-making when he had to accept the fact that, as far as Maude Templeton was concerned, he simply could not think straight.

They were all sitting waiting politely for him to speak, passing the food around amongst themselves in silence. Maude was even—God help him!—placing food on his plate and buttering his bread for him as if he was her father, or her husband or something.

'Thank you,' he said curtly, wanting to snub her. Clear

brown eyes met his for an instant and then the corners crinkled into a smile. Now she was feeling indulgent with his megrims, no doubt! Why wasn't she reacting to what happened last night? He had kissed her, in the street. Down an alley like a whore, he flagellated himself mentally. She should either be angry with him, or bashful, or flirtatious this morning, but, no, Lady Maude Templeton was none of those things. That kiss appeared to have made no impression whatsoever.

Well, it had on him. Damn it, he felt like a seventeen-year-old in the throes of his first infatuation. 'Pass the Stilton,' he said, perversely choosing the platter furthest from him. It was duly passed, he cut his cheese, then looked up. The three of them were regarding him solemnly, like children waiting for grace to be said. His sense of humour, like a cat twitching its tail, came to life.

'Lady Maude,' Eden said politely, his face perfectly straight, 'perhaps you would be so good as to give us your impressions of Miss Jones?'

'Me?' As he had hoped, she was somewhat discomposed by being asked to start.

'Ladies first.' She shot him a glance that told him she knew he was playing with her and unfolded her notes.

'Her voice projected well, she moved gracefully, she responded well to Mr Gates and her timing of the comic lines was perfect. She also looks young enough to play the ingénue for some time to come, unlike Miss Lewis. Oh, yes, and she was the first to go on, you barked at her, and she did not lose her nerve.'

'You base your assessment on the fact that she is not terrified of me?'

'Well, it helps, I should imagine,' Maude replied. 'Awe and respect are doubtless essential, but terror would be a handicap and you make Miss Lewis's knees knock.'

Eden swept the table with a glance, vowing to sack whichever of the others betrayed so much as a glimmer of a smile. Howard had his mouth full of pie and Gates, an actor to his toes, projected nothing but earnest attention. Awe and respect indeed! Little cat.

'Well, do either of you have any comments to make on the stability of Miss Lewis's knees?' he enquired dangerously and was answered by hastily shaken heads. 'I'll take them both, Jones and Lewis, on a month's trial. Satisfied?'

All three nodded and Maude smiled; not, he noticed, a smug feminine smile of triumph, just one of approval. 'What a good idea.'

They finished the meal more comfortably, Howard and Gates relaxing enough to exchange gossip about colleagues at Drury Lane. Maude, he noticed, had fallen silent again. Eden looked up and caught her watching him, uncertainty in her eyes.

'Mr Hurst, might I have a word with you? In your office?'

Ah, so here came the recriminations for last night. Knowing perfectly well he had no grounds on which to defend himself, Eden followed Maude's straight back down the corridor. He did not want her to leave, he realised. If he had driven her away, it was going to leave something perilously like a gap in his life. Which was ridiculous. It implied a weakness, an unfulfilled need, and he had neither of those things.

'Maude.' He waited until she was seated, then went round to take his own chair. It felt as though he was taking refuge behind a barrier.

'I was thinking about the charity event I have volunteered to organise for the committee,' she said, extracting even more notes from the bundle of sheets in her hands. 'Eden?'

'I'm sorry, a moment's inattention.' A charity event? Not tearful distress, not angry recriminations?

'We've had a ball, and a garden party, but I wanted to do

something different this year. And I thought we could hold it here, in the theatre.'

'A charity performance, you mean?' Eden pulled himself together and reached for a pen and paper.

'Not exactly. I wanted to rearrange the stalls and the galleries, set tables out for dining and the acts would all be amateur ones, from members of the audience. I would encourage people to dress up as their favourite characters as well. We'd need a string band and a pianist to accompany those people who wanted to sing and to provide interval music, of course…'

'How many guests?' Eden asked, suppressing his instinctive refusal. Turn his theatre into a cross between country-house theatricals, Astley's Amphitheatre and a vast dinner party?

'Two hundred invitations?' Maude ventured. 'We must make it exclusive.'

'Rip out the stalls?' He was losing this before he'd even begun to object, he knew it. But somehow she was mesmerising him and all he wanted to do was please her.

'Take them out, carefully. We've got some carpenters amongst the men, they'll help your team. The theatre won't need to be closed to the public for more than one night.'

He ought to say no. That was the sensible, prudent thing. He did not support charities, yet somehow she had inveigled him on to her damn committee. He did nothing to compromise the commercial success of the Unicorn and here he was, contemplating an exercise that would cost him goodness knows what. He had a reputation as a hard man and yet he was yielding to a woman who did not even *try* to wheedle concessions out of him. This was dangerous insanity and he was going to refuse.

'Yes, all right. When?'

Maude jumped to her feet and for one, breathless moment, he thought she was going to come round the desk and kiss him. 'Oh, thank you!' She sat right back in her chair again, Eden told himself he was a fool, and Maude drew out her memorandum book. 'Is three weeks too soon?'

Eden studied his own diary. It would give them a break in the run of *Her Precious Honour*, but that was no bad thing—it would give the cast a rest. 'No, that is fine. But can you do it in time?'

'Making things happen is my *forte,*' Maude said with a smile that became, he thought, a touch wry. 'I nearly always achieve what I set out to do.'

'Only nearly?'

'I—' She broke off and the sadness he had seen in her face that morning came back, touching her beauty with a haunting shadow.

'Maude.' Eden reached out a hand, not knowing why and she put out hers to meet it. Their fingers clasped across the stacks of paper on his desk, curled into each other, held. 'Maude, I—'

'Darling!' The door banged back on its hinges and in she swept, Madame Marguerite, scarves flying, gems glittering, her timing, as always, perfect. 'Eden, you absolutely must—oh. And who is this?' She produced one of her carefully graded smiles, this one for lovely young women who might be a threat, but on the other hand, might simply be admirers.

'Lady Maude, may I introduce Madame Marguerite? Madame, this is Lady Maude Templeton. I told you she is investing in the Unicorn.'

'Lady Maude, I'm so pleased to meet you.' One of her less haughty greetings, thank goodness. Apparently she was moved to be pleased. Eden helped her to a chair and resumed his.

'Lady Maude has asked me to join the committee of her charity, if you recall, Madame.'

'But of course. So worthy—you must add my name to the donations list,' she said airily.

'Thank you so much, Madame.' Maude whipped out a notebook and pencil. 'For how much?'

To Eden's vast amusement she sat there, pencil poised, smiling at Madame, who, he knew full well, had intended to forget all about it the moment she was out of the door. He was sorely tempted to sit there and see what happened, but for the sake of peace and quiet suggested, 'Twenty guineas? I'll arrange it, Madame.'

'Thank you, darling.' She smiled at him, her famous blue eyes wide and glorious. 'I can always rely on darling Eden,' she added as an aside to Maude.

'I am sure you can, ma'am. May I say how very much both my father, the Earl of Pangbourne, and I, admire your performances?'

'I am charmed to hear it. I must, however, be on my way. Eden—'

He got up to open the door. 'You came in to say there was something I must do?'

'Oh? Did I?' she said vaguely. 'Never mind, darling, I am sure I'll remember.' She swept out on a cloud of Attar of Roses and a rustling of silk.

Eden went back to his place behind the desk. 'That,' he said superfluously, 'was Madame Marguerite.'

'I was very pleased to meet her,' Maude said. 'She's your mother, isn't she?'

Chapter Thirteen

'**M**y mother?' There did not seem to be any point in lying about it. It was not as though he was ashamed of it, exactly, more that he found it much easier not to think of Marguerite as his mother. There were no expectations then. 'Yes.'

'It is not widely known?' Maude did not appear shocked. But then, she was a lady, and ladies were bred to disguise their feelings.

'Not known at all. How did you guess?'

'I can glimpse a resemblance. Not in colouring, of course. Your presence, perhaps. And yet you both remind me of someone else—I do wish I could think who.'

'She prefers it not to be known,' Eden said, his voice as neutral as he could make it. 'I am somewhat old to be comfortably acknowledged as her son. People would do the arithmetic, you see.'

'But in private—'

'No.' He shook his head. 'Outside the theatre we lead separate lives.'

'Oh. I am so sorry.' That was the second time she had expressed pity for him, and pity was not something his pride would accept from anyone, even if, for some reason, he wanted to pour the whole story of his childhood out to Maude and have her, in some way he could not imagine, make it better.

Eden shrugged. 'She is exhausting enough as it is.'

'Yes, but—' She must have seen something in his face, for she broke off, hesitated, then asked, 'Your father—she married him in Italy?'

'La Belle Marguerite,' he said, inserting the shield of irony into his tone, 'has never found any man worthy of marriage.'

Maude frowned, as though she was untangling a puzzle, not, oddly, as if she found herself disgusted to be having this conversation with a bastard. 'So your father—' She tried again. 'You said he would not speak to you, but did he not even—?'

'He refused to acknowledge me.' She might as well have the lot, see just who her business partner was. Or, more to the point, was not.

'Bastard,' Maude commented. 'Him, I mean. Is it true he is a prince?'

'So you had heard the rumours? He was. He died last year. When I was fourteen, Madame decided I might be of some use to her. She descended on the palazzo, swept me up against very little opposition—as you may imagine, his wife was happy to see the back of me, even if I was relegated to the stables along with the rest of his by-blows—and set me to learn about the theatre.'

'She had just left you with him?' Maude looked more appalled at that than anything else.

'She was sure I would be much better looked after there rather than being dragged around Europe in the wake of her career. And I learned fluent Italian—so useful.'

'And a baby and then a small child would be such an inconvenience with her career and her lovers, I suppose,' Maude said savagely, startling him. 'How she could!' She sat in silence for a moment, staring down at her tightly locked hands. 'I beg your pardon, I should not speak so about your mother.'

'Don't apologise. I do not love her, she does not love me. I am her business manager, she is my leading actress. It is business. I understand her very well; she, I think, understands me not at all.' Maude simply stared at him, her face appalled. 'What?' he flung at her. 'Are you shocked? Do you think I should have loved her, so that she had the power to break my heart?'

'Of course she broke your heart,' Maude said fiercely. 'Of *course* she did. Do not tell me you do not believe in love, just because it hurts too much. It hurts because it is important. It hurts because it is all there is. Don't pretend to me you are not capable of love.'

Eden stared at her, furious, confused, disorientated by her attack. He had told her the sordid truth about his birth and somehow he was at fault for dealing with it well? Then he saw her eyes, the sparkle of unshed tears, and something inside, something cold and hard that he had thought impregnable, cracked. What did she want from him? What was hurting inside him? Something trying to get out, or the pain of emptiness? Her heart seemed big enough to grieve for him— didn't she realise that he had built a wall around his? That he had nothing to give her? *Only more pain*, he thought as he went to her.

'Maude. Maude, don't cry.' He crouched down beside her chair and put his arm around her shoulders. Hell, she was so determined, so positive, she seemed sturdier than she was. Under the weight of his arm her shoulders were fragile. 'Don't cry. I won't know what to do if you cry.'

Tantrums, scenes, furious tears, manipulative tears, crocodile tears. He knew what to do with those, he had enough practice. But these unshed tears, tears she was fighting not to let spill, these almost unmanned him.

'You…you could give me a handkerchief,' she suggested
shakily. He pulled a large one from his pocket and handed
it to her. 'Thank you.' She blew her nose like a boy and
scrubbed at her eyes. No, these tears weren't for show, weren't
to manipulate. Her nose had gone pink and her eyes were
bleary and she was not sparing a thought for how she looked.
'Sorry. I don't cry, you know.'

'No, of course not.' He did not know whether to get up
and leave her to compose herself or not. He wanted to stay,
he ought to go. Eden remained where he was on his knees
beside the chair.

'It upset me,' she explained, looking at him directly at last.
'I hate it when people are cruel to anyone who is helpless—
children, animals, our soldiers when they were too sick to
fend for themselves.'

'I'm not helpless,' he said.

'Not now. Our soldiers have scars, limbs missing, eyes
gone. We can see their scars, do something with them. Where
are yours, Eden?'

'I am not one of your charity cases,' he said, not answering
her, rocking back on his heels because otherwise he would
kiss those tear-filled eyes, stop her looking at him like that.

'No.' Maude nodded. 'No, you are not. You have done all
this, all by yourself. You do not need charity. But don't tell
me not to pity the child that you were, or feel anger for him,
because I do. And don't tell me not to try to convince you
about love, because I will not stop trying.'

'Are you going to get out your Bible and preach to me,
then?' he asked bitterly. The priest at the palazzo had done
that often enough.

'No.' Maude folded up the handkerchief and regarded him
solemnly. 'It is up to you what you do with your love, and
you can put some of it into religion if you want to. I simply
intend to convince you it exists.'

'Why?' Eden got to his feet and stood looking down at her. This was dangerous, this could tear him apart.

'Because you are right in front of me, and we are friends and partners, so it behoves me to do something about you,' she said firmly, getting to her feet too and beginning to shuffle her papers together.

'Just like that?'

'Yes.' She nodded, tapping the edges of the pages on the desk to align them. 'When I see something that needs to be done, I do it.'

'And I have no say in the matter?' Eden found he was smiling at her. He received a watery smile back.

'Of course you do. You get to have free choice what to do with your love when you find where you have buried it.' *I know where it is, I have walled it up where it cannot hurt me. Or you, Maude. Oh God, I could hurt you so much.*

She picked up her memorandum book. 'Are you going to the Hethersetts' ball in three days' time?'

Conversation with Maude was like fencing lessons, you never knew where she was going to attack next. 'No,' Eden said baldly, a wary eye out for the next feint.

'But you have been invited?'

'Yes.'

'Excellent. We have a committee meeting tomorrow afternoon—I did tell you, didn't I? We need to discuss our plans for the theatre event and also tactics for taking advantage of the ball. It is very useful having another handsome man on the committee; you can woo all the rich widows, they are impervious to Jessica, Bel and me.'

'*Our* theatre event?'

'Ours. The others are going to be *so* pleased with us. Now, don't forget, the Standons' house at half past two. Goodbye.' He was still standing regarding the door panels when she popped her head round again. 'And don't forget to accept Lady Hethersett's invitation.'

'Mr Hurst is attending today's meeting,' Maude remarked, standing in the Standons' hall while Jessica supervised the footmen hanging a portrait.

'Excellent,' Jessica responded, her attention on what the men were doing with the heavy frame. 'Careful! Don't let the cloth slip off until it is up there, I don't want to risk damaging it. It is Gareth's papa,' she added to Maude. 'There's his mother, behind you. They were in the country house, but not well displayed, and absolutely filthy. I had them cleaned and I think they will look good here.'

Maude turned to study the portrait of the late countess, severely lovely in piled white wig and sky blue satin. 'Beautiful.' She turned back as the footmen pulled at the swathing cloths on the matching portrait. 'Oh, my God.'

'What?' Jessica blinked at her, puzzled. 'I think it is a very handsome portrait.'

'Yes, it is,' Maude agreed. 'But don't you see the likeness?'

'To Gareth? Well, of course, he's much more like his mother at first glance, but there's something about the way he stands.'

'Have you got a *Peerage*?' Maude asked urgently. Why on earth hadn't she seen it before?

'Yes, of course. Here, I'll show you.' Still looking bemused, Jessica led the way to Gareth's study. 'There, several editions, in fact.'

Maude pulled out the one that looked the oldest and flicked through her pages. 'Ravenhurst, Dukes of Allington...here we are, marriage of Francis, second duke, to Francesca. Son Francis 1750, that's Bel and Sebastian's father, then a big gap up to Sophia, 1761.'

'That's Gareth's mother,' Jessica said. 'Apparently Francesca was quite ill after the birth of the heir.'

'Then Augustus, that's Theo's father the bishop, then... Aha! Margery, 1767.'

'Why, *Aha*? I've never heard of her.'

'Exactly. Let's see what happens to her.' Maude began to pull out volumes, opening them in date order. Finally, when she checked the final one she said triumphantly, 'See? *Nothing* happens to Margery. No marriage, she isn't dead. So where is she?'

'I have no idea.' Jessica perched on the corner of Gareth's desk, apparently set on humouring her friend.

'She's La Belle Marguerite and she's Eden's mother.'

'*What?*'

'He told me yesterday she was his mother. His father is, as the rumours say, an Italian prince. Marguerite—or Margery—abandoned the child with his father, who left him to the servants to bring up. She only claimed him years later.'

'How awful, poor child,' Jessica said compassionately. 'But that doesn't make her Margery.'

'One, she gave him the surname Hurst—half of Ravenhurst.' Maude ticked off points on her fingers. 'Two, he's been reminding me of someone, I just couldn't put a finger on it. Three, when he came into the box that evening you were all there, Papa mistook him for Gareth, when he saw him in silhouette in the doorway, and, four, look at the portrait of Lord Standon in the hall.'

'There *is* a scandalous aunt in the family, I know that,' Jessica said. 'Gareth is mildly curious, but apparently even Sebastian doesn't know the story—the older generation just refuse to speak of it. Do you think Eden knows?'

'He is very unruffled about associating with Bel and Gareth, who are his first cousins, if he does,' Maude said.

'But then, Eden is unruffled about most things, except attacks on his control of the Unicorn. I will ask him.'

'Maude, you can't, not just like that! If he knows, he hasn't said anything, so he wants it kept secret; if he doesn't, think what a shock it would be.'

'Yes, I can. And, Jessica, don't you see, Papa can hardly object on the grounds of breeding—an Italian prince for a father and a duke for a grandfather, for goodness' sake.'

'You are overlooking the minor detail of a lack of a marriage certificate to link the two,' Jessica said wryly. 'It doesn't make it better; in some ways, it makes it worse.'

'True.' Maude swallowed, feeling as though she had been punched in the stomach. For one moment she had thought it would all be fine now. Of course it wouldn't. 'It has been such a big secret, what happened to Margery. Bel and Gareth's parents—all that generation—are going to be furious.' She began to put the books back on the shelf. 'I've got to find some way to make Eden acceptable to Papa.'

'You've got to make him fall in love with you first,' her friend added with brutal honesty.

Maude thought about confiding in Jessica. Perhaps she would understand what that strange, gentle kiss in the darkened alleyway had meant.

'Oh, there's the front door knocker, the committee is arriving.' Jessica hopped off the desk and became, once more, a dignified countess. The moment was lost.

'Go and greet people in the hall. I'll stand under the portrait and try to get Eden to talk to me there so you can see,' Maude urged as the Reverend Makepeace's fluting tones reached them.

Eden was exactly on time. Several of the others, more familiar with the household and less on their society manners, had arrived earlier and were gossiping in the dining room. 'Lady Standon, I apologise, I have kept you waiting.'

He glanced towards the open door and the sound of voices as he handed his hat and coat to the butler.

'No, not at all, they are early, Mr Hurst. Ah, there's Maude, she will show you the way.' Jessica smiled, affecting just to notice Maude poised under the portrait. Maude smiled and held out her hand to him, turning so that he was forced to stop and stand in three-quarters profile to Jessica, just like the figure in the painting. Maude saw her friend's eyes narrow and she nodded, just as her husband strolled downstairs.

'Maude, good afternoon. Hurst.' Gareth held out his hand and Maude slipped away to stand with Jessica, regarding the two men standing under the portrait.

'I think you are right,' Jessica whispered. 'There is a resemblance. Are you going to tell the other cousins?'

'How can I?' Maude murmured back. 'That is up to Eden and I have no idea whether or not he knows.'

Maude found herself watching Eden during the committee meeting. He was managing to control any surprise at Bel taking the chair, although she could read him well enough to see his impatience at Mr Makepeace's long, and rambling, report.

There was no disguising the fact that Mr Makepeace and Lady Wallace were treating Eden with some reserve. Presumably neither really approved of his presence on the committee.

'Now then, tactics for Lady Hethersett's ball,' Bel announced. 'She tells me that several ladies who are on our list as potential sponsors, but who have so far eluded us, will be attending.'

'And both I, and Dereham, will be absent,' Gareth remarked. 'So the duty of charming the ladies is, I am very happy to say, all yours, Hurst.' There was the slightest edge to his voice.

Eden's eyebrows rose. 'That sounds hazardous. Might I

remind you, Standon, that while you and Dereham are safely married, I am perilously single.'

'We are not asking you to propose to them, Mr Hurst,' Jessica said, with a dimpling smile. 'Just flirt. You can flirt, can't you?'

There was silence, broken only by Mr Makepeace's faint cluck of disapproval. Eden regarded Jessica steadily. How he did it, Maude had no idea, but somehow those cool brown eyes gained heat, the severe lips softened and, 'I never flirt, Lady Standon,' he said, his voice somehow huskier than before.

Jessica, sitting next to her own husband, blushed like a peony.

It seemed to Maude that the committee held its collective breath, then Jessica burst out laughing. 'Mr Hurst, that was outrageous! If you can make the toes of a happily married lady curl in her slippers like that, I shudder to think what havoc you can wreak on Lady Hethersett's guests.'

'Ma'am?' Eden looked blank.

'An excellent demonstration of just what is needed,' Gareth commented, his tone steely. 'I need hardly add that should you make my wife's toes curl again, there will be hell to pay?'

Eden inclined his head gravely, Mr Makepeace looked shocked and Lady Wallace was seized with a fit of coughing. Bel consulted her list again, 'There are also some gentlemen... I will distribute them amongst the ladies of the committee later and we can agree tactics over tea. Now, the next item on the agenda is our fund-raising event. Maude?'

'Mr Hurst and I have a suggestion,' Maude said, blithely ignoring Eden narrowing his eyes at her. 'Mr Hurst is very kindly prepared to allow us to use the Unicorn for a gala evening with music and refreshments. The special attraction is that the entertainment will be provided by the guests themselves.'

She explained in detail, conscious of Eden sitting silent, occasionally jotting down a note as she expanded the idea far beyond the bare details she had sketched out for him. Was she going too far? she wondered, braced for him to protest.

But he made no complaint, sitting calmly while the others exclaimed and praised, enthusiastically joining in to identify those leaders of society who must be persuaded to take part in this novel entertainment in order to ensure that everyone would be clamouring for an invitation. It seemed the novelty of the scheme was enough to overcome their reservations about Eden, at least for the moment.

When they finally finished the meeting and tea was served, Gareth made his way over to where Maude was talking to Eden.

'We have some skilled carpenters amongst the men—I have several employed renovating some houses I own,' he remarked. Maude held her breath, hoping this was an olive branch. 'I can bring them over, Hurst, give your men a hand. I'll supervise, if that will free you up for anything more technical.'

'Thank you.' Eden's voice was cool. 'I would be grateful for the men, but I, and I alone, supervise anything that happens in my theatre.'

'I wonder, then,' Gareth remarked, his eyes flickering to Maude, 'that you tolerate Lady Maude's interference.'

'I do not have to.' Eden sounded, to Maude's anxious ear, faintly amused. 'Firstly, Lady Maude does not interfere, she makes interesting and constructive suggestions. Secondly, we have established very firm boundaries for our partnership.'

'Amazing,' Gareth drawled, helping himself to a macaroon. 'You must be the first man, including her father, to impose any boundaries whatsoever on Maude.' He sauntered off and began to talk to Lady Wallace.

Maude could feel the tension coming off Eden like the heat from a fire. 'He presumes a lot on old acquaintance, does he not?' he enquired, his dark eyes following Gareth's progress.

'No, not at all, he is simply teasing me.' Maude blinked— a low sound, not unlike a growl, was surely emanating from Eden's throat. It could hardly, since there was no large dog in the room, be coming from anywhere else. 'I told you, we have known each other since childhood,' she added hastily. 'I tease him just as much.' It was not jealousy, that was too much to hope for, but the very fact that he wanted to defend her filled Maude with a warm glow.

'Would you drive me home?'

'Unchaperoned?'

'I happen to know you drove yourself in an open carriage,' she said. 'A curricle, perhaps?'

'And how did you know that?'

'You were cold when you came in. Colder than would be accounted for by being in a closed carriage—I was standing close to you in the hall, if you recall. And you were wearing a caped driving coat, which seemed a little excessive for a passenger.'

'Admirable deduction. I was driving my new phaeton.'

'Then, may I drive with you? It is quite unexceptional to be alone with you in an open vehicle, after all.'

'You will be cold.' But he was smiling, just a little.

'I will borrow Jessica's furs. Wait for me.'

'What is it, Maude?' She looked down at him in surprise from the carriage seat into which he had just helped her. She was not quite certain, for his eyes were shaded by the brim of his hat, but Eden was amused.

'What?'

'Whatever it is you want to quiz me about in private.' Eden went round and climbed into the phaeton, took the reins from the waiting footman and gave the pair the office to start. 'I can't believe that you have just had a sudden fancy to drive through London in the chill of a February afternoon to take the air.'

'I wanted to ask you something highly personal,' she confessed, watching the street unfold between the pricked ears of the bay leader.

'Ask then.' He glanced sideways. 'I won't promise to answer.'

'Do you know your mother's real name?' There was no point in beating around the bush, and sooner or later, they would have to confront the issue of his family.

'Yes.' The leader shied at a yapping mongrel on the pavement and Eden collected him with his voice and a touch of the whip. 'I suppose you are wondering if I know that I have just been sitting down with two of my cousins? Are they aware of who I am?'

'No, only Jessica. She was with me this afternoon when I saw a portrait of her father-in-law and realised why you so often seemed familiar. I looked in the *Peerage* and found your mother,' she added.

'Will you tell them?' Eden sounded merely interested, as though they were speaking of someone else.

'No, not unless you wish to, and I will ask Jessica not to say anything. She is very discreet.' Maude hesitated. He was not pouring out his confidences, but on the other hand, he had not rebuffed her. 'How did you discover the connection?'

'When we were packing to come to England, I found some papers that made me suspect. I have not challenged Madame on the subject. It would not be worth the effort—she always refuses to discuss the past. I do not think the resemblance is such that it is immediately obvious.'

'No, it is something about the way you move, the way you hold yourself, I think. I know them very well, so perhaps it is more obvious to me.' Still he did not react, yet Maude had the feeling she was walking on eggshells.

'Would you not like some family?' she persisted.

'You think they would acknowledge me? I think not. Besides, the question is irrelevant. Unless Madame wishes to make known her identity, I cannot speak of it.'

'Oh. I had not thought of that.' Maude fell silent, brooding on this latest complication. They were almost in Mount Street. 'Do you dance?'

Eden reined in the pair at her front door. 'Do I dance? There are times, Maude, when I find yourself baffled by the workings of your mind. How do we get from my parentage to dancing?'

'We do not. But there is no point in pursuing a topic of conversation you are obviously unwilling to discuss and I want to know whether you will dance with me at Lady Hethersett's ball.'

'Yes, I dance. And, yes, it will be a pleasure to dance with you at the ball, Maude.' The front door opened and a footman appeared. Eden glanced at him and added, his voice lower, 'But do not try to extend your campaign to make me admit the existence of love to a scheme to have me embrace all my family—they would not thank you for introducing a theatrical bastard to their fireside, believe me.'

'They already acknowledge you for what you are, not where you came from,' Maude said. 'The Ravenhursts—the ones who are my friends—are more open minded than perhaps you believe.' He made no response, and besides, James was already coming round to help her down. This was not the time to pursue it. 'Thank you, Eden, I enjoyed my drive.'

Chapter Fourteen

The bays fidgeted, testing his control as though his own tension was reaching them. Eden turned them towards Hyde Park. It would be relatively free of crowds now and he could work out the horses' fidgets and his own unsettled thoughts in privacy.

He had come back to England, settled into the fringes of society, confident that the secrets of his birth would remain just that. Secret. Lady Margery Ravenhurst had fled the family home at the tender age of nineteen—it was safe to believe that none of her family would recognise her now, a woman in her mid-forties.

Discreet observation of the myriad Ravenhurst clan had convinced him that with his Italian looks he had no reason to fear exposure either. Frowning, he realised how betraying that word was. There was nothing to *fear* from the Ravenhursts, not in the material sense. And yet it would hurt his pride, he realised, if there was the slightest suspicion that he was courting acceptance, presuming on the connection.

Eden swung the team in through the gates and let them extend their trot across the scuffed tan surface. Trust Maude to see a likeness that he was not even aware of himself. But then Maude looked deeper into him than anyone else ever had. She thought, bless her, that there was something about him worth humanising, worth teaching to love.

And he let himself be seduced and weakened by her friendship, her concern, just as he was constantly tormented by desire for her. She saw him as a crippled being to be rescued, taught love, sent out again into the world like a bird with a mended broken wing. But she assumed he wanted to feel love, that he was capable of it. Love was something you were born into, grew up with, surely? Not something you could learn.

The leader broke into a canter and was ruthlessly brought back to a trot. If he could control nothing else today, he could damn well control his horses. What would it be like to belong to a family like the Ravenhursts? So many of them and yet such a tight-knit clan, gathering in new members by friendship or marriage. It would be suffocating, he told himself. And weakening. And yet seductively warm.

Warm, like Maude. But Maude was special and he was not, he was all too bitterly aware, worthy of a woman like that. He could only hurt her, they were so different and he so scarred. He should send her money back, end their partnership, he knew that, but still he wanted to hold out cold hands to the glow of her smile and her honesty and her concern. Just for a little while longer.

'Papa? Are you ready?' Maude put her head around the door of her father's study, surprised not to find him waiting in the hall, foot tapping, one eye on the clock.

The earl was sitting at his desk, a letter in his hand, staring at the fire. Maude pushed the door wider and he looked up. 'Sorry, my love. Did you say something?'

'I asked if you are ready to go to Lady Hethersett's, Papa.' Maude went up to the desk, anxious. 'Are you unwell?' He looked uncharacteristically melancholy and suddenly, frighteningly, older.

'Unwell? No, my dear. Just rather...sad. That friend of your mother's—you recall I told you she was ill? Well, now it seems she has died.' He sighed, folding the heavy sheets of paper under his hands. Maude looked down at them, seeing for the first time how prominent the veins were becoming, noticing the age spots, and placed one of hers over his.

'I'm so sorry, Papa. Let me go upstairs and change and we'll spend a quiet evening together.'

'What! Nonsense, you'll do no such thing. It's years since I saw her, we never corresponded more than a note at the turn of the year. No, I'm just a little melancholy, thinking of times long past, that's all.'

Thinking of Mama, Maude thought, squeezing his hand. 'Yes, but I will—'

'No. You run along and enjoy yourself. I am going to go to the club, I'm not good company this evening, but I'm quite all right.' He beetled his heavy eyebrows at her. 'And I don't want you sitting at home when you could be out there snaring that highly eligible son-in-law for me. You give my apologies to Henrietta Hethersett now.'

'If you are certain, Papa,' Maude dropped a kiss on his cheek. 'But I'm not promising a highly eligible son-in-law, I'm afraid.' Her conscience gave a painful twinge at the thought of just how ineligible the man of her dreams was.

'You're a good girl. Just go and find a good man—I only want you to be happy, Maude.'

Papa really meant it, she knew he did, Maude thought as she climbed, alone, into the carriage. But could he possibly conceive just *who* it might take to make her happy?

'All by yourself, child?' Lady Hethersett tut-tutted indulgently as Maude reached the head of the receiving line.

'Papa is indisposed, ma'am.' Maude dropped a curtsy and smiled back. ' He asked me to give you his apologies. I will find Lady Dereham or Lady Standon at once,' she added meekly.

However, an airy wave when she saw them on the other side of the great reception room that led on to the ballroom was quite enough to fulfil her promise to Lady Hethersett, Maude decided. Just beyond a potted palm she could see Mr Worthington, an elderly gentleman who was on her list of potential benefactors for the charity. If she added him to her collection, she could relax and enjoy herself for the rest of the evening with a clear conscience.

Ten minutes later she was wondering if she was ever going to extract either money, or herself. 'Disgraceful, the number of sturdy rogues sponging upon the Poor Relief,' Mr Worthington was saying indignantly. 'The charge upon property owners in every parish is outrageous!'

'Exactly,' Maude interjected. 'And so many of these men are returning soldiers from the wars. Now, a very modest donation of one hundred guineas to our charity will prove a excellent investment in removing these men permanently from becoming a charge upon the parishes.'

'Hmm.' He eyed her dubiously. 'Investment, you say?'

'Absolutely,' Maude said. 'Of course, it takes a gentleman of experience and foresight such as yourself to appreciate that…' Her mind went blank. Just the other side of the arrangement of greenery she could see a pair of broad shoulders and hear Eden's trained voice.

'Of course, Lady Lucas, I can offer inducements beyond my, no doubt, imperfect arguments as to why you should become a patron.'

'Inducements? Why, Mr Hurst, you *do* interest me!' Lady Lucas, the wife of a notoriously indolent and neglectful husband, was a sprightly blonde with a roving eye. And, Maude saw as she shifted her position slightly, those wide blue orbs were fixed on Eden's face. Lady Lucas moved closer and rested one hand on his forearm. 'Do tell—or should we go somewhere more private?'

'No need.' Eden laid his own hand over hers, then raised it to his lips. 'I can rely upon your discretion?'

'Oh, yes, Mr Hurst, I am very, very, discreet.'

Trollop, Maude thought, torn between admiration for Eden's technique and indignation at Lady Lucas.

'If you promise not to tell a soul—' Maude strained to hear his lowered voice '—there is going to be a very interesting event at the Unicorn in a few weeks, and I can make certain that you have the very best box.'

'A private box?' Lady Lucas managed to imbue the phrase with overtones of delicious impropriety.

'Oh, yes,' Eden purred, 'Very private.'

'Two hundred guineas.' Maude started, then realised that leaving Mr Worthington to brood on her words appeared to have done the trick. 'Here you are, my dear, a note for my bankers.' He pressed the paper into her hand. 'No, no, do not thank me. Now I must find Lady Smythe, I have promised her a hand of whist.'

As she tucked the note into her reticule, Maude craned to see what was happening with Eden and Lady Lucas, but both dark head and blonde had vanished.

'What's the matter?' Bel asked, appearing at her side. 'You look as though you've lost something.'

'Eden. I last saw him reducing Lady Lucas to putty with promises of a very private box at the theatrical event. And now they've vanished.'

'And you are wondering if he has been swept off to demonstrate his um…credentials? Don't worry. See—he is over there, flirting desperately with Mrs Hampton-Wilde. He really is very good at it; look at her, she is positively quivering. He throws himself into it with far more enthusiasm than Ashe does when I nag him into trying to charm money out of ladies, poor dear.'

'Eden appears to have a natural talent for it,' Maude said darkly.

'Jealous?' Bel smiled wickedly. 'Never fear, he has not seen you yet; when he does, I am certain he'll have eyes for no one else. That gown is stunning.'

'It is rather, isn't it?' Maude allowed herself to be distracted into contemplating her gown. It was cut perilously high under the bust, and perilously low above it, modesty being preserved only with a yellow rose at the centre and a thin ruffle of lace. The underskirt of soft white satin was quite unadorned, but the overskirt of almost transparent gauze was finished at the hem with a double row of rosettes, each with a rose at the centre.

'I love those short sleeves, so intricate.' Bel studied them. 'I've never seen anything quite like it. But how on earth you are going to stay within the bounds of decency if you dance anything energetic, I have no idea.'

'It's very tight, I won't fall out,' Maude whispered. 'And you can hardly criticise.' Bel was dashing in pomona green with a plunging back and fluttering overskirt with high side-slits.

Bel looked smug. 'Ashe *adores* it. He wanted to stay home when he saw it. Oh, look, Mr Hurst is making her blush. Are you going to drift past and see if you can put him off his stroke?'

'Certainly not,' Maude said. 'I am going to see if I can make *him* jealous. And there's the very man.' She let her eyes widen as she caught the gaze of Major Sir Frederick Staines, then dropped them in apparent confusion.

'Careful,' Bel warned, 'he's the most terrible rake.'

'I know. Perfect.' With a laugh, Bel moved on. 'Oh, good evening, Sir Frederick.'

The major was tall, blond, smoothly good looking and perfect for her purposes.

'Lady Maude. May I say how very lovely you are looking this evening?' She dimpled at him. 'Might I beg the honour of the first waltz? And perhaps something later?'

'I would be delighted.' Maude consulted her dance card. 'The first waltz and the fourth set of country dances, then.' As she hoped, he stayed by her side, his eyes a little too brazen in their admiration of her neckline. 'Listen! The orchestra has started.'

The major promptly offered his arm to walk her into the ballroom. With perfect timing they found themselves halted at the doors to the ballroom by a knot of elderly chaperons who were greeting each other loudly right next to Eden, still in attendance on Mrs Hampton-Wilde.

Maude looked up at Sir Frederick, a slight smile on her lips, and was rewarded by him returning the look with one of cheek-warming intensity. 'Oh, Sir Frederick,' she said lightly, 'you quite put me to the blush, you wicked man.'

Out of the corner of her eye she was aware of Eden's head turning, felt the impact of his eyes on her. As she hoped, the major bent over her, murmuring flirtatious nonsense and she laughed, rapping him on the sleeve with her fan in mock reproof.

'Lady Maude.'

'Mr Hurst! My goodness, you made me jump. Good evening, Mrs Hampton-Wilde.' The other woman bowed, her lips pursing in displeasure at the interruption.

'Might I ask for the honour of a dance?' Eden asked. Maude smiled and nodded. 'The first waltz?'

'I am engaged to Sir Frederick for that set. Perhaps some country dances later?'

'Might I see?' Eden reached for her dance card almost before she lifted her hand. Beside her the major stiffened. 'The supper set and the last one?' He was writing, E.H., even as she agreed. *Perfect.* And even better was the way he was looking at Sir Frederick with cold, hard challenge. He did not like to see her with the other man, that was plain, even if he was unaware of just what that implied.

Although, Maude mused, as her hand was claimed by Lord Nashe for the first set, a quadrille, it could simply be that Eden was aware of Sir Frederick's reputation and would have been wary of his attentions to any young lady he knew.

Still, even if he was not consumed by burning jealousy, it was a good start to the evening and she could not brood upon it any more now—the first of the figures, the *Grand Ronde*, was underway. Maude smiled at her partner and set herself to follow the complex patterns of the dance.

Eden set one shoulder against a pillar and watched the promenading couples through narrowed eyes. Maude was not, thankfully, dancing with that rake Staines, although she would be, he'd seen the initials on her card. The man wasn't safe for her to be with; he was a regular visitor to the Unicorn, to be found in the Green Room after a show, propositioning the girls of the chorus or in a box with some companions and two or three bits of muslin.

Was Maude aware of his reputation? And what the hell was she doing here without her father, or a proper chaperon? She was too damn free and easy, that was the trouble…

He listened to his own thoughts and smiled grimly, hardly noticing the expression of alarm on the face of a bold young lady who had been staring at him as she passed. Damn it, he sounded like her guardian, or her elder brother, which was thoroughly hypocritical of him, considering he was encouraging her in unconventional behaviour—dining in her box, walking home through the streets. Kissing in alleyways.

But that was with him. She was safe with him—give or take a kiss. Thoughts of those kisses occupied him through the entire set. It occurred to him that association with Maude Templeton was turning him celibate—in action if not in thought. Which was, Eden mused, odd. He was well aware that his appetites, while well regulated, were more than healthy. So why was he avoiding the usual houses where such things could be discreetly satisfied?

Maude, twirling in the middle of the set, turned her head, laughing in response to something her partner was saying to her, and Eden caught his breath. No, he had not lost interest in sex, he had simply lost interest in any other woman than Maude.

Hell. This was more serious than he had imagined. There was a strange sensation apparently lodged under his breastbone, his normally clear mind was in turmoil—and she, quite obviously, had no ideas in that direction whatsoever. She would hardly been so comfortable alone with him if she had.

Maude knew all there was to know about his parentage, so she must, being very much a member of the *ton* herself, have no thought at all of any other relationship than the one they had now.

Eden conjured up, with no difficulty whatsoever, the feel of her mouth under his, her body against him. It was not that Maude was not responsive when he kissed her, but she was most certainly not abandoned to passion. It was almost as though she was curious. Perhaps that was it; a well-bred young woman had few opportunities to experience passion and she thought he was safe enough to experiment with a little.

Painfully, an entire new set of emotions were being born—possessive, protective desire, warm liking, the need to be near her. He had never let himself get close to a woman before and there was no one to ask if these were normal feelings.

He had resolved to simply get used to her being around and that was proving impossible. It was impossible, too, to be unmoved by the sight of Sir Frederick Staines waiting for her as she walked off after the completion of the quadrille. Eden looked at his own card. A waltz. Now he was going to have to stand and watch her revolving in the arms of that man.

Eden glanced to either side and realised he was behind the chairs occupied by a group of wallflowers, half a dozen young women watching with ill-concealed envy as their more fortunate sisters took to the floor. He stepped forward, selected the plainest girl he could see and stopped in front of her.

'I regret we have not been introduced, but may I have the honour of this dance?' It was improper on his part, and outrageously fast on hers, but the young woman, sandy haired, befreckled and gawky, jumped to her feet with alacrity.

'I would love to, sir.' She could, he realised with considerable relief as they reached the floor, dance. In fact, despite her height and her surprise at being snatched from the sidelines, she moved very gracefully.

'I am Eden Hurst,' he said after the first few steps.

'Angela Hunter. I haven't been approved to waltz by a Patroness, you know,' she added, biting her lip.

'It's all right, you can simply say I snatched you on to the floor and you were far too well behaved to resist,' Eden said, sweeping her round a corner. 'Everyone will blame me, I have a shocking reputation.'

'Really?' She grinned. 'What fun.'

Now that he could see Maude, it was a simple matter to steer his partner so that they were dancing close to her and Staines. He couldn't hear what the man was saying to her, but at least if he saw any distress on her face he was near enough to intervene.

And then Maude saw him. Her eyes widened, she smiled, then she saw his partner and she frowned. She was puzzled. Good. He fully intended that she should be, it might take her mind off that blond Lothario.

They appeared to be in perfect unison. *It was a wonder the swine can concentrate on his steps*, Eden thought savagely, *because he seems to be fixated on her breasts*. And that damn gown, the soft satin moulding her long limbs as she twirled, fleetingly outlining every lovely line.

Miss Hunter was mercifully quiet, content, it seemed to dance in silence. Glancing down, meeting her eyes and smiling, Eden decided he liked the girl. She didn't deserve to be stuck with no partners, or used by him as a stalking horse. As the set swirled to its end, Maude still happily chatting away to Staines, Eden felt his partner tense in his arms.

'What's wrong?'

'Mama,' she said grimly, nodding towards a tall matron with feathers in her coiffure.

'Never mind.' He spotted Jessica, standing talking to Lord Dereham. 'Come and meet some friends.' Miss Hunter, looking bemused, allowed herself to be led towards them. 'Lady Standon, may I introduce Miss Hunter?' Over the top of the sandy head, he mouthed *Find her partners* at Jessica.

She picked up the cue and smiled. 'Do join us, Miss Hunter.' They strolled off and a few moments later Eden saw Jessica introducing Miss Hunter to a lively group of young men, two of whom seemed to be asking her for a dance.

'Who were you dancing with?' He turned to find Maude, charmingly flushed from the exercise.

'A wallflower,' he said, controlling his breathing. 'Nice girl, a Miss Hunter.'

'Oh, that was kind of you.' Maude beamed at him. 'So many men just ignore the poor things and the more they are ignored, the worse it gets.'

It was tempting to bask in her approval. 'Kindness did not come into it,' Eden said, some evil genius prompting him to honesty. 'I wanted to keep an eye on Staines and I had no partner. He is not someone you should be associating with.'

'Indeed?' Maude's chin went up. 'I like him. He is charming, good looking and an excellent dancer.'

'He's a rake and a libertine.'

'You exaggerate. He's a shocking flirt, that is all,' she said haughtily. 'And I am well able to take care of myself, thank you.'

'He propositions the chorus girls and he brings birds of paradise into his box at the theatre,' Eden snapped.

'Oh, my *goodness*!' Maude assumed an expression of exaggerated shock. 'How *dreadful*! I am sure you have never so much as *spoken* to one of the muslin company yourself—have you, Mr Hurst?'

'I—damn it, Maude I'm only—'

'Interfering?' she enquired sweetly. 'Really, Eden, anyone would think you were jealous. Ah, there's my partner for the next set. Do excuse me—and please, do carry on your good work amongst the wallflowers. I am sure they will be most grateful.'

Jealous? Eden stood staring after her as she walked towards the young gentleman who had come to claim her hand, the skirts of her exquisite gown swishing slightly with the sway of her walk. Jealous? He certainly felt possessive, and foolishly hurt and— But if he was jealous, that had to mean that this was more than desire, more than friendship. That strange new sensation was making his chest tight again.

He turned his back on the dance floor and walked out, along a passageway, through the doors at the end and on to the cold deserted terrace. Was he developing a *tendre* for Maude? No. No, he could not be doing anything so foolish. He had no idea how. He might as well wish for the moon.

Chapter Fifteen

Well, that was either a big step forward, or a total disaster, Maude thought, joining hands across and promenading down the set. She had certainly succeeded in making Eden embarrassed and angry, but whether he was jealous, and if he was, what he would do about it, she had no idea. He seemed to have vanished from the ballroom.

By the end of the country dances, and the set that followed them, there was still no sign of him and the next set was the supper dance, the first he had put his name to on her card. Some of Papa's choicer expressions ran through Maude's mind. Well, she had plenty of married friends she could join for supper, but as for this set, she may as well go and sit with the wallflowers.

'Lady Maude?' She let the pent-up breath sigh out of her before she turned around. Eden was unsmiling, but at least he was there. 'Our dance, I believe?' He bowed.

'Sir.' Maude dropped an entirely proper curtsy and held out her hand. 'You are freezing!' Even through the fine kid of her white gloves, she could feel it.

'I apologise.' He placed the other hand at her waist, lightly, as if he did not want to press the chilly palm against her. She had forgotten this was a waltz. 'I was out on the terrace.'

'Why?' They began to move in unison with the other couples close around them. 'It is so cold tonight, foggy.'

'I was recovering my temper,' Eden said, his tone conversational.

Maude studied the diamond pin in his cravat. 'Oh?' She did not want to bicker, she wanted to be quiet, in his arms, moving to this loving, lilting music.

'I have never been accused of jealousy before,' he continued, spinning her so that their thighs touched momentarily and her swirling skirts flew around his legs and then away, like seaweed caught by a wave.

'No?' It was a very beautiful diamond. And she could smell him, his cologne, the scent of clean linen, cold skin, hot man. She shifted her gaze upwards, as far as it felt safe. Up to his chin, close shaven, up to his mouth. A mistake. It was too sensual, too masculine, too tempting. 'I am sorry,' she ventured. 'I was mistaken, of course. Why should you be jealous? I just wanted to hit back because you were criticising me.'

Those tempting lips curved—almost a smile. 'You were not mistaken, Maude.'

'I was not?' She looked up, startled. Eden was definitely smiling now, more than a little ruefully.

'No. I am jealous, but, of course, I have no right to be.'

'I... I do not mind, if you are,' Maude ventured.

Eden looked down at her, the smile fading, his eyes fathomless. Somehow they were still dancing, had not collided with anyone; somehow he must be concentrating, which was more than she was capable of.

His lips moved. 'Oh God, Maude.' Was that really what he had said? He sounded desperate. Her heart thudding against her ribs, Maude held her breath. Eden tightened his hold and swept her round, across the flow of the dancers and then off the floor and through the door at the end of the room.

'Eden?' They were in a deserted passageway. Without responding he lifted a branch of candles from a side table, took her arm, guided her along the passage and out into the cold, foggy night air. She shivered as he released her to cup his hand around the wildly guttering flames.

'It is warm in here.' He flung open one of the glazed doors that opened on to the terrace and stepped through. Maude followed and found herself in a small sitting room. Eden dropped the latch on the terrace door, dragged the draperies closed and then strode across the room to turn the key in the door.

'Eden?' He was walking around the room, setting the candle flame to the others on mantelshelf and side tables.

'We need to talk.' He came to stand in front of her, frowning.

'Yes,' she agreed. He looked so grim, but then Eden rarely smiled.

'My feelings for you have become—' He broke off, searching for a word. 'Inappropriate.'

'How?' Maude managed to say.

'I desire you.' He said it as if he was admitting to murder or fraud.

'And I, you,' she confessed. 'I do not find that at all inappropriate.'

'You do not, *Lady* Maude?' he enquired, his voice grating on her title.

'We are both grown up, we can make our own choices.' Desire, that is what he had said. But not love. Did he not love her yet, or not recognise that he loved her?

'Damn it.' Eden turned abruptly away, went to stand with his back to her, one hand on the mantelshelf. 'You know this is something we cannot choose to act upon.'

'Because you would leave me before one night was out?' she asked softly.

'Because I would not want to leave you at all,' Eden replied, still staring down into the cold hearth. 'It is novelty, that is all it is. It has to be. You are a beautiful woman, a virgin I have come to know as I know no others. I tell myself that of course I want you, and that of course I must not touch you.'

'Because I am a virgin or because of who I am?' If only he would turn around so that she could see his face. But perhaps it was easier to speak calmly, frankly, to his unresponsive back. Whatever she did, she must not blurt out her true feelings for him or he would be gone.

'The former overrides everything else,' he said drily.

Maude bit her lip, wondering what to say, what to do, to reach him. 'I find I am not so attached to my virgin state as I once was,' she said carefully.

That brought him round to face her, at least. But he kept the width of the hearth between them. 'And what if you found yourself with child? Just another inconvenient bastard?'

'If we were so careless, then I suppose I would marry you. A child deserves to be loved by both its parents,' Maude said, calmly, her eyes on his face.

His face stark, Eden took a step back. So, that answered that, the thought of *marriage* produced a physical response of rejection. Feeling slightly queasy, Maude waited to see what he would say.

'You are so tired of your family and your friends that you wish to exile yourself from polite society?' he enquired, one dark brow lifted.

'That was not a proposal,' Maude retorted, stiffening her spine. 'It was an observation upon a theoretical situation.' From somewhere she found a smile. 'Why did you bring me here if you do not want to be tempted, Eden?'

'Because when I am with you, my rational processes of

thought appear to be in as much of a fog as shrouds this house.' He turned his back again. 'I'm a danger to you and to my own peace of mind.'

The bitterness reached somewhere deep inside her. She had been certain that she should not take that first step towards him, should let him come to her, but she could not bear it.

'How could you be a danger to me, Eden?' It only took two steps past a side table to be close enough to touch him. 'You are my friend, you would not hurt me.' She lifted one hand and laid it lightly on his back. At her touch the long muscles went taut and she heard the sharp indrawing of his breath.

Eden turned, so fast that she could not step away, so close that she had to tip her head back to look up into his face, but he did not touch her.

'You are such an innocent. If I make love to you, Maude, you will most certainly be hurt.'

'I am not such an innocent that I do not know what would happen and that, yes, it does hurt the first time.' And very frightening that sounded.

'That is not what I meant,' he said gently. 'I would hurt you here—' he lifted one hand and brushed her temple '...and here.' For a fleeting moment his palm rested over her heart.

'Life hurts.' Maude caught Eden's hand in hers and held it a fraction of an inch above the bodice of her gown. He could have pulled free easily, but he left it, passive in her grip. 'Regrets hurt. My mother said to me once that the things she regretted were the things she did not do, not those that she did.'

And then, just when she thought she could not bear the suspense a second longer, he kissed her. It was not like either of the times he had kissed her before, she realised, dazed, hardly able to comprehend that it really was happening. Now it was neither an angry assault, nor a fleetingly gentle caress. He was intent, it seemed, upon reducing her to utter and complete collapse and she sensed he would devote however much time was necessary to the task.

Maude tried to keep some hold on reality. Eden had one hand firmly in the small of her back, the other, still held in hers, crushed between them. He seemed to be utterly focused upon what he was doing, carried away by his own desires. There was a faint thread of common sense that was observing what was going on and attempting to communicate rationally with her. It was doubtful, it commented, that he was as completely at the mercy of his senses as he seemed. Certainly he was not as adrift as she was.

Maude gave her commonsense a firm push away. This was not the time for it. This was the time to strengthen Eden's desire for her and show him that she wanted him with at least as much fervour.

Maude made herself relax, allowed herself to feel, gave her instincts permission to do just as they pleased and discovered, too late, that they did not need any encouragement whatsoever from her. If she had any illusions that she was in control, of either herself, or of Eden, she was swiftly disabused of them.

Eden's mouth was an instrument of the most subtle form of torture. Should kissing be like this? It was at once soft, sensual, gentle and yet demanding and hot. His mouth was both hard and sensitive. His lips slid slowly over the seam of hers, his tongue flickering out to nudge, insistently, at the join until she opened to him with a little gasp. There was nothing tentative about the invasion of her mouth—the firm, mobile moist heat of his tongue filled her, probing, licking, teasing. Thrusting.

It was overwhelming that one small piece of flesh and muscle could dominate her, demand, orchestrate her body's response so she began to sway against him in the rhythm of the thrusts. He was thinking about driving into her body, possessing her fully, she realised that. This intimate joining of mouths was simply a metaphor for that total possession.

Jessica and Bel had tried to warn her about this, and she had refused to listen. This was more than kissing—her whole body was reacting, changing. Her breasts ached and throbbed, heavier, fuller, the nipples fretting against the crisp lace trimming, throbbing with a pain that was almost totally pleasure. Deep in her belly, low where her thighs joined, the ache became a pulse, a demanding drum beat. Maude made a little inarticulate sound against Eden's mouth and he lifted his head to look down into her face.

In the candlelight his pupils seemed wide and dark, his face hawk-like, even more beautiful, fine-honed with concentration. 'Maude,' he said, his voice husky. *'Maude.'* He buried his face in her neck, his tongue, then his teeth, fretting at the shivering, sensitive skin as he followed the line down, down to her collarbone, tracing the dip with the very tip of his tongue while she sobbed with the building tension.

She needed *something*, something that would come from this, but she did not know what, did not know how to find it. Did not understand. But he did. 'Eden,' she whispered, her lips against the silky thickness of his hair as he bent lower, found the swell of her breasts, found the low edge of the bodice and ran his tongue under it, touching the straining, hard peak of her right nipple. 'Eden, please…'

Maude clutched his shoulders, shaking, adrift, feeling only the heat and the strength of him. She was leaning back against the table and there was cooler air on her legs. His hand was slipping up under her skirts, stroking up the length of her legs to the mound between her thighs. He cupped it and it felt so right. There was no shame in his touch, only the need to arch against him, seek the point of twisting, aching tension and make it stop, somehow…

He took her mouth again, just as one finger slid through

the damp tangle of curls and found the hard knot at the centre of her torment. His tongue thrust, the teasing pressure intensified and everything fell apart into darkness and light and blissful pleasure.

'Maude?'

She stirred, her body limp and heavy and at peace again. 'Eden?'

'I'm here, I've got you.' He was holding her on his lap, sitting on one of the sofas that flanked the fireplace. He lay back against its support, cradling her, and the softness she could feel under her cheek was the linen of his shirt, the solid rhythm, his heartbeat. 'Are you all right?'

'Yes.' She supposed she was. That she would be...eventually. She felt wonderful and strange and very shy. Maude snuggled closer. Eden smelt different. His skin was saltier. There was a faint, intoxicating sensation of musk in the air. Arousal, she realised. Hers, his. Theirs. And his had not been satisfied.

'Eden? What about you? Tell me what to do.'

'No.' She felt the shake of his head. 'We're in enough trouble as it is. We are going to sit here while you collect yourself and then I am going to sit over there until *I* collect myself, and then we are going back into the ballroom.'

Maude rubbed her cheek, cat-like, against his lapel. 'I did not know about that, about what just happened.'

'I realise that,' he said grimly. Eden's body was not relaxed now, holding her. And his voice was no longer tender. Maude felt him shift his grip, felt the exciting bunch and flex of thigh muscles under her and then he stood with an ease that should have surprised her, yet seemed quite natural. This was Eden after all. He could do anything.

Anything but fall easily in love with her, it seemed. He set her down on the sofa and went to take the one opposite. Even in candlelight Maude could see just how aroused he was. To her shame he saw where she was looking.

'These evening breeches are not designed for concealment,' he observed, sitting and crossing his legs. 'Let us sit and discuss unpleasant things for a while.'

The haze of satisfied desire was fading rapidly, leaving Maude staring at reality. 'No doubt you can think of several,' she managed to say.

Too soon, the voice in her head whispered. *Too soon*. That had been desire, pure carnal lust. Not love. Was it even, on his part, much to do with affection either? And she had melted at his touch, all her careful, foolish, strategy in ruins. *I had no idea*, Maude's thoughts whispered. *None*.

Her friends had cautioned her, and in her innocence she had failed to understand. Thinking she could manage a man with the sensual experience and the lack of social constraints of Eden Hurst was like thinking she could ride a wild horse bareback. And now she had fallen. And he had made love to her and remained in control. She had laid her desires open and he had sated them and murmured not one word of affection as he did so. And he had been right—in the morning, when she could think clearly, she knew this was going to hurt a great deal.

Maude clenched her hands together. What had she said to Bel? *I have enough breeding for both of us*. She was Lady Maude Templeton, daughter of the Earl of Pangbourne, and she never, ever, ran away from anything or anyone.

Eden drew in the same deep, calming breaths he used before stepping out on to the stage or dealing with a difficult negotiation, then he conjured up the face of the Earl of Pangbourne and imagined his expression if he discovered that his daughter had been making love with Eden Hurst. That was a start, enough to chill anyone's ardour. If he needed anything else, he could remember that he was the bastard son of a disgraced Ravenhurst and had nothing at all to offer her, certainly none of the things that she deserved.

The trouble was, whenever he looked across at Maude, whenever he drew breath and caught the scent of warm, aroused woman, lust grabbed him again with hot claws.

Why couldn't he resist her? He could resist any other woman on the planet. It was merely sex, he tried to tell himself, an appetite to be controlled just as one would control hunger or anger. But somehow, with Maude, it was mysteriously more.

'That will not happen again,' he said, deliberately harsh, wanting to see her flinch, wanting to repel her.

'No. I can imagine it was very unsatisfactory for you,' she said softly. 'But thank you for being so careful.'

'It was far from unsatisfactory,' he said, charmed into truthfulness. She should be weeping, or having the vapours, or throwing the china at him in reaction by now, not being sweet and understanding and—and Maude. 'It was beautiful to hold you in my arms and to see your pleasure, a privilege that you trusted me.'

That sweet, dazed bliss, the knowledge that he had given her that, overwhelmed the desire simply to take her, thrust into her body, find his own release. It was working now, he could feel the brute nagging lust subside into something that was a warm, regretful glow.

'I think we should go back now, have some supper before we are missed.'

Maude nodded and got to her feet, grabbing at the arm of the chair. 'Oh my, my legs are so shaky!'

Eden reached for her, then snatched his hand back. Better not to touch her, not while they were alone like this. He saw the look of comprehension on her face and winced inwardly.

He should have been strong for both of them, but even now, he could not truthfully tell himself he was sorry.

'If you go first,' he said, unlocking both doors, 'and then take the door on the right in the corridor, that opens up into one of the retiring rooms. I'll go out of the door we left by.' He snuffed out the candles as she left with a terse nod. 'Wait for me by the door to the supper room.'

Alone, he stood trying not to think and then found his right hand was pressed to the centre of his chest as if to soothe the pain there. But why was he in pain? Why did he feel as though he had just lost something?

Chapter Sixteen

'Maude? What has happened?' It was Jessica, right behind her. 'Where have you been?'

'What do you mean?' Maude retorted, too flustered to be anything but defensive. 'I'm hungry, that's all.'

'You and Mr Hurst vanished over half an hour ago,' Jessica said. 'And you look…different. Have you—? No. No, I refuse to believe that even that man would do such a thing in the middle of a ball.'

'What do you mean, *even that man*?' Maude managed to keep her voice down to a furious hiss with difficulty.

'The man's a notorious rake,' Jessica hissed back. 'But I never believed he'd debauch a virgin. I should have spoken to your father. I am never going to forgive myself if I find he has—'

'Well, he hasn't. Unfortunately,' Maude snapped, perilously close to tears all of a sudden. 'I had been going to talk to you, ask your advice, but now, I never want to speak of it again to you.'

'Of all the naïve, headstrong, romantic idiots.' Jessica shook her head in disbelief. 'How you—'

'Maude, are you all right?' It was Eden, tall and broad and *here*, just when she needed him.

'No, I am not all right,' she said, taking his arm. 'I would like a glass of champagne, please. And I want to sit down somewhere where I will not be nagged at by hypocritical friends,' she added in a fierce undertone to Jessica. 'I was there when you came back from Gareth's bed at eight in the morning in your evening gown—remember?'

She had never once exchanged a cross word with Jessica and now, here they were, hissing at each other like the start of a cat fight. Unable to bear the expression of shock on her friend's face, Maude whirled round and walked into the supper room.

'Sit.' Eden had found a table. 'Wait there and do not pick any more quarrels until I get back.'

Maude sat, feeling dizzy with reaction and trying to look as though she was having a wonderful time and the only concern she had in the world was what delicacies her partner was going to bring her.

'Here.' Eden put a filled plate in front of her and sat down. 'Eat.'

'I can't. I want some champagne.'

'Eat,' he repeated, filling his own glass and leaving hers empty.

Maude forked something up and chewed it with dogged determination. 'I've quarrelled with Jessica,' she said, sick at heart.

'You'll make it up,' Eden said. 'Please eat some more, you've gone white and it is worrying me.'

A spark of humour surfaced. The poor man was obviously used to dealing with Madame Marguerite's spectacular tantrums, but pale-faced female misery was outside his experience. 'I don't expect this is the usual result of one of your interludes with a lady, is it?'

'No,' he confessed. 'But everything to do with you is un-usual, Maude.' She smiled at his serious face. 'What are we going to do about this?' he asked. She had the feeling the question was to himself, as much as to her.

'Nothing?' she ventured. 'See what happens?'

'Maude.' He leaned closer under cover of pouring her some wine. 'We are having trouble keeping our hands off each other. It does not take much imagination to see what will happen next if things carry on as they have been.'

'We will not meet unchaperoned,' Maude said. 'Then things will calm down again.' From the quizzical lift of his eyebrow she could see that she was not convincing him of that. 'There will be so much work for the theatrical entertain-ment that we will not have time to think of anything else.'

Eden shook his head, but made no further comment. In silence they ate, sipped their wine and, and, Maude thought sadly, were alone with their thoughts.

'Lady Maude?' She looked up, startled to realise where she was, and found herself looking at the enquiring face of Mr Hethersett, her hostess's elder son. 'We have the next set, but if you are still engaged...'

'No, I have quite finished. Thank you so much, Mr Hurst.' He was on his feet, assisting her with her chair, putting him-self between her and her new partner to give her precious seconds to collect herself. 'Thank you,' she whispered again. There was still the last dance to come.

Mr Hethersett, a ponderous young man, was hardly the liveliest of partners for a vigorous country dance. Maude had to concentrate on her footwork, so much so that it was not until she was facing her and had to join hands for a round, that she realised that Jessica was dancing too.

Their eyes met, Jessica's distressed and hurt, before the dance separated them. Maude stumbled over her partner's tardily withdrawn foot and continued down the line, blankly miserable not to have the support of the one friend she had always thought would be with her, come what may. Would Jessica really go to Papa? Somehow that was less important than quarrelling with a dear friend.

The set drew to an end at last, Maude dropped a hasty curtsy to her partner and craned to see where Jessica was. She would go to her now—but, no, at the far end she could see her on Gareth's arm. Leaving.

Maude felt like fleeing the ballroom too, but something— stubborn pride? The need to be in Eden's arms one more time?—kept her there, dancing and chatting and smiling. When he came to claim her hand for the last dance, Maude was ready to drop.

'Do you want to dance?' he asked, pausing at the edge of the floor. 'You look...tired.'

'A gentleman should not say such things to a lady,' she said in a rallying tone. 'We are always radiant.'

'Well, I am not a gentleman and you are not radiant.' He turned back and led her to an alcove. 'Let us stay here, in plain view. Besides, I have something to give you.'

'You have?' He was taking something from the pocket in the tails of his coat, a dark morocco jewellery box. Maude's heart turned over with a thump. 'Eden—'

'I put it in this because otherwise I would be sure to sit on it and squash it,' he explained, placing the box in her hand. Maude opened it. Inside, nestling on red plush, was one marchpane sweetmeat. Her heart thumped back to its normal location. 'You did not eat any at supper,' he explained, his face serious. 'I came away from the jewellers with that box empty because I had taken a pair of Madame's earrings to be cleaned.'

Maude looked down at the small yellow-and-green confection and then up at his face. For one startled moment she had thought he was going to give her jewellery and instead he had given her marchpane.

'Sugar's good for the nerves,' Eden added, his eyes smiling into hers. 'We make sure nervous actresses drink sweet tea.'

'That was very thoughtful, thank you,' she said, meaning it. He had remembered that she liked it. Something out of the corner of her eye made her turn her head. 'Oh dear, people are looking.'

'They think I am about to fall to one knee, perhaps, and they are ready to faint with shock or rush forward to rescue you,' he said sardonically. 'I suggest you eat it immediately, which will confuse them, if nothing else.'

Maude popped the sweet into her mouth, shook the dusting of sugar out of the box and handed it back. The curious onlookers turned away, some of them smiling. That fast Lady Maude again! She could almost hear them saying it.

'Now, let us dance,' she said, laying her hand on his arm. 'I think we waltz rather well together.'

'You feeling all right, my lady?' Anna placed the breakfast tray on Maude's knees and peered at her. 'You look proper peaky this morning.'

'I didn't sleep very well.' That was an understatement; she doubted if she had slept a wink all night.

'I knew I should have let you lie in, no matter what you said,' the maid pronounced, pulling back the drapes. 'Eight o'clock is no time to be getting up the morning after a ball. You've got dark circles under your eyes.'

'I must see Lady Standon first thing this morning,' Maude said, wrapping her fingers tightly round her chocolate cup for the comfort of the heat. She had to make thing right with Jessica. 'And then we will go to the theatre.'

There was a noise from the landing. Rainbow appeared to be arguing with someone, which was unprecedented.

'Anna, go and see what on earth is going on...' Maude began, but the maid was already round the screen that shielded the bed from the door.

'Oh, Lady Standon! But my lady said she was coming to call on you this morning...'

'You see, Rainbow. I knew Lady Maude would be awake, so you can stop looking starchy and let me in,' Jessica said firmly. 'Anna, I want a private word with your mistress.'

Maude put down her cup and slid out of bed. 'Jessica?'

'Oh, my dear!" Her friend flew round the screen and caught her in a warm embrace. 'I've been perfectly miserable—how are you?'

'Miserable too. Jessica, I am so sorry, I should never have said you were hypocritical, or mentioned that morning, or been cross at all. I know you are worried about me.'

'Oh, I am!' Jessica sat down on the edge of the bed, her arm around Maude's shoulders. 'But I wouldn't tell Lord Pangbourne, I promise.'

'I know. Jessica, I should have listened to you and Bel—it's like riding a tiger, isn't it? How do you get off it again safely?'

'What is?' Jessica was looking bemused.

'Sex,' Maude said bluntly. 'I thought there was kissing. And then there was bed and he'd...you know. I didn't know there was all that stuff in the middle! How on earth do you *think* with that going on?'

'You're not supposed to,' Jessica said, unsuccessfully fighting a smile.

'But I need to think, I need to plan and see what is happening and judge how he's feeling. And when he...we... My mind just turned to jelly.'

'Maude, you can't do this like planning a complicated social event, with a list for this and that and things to be done that will get you a result. Either the man falls in love with you—and Heaven help you both if he does—or he doesn't. Now tell me, what exactly happened?'

Looking back, it wasn't all very clear, but blushing rosily, Maude did her best to explain.

'Oh, my,' Jessica murmured. 'Well, I take back what I said about him—the man has enviable self-control. Now listen, I am going to be very, very frank about things because I do not want you being taken by surprise again. Not,' she added, 'that I hope you ever find yourself in that situation with a man you aren't married to.'

'You did,' Maude pointed out.

'I married him, and very eligible he is too,' Jessica retorted. 'Now listen, and if you do not understand, ask me questions.' She looked around. 'But ring for a jug of chocolate first, I am going to need it.'

'Her ladyship's back, Guv'nor.' Howard put his head round the office door. 'Bloody hell, you look rough this morning.'

Eden growled and put down his pen. 'Send someone with some hot water.' She was here? The day after the ball? After what had happened? 'What's she doing?' he called after the stage manager.

'Prowling up and down the aisles with a tape measure, a notebook and that maid Anna. I'll send Millie with the water.'

Eden stripped to the waist and took his shaving gear from the cupboard. The face that glowered back at him from the glass had a heavy growth of stubble, dark circles under its eyes and hair that had been raked by his fingers into wild disarray. Perhaps he should walk out looking like this, then she would see the real him, the unworthy, uncivilised creature under the veneer.

There was a tap on the door, Millie came in, gave a started squeak, set down the hot water jug and scuttled out. Eden set to work restoring the image he so carefully cultivated:

controlled, polished, unapproachable and impregnable. The razor slid through the soap foam on his face, slicing away the whiskers, leaving a clean, smooth track in its wake. If only he could cut away last night as easily. But Maude was under his skin now, too deep to reach without cuts that would be agonising.

When he was finished, hair slicked back, neckcloth tied, he strode out of the room without giving himself time to think.

Maude was on stage, bent over the table, drawing on a large sheet of paper. He walked silently across and looked over her shoulder. It was a rough plan of the theatre. 'Good afternoon, Mr Hurst,' she said, running her pencil carefully along a ruler's edge. He could have sworn he had made no sound.

'Good afternoon, Lady Maude.' She turned her head, her hands still resting on the table, and smiled up at him and he realised what had been making him dizzy all those times he had thought himself unwell. Maude. She looked tired, but the unhappiness had gone from the depths of those big hazel eyes. 'Have you made up your quarrel with Lady Standon?'

'Yes—how did you know?'

'You don't look sad any more. Your friends are important to you, aren't they?'

'Oh, yes. Very.' Eden tried to imagine feeling that desperate at falling out with one of the men he counted his friends. He could not. The only person that touched his emotions in that way was standing right in front of him. How did she manage it, that emotional connection to so many people? It seemed to give her such pleasure and yet, to bring her such pain as well. He thought of the network of Ravenhurst cousins, that big family, and pushed away the momentary yearning to be part of it. Childish weakness.

Maude straightened up, put her fists into the small of her back and stretched. 'I had a note from Bel—Lady Dereham—

she has taken your Miss Hunter under her wing, says she does not deserve to be a wallflower and she intends to promote her as an original. Bel also says I am to congratulate you upon your perspicacity.'

'Miss Hunter?' He stared blankly at her. 'Oh, the gawky girl.'

'Yes, the one you picked on as a stalking horse in order to follow me round the dance floor glaring at Sir Frederick,' Maude said severely. 'I shall not disillusion Bel and tell her you ruthlessly scooped up the nearest unfortunate young woman.'

She turned back to her plan, sucking the end of her pencil until he removed it from her. 'You'll make your tongue black. What are you doing?'

'Planning out the tables and so on for the special event. We'll have to think of a name for it. Which blocks of seating may I have removed?'

'Let me see.' He joined her, shoulder to shoulder, at the table. 'I see you have drawn sight-lines in. We could take these and these, put the buffet tables here, the string band in this large box here...'

Somehow, working on such a practical task with Eden, the restraint between them eased. They sat on stage while the work of the theatre went on, sketching, thrashing out problems, occasionally getting up to measure something or go down into the stalls to check the view.

Maude felt warm, happily relaxed with him and he did not seem to try to avoid touching her, or appear awkward with her. Whether that meant that he simply discounted what had happened and could put it behind him, or whether he was a far better actor than he had let her suspect, she did not know. It was simply happiness to be with him like this, doing something practical, seeing his mind work, watching those big, sensitive hands as he sketched out ideas in the air or on paper.

'We'll need the stage in ten minutes or so, Guv'nor.' It was one of the hands, standing looking up at them from the orchestra pit. 'Got to get set up for this evening.'

'Lord, is that the time?' Eden was sitting on the edge of the table, legs swinging, hair loose on his shoulders, as relaxed as she had ever seen him. A pang of love and longing struck Maude with almost painful intensity. She must have made a sound, for he turned his head to look at her and their eyes locked. There was that look again in the dark depths, the look that made her breath hitch in her throat and her pulse stutter.

'Eden—'

'Late afternoon post, Guv'nor.' It was Millie, balancing a pile of correspondence.

'Put it in the office,' Eden snapped. 'I am working with Lady Maude.' The moment, and whatever it had held, was gone.

'It is all right,' Maude said. 'We have finished for today, after all. Please, make sure there isn't anything important.'

Eden tossed the pile on to the table and sorted through it rapidly. At the bottom, a large letter on thick paper covered in seals crackled importantly. He ran his thumb under the wax, sending red fragments flying, and smoothed it out. Something about the quality of his stillness caught Maude's attention as he scanned the letter again and then a third time.

'Is something wrong?' she asked, unable to bear the suspense any longer.

'Wrong? No, far from it. It is the agents for the Unicorn. The owner has died and they ask if I wish them to approach the heir with an offer to purchase.'

'Who is it?' Maude came to his side and put her hand on his forearm. Under the fabric of the sleeve she could feel a vibration. It seemed to pulse up her arm, infecting her with his tension.

'They do not yet know. The solicitor dealing with the will is to write—they expect to know in a week or so.' He looked up, his eyes burning with a fierce excitement. 'They will sell, surely? Why should they want a theatre? It is something you set out to acquire, not something you keep if it comes to you by accident.'

'You are right, most people would want to realise the asset as soon as possible, especially if they have an inheritance to deal with. Oh, Eden, I'm so pleased for you—the Unicorn, yours, at last.'

'I must not count on it, not until it is certain,' he said soberly, then caught her eye and grinned. 'Oh, to hell with caution! Maude, it is going to be mine, I know it.' And the next thing she knew he caught her around the waist, lifted her in the air and was whirling around the stage in dizzying circles, laughing up at her. 'Yes, yes, yes!'

Maude laughed back, safe with his hands spanning her waist, safe with his strong back holding her up, as dizzy as he was with joy.

'What on earth are you about, darling?' The trained voice from the wings brought Eden to a halt, the laughter dying out of his face. Slowly he lowered Maude to the floor, released her and stepped back. 'Auditioning for the *corps de ballet*?' Madame Marguerite enquired, strolling on to the stage. The feathers in her hat swept down to the shoulder of her deep plum-coloured gown, diamonds winked and flashed at ears and throat, her skirts swished across the boards. She looked, quite simply, magnificent and Maude, her hair in her eyes and her skirts in disarray, felt like a thirteen-year-old romp caught playing with the village boys.

'Celebrating,' Eden said flatly.

'I hardly dare ask what, darling,' Madame said, running

a critical eye up and down Maude's tousled figure. 'But it is Lady Maude, is it not?'

'Madame,' Maude rejoined politely, resisting the urge to tug at her skirts and push back her hair. She was not going to react like a naughty schoolgirl, whatever the provocation.

'Well now, and when were you going to tell me this happy news?' Madame Marguerite enquired. 'I do feel, Eden darling, that a quiet word would have been more appropriate—every stage-hand must know by now.'

Oh, my God! She thinks we have become betrothed, Maude thought, hardly knowing where to look. Of all the hideously embarrassing misunderstandings.

'I saw no point in telling you until we know the theatre is definitely on the market,' Eden said. Whether he had understood what his mother had assumed, Maude could not tell, but she could only admire the delivery of the line.

The actress produced an exaggerated start of surprise. 'The *theatre*?' she enquired, in ringing tones, managing to make three dramatic syllables out of the word.

'Yes.' Eden began to gather up the letters. 'The owner has died and the agents are finding out if the new owner will sell.'

Madame appeared momentarily speechless; not a state, Maude guessed, she was often reduced to. It did not last long. 'Eden darling, a word, if you please.' She swept Maude with a look that was assessing and speculative. 'Lady Maude,' she said coolly, before she swept off stage.

'I must be going.' Maude tidied her hair by touch. 'Anna!'

'Here, my lady.' The maid hurried out of the wings with Maude's muff and bonnet. 'I've called the carriage, my lady, seeing what the time is.'

'Thank you.' Maude looked across at Eden, his face as cool and unreadable as it usually was. 'I will see to the invitations, which will take a day or so. Shall we call it *The Unicorn Musicale*?' He nodded, unsmiling. He must be thinking about Madame's false assumption that they were betrothed. He would be feeling trapped by that, coming so close on the realisation of how much she desired him.

There was an ache inside her, not just embarrassment, but something else. The sudden change in him hurt, she realised. Whenever she believed they were getting close, Eden brought down an intangible barrier and retreated behind it. Was he truly so unable to love, to make himself open to another person, to trust her enough to make himself vulnerable? She needed love, and she would sacrifice everything for that. But lack of it would kill her spirit, she knew it. It would be better to put some distance between them, just for a little while.

'I… I may not come to the theatre for a day or so, there is so much to do for this. I will send notes, of course. And you will let me know if there is any news?'

'Of course.' *He agrees so readily, he is relieved that I am going.* Her heart sank a little. 'I will see you at the special committee meeting we arranged for planning the event?'

'Next week? Yes, of course. Goodbye, Eden.' Maude paused, tying her bonnet strings. 'I'll be thinking about the Unicorn, and wishing you luck.'

Chapter Seventeen

'Madame?' Eden closed the door of his office behind him and went to sit in the high carved chair. He felt decidedly unfit for dealing with his mother in one of her moods. His body was still jangling with nerves and arousal from being around Maude, the thought that he might have the chance to buy the theatre was threatening to fill his brain to the exclusion of all else, and, on top of it all, his leading lady was leaping to quite ridiculous conclusions.

'What are your intentions towards Lady Maude Templeton?' she enquired.

'Intentions? To continue with my existing partnership with her. Her insights are useful and I find the charity work she has involved me with surprisingly interesting,' he said coolly, instinct warning him against allowing Madame any hint of his feelings.

'Don't try to cut a sham with me, Eden. Any fool with half an eye can see the pair of you are like April and May,' Marguerite retorted. 'Are you sleeping with her?'

'No.' Eden got a tight rein on his temper. 'You are speaking about an unmarried lady of quality.' It was probably not the most tactful of observations to make to someone who had been a lady of quality herself, before she had turned her back on her family and her chances of a respectable marriage.

His mother's eyes widened, and he was seized with sudden doubt. She was a great actress, but could she really counterfeit that flash of pain? Had that scandalous split with her family not been her choice after all? 'I am fully aware of that. And what a catch! Marry the girl, for Heaven's sake, Eden. Think about her dowry, her connections!'

'Think about the Earl of Pangbourne's response when a bastard theatrical manager turns up asking for his daughter's hand in marriage. Horsewhips would feature, I imagine.'

Marguerite shrugged. 'Then get her with child—he won't refuse then.'

If we were so careless, then I suppose I would marry you, she had said. And, *A child deserves to be loved by both its parents.* He eyed his own parent, that uncharacteristic feeling of sympathy quite gone. 'Debauch her, in effect, so I can marry her for her money?'

'A sensible strategy.'

'A despicable one!' he said hotly. The pain of the heavy carving biting into his clenching hands cut through the wave of red anger that her suggestion provoked. 'Lady Maude is a friend.'

'She's in love with you,' his mother said. 'She'll be willing.'

'There may be some physical attraction between us,' Eden conceded through clenched teeth, 'but she is not in love with me. And,' he added before she could say anything else, 'I am not in love with her.'

May I be forgiven for that lie. Even as he denied it, he recognised the emotion that was possessing him. He loved Maude. How had that crept up on him, overwhelmed him without him realising? When had he fallen in love, so disastrously, so hopelessly? With that first kiss? The second?

But she, with her gift for friendship, her passionate defence of the wounded and needy, she was simply encompassing him within the fortunate circle of those she cared for. She was not going to give her heart to someone as unworthy of it as he was. And if she did, then she needed protecting from herself. And from him.

'Sentimental fool,' his mother observed, getting to her feet in a flurry of silks. 'I came in today because I was beginning to wonder if you were ever going to visit me. Now I can see why I have been neglected. You will want to start rehearsals soon, I imagine?'

'Yes.' He had been intending to call on her that evening. Not to do so now would be childish and he was not going to add that to the list of failings that seemed to be written in letters of blood on his lids whenever he closed his eyes. And an evening doing a read-through with Madame would most certainly distract his mind from the shattering realisation that he had fallen in love.

But I don't believe in love, the old, hard, cynical part of his brain protested. Everything that he thought he was, was false, it seemed. 'I will bring the script round this evening. May I see you to your carriage, Madame?'

'Thank you, no. You will take supper?'

'Of course. Thank you.' He opened the door for her, then went back to sit behind his desk. After a minute, he put his elbows on the green leather and dropped his head into his hands and tried to think, not to feel, not to hurt. Just to think.

Maude did not love him, of course not. What was there to love? A cold, hard man—out of her world, out of her class. She desired him, as he did her. That physical spark between them had been unmistakable from the very first touch. She was innocent, but not a child—she was old enough, she would say, to know what she wanted. And she wanted him—as a friend and as a lover. Apparently she saw something in him that would be worthy of her friendship, worthy of her attempts to make him admit that love, in its widest sense, existed.

Well, she had done that. He believed in love between a man and a woman now, that was for certain. And in that one sentence asserting a child's right to be loved by its parents, she had, somehow, convinced him about maternal love too. He could imagine Maude with a child in her arms. His child. He could almost feel the love flowing from her. She had shown him how she loved her friends and what misery it plunged her into when they were at odds.

She was every dream he had suppressed for years and the best thing he could do for her, the only way to show her his love, was to deny it and, by denying it, protect her. Honour demanded it, pride dictated it.

Eden allowed himself to imagine calling on the Earl of Pangbourne, telling him he loved his daughter, setting out for him what he could offer her in life. The loss of her status, the loss of her friends, the loss of the brilliant marriage she would one day make. His love, the emotion he had only just discovered, was made null and void by his theatre and the stigma of trade, his bloodlines. It was not going to happen and he was going to have to learn to live with it.

Maude found more than enough to busy herself with over the next seven days. She should have had no time to think about Eden or those moments of bliss in his arms or the sobering reality of his reaction to Madame's assumption of their betrothal.

There were balls and parties and soirées to go to, morning calls to make, clothes to buy, invitations to write for the *Musicale* and there was committee business for the charity.

All in all, she should not have had room in her brain to think of anything else and she should have dropped exhausted into her bed every night. Instead, Maude found herself falling into a daydream about Eden's mouth with half an address written, or worrying about the ownership of the Unicorn in the middle of thinking about a new ballgown or tossing and turning long into the small hours, her body aching for the touch of his hands.

They exchanged notes almost every day, innocuous, practical letters about food and musicians, doormen and footmen, lighting and menus that she would not have blushed to have shown to anyone. Even so, all Eden's notes to her ended up tied with red ribbon, at the bottom of a hat box.

By the morning of the special committee meeting to discuss the *Musicale*, Maude was feeling almost light-headed with lack of sleep and distraction. When she was shown into Bel's boudoir an hour before the meeting she sank down in her usual chair with a sigh of relief, only to be jolted upright by Bel. 'Maude! What on earth is the matter with you?'

'I'm tired, that is all.' She sank back and closed her eyes.

'You are white as a sheet and I could swear you have lost weight. I thought so at the Petries' party the day before yesterday, but the light was so bad I thought I must be mistaken.' Maude heard Bel move to sit next to her, then her hand was lifted and enfolded. 'It isn't just weariness, is it? What's wrong?'

'Nothing—and everything.' Maude opened her eyes and sat up, managing a smile. 'I am busy, but that isn't it. I haven't seen Eden for a week and when we parted it was... difficult. We were celebrating because he thinks he has the chance to buy the Unicorn and Madame Marguerite came in and thought we were happy because we were betrothed. He changed, Bel. I have never seen a man change so rapidly. One moment he was laughing and warm and happy to be with me and the next—cold and distant. He was obviously appalled by her mistake. I said I wouldn't be at the theatre for some time, that I had a lot to do, and he accepted that so easily. And yet, only the night before we…he… Oh, damn! I am not going to cry.'

'You were lovers?' Bel asked, her grip on Maude's hand tightening. So, Jessica had not betrayed Maude's confidence.

'No, not fully. No doubt he regrets even that now.'

'Will he be here this afternoon?'

'He said he would be.' Maude blew her nose briskly. 'Do I look as awful as I feel?'

'Not your best,' Bel admitted. 'Shall we do so something about it?'

'No.' Maude shook her head. 'I don't want to be powdered and pinched. I will smile a lot, no one will notice.'

'I don't know about that,' Bel began, then looked up as the boudoir door opened to admit Jessica, another young woman at her heels.

Maude stared at her. There was something very familiar about the red-haired, elegant stranger. Then she smiled. 'Elinor!' Both Bel and Maude hugged and kissed and exclaimed over the latest Ravenhurst bride.

'You look radiant!' Maude pulled Elinor, whom she had last seen looking the epitome of a drab bluestocking spinster, down on the sofa beside her. 'I wasn't expecting you yet—where is Theo?'

'Talking to Ashe and Gareth downstairs. We only landed two days ago.'

Elinor had married her cousin Theo Ravenhurst in France the previous year and they had embarked on a prolonged Continental honeymoon combined with a buying trip for Theo's art and antiquities business.

Someone else who managed to be in trade and remain respectable, Maude thought with an inward sigh.

'Tell me all the gossip,' Elinor demanded, waving aside

Bel and Jessica's questions about the exact state of Paris hemlines and where she had bought her bonnet. 'Talk to Theo about fashions—he makes me buy clothes; he threatened to burn all my old ones.'

At least, with the three others engrossed in their conversation, Maude was able to avoid any more comments about her wan complexion. She slipped out of the room while they were still talking and went downstairs to curl up on a window seat, shielded by the curtains, where she knew she could watch the comings and goings in the dining room unobserved. For some reason she felt shy about seeing Eden again; when the room was full she could emerge and mingle at a safe distance.

As she thought it, he came in carrying a portfolio and a roll of paper, Lady Wallace at his side. His willingness to throw the resources of the Unicorn into supporting the charity seemed to have overcome her suspicions of him.

Maude watched him, indulging in the luxury of just being able to stare unseen. He unrolled what she guessed, from the questions Lady Wallace was asking him, was a plan of the stalls and stage. Their voices just reached Maude from her hiding place at the far end of the long room, Eden's low, rich, sending shivers down her spine, the older woman's bright and chatty.

He anchored the corners of the plan with piles of paper, then looked up, his head cocked to one side, as though straining to hear a distant voice. When Lady Wallace stepped out for a moment, Eden turned slowly on his heel, his eyes scanning the room, then he walked straight towards her. He could not see her, surely? Maude held her breath, dropping the edge of the curtain she had been peeping through and feeling quite ridiculously flustered.

'Hello.' Eden stood in front of her, his mouth quirking at the sight she presented, curled up like the parlour cat on the window seat. 'Move up?'

Obediently, Maude swung down her feet and sat up to give him room to join her, so close she could feel his body heat and inhale the achingly familiar scent of him. 'How did you know I was here?'

'I seem to be able to sense your presence when you are in a room,' he said. 'Maude, are you all right? You are very pale.'

'I'm a little tired,' she confessed, catching at an excuse for her behaviour. 'Elinor Ravenhurst and her husband Theo have returned from France, so I came down for some peace and quiet before the meeting.'

'And now I have disturbed you,' he said, running the ball of his thumb gently along her cheekbone. 'You've lost weight, Maude.'

'Some, I think,' she confessed. 'I've been overdoing it, I expect.' He cupped her face in both hands, looking at her with dark, fathomless eyes. 'You...you haven't disturbed me, Eden.'

'Have I not?' As though drawn by something he saw in her face, he leaned forward and touched his mouth softly to hers. 'I am sure your friends would say that was a good thing. I am quite certain I should agree.'

'I meant,' Maude managed to murmur against his lips, 'that you do disturb me, but I do not mind.'

The lavish folds of green velvet hid them from the room. Outside, the garden was deserted. They could stay here, in their private hiding place, for hours, barely touching, speaking with their eyes—and perhaps she could learn what his were saying.

'Where is Maude?' It was Jessica, answered by Bel.

'I haven't see her since we were upstairs.'

'I have lost Mr Hurst, too,' Lady Wallace added. 'He was here just a moment ago.'

'Leave this to me,' Eden said quietly, emerging from the curtains. 'We are here. Lady Maude was feeling a trifle faint—the cool of the window seat has revived her, I am glad to say.'

He offered her his hand and she stood, feeling quite shaky enough to give credence to Eden's assertion that she was un-well. 'I'm sorry to keep you waiting,' she apologised, taking a empty chair next to Mr Makepeace. Her friends, thank Heaven, appeared to have decided that it was best not to draw attention to her any further and the meeting began.

As the discussion unfolded, Maude began to feel better, although whether it was the praise heaped upon Eden and herself for their work so far, or the gentleness of his caresses that seemed to linger on her skin, she did not know.

'We have had over a hundred acceptances already,' she said, when it was her turn to speak. 'And at least a dozen offers to perform. I do think that members of the commit-tee should each present a piece.' She said it, part seriously, part in jest, but to her surprise everyone nodded their agree-ment except Eden.

'I will be directing,' he said firmly. 'I never perform.' And nothing could shift him from that position. Watching him from beneath her lashes, Maude had the distinct impression that the thought of performing made him nervous. Which was rather endearing, considering how confident he appeared on stage and how forcible his presence could be.

It seemed that very little now remained to be done. Those things she had thought of and had made a note of to raise in the hope that others in the group would take on, had all been swept up already by Eden and organised with ruthless effi-ciency. He and Ashe had their team of carpenters, augmented by some of the handier of the soldiers, drilled with military precision to strip down and rebuild the stalls in hours, the theatre orchestra were practising interval music and the pia-nist was well prepared and confident of accompanying what-ever the amateurs might decide to sing.

It seemed that all Maude's excuses to keep her mind busy had gone. Which meant, she realised, that she was going to have to think about what had just happened with Eden and decide what to do next. She was frightened, she realised, as the meeting broke up and transformed into a tea party. Frightened that she would somehow misread Eden's intentions and feelings, might scare him away by revealing her true feelings for him to soon. Or leave it too late.

'Come to the Unicorn tomorrow, Maude,' Eden said to her as they stood to one side, sipping tea. 'I have missed you.'

'And I, you.' She did not look up at him, content to feel him so close beside her, unwilling to confuse herself further by trying to read his expression.

'And we need to talk, I think,' he added, as much, it seemed, to himself as to her.

Yes. Maude drew in a deep breath, down to her toes. *Time for the truth. Courage, Maude.* 'I'll come tomorrow,' she promised.

'Maude, I would like to speak with you in my study, if you have finished your breakfast.' Lord Pangbourne folded his newspaper and fixed her with such a beady eye that her over-active conscience produced an uncomfortable twinge. Could Papa, in some way, guess what she was intending to do today?

'Yes, Papa, of course.' Another white night had produced the resolution that she was going to tell Eden she loved him and see what his reaction was. Not enthusiastic, she feared. He would see the barriers to their happiness even more clearly than she could—and that was assuming he wanted to marry her anyway and it wasn't all just desire mixed with friendship.

She still had not decided what words she would use. How did you propose, in cold blood, to a man?

Still pondering, she followed her father out of the breakfast room and into his study. She loved that room, dark and full of books and smelling of bay rum, brandy and leather.

'Sit down, my dear.' He took his seat behind the desk and unlocked a drawer. 'You recall me telling you that an old friend had died?'

'Yes,' Maude nodded, wondering what this was about.

'And I also told you that this lady, Sarah Millington, almost became your godmother?' Maude nodded. 'Well, my dear. It seems she has left you a legacy and one that I think will startle you as much as it has me.' Lord Pangbourne lifted a packet from the drawer and unfolded a sheet from the top. 'Here. Read for yourself.'

It was an extract from a will, copied in a heavy black hand. Maude tilted the page to catch the light from the window and read.

To Maude Augusta Edith Templeton, only child of my beloved friend Marietta Templeton, Countess of Pangbourne, née Masters, I leave the freehold and all the curtilage, appurtenances and rents of the property known as the Unicorn Theatre, Long Acre, London...

Maude read it again, half-convinced she was seeing things. But, no—she was the owner of the Unicorn Theatre. Eden's theatre. Her hands shook as she refolded the paper, trying to imagine what this was going to mean.

Chapter Eighteen

'But how on earth did she come to own the Unicorn?'
Maude asked, emerging from her muddled thoughts.

'Sarah Millington, as a young woman, left her respectable home to go on the stage. A scandalous thing, of course, but I suspect there was some sad story behind it—a seduction, perhaps.' Lord Pangbourne settled into his chair, his expression unfocused as though he was looking back down the years. 'Your mother, before I was courting her, was stagestruck. She wanted to act and of course, that was quite impossible. But she found ways to meet actors and actresses, Sarah amongst them.

'Sarah became a great friend, but she never forgave herself that she introduced Marietta to a certain young actor and that they fell in love. Naturally, it was quite hopeless. They tried to elope, were caught at Hatfield, and to prevent a scandal her father sent her away to his aunt in Wales. The young man was killed the following year in an accident with falling scenery and Marietta was allowed back to London, where we met. I courted her and she agreed to marry me.'

'I thought…you always seemed so much in love,' Maude ventured. *Poor Mama! How would I feel if I was dragged away from Eden, just when we thought we were safe? How had she heard the news of his death, so far away from her?*

'I believe we were, although I never fooled myself that I was the great love of her life,' her father said, smiling ruefully. 'We were very happy, and when you arrived, even happier. Anyway, your mother kept in touch with Sarah, but after the near scandal they were very discreet, even after our marriage. Unlike many actresses Sarah was careful with her money, retired at the peak of her modest success and bought property. The Unicorn was one of her purchases.'

'It wasn't the theatre where the young actor was killed?' Maude asked, suddenly chilled. *If I have been standing on the very stage where Mama's love died...*

'No.' Her father shook his head. 'No, I do not think I would be comfortable there either, if that were the case. He was on tour—Norwich, I think. But he acted at the Unicorn, often. That was where your mama first saw him.' He gave himself a little shake and seemed to come back entirely into the present. 'You see why I was not entirely surprised at your interest in the theatre and why I was not inclined to forbid it to you?'

'Many other parents would have seen it as *exactly* the reason to forbid me,' Maude observed, thinking how very fortunate she was in her father.

'I do not expect you to fall in love with an actor,' Lord Pangbourne said with a smile. 'You are far less sheltered than your mama, you have met many more gentlemen and you are old enough not to have fairytale dreams, I am sure.'

Oh, indeed, this was not a fairytale! Maude glanced at the clock. There was an hour before she could reasonably set out to the Unicorn, time to think.

'You will sell to Hurst,' her father observed. 'He'll be delighted. But talk to Benson, make certain the price is right. This is business, not friendship.'

'Yes, Papa. Perhaps I will. Although the rent would be

useful.' Oddly, one part of her could discuss this rationally while the other was confused and uncertain.

Her instinctive reaction was against the idea of selling the Unicorn. She loved it, partly because it was Eden's passion, partly for some atmosphere of its own. And now it was *hers*. If she married Eden, it would become his, along with all her property, of course, that was the way the law worked. A stab of anxiety warned her that it was a powerful incentive for him to marry her. Part of her did not want to believe that it might influence him, part knew that she was dealing with a man who had grown up rejecting love, focused only on his ambitions. She must not tell him until she had spoken to him today about her feelings.

But then she would be deceiving him by keeping the knowledge of something so important to him secret. Or she could to sell it to him first and then speak of her love...

But she did not want to sell it. Somehow that theatre had dug itself under her skin and into her affections. And it would have had such emotional resonance for Mama: that was why Sarah had left it to Marietta's daughter. Mama would not have wanted her to sell it, to lose that link to her first love. Yet, she would have wanted Maude to be happy with the man she loved.

But Eden was more important. More important than anything, surely? And he wanted the Unicorn with a passion. And she loved him—so shouldn't she give him what he wanted, unconditionally? Confused, Maude opened the copy of the will and stared at it again as thought the black letters would somehow tell her what to do, what was right. They were absolutely no help whatsoever. One thing she knew: she could not see him today, not with the shock of this so fresh in her mind.

'I want to go down to Knight's Fee, Papa,' she said, suddenly certain that she must get away. 'I've been overdoing it, I feel tired. I'll go down this afternoon, if you don't mind.'

'Of course, my dear.' He smiled his understanding, leaning across to pat her hand. 'I expect this story about your mother has upset you a little. How long will you stay?'

'Just a few days—until Tuesday, perhaps.' That would give her time, surely, to decide what to do. She could not take any more, not with the *Musicale* looming in only eight days' time. 'I'll go and write to the committee, let them know where I am.' And, somehow, manage a note to Eden to account for her absence when it had been obvious that he had wanted to speak to her seriously about something. The excuse of her health would convince him, however reluctant she was to deceive him.

...and so I think the sensible thing is to go down to the country for a few days and rest and get some fresh air. I will be back on Tuesday next week, so do not think I have abandoned you and the Musicale *entirely! Maude.*

Eden looked down at the note, fighting the irrational disappointment. He had wanted to see Maude because he was going to do the sensible, honourable, thing and tell her that he was becoming too fond of her for prudence and that after the *Musicale*, they should keep a greater distance. And here she was, distancing herself. Excellent. That was what he told himself. But it was not true, of course. He should do what was right for Maude, yet he simply wanted to be with her, and to hell with the risks of that proximity.

And yet this note did not ring true. Yes, he could believe that she was tired, perhaps even unwell. Yesterday he had wanted to hold her in his arms, he had wanted the right to carry her to her bed, tuck her up, pamper and coddle her until the roses were back in her cheeks and she was answering him back with her usual spirit. But if she was unwell, it was not because she had been overdoing things. Maude Templeton was perfectly capable of dancing 'til dawn every night of the week. There was something wrong and he knew, in his heart, that it was to do with him.

Eden studied the abrupt signature. There were tiny marks on the paper as though she had made several false starts at ending the note. What had she almost said? Had she been on the point of sending him her love? His hand clenched around the note, crumpling it as he sneered at himself for such a foolish dream. More likely Maude had wrestled with endings that would show her desire to set a proper distance between them, had failed to find something suitable and had simply put her name.

She liked him and he did not subscribe to the convenient fiction that unmarried young ladies were not possessed of any feelings of passion or desire separate from those of chaste love, so why should she not want him as a lover? But love? Did she share that overwhelming feeling he had only just discovered for himself?

Maude knew him too well, had seen into the space inside him that he had never realised was there and which he now knew was an inability to care for another person as she should be cared for. With so much love herself, she must not put herself into the power of someone who could only take from her, never give as she deserved.

He looked down at his big, scarred hands holding the scrap of paper, the hands of a man who worked for his living. She was a lady. And he was not a gentleman. Somehow, knowing that he was a Ravenhurst, and yet being outside that charmed circle, made it worse, not better, and even their cautious friendship would be withdrawn if they realised that a black sheep from the wrong side of the blanket was compromising Maude.

Of course she could not love him. Carefully he smoothed

out the note and laid his blotter on top of it, then got up to go and make someone else's life hell. And tonight he would go and seek some undemanding, uncomplicated professional female company and put Maude Templeton out of his mind and his heart and his soul.

'Aah.' Maude let out a long sigh and felt her shoulders drop as she relaxed. Coming home to Knight's Fee always did that. The remains of the ruined tower of the long-abandoned castle poked up from the wood that clothed the hill slope and the old house sprawled beneath it, dreaming above its water meadows in the countryside.

Her father joked that each succeeding generation of Templetons had studied architectural developments carefully, then had built a wing, or made some alteration, in the least distinguished style of their time. Yet for all its rambling layout and lack of coherence or sophistication, the whole was a simply charming, unpretentious home.

Here the smoke and fogs that beset London gave way to clear skies and the air had a freshness that had Maude itching to find her boots and go for a long walk.

Would Eden like it here? She had no idea what he thought of the English countryside, so very different to the land he had grown up in. Would she ever be able to show him Knight's Fee, walk with him through the woods where soon the primroses would cluster under the beeches, and bluebells fill sunlit glades heady with their scent and the drone of the nectar-drunk bees?

'Mrs Williams, good afternoon.' The housekeeper came bustling into the hall, her face wreathed in smiles. 'An impromptu visit, I'm sorry I didn't send warning. Now, tell me, how does everyone go on?'

The housekeeper's news kept Maude distracted for a good

hour while they sat and drank tea and Mrs Williams made efforts to tempt her to buttered scones and jam.

'You need fattening up, my lady, you're too pale. I'll get you the creamiest milk from the dairy for your breakfasts and tell Cook to make some sustaining dishes. That London life isn't good for a young lady like yourself—you need the fresh air and proper wholesome food to put roses in your cheeks.' She cocked her head to one side like an inquisitive blackbird. 'But I expect all the young gentlemen will be pining if you are away for long.' Maude felt herself blush, and the housekeeper, who had known her all her life, chuckled richly. 'Or just one young gentleman, perhaps?'

'It's all right, darling. It happens to the best of gentlemen, you just lie back, sweetheart, and we'll soon have your sugar stick sitting up and taking interest.' Mrs Cornwallis's latest acquisition, a tall, buxom blonde with big blue eyes and absolutely no resemblance to a certain hazel-eyed brunette, reached out and trailed a hand expertly up Eden's thigh as he sat on the edge of the bed and grimly contemplated an apparently celibate future.

He had chosen this girl—Sally—quite deliberately, as a complete contrast to the woman who was haunting his mind and obsessing his body. Far from being incapable, his state of arousal had been uncomfortably insistent, right up to the moment he started taking his clothes off and was faced with the reality of the woman on the wide bed.

It now appeared that something that felt uncomfortably like his non-existent conscience was preventing him from making love to anyone else but Maude. If nothing else, it was convincing proof that he was in love, Eden thought with grim humour. No one had told him about these inconvenient aspects of the condition.

He took hold of Sally's skilfully exploring hand and placed

it firmly on the coverlet. 'Don't trouble yourself, I've just concluded that what I need is a brunette,' he said with a wry smile for his own predicament. 'You'll be paid, never fear.' He felt the bed shift as she came up on her knees behind him, pressing the whole curvaceous length of her torso against his naked back and whispering tantalising suggestions in his ear. 'No, I don't think your brown-haired friend Jeanie joining us would help, either.'

He could only hope, he thought as he found his shirt and pulled it on, that once he had spoken to Maude, had finally put an end to their strange relationship, that he could accept her loss and get back to something approaching normal. He was not cut out for self-denial, that was certain, he decided, tossing money on to the side table and finding a reassuring smile for the pouting Sally. He wasn't cut out either for having his mind fogged with daydreams of unobtainable women, not since he had mooned after Guilia, the cook's seventeen-year-old daughter when he was thirteen.

'Damn it, Maude,' he muttered, jogging down the staircase into the brothel's reception hall, 'why don't you come home?'

Maude woke to sunshine and a soft breeze. A perfect day for a walk to her favourite place for thinking, she realised with relief, cajoling a small picnic basket out of Cook, who grumbled that she'd wanted to make sure her ladyship had three good, solid meals, not mimsy cold stuff, even if it did include her special chicken pie and a big slice of fruit cake.

She then had to fight off Mrs Williams' attempts to send her out with a footman at her heels to carry the basket and protect her from nameless dangers in her own woods. Finally, sturdy boots laced up, an ash stick in one hand and the basket in the other, Maude was able to escape out through the kitchen garden and up the steeply sloping path to the castle ruins.

Panting slightly, she scrambled up the last few feet of rough path and on to one of the slabs of stone that lay scattered around what had once been the little castle the first Templeton had built to lay claim to this land. It was a favourite spot, flat enough to sit, south facing to catch the sun and with a view out over the wide acres down to the river. The sight of it brought a pleasure that was almost painful in its intensity.

Could she give this up for Eden? If he loved her, she would have to, for her own world would shun her and she could not expect him to visit Knight's Fee in a hole-and-corner way, as though she was ashamed of him. Her first euphoria on discovering that he was a Ravenhurst had given way to the realisation that this only made things worse. Their very prominence, her close relationship to them, emphasised all too clearly Eden's circumstances. She had wanted to rush to her friends, tell them all about their charismatic new cousin— now she found herself desperate to keep it secret from them.

Papa would never cast her off, she was sure of that, but he was a man with a position to maintain, prominent friends and associates—he would have to show his disapproval of the match in public.

If Eden loved her: that was the key. She would tell him, she was decided upon that. Tell him, straight out, how she had loved him since she had first seen him, how she had come to the Unicorn to be with him, beg him to tell her the truth about his feelings. If he did not love her, then she would sell him the Unicorn, keeping her identity a secret and… And what?

Maude sat down on the bare stone, drew up her knees and rested her chin on them. Retreat here to Knight's Fee and become a country spinster? A society marriage with both partners frank about the absence of love between them was one thing—to marry one man while nursing a broken heart for another, was something else.

* * *

Maude stayed all day, high on the hillside, occasionally stretching her legs to walk through the woods, always coming back to her eyrie. She ate her lunch, more hungry than she could remember being for weeks, then amused herself luring a robin close with crumbs. He proved a willing confidante, cocking his head to listen as she talked to him, flying down with a whirr of wings to hunt through the grass before coming back for another fragment of cheese.

'I can't tell Eden about the Unicorn until I know how he feels,' she explained when the robin flew up to perch on the basket handle, watching with black beady eyes. 'Otherwise how will I ever be certain that it did not influence what he says? He is passionate about that theatre. And ruthless.' It was hard to have to believe that about the man she loved, but this was no time to delude herself about the darkness in him that she so much wanted to overcome. 'Passionate and ruthless enough, perhaps, to marry me to get it.'

The bird was a good listener, but not much use for helpful advice. 'I should wait until after the *Musicale*, don't you think? Or before?' The trill of song from a perch in the hawthorn bush gave no guidance. 'After,' Maude decided. 'If he says *no*, I don't think I'll have the courage to stay in London. Oh, robin, if Eden doesn't want me, do you think I'd ever find someone as kind as Papa instead, like Mama did?'

Why the tears should come then, Maude did not know, but it seemed she could not stop them, letting them flow unchecked down her cheeks, blurring the view of the valley. 'Eden.' She hugged her knees tighter, bent her face to them, letting the moisture soak into the fine wool. 'Oh, Eden, I love you so much.'

Chapter Nineteen

'You look so much better!' Jessica enfolded Maude in a huge hug. 'It must be all that country air.'

'All that country cooking, to be truthful,' Maude smiled. 'It is a miracle I can get into any of my gowns. How is everything and everyone?'

'Every*thing* is fine, if you mean the *Musicale*. As for every*one*, we are all well, thank you. The only person who is not very well is Mr Hurst.'

'Is he sick? An accident?' Maude could make no attempt to hide her anxiety.

'Far from it. So far as one can tell, he's as strong as a horse. No, it's his temper. I swear the man has not smiled since you left and the slightest error or omission amongst his company, or the men, is dealt with in a manner which brings the Grand Turk vividly to mind. As for the ladies, he endures our shortcomings with a courtesy that will probably induce frostbite before much longer—I cannot begin to tell you how glad we all are that you have returned to tame the beast.'

'Oh.' Maude could not help the smile that spread across her face. 'Do you think he missed me?' Then her fragile confidence dipped again. 'Or, perhaps he is annoyed that I left him with all the work.'

'I rather suspect the former.' Jessica grinned. 'The man thrives on work. No, I think he has been pining, although Eden Hurst's version of that condition ensures that all around share in the misery.' She pulled Maude down to sit beside her. 'Has he said anything to you?'

'Nothing definite,' Maude said with a sigh. 'But he is so gentle with me, so tender—and he seems happy, and able to show that happiness, when he is with me. And then, something happens to remind him of who we are and it all vanishes. Or perhaps it is true, what he says, and he simply does not know how to love and that can never be cured.' She drew a deep breath. 'I am resolved to tell him, Jessica, tell him exactly how I feel about him. But not until after the *Musicale*. May I tell Papa that I will stay on for a while with you that evening?'

Her friend nodded, her eyes not leaving Maude's face. 'Oh, Maude, I really do not know what to hope for the best.'

'Hope for my happiness,' Maude said fiercely. 'Mine and Eden's.'

They sat, hand in hand in silence for a while until Bel breezed in, shedding her furs into the arms of Jessica's butler.

'I have the final list of performers,' she crowed. 'And there are three of the Almack's patronesses upon it! Lady Cowper, Princess Esterhazy and Lady Jersey, would you believe? I cannot prevail upon any of them to tell me whether they will perform together or individually, or what indeed, they intend to do—but such a coup!'

'Maude, darling—I'm sorry, I didn't see you.' Bel swooped for a kiss. 'You look so well. Now, what are you going to do on the night? Jessica, Elinor and I plan to sing together and Ashe is going to teach Gareth a rousing military song with some of the soldiers as a chorus.'

'I hadn't thought,' Maude confessed. 'Recite something, I suppose.' As she said it, she remembered that moment when Eden had stood on the stage below her box and spoken one line from Romeo and Juliet. Dare she? Could she find a passage that would tell him what she felt and yet be something that she might speak before an audience? 'Shakespeare,' she added, vaguely. She could not act, but she could recite and Eden had said she had good projection.

'So serious.' Bel pulled a face. 'Still, I suppose we have lots of songs and comic pieces. Tomorrow we are going to the theatre to run through the order with Mr Hurst. Will you come?'

'Yes.' Maude nodded. That would be best. She did not trust herself to be alone with Eden and not tell him how she felt, tell him that she owned the theatre and he need no longer worry about it. Her friends would be more than adequate chaperons.

'We cannot rehearse, that is the trouble.' Bel stood in the centre of the fore-stage, a list in her hand, and addressed Eden, who was standing in front of the stalls looking up at her. 'I mean, *we* can, but I can hardly ask some of the guests how long they will take.'

'It doesn't matter,' Eden said. 'Give me the list, with what you've got, and I will work out the timings as best I can and then improvise on the night. If necessary, the orchestra can cut all its pieces—or add things in if we are running short.'

'Mr Hurst, you are quite wonderful,' Bel said, beaming at him.

'And you, Lady Dereham, are offering me Spanish coin,' he retorted.

'Oh, no, Mr Hurst,' Jessica added, laughing at them as she and Elinor joined Bel. 'We all think you are wonderful.'

'*All* of you?' His dark brows rose as he scanned the three of them.

'Lady Maude too,' Bel said, slyly, looking into the wings where Maude was standing, content to be at a safe distance. She had slipped in without Eden seeing her.

'She is here, then?' It seemed to Maude, as she stepped out of the shadows, that Eden's expression lightened, the corners of his eyes creased into a smile, his lips curved, even as he bowed punctiliously. 'I see you are in good health, ma'am.'

'Thank you, yes. Good country air and food and I am quite myself,' she said lightly, moving to join the others. He watched her walk across the stage, his eyes locking with hers as she reached Bel's side.

'You will take tea with me?' Eden asked, still speaking directly to her.

'We would be delighted, Mr Hurst,' Jessica said briskly, her voice cutting across the tension between them.

'In my office, then. Lady Maude will show you the way, if you will excuse me.'

Maude led the way into the square room, amused, despite her preoccupation, at the reaction of the others to the mass of prints and playbills on the walls and the drama of Eden's great carved chair. They flitted about the room, peering at the pictures, the shelves of books, the heavy black opera cloak with its scarlet lining swept around the shoulders of a bust of Shakespeare.

She watched them, standing beside the chair, her hand absently caressing the great eagle that crowned the back. Eden entered quietly and joined her while Bel and Jessica went to help Millie find space for her tea tray.

'You came back,' he said, softly, resting his left hand, the one with the diamond ring, on the eagle's claw.

'Yes. I never meant to stay away for long.'

'There is much I must say to you.' His dark eyes seemed to suck her in as though she was gazing deep into a woodland pool. There was tenderness there, and anger and a haunting sadness. 'I missed you, Maude.'

'And I you.' Somehow their fingers had drifted together, meshed, locked. His hand was warm and dry and she could feel the calluses on his palm, the hardness of the ring. 'Eden...'

Behind them Bel cleared her throat and Eden turned, smiling. 'Would you pour, Lady Dereham?' and the moment had gone.

They had gathered round the tea table and were discussing the final details when suddenly the light flickered, dimmed, almost vanished. 'What on earth?' Elinor gasped. Then, as suddenly as they had faded, the gas lights were glowing as brightly again.

Eden got up and checked the lamps. 'Strange—this has not happened before. I can only assume the gas pressure dropped for a moment. Will you excuse me, ladies? I must check that no lamps have gone out completely anywhere.'

'I don't like the things,' Jessica confided as the door closed behind Eden. 'I know they give a stronger light, but the smell gives me a headache.'

'They must be safer than oil or candles, though,' Bel suggested. 'You can't knock them over like oil lamps and the flame is enclosed.'

'That's true. But then there is the disturbance and cost of having to have the pipes put in everywhere,' Jessica countered. They were still discussing it when Eden returned.

'Inexplicable. If it happens again I will have to speak to the gas company—we cannot risk being plunged into gloom in the middle of a performance.' He looked around the four faces as one by one they finished drinking their tea and began to gather up their possessions. 'Is there anything else I can assist you with, ladies?'

'No, thank you. I think everything has been organised to

perfection.' Jessica retrieved her umbrella. 'We will see you on the afternoon of the *Musicale*, then?'

'Lady Maude?' She stopped, biting her lip, then turned with a smile.

'Mr Hurst?'

'Could you spare me a few minutes? There is something I would discuss with you.' Maude's heart seemed to jolt in her chest. Eden looked almost vulnerable, standing there, waiting for her response. But she could not risk being alone with him, not yet.

'I am sorry, but I must go now, the others are waiting for me.' She gestured towards the door as their voices faded away down the passage. 'After the *Musicale*, Eden. We will talk then.'

'Very well,' he said sombrely, as though she had given him bad news. 'You had better hurry, don't keep your friends waiting.' And somehow she forced a smile on to her lips and walked away.

It was like throwing a party to celebrate his own breaking heart, Eden thought as he stood on the stage at the Unicorn and surveyed the ants' nest of activity that was transforming his theatre.

Men in shirtsleeves were everywhere, scarred soldiers, some limping, some with only one arm, mingled with his own carpenters and riggers while their noble lordships, Dereham and Standon, apparently enjoying themselves enormously getting sweaty and filthy, checked their work against Eden's master plans.

Behind him, the scene painters and the scenery shifters were working to create the backdrop under Theo's direction and in the boxes two dozen footmen, loaned by the various committee members, flapped tablecloths and clattered silverware under the command of his butler.

Backstage the Green Room had been transformed into a base for the caterers, his own cook supervising the men from Gunther's while Millie, white with excitement at the responsibility, was in charge of the ice boxes and their precious contents.

Maude was with her friends, arranging flowers and deciding on where the swags of greenery were to go. She was avoiding him; her smile, when they found themselves close, was strained. He, thankful for small mercies, knew no one expected him to smile at them; he rather thought he had forgotten which muscles were used.

Eden found his mind wandering to Maude again. What did she feel for him? Could she possibly share the emotion that was wrecking his sleep, leaving his body aching with unfulfilled desire and his thoughts flinching away from the knowledge of the pain to come? Would it be better if she did not—or worse? Better, he told himself. Then only he would be hurt. If she loved him, the knowledge could only bring him a second's happiness.

All around him activity was slowing, men were stopping, standing back to eye what they had achieved, slap each other on the back. It was done. Even the ladies seemed satisfied at last, putting down scissors and wire and reaching out for one last tweak at vases of nodding blooms.

Now all that remained was to clear away the tools, sweep up and for the caterers to take over. Eden raised his voice. 'Thank you! I suggest that everyone who is not involved in catering or cleaning leaves now. Beginners…that is, the committee, back here at six, if you please.'

Three hours for them to bathe and dress and rest. Three hours for him to transform himself as his theatre had been transformed and to show Maude, so very clearly, that the notorious Eden Hurst was not a suitable companion for her.

* * *

'What on earth are you doing, my dear?' Lord Pangbourne enquired with a chuckle, emerging on to the first floor landing to find Maude clutching the balustrade and muttering.

'Practising my piece for this evening,' she said. 'Oh dear, I wish I had joined in with the others; my singing might be poor, but at least no one would have known if I had just mouthed the words.' But it was not the act of performing that was making her insides tie themselves in knots and her hands shake, it was the thought of what Eden's reaction to what she was saying might be.

'You will be fine,' her father said firmly. 'What are you performing?'

'Just a short piece from Shakespeare,' Maude said vaguely. She had said little more than that to Eden, other than to add, 'It will only take a few minutes. I will go at the very end, before the string band's last piece', before escaping under the pretext of taking delivery of the hothouse blooms.

'Most suitable, I am sure. You look very lovely,' Lord Pangbourne added. 'That soft green suits you.'

'Thank you, Papa.' She had chosen the gown with care, selecting a simple column of green silk over an underskirt of soft cream crepe. Anna had piled her hair high, dressing it with pearls to match those in her ears and circling her throat.

It was, Maude thought, considering her appearance with ruthless detachment, the most elegant and also the most seductive garment she possessed, the low bodice cupping her breasts, the cunningly cut sleeves seeming on the point of slipping from her shoulders. If everything went well, they would slip from her shoulders under the pressure of Eden's hands and his mouth would find the lush curves they guarded. And if she failed, then Anna would unfasten it with care, hang it up to air and then fold it away again in silver paper and lavender—she would never want to wear it again.

* * *

Two hours later she was sitting applauding her male friends and their soldier chorus while the Unicorn shook with cheers and clapping. 'It's a wild success!' Jessica was on her feet, clapping. 'Everyone is loving it.' She collapsed back again on to her seat and fanned herself. They were using the Templeton box for their party so they had the best view of the whole theatre. Some people were promenading, others seated, eating. Parties had taken boxes and had crammed them with their friends and the wine was flowing like water.

Ashe had had the idea of charging for champagne, deliberately inflating the price, and guests were vying to be seen buying with a lavish disregard for cost in support of the charity. The rows of bottles in front of parties was becoming a matter for competition, and it was certainly helping the amateur performers overcome their nerves, adding an extra dimension to some of the more comedic pieces as performers literally tripped on to the stage to roars of laughter from their friends.

But the ladies, and most of the older men, were providing enough dignified entertainment to leaven the jollity and Eden was managing the order and presentation of the acts with flair.

He was also playing his role of showman to the hilt. Maude had told him she would like to see his impersonation of the old-school actor-managers and now she was wondering if he had remembered that and had dressed accordingly.

She watched, a fond smile on her lips, as he walked out to introduce the next act. 'My lords, ladies, gentlemen! The lovely, the distinguished, the talented Lady Patronesses of Almack's!'

They filed on, grouped themselves with the elegance of three Greek goddesses at the centre of the fore-stage and bowed. Jessica craned to see the four who had not agreed to perform. 'Mrs Drummond Burrell is sucking lemons,' she reported. 'I am sure she wishes now she had agreed to take part.'

But Maude was watching Eden signalling to the string band to strike up the accompaniment for the song. His hair was glossy with oil, curled, dressed so its length was very obvious. His skin was golden in the gas light, his eyes so dramatically dark that she knew he must have outlined them with kohl. He had never looked so Italian and in his flamboyantly frilled shirt and his jet-black suit of tails she thought he had never looked quite such a dangerous male animal before either. Diamonds winked everywhere, including both ears, and the audience seemed to love him. He exactly fitted their mood for the evening—different, exotic, decidedly scandalous—and his uncompromising control of the stage seemed to steady the nerves of the most anxious performer.

Ashe, Theo and Gareth came in, larger than life after their success, grinning and demanding praise for their act. 'And we have a surprise for you,' Ashe added, flinging the door to the box wide. 'I give you Her Serene Highness, the Grand Duchess Eva, and Lord Sebastian Ravenhurst!'

Maude was so swept up in the excitement of the new arrivals and the need to find chairs, settle them in the box, explain what was going on and demand news, that her planned half-hour of quiet rehearsal, when she had intended to slip away backstage by herself, was quite forgotten.

Eva, magnificent in ruby silk, waved to her friends all around, in between explaining their unexpected arrival. 'The wind in the Channel was just right, we seemed to fly across, then the children were so good we just pressed on from Dover and arrived at five this evening and of course you'd told us about this in your letters, so we put the children to bed, got changed and here we are.'

'Aren't you exhausted?' Bel asked over the clamour of a demonstration of Scottish sword dancing by three officers of a Highland regiment.

'Not in the slightest,' Eva pronounced. 'Who have we missed?'

'All of us except Maude, and she is the last act.'

The officers left the stage to cheers and Eden walked back on. Eva raised her quizzing glass. 'What a very dramatic young man.' Maude saw Jessica kick Eva's ankle warningly. 'Are we supposed to pretend he doesn't exist?' she asked provocatively with a sideways look at Maude.

'What have they been telling you?' Maude asked, resigned to Jessica and Bel having regaled Eva with the entire story, episode by episode, in their letters.

Instead of teasing her, Eva lent over and touched her cheek in a fleeting caress. 'That you have lost your heart and it is hard for your friends to see how it is not going to be broken.' Maude swallowed, shaken by the tenderness in Eva's voice. The Grand Duchess could be so autocratic and overwhelming that the gentle understanding in her eyes brought tears to Maude's own. 'There are those who said I made an unequal marriage—the bridegroom included,' she whispered. 'But love gives you courage.'

Maude hung on to those words as the evening passed and the moment arrived when the act before her own came on to the stage. 'You had better hurry down,' Bel whispered.

'No, I am staying here,' Maude said, getting to her feet. 'Please can you all move back a little and dim the lamps on that side?'

Puzzled, they did as she asked. Maude stood back in the shadows, waiting. Lady Calthorpe and her daughter came to the end of a charming duet and Eden walked back on stage.

To Maude's eye he was puzzled, obviously wondering

where she was, but, with a glance back into the wings, he announced, 'Lady Maude Templeton!'

There was silence, then Maude stepped to the front of the box in the light of the only remaining lamp and spoke Juliet's words, her voice clear across the crowded space.

Gallop apace, you fiery-footed steeds,
Towards Phoebus' lodging...

Chapter Twenty

"…come night, come Romeo, come thou day in night;
For thou wilt lie upon the wings of night,
Whiter than new snow upon a raven's back.
Come gentle night, come loving black-browed night,
Give me my Romeo…"

The theatre was hushed as Juliet's words, the plea of a woman whose lover has been wrenched from her by a cruel twist of fate, who knew all too bitterly the barriers keeping them apart, floated out above them.

Maude spoke them from her heart, her eyes locked with Eden's. He stood, stock-still, looking up at her, his face white.

"…and when he shall die,
Take him and cut him out in little stars,
And he shall make the face of heaven so fine,
That all the world will be in love with night…"

It was almost ended, he was still there, still intent upon her lips.

"O here comes my nurse…what news?"

And Maude stepped back into the shadows and into Eva's arms. The silence stretched on, then the applause broke out and the tension was broken.

'Wonderful!' Bel was openly mopping at her eyes, the others clapping. Lord Pangbourne beamed proudly as Sebastian put a chair forward and Maude sank down, her legs trembling. *Give me my Romeo.*

The string band began to play incidental music, the audience to gather itself, talking at the top of its voice. Laughter rose up to the box as the stalls began to empty. It was over— and it was just beginning, Maude told herself.

'Maude and I will stay on a little, Lord Pangbourne, just to thank everyone who has worked so hard behind the scenes,' Jessica was saying. 'Is that all right?'

'Of course.' He was still beaming proudly. 'And you say you cannot act, Maude. I have never heard better, I declare.'

'Ah, yes, but you were not acting, were you?' Eva murmured in her ear.

'I'll just go down and have a word with Mr Hurst, thank him for managing the stage so well,' Maude said, slipping to the door of the box. She hurried down the stairs, held up every few paces by people wanting to congratulate her upon the evening or her recitation. Finally she made it to the door off the lobby and made her way to the wings.

Eden was there, giving orders to the stage manager and the hands. 'Everyone help the caterers,' he was saying. 'The rest can be dealt with tomorrow. Lord Standon is taking care of the money; someone find him and carry the strong box to his carriage.'

Maude waited, enjoying seeing Eden work, the effortless way he covered everything that needed to be done. Finally the workers trooped off to their tasks and he turned and saw her.

'Maude.' It was there in his face, all the hope and despair and doubt that was whirling inside her. 'Maude, that was…'

'Hurst, my dear fellow. A triumph! I am very impressed, very impressed indeed.' It was Papa, marching across the stage, hand outstretched to wring Eden's. He turned and nodded briskly at Maude. 'Telling him the good news about the theatre, my dear? That's the way to round off the evening, indeed it is!' He dropped a kiss on Maude's cheek. 'Now, don't you and Lady Dereham stay here all hours, will you? You need your rest.'

'What about the theatre?' Eden asked, his voice ominously quiet as the earl disappeared from sight.

'I… I know who owns it.'

'And you were about to tell me?'

Some demon of truthfulness had Maude shaking her head. 'No… I mean, yes, I was going to tell you, but not just now. You said you wanted to speak to me.'

'And how long have you known who owns it?' He made no move to come closer.

'A week. Just over. Eden—'

'Would you be very kind and wait for me in my office, Lady Maude?' he asked with awful politeness. 'I doubt that we will want to edify the stage hands with this discussion.'

'Yes, of course.' Maude walked stiffly past him. He was furious, she could understand why. But it wouldn't last, once he understood…

Eden stood outside his own office, hand on the door. He had made himself stay and organise things until his stage manager could take over and then he had walked back here, still not allowing himself to think about what Maude's knowledge meant.

Gritting his teeth, he walked in, closing the door behind

himself and turning the key in the lock. Maude was sitting
in an upright chair, her hands clasped in her lap, her chin up.

'You know who owns the Unicorn?' he asked.

'Yes.' She swallowed. 'I do.'

'What?' Maude met his eyes defiantly. 'You bought it?'
The sense of betrayal was like a blow.

'No, I inherited it from a friend of my mother. She was an
actress. I did not know until last week she was the owner.'
But she had known last week, had known it and had not told
him, even though she knew he was waiting anxiously for
that very piece of news.

'Why did you not tell me? You know I want to buy it. You
know how much it means to me.'

'I did not think I wanted to sell it,' she said. 'I thought I
might keep it, as an investment. Then it would be safe for
you.'

'You could have invested the money,' Eden said, furious,
something very like fear gripping his heart. 'If you keep it,
when you marry it goes to your husband. You know that, it
is the law. God knows what *he* will do with it.'

'I wouldn't…' She swallowed. 'I would not marry someone who would do that.'

'Indeed?' Eden demanded, his voice sceptical in an effort
to hide the hurt of thinking of Maude as another man's wife.
'You'd put that in the marriage settlements, would you?'

'No,' she snapped, on her feet in a swirl of silks. 'No, because I only want to marry you.'

'You—' Eden knew he was staring, couldn't find the
words. He tried again. 'You want to marry me? Impossible.'
She couldn't be doing this to him, not on top of that speech
this evening, not when he had screwed himself up to renounce
anything to do with her.

'Why is it impossible? Are you married already?'

'No, of course not. You know why you cannot marry me.

Look at me.' He took a stride forward, seized her arms and pulled her back against him, forcing her to look at their images in the long glass. 'And look at yourself.' The contrast of her simple, lovely pearls, the elegant, understated lines of her gown and the glitter and tawdry tricks of his own appearance. 'You are a lady, of the *ton*, a *virgin*, for God's sake. I am a bastard, a theatre manager, a rake with a notorious reputation. Just because you desire me—'

'I love you.' Maude spoke the words to his image in the glass, her voice steady. 'I love you, Eden. I was going to tell you that tonight. That is what those words I spoke tonight were for.' Then her voice began to shake and she twisted in his grip. 'How much closer could I get to telling you I loved you in front of the whole damned *ton*?'

She loved him? Eden's heart seemed to turn to water in his chest, something—joy?—was struggling to surface against the fear for what this could mean, the impossibility of it. And there was a little nagging voice that would not be silenced. 'When, exactly, were you going to tell me about the theatre?' he asked.

Maude was so still in his arms, her face pale and very lovely as she looked up at him. 'After I told you how I felt,' she whispered. 'Eden, tell me how you feel about me—I can't bear it, not knowing. I have loved you for so long, ever since I first saw you. My love—'

Her words made no sense, he shook his head, grasping the one thing that was clear. 'Why wait to tell me you own the theatre?'

'Because…because I wanted you to be thinking just about us, not to be influenced by the Unicorn.'

'Influenced?' A coldness gripped him. 'You were not sure whether I would tell you the truth about my feelings for you if I knew? You thought I would pretend to love you to gain the Unicorn?'

'I was not certain. You are so passionate about it.'

'And if I said I did not love you? You would punish me by keeping the ownership secret?'

'No!' Maude gave a little push against his chest as though to push away the very thought. 'I would have told the agents to sell it to you and not reveal the owner.'

'I see.' Eden was not sure he believed her—a woman scorned would have to be a saint to do such a thing when she could hold such a weapon against him. 'So, you love me, you say, but you do not trust me.'

'Eden, I have loved you for a year and known you for a few weeks. I trust you, of course I do, with my life, but this is so important to you.'

'If I loved you, Maude,' Eden said slowly, 'and burning down the Unicorn was what it took to have you, then I would light the match myself. If you do not know that about me, you know nothing.'

Her eyes were huge and shimmering with tears she was too proud to shed, her mouth, soft and vulnerable. She was everything he wanted and he had told her the truth: he would destroy the Unicorn if that was the only way to have her, if that was all it would take to make him eligible for her.

But if she could not trust him... And she was right not to. She sensed the haunted darkness inside him, the unworthiness. And then through his misery he saw that she had indeed handed him a weapon, the one he needed to convince her he did not desire her for every reason a man could desire a woman. He tried to feel glad, glad that here was an excuse to break with her, one that would surely cut the tie between them with the sharpest knife.

'I realise,' he said harshly, 'that for a lady like yourself to admit desire for a man like me it might be necessary to dress it up as an elevated emotion, as love.'

'No,' Maude whispered. 'Oh, no, Eden.' Her hand fluttered at his breast and the need to hold her, rain kisses on her, was agony to resist.

'I would enjoy taking you as a lover, Maude, but if you think I am insane enough to entangle myself with a society virgin just for that, you are far and away wrong. I have no desire to find myself called out by your friends, my cousins.'

'You don't love me?' she asked. 'No, I can see that you do not. You cannot find it in you to forgive me my lack of trust.' There was bleakness in her eyes now, pain. 'I will go now and send Benson round in the morning to discuss selling the theatre to you.'

'You want me to buy back your investment as well?' he asked, wondering why he was still able to speak of such matters when he had just denied his own feelings and wounded Maude to the very heart. But talking of business suited the image he wanted her to have of him. It was the true image, after all. In a day or two she would be grateful for her escape, he had to tell himself that.

'No.' She pushed back out of his arms and he let her go. The last time he would hold her. 'I will not come to the theatre again, I will not interfere. I do not think I could bear to return. But should I consider marriage in the future, I will sell my investment back, never fear.'

Maude opened the door. His last chance to say those three words. He was hurting her now; to say them would be to ruin her. This, if ever, was the time to pretend to himself that he was a gentleman. Eden held his tongue. 'Goodbye, Maude.'

She turned, looked back and now he could see one tear sliding down her cheek. 'Goodbye.' Then she was gone.

She should go home, or at least to Jessica's. Maude passed down the passageway like a ghost, her surroundings as insubstantial as a dream, She had told Eden of her love and he had rejected her. She had shown her lack of trust and wounded him—but surely, if he had loved her, he would have told her so, despite that?

Her mind could hardly touch the hurt with thoughts; she knew she could not speak of it to anyone, not yet. Maude came up against a closed door and stopped, disorientated, before she recognised that this was the dressing room where she and Eden had found the two lovers. It would be deserted now, she could sit in there a while. Time would pass and perhaps she would be able to think what to do next, where to go.

How long she sat there in the dark, she did not know, nor what she had been thinking about. Her consciousness just seemed to be full of pain, a dull, bruised ache that stabbed like a knife wound if she let her thoughts drift to Eden.

But her limbs were cramped and she felt so tired. Maude got to her feet and went out again into the silence that seemed to fill the old building. She should go now; the stage door-keeper, who doubled as a night watchman, would find her a hackney. She felt her way through the darkness until she realised where she was. This was the door to Eden's office.

Just once more, she told herself, pushing it open and finding by touch the box of Lucifers he kept on his desk. She had never lit the gas before, but she had seen Eden do it. Maude struck a light, then turned the tap, jumping as the gas lit with a loud *pop*. His great chair loomed out of the shadows and she went to sit in it, curling up under the grasp of the eagle's claws. She would just rest there for a few minutes, absorbing one last memory.

She was so tired, as though she was ill. Perhaps a broken heart *was* an illness. So very tired. Maude's head drooped and she slept. Above her, the shadow of the eagle on the wall dipped wildly as the gas flame fluttered and dimmed, then strengthened again.

* * *

The shouting brought Eden bolt upright in his bed. Hell—
had he managed to sleep after all? The noise was approaching his room, raised voices, three at least. The candle on the
nightstand had almost burned out, but gave enough light for
him to see the face of his watch: three o'clock.

He flung back the covers and got out of bed, stark naked,
just as the door banged back.

'You cannot go in there! My lord, my lord, I will have to
call the Watch!' Greengage, his butler, was giving ground
before the bulk of a much larger, taller, older man whose arm
was held by one of the footmen, quite ineffectually, for he
was being towed along despite his efforts.

'Sir, I tried to stop him, but he has run mad, I think!'
Greengage gasped. 'I'll go for help, sir.'

'No.' Eden had seen who the furious intruder was. 'Leave
us.'

'But—'

'Out!'

'Where is my daughter?' Lord Pangbourne advanced on
Eden, clenched fist raised. 'Where is she?'

'Not here, my lord.' Eden moved quickly, catching the
earl's arm as he stumbled. 'Is she not with Lady Dereham
or Lady Standon?'

'No, I went there first, when she was not returned by one.
And to Lord Sebastian's house, too. That left only you.'

'I give you my word, she is not with me and I have not
seen her since she left my office at the Unicorn.' The older
man's eyes were fixed on him with painful intensity and he
felt his colour rise. 'I realise that I am not a gentleman, that
you may not be willing to accept my word, but I give you
leave to search this house, cellars to attics.'

'Of course I take your word, Hurst, damn it,' Lord Pangbourne snapped. 'Do you think I would allow Maude to as-

sociate with you if I did not consider you a man of honour? Your parents may have acted without much; that's not to your discredit. I make my own judgements about men. But where is she?' he asked, suddenly looking desperately anxious and vulnerable.

'We parted…angrily. It may be that she is still at the theatre, I can think of nowhere else. I'll go, right away.' Eden went to drag on the bell pull, his heart pounding. *Maude.*

'I'm coming, too, and for God's sake, put some clothes on, man.' The earl sounded more himself.

Greengage burst into the room, a poker in his hand and the footman on his heels. 'Sir!'

'Put that damn thing down, get a carriage harnessed. *Fast!*' Eden threw open the clothes-press door and began to drag on clothes.

The pair skidded into the theatre yard. Eden was out of the carriage before it came to a halt. 'There is no light in the stage-door office.'

The stench of gas hit him, even before he got the door properly open. In his cubby hole, Doggett lay slumped over the table, his face strangely flushed. The gas lamp hissed, unlit. Eden turned it off. 'Drag him out into the air,' he snapped, his heart turning to water inside him, even as he began to run. 'I'll find Maude.'

He hardly dared think, lest fear freeze him, could not strike a light to search by for fear of igniting the gas. His brain was already clouded by the fumes as he ran down the passageway, into the Green Room. It was empty, its gas lamps turned off. The office, she might have gone there.

Eden ran, shouldered open the door into the dark room, hearing the hiss of gas, choking as the fumes hit him. For a moment, as he turned the tap off, he could see nothing, then the huddled form slumped over the desk came into focus.

'Maude! Maude!' He half-lifted, half-dragged her, a dead weight, out into the corridor. But he could not see, and the fumes were making him choke. Eden pulled her over his shoulder and ran for the yard and the clean, fresh air.

'You have her!' Lord Pangbourne started towards them. Beside the carriage the groom knelt over Doggett. 'That poor old fellow's gone. But she is all right? Tell me she's all right!'

'I don't know.' Eden lowered Maude on to the damp flags. 'She's not breathing. I think she was breathing when I found her.' The fear was washing over him, the despair clutching. She had come back for him, gone to his room, and he had not been there for her and now she was dead. 'Maude! My love, darling, speak to me. Maude!' Desperate, he slapped her face, jerking her head back and forth, but there was no response. Eden bent, covered her mouth with his and breathed hard down into her lungs.

He could taste the gas as he worked, masking the scent and the taste of her. Desperate he kept going, aware of the earl's sobbing breath beside him. It was no good, she had gone. Eden sat back, feeling the tears begin to roll down his cheeks. 'Maude, oh, my love, my love.'

And then she coughed, a pathetic, tiny noise like a half-drowned kitten. Eden snatched her up, pulled her against his shoulder, patting her back hard while she gasped and choked and then, at last, clung to him. 'Eden...' Her eyes were closed, but she breathed.

Lord Pangbourne threw his arms around the pair of them and they rocked together in the chill morning while Eden cried tears of incredulous joy and the older man wept unashamedly.

Chapter Twenty-One

'Eden.' Restless, Maude turned her head on the pillow. Her head ached appallingly, her stomach hurt as though she had been sick and somewhere, in the back of her mind, she knew that something was terribly wrong.

'Hush. Try to drink this, dear.' Jessica's voice. Maude opened her eyes on her friend's anxious face. 'There, you'll be all right soon, try to drink a little. Jane, come and help Lady Maude sit up.'

Between them they pulled her up against the pillows and the maid held a glass of barley water. Maude sipped, choked and sipped again. 'What happened?'

'Do you remember being in Mr Hurst's office? The gas pressure must have dropped and your light, and that in the stage-door office, were the only ones lit. The flame went out and when the pressure came back the taps were still open. Gas poured out and nearly killed you. If your father and Mr Hurst had not arrived in time and found you and the stage doorman…'

'Doggett?' Maude recalled his lined, cheerful face. Jessica shook her head. 'Oh, no.'

'He was an elderly man; his heart must have given out.'

'Eden saved me?' She could remember, as though in a swirling nightmare, his voice, her father's presence. She could recall the pressure of his mouth, but not a kiss. She could remember his words. Or a dream of his words.

'Yes, he found you, brought you out, breathed air into your lungs until you started breathing again by yourself.'

'Where is Papa?'

'We made him go home, once it was obvious that you were no longer in any danger. He was very much upset and distressed and the doctor said he must rest. Gareth has gone with him.'

'And Eden?'

Jessica smiled. 'He is here, outside your door where he has been for the past ten hours. I can't move him. Do you want to see him?' Maude could only nod. Her friend got to her feet. 'I should stay and chaperon you, but I really think even the most notorious rake is safe alone with you at the moment.' She opened the door. 'Mr Hurst, Maude is asking for you.'

Maude struggled up further against the pillows, pushing her tumbled hair back from her face. Eden deserved her thanks, if she could only find the words and then, no doubt, he would go.

He stopped inside the door and just looked at her. His face was strained and smudged with dirt, he did not look as though he had slept and the expression in his eyes made her breath catch in her raw throat. Maude held out one hand, silent, and he came, not to take it, but to catch her up in his arms, pull her into a fierce embrace. 'Oh, my God, Maude, I thought I had lost you.'

She clung, then pulled back, staring at his face. His eyes were red, as though he had wept, and in their darkness was emotion so deep she caught her breath. 'Eden? I can remember you speaking to me, calling me back. You said—'

'Maude, my love,' Eden said, with so much sincerity she

could not doubt him. 'My love, my darling, my heart.' His mouth, taking hers, was gentle; she felt him tremble under her spread hands and her heart soared.

'You love me? Oh, Eden, I knew, I sensed it. I am so sorry I did not seem to trust you—I was afraid. I love you so much, please forgive me.'

He sat back, taking her hands tight in his. 'It gave me the excuse I needed. Maude, I had to tell you, last night, tell you that whatever it was between us had to end. That I could not—' He broke off, closed his eyes and continued. 'I could not love you.'

'But you do?' Puzzled, she stared at him, cold apprehension touching the edge of her burgeoning happiness. 'Do you mean you did not realise you loved me until I almost died?'

'No. I knew I loved you, I have known that for days. But I know I should not, and I must not. Maude, this cannot be. It was bad enough, loving you, but I knew it would be worse if we both knew.'

'I don't understand.' But she did. Eden did not think he was good enough for her. 'I am old enough to marry without consent, if that is what it takes. Eden, no one can stop us.'

'I can,' he said grimly. 'Do I need to remind you that I am illegitimate, in trade and I have a shocking reputation?'

'And most of the men whom I know had a shocking reputation, until they were married,' she protested hotly. 'I love you Eden; if that means I have to put up with some snubs and a shorter list of invitations, well, to hell with them! They aren't people I want to know in any case.' She looked at his face, set in stubborn lines of absolute determination. 'Eden, kiss me and then tell me you don't want to marry me.'

'Of course I want to marry you,' he retorted. 'I want to live the rest of my life with you. Damn it, Maude. Don't look at me like that. I am trying to do the right thing, not drag you down, cut you off from your friends.'

His kiss was hard, fierce, angry. It made no concession to the fact that she was ill or frail and it spoke more strongly than he ever could of just how he felt for her.

Maude pulled him down to lie with her on the big bed, opening her mouth to him, inciting him to deepen the kiss. His tongue slipped into the moist warmth of her mouth, taking, claiming, and she groaned against the impact, scrabbling to push away the bedclothes so she could feel the length of his body against hers.

She could feel him trying to resist and yet he helped her, his big hand coming up to cup her breast through the thin nightgown, his thumb fretting at the nipple until she writhed against him. The heat was pooling deep in her belly, wanton, excited, and Maude pushed her hips against the hardness of his pelvis. And then he rolled away from her to sit on the edge of the bed, his head bowed, his hands raking into his hair.

'No! Maude, let me retain what glimmerings of honour I possess, what pride I can salvage from this. It would be wrong of me to seek to wed you, I would be blamed, and rightly, for taking you away from everything that is your life and your birthright.'

Shaken, Maude pulled her nightgown into some kind of order. She had lost him and she should be sobbing her heart out, but oddly she was angry, furiously angry.

'Your pride?' she demanded. 'You would stand on your pride and break my heart? You would sacrifice what we are and what we could have because of your damned pride? You would end the lives of the children we would have together before they are even conceived? For pride? Where is the honour in that—or do you truly not have any? You had a hard start in life and you rose above it to become the man I admire and love, but you wear your bitterness like a badge to warn people away in case they hurt you. You did not disbelieve in love—you are afraid of it.'

Eden swung round, his face stark. 'Maude—'

'Go away. I don't want you here. You saved my life and I thank you for it. I will love you until I die, but I never want to see you again if you can throw that away for pride.'

He got to his feet, slowly, as though it hurt him to move. 'Maude, I want only to do what is best for you.'

'What you, in your arrogance, think is best,' she retorted. 'You admired my intelligence, I thought. Well, you do not admire it enough to allow me to use it, or my independence, it seems. Goodbye, Eden.'

The door slammed behind him, every iota of his cold control gone, taking her hopes and dreams and future with him.

Eden spent the next twenty-four hours in a sort of blind fury of shock. By sheer will he got the Unicorn functioning again, Doggett's funeral arranged and his widow and family cared for and then, alone in his bedchamber, he let himself recall Maude's words.

Pride and honour. He had thought them the same thing, but it seemed she did not. She loved him, wanted to marry him, to have his children. He did not deserve her, he knew that, listening again and again to her words in his head.

Gradually something like hope began to penetrate the darkness. If he could marry her without making her give up everything that made her life what it was—her loves, her loyalties—then he could marry her with honour. Doggedly Eden set himself to work out exactly what Maude would need if she were to marry him and to keep everything of her present life that she valued.

First, he must believe what she told him—a few snubs would not hurt her. But her friends meant a great deal to her and the closest of those, the dearest, were the Ravenhursts. If he married Maude, then the hope of keeping his parentage secret would vanish under the pressure of society's intense curiosity. The Ravenhursts would hate the revelations about their aunt and Maude would know she had contributed to that. And they, surely, would never forgive him for the blow to their family and what he was doing to Maude.

And she adored her father. To give Maude what she wanted, what she deserved, he was going to have to sacrifice his pride and lay himself open to the risk of hurt and rejection, the loss of the dream of friends and family he had not ever dared to acknowledge he needed. And he had to learn to forgive. Hope, and her words, must be enough to make this work. He had thought himself able to organise anything— well, now was the time to prove it. Eden pulled paper and pen towards him and began to write.

Promptly at eleven the next morning he walked up the steps to the Earl of Pangbourne's front door. Maude, he knew, was still at the Standons' house. Jessica, bless her, was keeping him up to date with little notes reporting that Maude was physically stronger and was out of bed. *But she is so quiet*, Jessica wrote that morning. *So very still.*

'Mr Hurst, to see his lordship. He is expecting me.' The Templeton's butler bowed him in, took his hat and gloves and then hesitated.

'My name is Rainbow, sir. We are all very fond of Lady Maude,' he said stiffly. 'His lordship tells me that you saved her life.'

'Yes, but it was my fault she was in danger in the first place,' Eden confessed, wondering at a butler of this superiority unbending to make personal comments.

'I'm sure it will not happen again,' Rainbow remarked, taking Eden aback. 'His lordship is in the study, if you will follow me, sir.'

The earl stood up as Eden entered and offered his hand. 'Come, sit down.'

'You are recovered, my lord?' Two nights ago he and this man had clung together, shed tears together, over Maude. Now he was shaken to find how much he was concerned about someone he hardly knew, how much he felt for him. It was as though Maude had ripped open a locked compartment in his heart, leaving him vulnerable to not just her, but to everyone he met.

'Yes, thank you. My doctor said it was shock and over-exertion, nothing more serious. You said in your letter that you want to talk to me about Maude, hmm? You'll take a glass of brandy?'

'Thank you.' It was early for him to be drinking, but Eden could only feel grateful for a little Dutch courage. He took the glass, sipped, waited for the older man to sit. 'I love Maude and I want to marry her.' The earl nodded, his face giving nothing away. 'She says she wants to marry me. But I cannot take advantage of that, not unless I know we will have your blessing and not unless I am certain that such a match will not compromise Maude's position in society and her relationship with her dearest friends.'

'As the daughter of an earl, there is not a lot that can compromise her standing,' Lord Pangbourne remarked, swirling his brandy.

'Marriage to a bastard half-Italian theatre manager might,' Eden said bluntly. 'Constant whispering, gossip, cuts will hurt her.'

'Very true. I will be frank with you, Hurst. I had you investigated before I allowed Maude to associate with you. I know who your parents are, I know the names of the society women you have slept with, I know as much about your finances as you do yourself.' Eden felt his anger burn, then subside as quickly as it had flared. Of course her father would do anything to protect Maude—so would he in his shoes. 'You're a rake, but you don't seduce virgins, you're a hard man at business, but you don't cheat, and you've a brain in your head.'

He took a swallow of brandy and regarded Eden over the rim of the glass. 'I wouldn't have gone out of my way to pick an illegitimate half-Italian in the theatre business for her though, I'll be frank.'

'Who would?' Eden enquired bitterly, provoking a bark of laughter.

'I'll tell you something about her mother, my Marietta. She was a wild girl—beautiful, intelligent, impossible to handle. She fell in love with an actor, tried to elope, but they were caught and separated. He died in an accident. I loved my wife, Mr Hurst, and she loved me, but I knew that her heart had been broken and it would never be whole again.

'I gave Maude as much freedom as her mother had been denied because that was what her mother would have wanted. I thought I saw something in her eyes when she mentioned you, so I set her boundaries, which I know she's kept to— even if she's bent them as far as they'll go, I'll be bound.' Eden felt a twinge in his newly found conscience, more, perhaps than a twinge, for the older man smiled. 'I see you have the grace to blush, sir! If you love her, and I believe you do, after seeing you the other night, then you have my blessing.'

Eden stared into the golden brown liquid in his glass. He had come prepared to beg, if that was what it took, and this extraordinary man had given his permission without hesitation. He found it difficult to make his voice work. 'I see you set more importance on your daughter's happiness than on society's strictures, my lord. I give you my word, Maude will never have cause to regret marrying me.'

Eden raised the knocker on the Henrietta Street house, aware that Madame would have finally drifted out of her boudoir and would be pecking at a little light luncheon by now.

He was shown through without ceremony and stood for a moment to admire dispassionately the picture his leading lady made. His mother. Coiffed, subtly tinted, dressed in the most feminine of gowns, she was posing even though she thought herself alone, finger at her chin, head tilted as she studied a fashion journal.

'Eden, darling.' She pouted as she became aware of him. 'Has all the fuss subsided at the Unicorn? I cannot be expected to work in such an atmosphere.'

'You mean the natural distress of the company over Doggett's death and the anxiety of getting the gas system to work more safely?' he enquired. 'Yes, all the *fuss* is subsiding.'

He sat and regarded her, wondering, even as he did so, which leading actress he could secure at short notice if what he was about to say sent her off into screaming hysterics. 'That was not why I called.'

'What then, darling?'

'When I was born, did you register my birth at any of the English embassies?' he asked.

'What? Yes!' Marguerite goggled at him, shaken off guard into frankness. 'Yes, of course I did—in Florence. And the chapel register at the palazzo. But I went to the embassy because I wanted you to be able to get an English passport if you needed one.' She stared at him. 'Why on earth are you asking?'

'You never gave me that passport after we arrived in England,' he pointed out.

'Didn't I?' She shrugged. 'It is around somewhere, I suppose.'

'And what name did you put in the embassy register?'

Marguerite became flustered. 'Name? Why, Eden Francesco Tancredi, of course.'

'My surname, Mother.' He could not recall ever calling

her that, not since the day she took him from the palazzo and told him sharply to call her Marguerite, or Madame, never Mother.

'Eden, I do not like you to call me that,' she began.

'I do not care what you want, *Mother*.' He smiled, his voice light, aiming to keep her off balance. 'What surname did you put?'

'I... Hurst, of course.'

'I suggest you tell me the truth,' he said. 'If necessary, I will contact the embassy directly, or tear this place apart until I find those passports.'

'Damn you, then.' She flung down her napkin and got to her feet, pacing angrily away from him. 'Ravenhurst. Is that what you wanted to hear? Is that going to make you any more acceptable to that chit of Pangbourne's? I never speak of my *family*.' She said the word as though it were a curse. 'Never, you know that. Why must you upset me, be so selfish, Eden?'

Selfish? He was about to throw the word back at her and then something stopped him. It was hard to know what, exactly. The memory of the affectionate concern he had felt for Maude's father came to him. It had felt good to care about the older man, to receive back his approbation, his trust. This difficult, demanding, selfish woman in front of him was his mother and in the depths of her eyes was, he finally recognised, pain and vulnerability.

'Mother.' It felt strange to say it like that, as though he meant it, as though it mattered. 'Tell me what happened, why you defied your family and left home.'

'No.' But it was half-hearted. Something glittered in her eyes and he pulled a handkerchief from his pocket and handed it to her. La Belle Marguerite took it, buried her face in it, exquisite paint notwithstanding, and wept. He sat, silent, not knowing what she would want him to do. Eventually she emerged, smudged, smeared and suddenly a middle-aged woman, no longer a diva.

'I fell in love,' she said. 'He wasn't good enough for the daughter of a duke, they said. They told him that and he accepted it, promised not to see me again, promised to go to the family estates in the West Indies. Abandoned me.' The handkerchief twisted in her hands. 'I ran away to catch him before he sailed, but I was too late. He had gone, but there in the inn was an acquaintance of his. So kind, so helpful. I couldn't go back, he told me. I was ruined. By the end of that night, so I was. But still I went home. I thought, you see, that I would tell them the truth and they would let me go after my love, out to Jamaica.'

'But they didn't?'

'No. They shut me up, presumably to see whether I was going to make things worse by being with child. When it was obvious that I wasn't, they told me that George's ship had gone down in a storm with the loss of all hands. So I ran away again, fell in with a travelling troupe at Dover—you can guess the rest.'

Eden felt sick with an empathy he had never dreamt he could feel. 'They cut you off?'

'Yes. The old duke made all my brothers and sisters swear they would never speak of me again. I came back to London, a few years later, determined to try to see my mother. Then I saw a report in *The Times* of a marriage in Jamaica. My George. So they had lied to me about that, all of them. It taught me a lesson, at least.'

'That you cannot trust anyone?' Eden queried. 'That you can lock away your heart?'

In answer she turned to him, put her arms round his neck and sobbed as though the heart he had never believed she possessed, would break.

'Mother,' he said gently when she recovered herself a little, 'I love Maude Templeton and she loves me. The Raven-hursts are her best friends, almost her family. If I am to have any hope of marrying her and not destroying everything she holds most dear, then I must tell them who I am and seek their recognition.' She moved convulsively in his arms. 'This is not the generation that lied to you and banished you, Mother. These cousins know nothing about that old story. They admire you for what you are now.'

Marguerite sat up, her face with its ruined make-up stripped bare of artifice. 'Then tell them.' She managed a smile. 'Will having a daughter make me look old, do you think?'

Eden's third appointment of the day was at the very superior town house that Eva, Grand Duchess of Maubourg, and Lord Sebastian Ravenhurst kept for their regular visits to London. He wished, as he was ushered through into the salon, that he was wearing his stage costume, the diamonds in his ears, the ironic disguise he had used all these years to hide behind.

All he had now was his real name, the counterfeit appearance of a gentleman and the love of a woman he would walk over burning coals for. This, as the double doors swung open on to the eight people ranged around the room, felt rather more dangerous.

'Good afternoon.' Lord Sebastian Ravenhurst greeted him from his position by the fireplace. Under the portrait of his father, the third Duke of Allington, he watched Eden with sombre, assessing eyes. 'You wrote to me and asked that we Ravenhursts who are Maude's friends gather here to meet you. Perhaps you would care to explain why, Mr Hurst?'

'Because that is not my name,' Eden said. 'My name is Ravenhurst and I am your cousin. Acknowledging me will bring you scandal and pain. You owe me nothing, certainly not recognition; by our grandfather's decree my mother, your Aunt Margery, forfeited that years ago. But you all, I believe, love Maude Templeton and I am here to beg you, on my knees if I have to, for her happiness.' He looked round, meeting eight pairs of serious, steady eyes in turn and waited on their judgement.

Chapter Twenty-Two

'I am not going.' Maude sat defiantly in her dressing room in an old afternoon dress and frowned at Jessica and Elinor in their full glory of ballgowns, diamonds and plumes. 'I told Bel I was not going.'

'You said that when you were still feeling so poorly after the gas,' Elinor pointed out. 'You can't mean to miss Bel's ball, surely?'

'I still feel poorly,' Maude said stubbornly, feeling not unwell, but harassed. She did not want to go anywhere where she might be expected to smile and flirt and behave as though her heart was not broken. Soon, she would make the effort. Soon, she would do her duty and go and find herself an eligible and suitable husband in cold blood and give her father the grandchildren she knew he longed for. But not yet. Not while there was the slightest danger that she might simply sit down and weep as the sadness and despair swept over her. It felt like a bereavement, not the end of a love affair, and she wanted time to mourn.

'You are perfectly well,' Jessica said briskly. 'It is not like you to be a coward, Maude.'

'I am not,' she retorted, stung. 'I am unhappy. Do you expect me to plaster on a smile and go and cavort at Bel's ball as though nothing was wrong?'

'Yes.' Jessica sat down with care for her silver net skirts and wagged her fan at Maude. 'It is the big event in the Season for Bel, and you owe it to her to turn up and look as though you are enjoying yourself. Your father is going.'

'I haven't got anything to wear,' Maude said, feeling cornered and guilty and miserable all at once.

'Poppycock.' Elinor jumped up and pulled the bell cord. Anna came in with a speed that showed she must have been waiting outside the door. Was everyone in the plot to harass her? 'Anna, your mistress is complaining she has nothing to wear, which means she is feeling well enough to go. Now, show us her wardrobe.'

Resigned, Maude got to her feet. To resist any further was perilously like sulking and she never sulked. It would hurt, but she supposed it was like getting back into the saddle after a fall. 'Very well. The new yellow gown, Anna.'

'Now that,' Jessica approved, 'is lovely, like autumn leaves. So clever, all those layers and the different colours and the way the hems are cut so it flutters. Your amethyst-and-diamond set with it, I imagine?'

'Yes,' Maude agreed, trying to get into the mood. She had bought this gown expecting that Eden would see her in it, the thought lending pleasure to the choice of every detail. Now it was just another gown.

But she dressed and let Anna pile her hair up into an elaborate knot within the tiara and pretended that she cared enough to make a decision on which side the one long curl should drop to touch her shoulder. She put on her new bronze kid slippers and slid the fine cream gloves up over her elbows and hurried so as not to keep her friends waiting.

Her reward was her father's face when she followed Jessica down the stairs to where he was waiting. 'Papa, I thought you were gone by now.'

'Lady Standon convinced me she could persuade you.' He smiled down at her 'How lovely you look, my dear.' He kissed her cheek. 'I've been worried about you.'

'I know.' From somewhere Maude found a smile and saw him relax a little. 'Now, shall we go and dance all night?'

It seemed to Maude, emerging from the end of the receiving line and hearing her name announced, that it would be some time before any of them reached the dance floor. Eva had attracted her usual crowd of admirers and friends and was holding court in the first reception room, Sebastian, Theo and Gareth at her side and a collection of some of the most notable guests, including four of the Patronesses, drinking champagne with them.

'Honestly,' Maude remarked with the first genuine feeling of amusement she had experienced in days, 'trust Eva to pick up all the best-looking men in the room.'

'Well, she can put mine down, for a start,' Jessica said with a laugh, watching Gareth responding gallantly to one of Eva's outrageous sallies. 'Here, let me help you with your dance card—and if you try to tell me you intend to sit a single one out, I will set Eva on you.'

'Yes, Jessica.' Maude submitted to having the ribbon tied round her wrist. They had been late, almost past the point of fashionable lateness, and behind them the flow of new arrivals had subsided to a trickle. Maude accepted a glass of champagne from a passing footman, having no difficulty ignoring the more conventional choice, for an unmarried lady, of ratafia.

'Lord and Lady Langford! The Marquis of Gadebridge!' the footman announced. 'Mr Ravenhurst!'

'Who?' Maude frowned at Elinor. 'Theo's over there.'

'There's more than one Mr Ravenhurst,' Elinor said, smiling. 'See?'

As she spoke the crowd parted, heads were turning, a buzz of comment swept through the room, overriding the gossip and laughter. And there, in the middle—tall, immaculate and looking exactly like Jessica's description of the dark angel from the chillier regions of Hell—stood Eden. The whispering fell silent; his expression was enough to make anyone think twice about any speculation within his hearing.

Then, just at the point where the silence became excruciating, Bel left her position at the head of the stairs and linked her hand through Eden's arm. 'Well, I think I might safely desert my post now, Cousin.' There was an audible gasp from all around. 'Have you met the Grand Duchess and your Cousin Sebastian? There are so many of us, I quite lose track of who has met who.'

Ashe beside them, she bore down on Eva. It seemed the crowd were holding their breath, then Sebastian stepped forward, his hand held out. 'Cousin.' Eden shook it, bowed to Eva, then was swallowed up in the knot of Ravenhurst men.

'Come on.' Jessica tugged at Maude's arm.

'No.' Her head was spinning. 'No, you go, I am going to sit down.' She waved her hand vaguely towards the ballroom and slipped away into the crowd before Jessica could catch her.

Inside the ballroom, people were unaware of the stir outside. The orchestra was playing a spirited tune for a set of country dances and Maude was stopped several times by friends eager to talk and gentlemen asking for the honour of a dance.

'No, thank you,' she kept repeating. 'I have been a little unwell, I am just going to watch.'

At last she reached the alcove near the end of the long room and parted the heavy swagged curtains that gave a fragile privacy to the space and its gilded sofa and chairs.

Later, couples would sit out there to cool off, flirt a little, but now it was empty. Maude sat down and tried to make sense of that had just happened.

Her pulse was racing, her breath came short as though she had been running and she felt dizzy. It was the shock of seeing him, of course, she told herself. She could—she must—regain some control. But what was he doing here, calling himself Ravenhurst, and why had the family accepted him, without any sign of shock or rejection? And what did it mean for her?

The curtains parted, the heavy fringing rustling a warning and Maude plied her fan, trying to look as though she was just sitting out in the cool.

'Ah, there you are.' It was Eden. He let the green velvet close behind him and stood looking at her while she got to her feet without any of her usual grace.

'Eden?' Then he held out his arms and she was in them, uncaring what had gone before, only that he was here, now, and she could hold him. 'Eden.' Her face was pressed into his shoulder, the edges of his waistcoat digging into her bosom, his fob chain pressing against her ribcage, his heart beating as hard as hers.

'Maude.' He set her back away from him. 'My darling, I can't kiss you with that damned tiara on, I'll put my eye out.'

She gave a little gasp of laughter. 'That is not the most romantic thing you could have said, Eden.'

'No.' He was smiling at her and hope began to grow in her breast, like a snowdrop pushing up through the snow towards the sun. 'No, but I hope this may be.' Before she could move, he was on one knee before her, lifting her hand to his lips.

'You accused me—rightly—of letting my pride stand before our love. I have the consent of your father to address you, I have the support of the Ravenhursts, your friends, in using my real name—their name—despite the fact that it is my mother's also. And I have her blessing to go and find her a daughter to love. I believe that if you will do me the honour of becoming my wife, you can do so without losing any of the friends that you value or the life that you are used to.

'Maude, you have taught me how to feel, how to love and I love you, with all my heart, with my life, with my soul.' He raised his eyes to hers and what she saw in them stopped the breath in her throat. 'Will you marry me?'

'Yes.' Maude tugged his hand. 'Oh, yes. Eden, I love you so much, stand up and kiss me—I don't think I can bear it for a moment longer if you do not!'

He got to his feet. 'There is going to be a hellish amount of gossip until people get used to me being a Ravenhurst. You are certain?'

'For an intelligent man, Eden Ravenhurst,' Maude said, throwing her arms around his neck and pulling his head down to hers, 'you sometimes worry about the most foolish things. People have been gossiping about me since I put my hair up for the first time.'

The touch of his mouth was everything she had been pining for and she opened to him, parched for his love, aching for his touch. The heat of desire flowed through her like licking flames and yet it was this embrace she craved, the gentle question in his caress, the question she could answer with the trust of her kiss, the completeness of her yielding.

Eden overwhelmed her, and this, she knew, was just the beginning of their journey. Maude abandoned herself to the taste of him, the heat and the hardness, the scent of him. Her love, her husband, her—

'Thank goodness!' Bel's voice jerked them both back to reality. Eden swung round defensively, Maude tight to his side. 'We'd lost you,' Bel explained, 'And we didn't know if Eden had found you or what you had said and your father is about to—oh, he's started!'

She held back the curtain and they stepped out to find the orchestra had fallen silent, and so had the guests, all facing towards the podium where Lord Pangbourne was speaking.

'...so I am delighted to announce, with all their friends here together, the betrothal of my daughter Maude to Mr Eden Ravenhurst.' Gasps, cheers, a babble of voices rose. He cut them off with a lift of his hand. 'Maude? Where are you?'

Holding tight to Eden's hand, Maude let herself be led down the length of the ballroom, the crowd parting in front of them, smiling and reaching out to pat Eden on the back, or touch her hand, or simply stare in amazement until they reached the podium.

'Papa.'

'Come up here, both of you.' Eden lifted her up, then came to stand beside her. 'I hope you've asked her,' her father said anxiously to him, provoking laughter from everyone close enough to hear.

'Yes, sir,' Eden said, smiling and lifting Maude's hand to kiss it. 'And she said *yes*.'

'Well, Lady Maude Ravenhurst, are you quite exhausted by your wedding day?' Eden put his arm around her, pulling her close as they looked out from her bedroom window across the darkness of the parkland towards the lights of Knight's Fee, where the wedding guests were still celebrating, late into the night.

'A little,' Maude said, running the tip of her tongue along her lower lip and watching with interest the effect that had on her husband. 'I might have to lie down in a minute.' Eden had amused her and touched her, in equal parts, by the propriety of his behaviour towards her in the two months since their betrothal was announced. It had not been easy for her. For him, knowing what to expect from lovemaking, it must have been a strain. But she rather thought they were going to reap the benefit tonight.

'Hmm, yes, of course you must lie down,' he said now, deeply serious. 'After all, you should try out this handsome new bed.' To Maude's vast relief Eden had been delighted with Lord Pangbourne's suggestion that they use the Dower House as their own country home and decorating and furnishing it had kept her jittery nerves under control. It could not do much for them now as he took her hand and led her towards the elegant canopied bed with its rose pink hangings and silken coverlet.

'I should leave you,' he added, managing to look concerned. 'You'll want to sleep. At what hour do you like to take breakfast, my love?'

'Eden Ravenhurst,' Maude said, taking a firm hold of his lapels. 'If you do not take all your clothes off, this minute, and then mine, and then make love to me, I am going to scream.'

'I think,' he said, his trained breath control suddenly all over the place, 'that it might be faster if we both undress together.'

It was not faster, but it was, Maude discovered, both fun and intensely arousing. She had not expected to find herself giggling helplessly as Eden hopped from one foot to the other as he dragged off his stockings or that taking off her corset would be such a ticklish endeavour or that they would find themselves suddenly still, the laughter dying out of their faces as they just looked at each other.

It was like learning a language with a complex grammar and vocabulary, Maude thought hazily, as she let her hands wander over Eden's long, naked body. There was what he looked like, how he felt, the textures of his skin, the contours of hard muscle and arching bone, the crisp friction of hair. There was the way he reacted to touch, to the caress of her breath, the tentative sweep of her tongue, the brave explorations of her hands.

He lay there, exotic and golden and beautiful, letting her touch and caress and wonder, doing nothing to alarm her, watching her with dark, heavy-lidded eyes while the pattern of his breathing changed and while his body stirred into rigid arousal.

'May I touch?' she asked, hand reaching a fraction of an inch above the heat of him.

'Yes.' He sounded as though he was gritting his teeth.

'Oh,' she murmured, fascinated by the soft skin over iron hardness, the movement, the...reaction.

'Maude?' She whipped her hand away. It sounded as though he was in pain. 'Oh, my God, Maude.' And he rolled her over on to her back, the silk slithering beneath her and his weight came down so that her body shifted, instinctively cradling him and his mouth found hers as she sighed and arched. He slipped a hand between their bodies to where she ached, where the heat and the moisture and the need focused in all their intensity, and stroked as he had that night that seemed so long ago.

Muted against his mouth, her pleas and sobs were answered, not as before with his wicked, skilful fingers, but the thrust of his hips. He stopped just inside her and lifted his head. 'Maude, look at me.'

She focused her eyes on his face, and saw every muscle strained with the effort of control, saw the love in his eyes, saw the question, and smiled. 'Oh, yes, Eden, love me.'

Her cry as he entered her was soft and the smile became a gasp of pleasure as he filled her, completed her, thrust long and hard and inexorable into her core until she shattered, sobbing in his embrace and heard his cry, muffled against her breast.

A while later, when she stirred against his shoulder, he

shifted her gently on to the pillow and propped himself up on one elbow to look down at her. His hair fell over his shoulder and she reached up to play with it. 'Well, wife?'

'Very well.' She should, she supposed, be feeling shy, but all she felt was wonderful. 'I had understood it was not very... that it took getting used to, at first.'

'So did I,' Eden said, thoughtful. 'Do you suppose we have a natural talent for making love to each other?'

'That must be the case,' Maude agreed, letting go of his hair and using the end of a lock of hers to stoke his nipple experimentally. 'Oh, look.'

'I believe everything is in working order,' Eden said. 'But we had better check again.' He dropped his head to nuzzle into the curve of her neck, and she could feel his mouth smiling. 'How long is it since I told you I loved you?' he asked, his voice muffled.

'Several minutes, I feel quite neglected.'

'Do you?' He sat up, frowning at her.

'No.' Maude shook her head. 'I feel very much loved. Eden, did I say how much I admire you for what you did—going to my father, confronting the Ravenhursts, making peace with your mother? I should never have lectured you about pride, I have too much myself, and yet you took my rejection and you forgave my lack of trust and you gave me—this.'

'Because I love you. You taught me how to love, showed me all the kinds of love. I thought that I could never be fit for any woman to love, that all I could give in return was dust and ashes and, eventually, pain. You saved me, Maude, healed me. I would give you my life; all I could give you was my pride.'

'And your love. I have thought of something else you may give me.' Maude reached out and pulled him down so his body slid against hers, fitted as though he had been designed for her. 'How many children would you like, Eden?'

She had been afraid to ask him that, afraid his own childhood would have killed that instinct in him. Then his mouth curved in that lazy, sensual, thoughtful smile that made her blood tingle. 'One for me, one for you, one for us. All to love.' His hand stroked down over the gentle curve of her belly. 'All made from love.'

* * * * *

DISROBED AND DISHONOURED
LOUISE ALLEN

Author Note

I was delighted to revisit the Ravenhurst cousin's part of the way through their adventures. *Disrobed and Dishonoured* is the story of what happens when a respectable young lady with a problem meets a rakish highwayman whose solution to her dilemma is anything *but* respectable. Jonathon's suggestion gets Miss Sarah Tatton out of one predicament and into his bed – which is no place for a virtuous young lady. Luckily for her she knows the new Lady Standon (wife of *The Shocking Lord Standon*) and through her he meets more of the Ravenhurst clan who throw themselves with characteristically unconventional enthusiasm into rescuing the ill-matched pair of lovers.

To the brilliant team at Mills & Boon with thanks for all their support.

Chapter One

July 1816, Norfolk

The man in the mask ran one hand down the neck of the ugly gray hunter. 'Patience, Tolly. One more to go and then it's oats for you and two dozen of the finest old brandy for me.'

The horse snorted, his ear flicking back to listen to his rider's voice as Jonathan slouched into the familiar comfort of the saddle, eyes narrowed against the late-evening light. It was past eight now and no traffic had passed along the lane for half an hour. Up to then business had been brisk and last night's wager seemed easily won. He dug a hand in his pocket and drew out the tokens he had claimed, proofs of a kiss from each of the first five women who passed down the lane on their way back from market in St. Margaret's to the villages of Saint's Mead and Saint's Ford.

There was a downy feather from the empty egg bucket of the country lass who had giggled and returned his kiss with relish; a tiny corn dolly from the elderly dame driving her donkey cart back, her baskets of straw plait almost empty, a twinkle in her eyes as she pinched his chin; a paper of pins from the thin-faced spinster who had blushed like a peony when he had respectfully saluted her papery cheek; and a promissory note for one ginger kitten (guaranteed of good mousing stock) from the farmer's wife who had roared with laughter and tipped up her round red face with cheerful anticipation.

Jonathan pinned the corn dolly to his lapel, stuck the feather in his hat brim and wondered which of his housekeepers would most appreciate a kitten. His pleasure in the evening's sport began to wane. He had another hour before he was due to join his friends at The Golden Lion for supper to present evidence of his success and the chances of the required fifth female happening along seemed increasingly poor.

Tolly lifted his head and pricked his ears. 'Hoofbeats,' Jonathan concurred. 'One horse—likely to be a man.' He nudged the gray through a gap in the thick hedgerow, drew the empty pistol, laid it along his thigh and waited.

'Despicable, hypocritical swine,' Sarah Tatton repeated, reining in her mare to a walk and dashing the tears out of her eyes with an impatient hand. Careering around the countryside sidesaddle in evening dress was far from comfortable now that her initial fury had simmered down, to be replaced by something approaching panic.

How could she have been so meek, so trustingly innocent? Eighteen months sitting in the country, perfecting her wifely skills in domestic management, needlework and entertaining, while Papa boasted to all and sundry of the excellent match he had made for his daughter—and what had she to show for it? Her linen cupboard was immaculate, her stillroom a marvel, she could play a sonata and hold her own in the most trying dinner-party conversation and, *finally*, her betrothed had deigned to turn up to discuss the wedding.

Sir Jeremy Peters might be only moderately good-looking and not possess a sparkling wit, but he was, as everyone had told her during the course of her second Season, *a catch* for the daughter of a country baronet with moderate looks and a moderate dowry to match. Wealthy, well-connected—she could not hope to do better to oblige her papa.

'Respectable?' Sarah swore under her breath. Half an hour in his company, during which he had congratulated her on her modest gown and presented her with a hideous string of lumpy freshwater pearls had made her heart sink; she had not remembered him as being so dull. But when she had gone upstairs to change for dinner Mary, her maid, had broken down in floods of tears as she fastened her gown.

'I've got to tell you, Miss Sarah. I cannot let you marry him, not even if it means my place,' she had wailed. What Sarah had heard took her breath away and left her sick and shaken. Sir Jeremy had assaulted Mary at the house party where he had proposed to Sarah and threatened that he would tell Sir Hugh Tatton that she had offered herself for money if she said one word of it.

So Sarah confronted her father with the fact that she had discovered her betrothed was the sort of man who would ravish defenseless young women—and Papa had dismissed the matter.

'Nonsense,' he blustered, slapping his newspaper down on his desk in irritation. 'Some young trollop looking to earn herself a few shillings, I've no doubt. Asking for it.'

'But no, Papa! This is a respectable girl.' She did not dare tell him who, not with the memory of the housemaid turned off without a character when Cousin William's visit had left her pregnant. Her father was of the old school when it came to domestic discipline. 'And even if it were the case that she was willing, you cannot expect me to marry a man of such loose morals.'

'A lady ignores such matters. It is her duty to remain faithful, above reproach, and to raise her children. Her husband may seek diversion elsewhere—'

'Diversion!'

He scowled. 'Diversion. It means nothing and no lady of refined mind should think of such things, let alone admit to knowing of them.'

'I cannot possibly marry Sir Jeremy,' she announced flatly.

'You most certainly will, my girl! I'm not letting a good match like that slip through my fingers because of some missish scruples. You marry him—or I will find out who has been filling your head with this scurrilous nonsense and see they suffer for it. Do you understand me?'

How could she find Mary a suitable new post, one where she would be safe from her father's wrath? If she had been in London she could have gone to a good agency, given her glowing references, but here, deep in the country, such a plan would have to be conducted by letter and Papa insisted on her chaperone reading all her correspondence.

And how she was going to be able to keep a civil tongue in her head over dinner she had no idea. She had stood outside the drawing room gathering her composure to enter when she heard the men talking inside.

'Modest virtue, that is the thing about Miss Tatton,' Sir Jeremy was saying. 'The assurance that one is marrying a virgin of impeccable upbringing and not one of those flighty girls who live for nothing but their beaux and their parties. How precious is a lady's purity! I searched long and hard before I was confident I had found such a prize.'

The hypocrite valued only her *virginity*? He debauched young women and yet he could say such things to her father who would smugly accept them?

Sarah turned on her heel. 'Tell Sir Hugh that I have a migraine and regret I will not be able to come down this evening,' she said to the footman. The moment his back was turned she was away to the stables.

Leaving the house for an hour or so at least gave her a

chance to cool her temper, but what to do now? Fear was beginning to overcome the fury as her imagination took hold, presenting her with a vivid image of what life with Sir Jeremy would be like. Her instinct was to run, but that was pointless; how would she live?

The question became academic as she rounded a corner and found herself staring down the barrel of a large horse pistol. 'Stand and deliver.'

A highwayman? They really said that? Sarah discovered her mouth was open and shut it. The figure confronting her was straight off any broadsheet telling the shocking stories of Dick Turpin or "Hell" Hawley. A big, ugly gray horse, a tricorne hat, a cloak thrown back over his shoulders despite the heat and a black mask covering the upper half his face.

She dragged Sir Jeremy's string of pearls over her head and held it out. He was welcome to them.

'No, I don't want those, sweetheart.' His voice was amused, educated and deep; it seemed to resonate at the base of her spine. A gentleman gone to the bad?

From somewhere she found her voice. 'What do you want then?'

'One kiss and a little token to show for it.' He urged the horse up alongside her mare and she realized it was not just the horse that was big. She made herself sit still and not flinch away.

And then she found she did not want to. 'A kiss?' He was clean-shaven, his teeth white as he smiled in the evening light. The breeze brought her not the rank smell of unwashed robber that she had been expecting, but the clean odors of leather and citrus. 'It is not gallant to jest! You may have the pearls and welcome.'

'No.' He took the pearls in an ungloved hand and dropped them back around her neck, holstered the pistol and leaned toward her, doffing his hat. 'I do not jest.'

His hair was dark brown, overlong, waving from the pressure of the hat. His eyes were green, shadowed by the mask, and yet when he smiled she could just see the laughter lines in the corners, the humor.

'Just one kiss?'

He nodded as she bit her lip in indecision, his mouth curving in a way that made her want to touch it. 'If you will grant it. I do not steal from women.'

What if she should kick her heels and send the mare plunging past him? He leaned down and took the reins as though he could read her mind. Sarah stared at him, wondering why she did not scream. He really was a very strange highwayman. And she was in a very strange mood. She was conscious of her heartbeat—that was trepidation, no doubt—but what to make of the warm feeling low in her belly or the fact that her lips were dry? Sarah licked them and saw his eyes follow the movement.

'Why have you a corn dolly in your buttonhole?'

'A token from the donor of my second kiss. It is a fertility symbol, I believe, but don't worry, kisses are harmless.'

An interesting definition of harmless! 'Very well. I have nothing better to be doing this evening, after all.' She tipped up her face, turning her cheek toward him and closing her eyes. And then she felt his breath warm on her skin and realized he really was only going to take what she offered and some madness seized her.

She opened her eyes and moved her head and met the hooded green gaze and his mouth found hers. 'Oh!' As she gasped his tongue slid between her lips and his free arm went around her shoulders and he lifted her against him so she was standing in the stirrup while the kiss went on…and on…and the warm evening world spun around her and his heat and the questing invasion of his tongue filled her senses and she gripped his lapels and touched her tongue to his and thought she would faint from the intensity of it.

And then she was back in the saddle and they were looking at each other as though the earth had just shifted beneath them. He seemed to be breathing rather heavily. She rather thought that if she did not loosen her stay laces that breathing would no longer be possible.

'Madam,' he said at last. 'I must thank you for giving me the most precious thing in your possession. May I ask for a token, also?'

Sarah took hold of three or four hairs that had come down from her topknot of curls, tugged them free and held them out to him. He bowed slightly and curled them with care around the corn dolly. He thought her kiss precious? A highwayman's opinion of her kiss was certainly more acceptable than Sir Jeremy's hypocritical valuation of her virginity.

'Sir, that is not the most precious thing I possess.' The words left her lips without conscious thought.

'It is not?' The green eyes rested on her face.

'No. I am a virgin.'

The gray tossed its head as though its rider had clenched his hand on the reins. 'Ma'am?' She saw him swallow.

'And that is something of a burden to me, just now,' she confessed.

'Indeed?' He looked, not shocked, but interested.

Somehow the story tumbled out. How she came to be recounting such intimate details to a complete stranger, a man—a rogue—Sarah could not fathom. Why she was not sliding from Daisy's back in a pool of embarrassment, she had no idea, but she did not even seem to be blushing. It could only be her desperation and the utter seriousness with which he was listening to her.

'In short,' she concluded, 'my father plans to marry me to

a lecherous, hypocritical excuse for a gentleman for whom
my only virtue appears to be my—well, my *virtue*.'

'If you were not a virgin, he would not be interested,' the
highwayman remarked.

'Well, I am, so there's nothing to be done about it.'

'You could have a frank discussion with a married lady,
discover some, er…details and inform your chaperone that
you have lost your virtue, describing the experience so she
had no doubts,' he suggested in a matter-of-fact manner, as
though they were puzzling over some trivial problem.

'There is no one I could talk to.' If only her good friend
Jessica was home from her honeymoon by now! She would
enter into this scheme with complete frankness, but it would
be another two weeks and that was too late. 'I do not think
that anything less than firsthand experience would do. I can
hardly make it up. But thank you, it was a very good idea.'
She sighed, feeling the tears beginning to well up in her eyes
again. She bit down hard on her lip to stop them; weeping
and moaning was not going to get her out of this fix.

The gray backed away and she glanced up at its rider's
face. Below the mask his mouth was set. He looked somewhat grim. 'I could help you.'

'Describe…*it*?' she faltered, finding she could blush, after
all.

'No. I doubt I could, from a woman's point of view. No,
more practically, we—'

'You want to take my virginity?' Her voice emerged as a
squeak. Daisy tossed her head, catching her mistress's sudden panic.

'No, but I could *almost* take your virginity.'

'Almost.' The light was beginning to fade and she was not
able to make out the nuances of his expression beneath the
mask. His tone was pitched somewhere between appalled
and amused.

'Almost. Just so you get the idea. Have you any knowledge of the theory, Miss, er...?'

'Sarah,' she said shortly. 'No, not much. I know it hurts and I know there is the danger of becoming pregnant and I have no desire for the former experience and certainly none for the latter.'

'I promise that neither would be the case.'

'Are you mad?' she inquired, more of herself than of him. He did not appear to be deranged and if he was an evil seducer, he was certainly going about it in a most original way. And she was beginning to find the preposterous, shocking suggestion positively...possible.

'I know you did not rob me just now, or ravish me,' she said, frowning at him in the twilight. 'And you could have done either, quite easily. I liked the way you kissed me, although I should not. You appear to be a man of principle, even if you do earn your living in an illegal manner.'

He shook his head, seeming to withdraw from the idea even as she became convinced. 'You are right, I was mad to suggest it. There must be some other way out of your predicament.'

Sarah contemplated her situation. She was not lacking, she felt, in either determination or imagination, but she could see no other way out of this. 'No, you are quite right: it is the perfect solution. And if you will not then I must find someone who will help me.' There wasn't anyone, of course, but she put every ounce of conviction she could muster into the statement.

Jonathan could feel his will being sapped by the intensity in the gray eyes fixed on his face. He believed she was in trouble, else why would she be riding alone in evening dress? She appeared to be in her right mind—which was more than he had been a moment ago as he had articulated, without thinking, the idea that had come to him.

There was an edge of desperation in her tone that convinced him that what she said of her betrothed was true and it was not simply a matter of a lovers' quarrel. And now that he had put the idea into her mind he feared she really would seek out another man if he refused her. And then there was that kiss. The taste of her like honey and roses and a hint of spice and the heat and the response that he would swear was instinctive, innocent—and deadly.

She had no idea, of course, of what he would be letting himself in for. No concept of the willpower it would take to go so far and then stop, to pleasure her just so far and no further. 'Very well.' Her expression made him smile. Her eyes widened with surprise, relief and apprehension in almost equal measure. 'I know an inn not far from here.'

'The Golden Lion.' She nodded. Of course, she must live hereabouts and know it. And be known, if only by sight. This would take some care.

He led her back along the woodland path he had come by, stopping at the shepherd's hut he had noticed earlier. 'We'll leave your mare here. There is shelter and water.' She let him lift her down, silk and light boning and warm, slender waist under his hands making his imagination run riot while he saw to the mare, conscious of Sarah's eyes on his back as he worked.

'What is your name?'

'Jonathan. Here, take this.' He swung off his cloak and tied it around her neck, flipping up the hood to cover hair and face, then boosted her up onto Tolly's broad back and swung into the saddle behind her. Ah, more torture, the soft weight of her on his thighs, the little wriggle she gave to get her balance, the scent of her body pressed warm to his chest.

'You are a successful highwayman then, Jonathan, to be able to afford The Golden Lion and yet resist my pearls?'

'Shall we say it is more of a recreation than a business?' he suggested, guiding Tolly toward the stable yard, puzzling about the woman in his arms. Not just out, certainly. Twenty-two or -three, he would guess, with some authority about her. Well-bred, respectable and, presumably, an obedient daughter up to the point her father introduced this undesirable suitor. He had never seen her before, which meant she did not move in his circles, but even so, to avoid embarrassment he rather thought he would keep his mask on.

He helped her down in the shadows and led her up the side stairs and to his room without being seen. 'Wait here. I'll not be long.'

His six friends were in the private parlor, cards on the table, bottles open, food spread out on the sideboard. They got to their feet, grinning, as he came in, still masked. 'Well,' Griffin demanded, 'have I won back the money I lost on yesterday's prizefight or am I out a dozen of my best cognac?'

'You're out.' Jonathan tossed his hat on the table. 'Here—a feather from a maid who'd taken her eggs to market and came back with a kiss to spare for me, black hairs from a fancy young thing with her nose in the air, a corn dolly from an old duck in a donkey cart and a paper of pins from a severe dame who is doubtless still blushing. Oh yes, and the promise of a ginger kitten should I care to collect it.'

'Damn me, I never thought you'd do it.' Lord Gray splashed port into his glass and downed it in one gulp. 'I wagered against you. Get some food and come and help me win it back.' He gestured at the litter of vowels on the table.

'No, I'll leave you to it.' Jonathan walked over to the sideboard, rubbing his back. 'Pulled a muscle somehow. Damn sore. I'll take some food up and see if bed will put it to rights.'

He retreated, with a laden plate and a wine bottle in his pocket, amid gibes about what had caused the strain and ribald suggestions for curing it.

* * *

Sarah perched on the edge of the bed and wondered if she had gone mad. If she had misjudged her man, she was in serious trouble. Even if she had not, she was deliberately setting out to ruin herself. And then there was the undeniable fact that she was about to commit acts of shocking intimacy with a man. A stranger.

What was almost more disturbing, she found her heart was beating with wild anticipation at the thought of it. She wanted him in almost equal measure to the fear. Her highwayman. Jonathan. She had never wanted a man before; at least she had never wanted more than a mild flirtation, a daring kiss to set her a-flutter for an evening, to be forgotten in the morning along with the champagne and the foolish flirting.

Now… She jumped as the door opened and he came in, locking it behind him. He handed her the key before putting a plate on the table and taking knife, fork and bottle from his pocket.

'Food first?'

That voice seemed to curl round inside her, making her hot and flustered and strangely jumpy. 'No.' *Eat? Is he mad?*

'Wine, then?'

'Yes.' That would help. She studied him as he eased out the cork. Long legs, broad shoulders, enough muscle to be a fighter and a smile on him that turned the hot, flustered feeling into a deep, disturbing, low ache. He still wore the mask and she was glad of it; somehow it made him less real. 'Thank you.' She gulped the wine and handed him back the glass. 'I am a little nervous, I confess.'

'Understandably. Do you still want to go through with this?' Sarah thought of Sir Jeremy, thought of Mary's tears, and nodded. 'We will proceed to the matter at hand then? Would you like to undress first, or shall I?'

Chapter Two

'You will have to help me.' Sarah got to her feet and turned her back. That was easier, she did not have to look at him. She tried not to flinch as his fingers, busy on the buttons, brushed the bare skin of her neck, then her shoulders, then were kept from her naked skin by her chemise. The gown sagged and she caught it, stepping out and standing there, his warmth at her back as he began to untie her stay laces.

'You are very adept at this,' she said, attempting to sound cool and sophisticated and aware she was achieving neither. The release of pressure on her ribs was not, oddly, helping her breathing at all. *I can still stop, I can still say no...*

'I have had a little practice,' Jonathan conceded. She could hear he was smiling. 'You can turn round now.'

He was standing there shrugging out of coat and waistcoat. Despite the mask she could see his eyes on her, a dark heat smoldering there. 'Will you untie my neck cloth?'

That brought her close, as he no doubt intended, her fingers clumsy on the simple folds. His clothes were respectable, but plain; she tried to concentrate on that while she unwound the warm muslin from his throat and pulled it free. He was waiting, it seemed, for her to unbutton his shirt, so she did that too, feeling a little light-headed as so much chest became visible right in front of her face. It was a very impressive chest, with flat, sculpted muscle and lightly tanned skin as though, perhaps, he had swum that summer or worked with his shirt off. He must undertake other, more honest, labor from time to time.

And then there was the hair, crisp and startling as it brushed her knuckles, growing thicker and more focused as she worked down, until it vanished into his breeches. Sarah undid the last button and tugged so the shirt came free. And then there he was, clad in nothing but buckskins and boots and there she was, feeling as though she was wearing nothing but a blush.

'It isn't compulsory to proceed, you know,' Jonathan said, watching her face. 'We can just have some supper and I'll escort you home.'

'Oh yes it is,' she retorted, suddenly sure, despite feeling more nervous than she could ever remember. 'It is this or marriage to the swine who raped my maid and then threatened her. Papa considers him such a good match in material terms that I cannot think of any other way than this to get free from him.' He still seemed to hesitate. Sarah swallowed down the lump in her throat . 'Are you going to take your boots off?'

That provoked a snort of laughter. 'But of course. It is *de rigeur* to remove one's boots before making love to a lady.' He sat and began to pull them off.

'You are a very strange highwayman.' She supposed she should remove her petticoats. Was there an etiquette to this lovemaking? Sarah stood there in chemise and stockings watching the play of muscle on Jonathan's back as he tugged. It was important to be able to describe the intimate appearance of her lover if she was to convince Mrs. Catchpole, her chaperone, of her ruin, she thought, finding strength in the reminder of why she was doing this.

'I have had a sad life,' Jonathan explained, glancing up and catching her staring.

'No doubt.' He was, thank goodness, retaining his breeches. The amount of bare man on display was already rather more overpowering than she had bargained on. For some reason she had thought this would all take place in the dark.

'Now, I have been wanting, for the past hour, to kiss you again.'

It was interesting, Sarah thought, striving for rational thought, how different a kiss was when there were so few clothes in the way. His arms around her seemed to caress her skin, she could smell his warmth and the intriguing male scent of sweat and plain soap and something citrusy and horse and leather, and he tasted of wine and man. And his mouth on hers was not smiling any longer.

Rationality slid away to be replaced by a need Sarah did not know she had. She was shocked by the intimacy of his tongue in her mouth, inciting hers to touch and invade in its turn and surprised to discover that without having any idea what she should be doing, she was twining into his embrace and pressing herself against the outrageously hard ridge that lay against her stomach.

She gave a gasp, startled and embarrassed and not a little fearful until Jonathan's hands came down to cup her buttocks, lifting her against himself, rocking her into the hardness until she moaned, the fear subtly becoming another kind of trembling altogether. 'Oh yes, sweetheart,' he murmured against her neck. 'Oh yes.'

She was on the bed, Sarah realized, as her chemise was lifted over her head, and then there they were, her against the pillows wearing nothing but her stockings and Jonathan leaning against the bedpost breathing hard and looking as though he was counting.

'Oh!' One arm across her breasts and one hand flat at the

junction of her thighs were not a great deal of covering, not when he was still in his breeches. He was watching her and she should be dying of shame—and part of her was and part of her was trembling with the need for him to hold her again. 'Aren't you going to take those off?' she blurted, suddenly anxious to have this over and done with.

He did, dropping them to the floor and making no attempt to cover himself. 'Oh,' Sarah said again. Her gaze skidded away, up his body, and met the masked green eyes. Now, his body naked, the mask seemed sinister and she swallowed, hard.

Something must have shown on her face, for he raised one hand to the black silk, hesitated, and pulled it off. 'Better?' She nodded, studying his face intently, fearful of finding something there that the mask had hidden, but the green eyes were clear and frank and his expression serious. Removing the mask made him look younger.

'Good,' he said, his mouth curving up into a slow smile. 'Are you all right?'

She managed another nod as he came and lay down next to her, pulling her against him. 'Stockings?'

'I like the stockings.' His voice, coming as it did from the valley between her breasts, was somewhat muffled.

'Oh.' She stroked his hair, then found the curl of his ear and played with that with one hand while the other pressed him to her breast and she became aware that she was whimpering softly and his lips and teeth had found a nipple and were tormenting it until she thought she would scream.

Then he released her and propped himself up on one elbow, smiling down. 'Is this what you had in mind?'

'Mind?' Sarah blinked at him. 'I don't think I have one.'

'Oh well, I'll just have to carry on then.' He moved down the bed and began to untie her garters while Sarah lay back, panting. She knew what happened with animals: the male pounced and it was all very hurried and rather violent. Not like this at all.

This seemed a little safer; he showed no intention of pouncing... 'Oh!' Jonathan was licking up her leg from her ankle, up to the back of her knee. Her legs, with no conscious thought from her, fell apart shamelessly, and with a chuckle he lowered his head between them as she tried to close them, feeling that she would die of shame. What had come over her? 'No!'

'Yes.' And his mouth was *there*, flicking and teasing a tiny point of intense sensation that seemed to dominate every other feeling. It was outrageous, inflammatory, something was going to break, shatter—she had to resist, to hold on, to... She shattered.

'Jonathan?'

'Welcome back.' He sounded pleased with her. 'More wine?'

'What was that?' Sarah blinked in the candlelight. Jonathan was off the bed, pouring wine, still shamelessly naked. Still very aroused.

'An orgasm.' He handed her the glass.

'But we didn't...'

'No. We don't have to,' he explained, comfortably matter-of-fact as he sat beside her and took his turn with the wine.

'But if we had been doing...doing everything?'

'Same result, some extra preliminaries.' He dipped a finger in the wine and dripped the red drops onto her left nipple, then bent his head and began to lick.

Sarah surrendered to the sensation, her hands clutching his shoulders as his hand slid down, touched where his mouth had been, his thumb circling the sensitised nub. Jonathan lifted his head. 'Relax.'

'I am!'

'More.' And he slid a finger into the wet heat, into the aching tightness and she arched, panting. Then another, and still his thumb wove its wicked pattern of arousal and her body clenched around the intrusion and her groping fingers found him and closed on mobile satin skin and bone hardness and heat and he moaned and thrust into her grasp as she lifted against his hand and there was darkness and stars and his mouth hard over hers as she screamed and he surged against her. And then a slow slide into oblivion.

Jonathan was asleep when she awoke. She lay there for perhaps ten minutes, just looking at him while her mind and her body returned to something like normality and the impact of what she had done came to her.

She was naked, in bed with a naked man with whom she had been utterly shameless, with whom she had experienced pleasure she had no idea existed. And now she was ruined. Sarah had no idea whether she wanted to laugh or cry, but she knew she had to go before he awoke, slip away, get to the hut and saddle up Daisy, ride home—all without him following her, discovering who she was.

She sat up and Jonathan stirred. No, she had to delay him. He would be alert in a second if she tried to creep out. One silk stocking curled across the rumpled bedspread. She eyed the man beside her, sprawled in utter relaxation on his back, arms thrown above his head.

So, she wanted to play games? Amused and aroused, Jonathan kept his eyes closed as silk trailed up his arm, caressed his wrists. How very sophisticated for such an innocent! He let her imprison his wrists, felt her fumble at the bed head. Then the knots tightened, something rattled and he was wide awake, straining to be free against bonds that did not yield one inch.

'What the hell!' Sarah was dressing, her hair scraped back

into a tail and tied with one stocking. The other, presumably was what was imprisoning him.

'I'm sorry, but I cannot risk you finding out who I am,' she explained, her face rather pale in the candlelight. 'I am very grateful.'

'Grateful!' he exploded, bucking futilely against the knots.

'It was wonderful and so…helpful. And I really appreciate that you did not take advantage of me.' She picked up his cloak and edged toward the door. 'I will leave the cloak in the hut.'

'Helpful?' Jonathan demanded of the door as it closed softly behind her. '*Helpful?*'

The storm that shook Saint's Ford Manor had subsided to merely hurricane velocity by ten the next night. Mrs. Catchpole eventually recovered from the hysterics brought on by her charge's careful description of exactly how a man's member felt when held in the hand and had braced herself sufficiently to assure Sir Hugh that, indeed, it would appear his virginal daughter had been deflowered. And what was worse, that the young woman was so far abandoned to propriety that she was threatening to tell Sir Jeremy about it, in detail, if she was compelled to persist with the betrothal.

Sir Hugh had subsided from puce to mottled crimson and stopped shouting long enough to agree that, to prevent scandal, he would inform Sir Jeremy that Sarah had changed her mind and there was nothing to be done about it. The spurned suitor had driven off in high dudgeon.

That had all taken until midafternoon. The rest of the day had been filled with recriminations, more hysterics, demands to know who the man was—and firm refusals by Sarah to say—and dire warnings of what would become of her should she prove to be with child.

She nearly blurted out that there was no danger of that and

bit her tongue, concentrating on looking determined—which she was—and ashamed of herself, which she most assuredly was not. What she was also feeling was an alarmingly awareness of her own body and an utterly immodest desire to do it all over again. And again.

Finally Sir Hugh had retired, muttering, to his study with a full set of decanters, Mrs. Catchpole had succumbed to a migraine and Sarah deemed it tactful to retire to her bedchamber for the night.

Mary, beaming with delight that somehow her mistress had routed the feared Sir Jeremy, was agog to know how she had done it, but all Sarah would say was that she had stood up to her papa and that finally he had accepted, with very bad grace, that she could not be forced into the match.

The maid left Sarah in nightgown and robe, a book of poetry in her hand, and went off to raid the cooking sherry in celebration.

Quite how Sarah realized she was not alone, she was uncertain. There was no sound, no stirring of the air—just a tingling down her spine. She put down the unopened book with care and turned, her fingers closing around the candlestick. A tall, masked figure materialized from the shadows in the corner by the window.

'Jonathan! How long have you been there?'

'An hour.' His voice sounded cold as he put up his hands to untie the mask, tossing it aside, his eyes not leaving hers.

'While I was undressing?' she demanded, then realized how foolish it was, after yesterday, to be indignant about that. 'How did you find me?'

'I followed the hoofprints of your horse, made some inquiries in the village. It was not hard.'

'No.' Her heartbeat was all over the place. 'You must have heard me taking to Mary; you know my plan succeeded, thanks to you.' He must have done more than listen; he had been there in her most private, feminine space, a space she had expected only a husband to enter. 'Why have you come?'

'To return these.' He tossed the long rope of pearls on to the bed and this time she could hear the anger in his voice.

'I'm sorry I tied you up.' Sarah found she was stammering more than she had when she confronted her father. 'I did not want you to find out who I was.'

'It certainly gave my friends considerable entertainment to find me tied naked to the bed by one silk stocking and a string of pearls,' he said, his lips thin.

'Oh no!' Sarah stared back, aghast. 'I thought it would be easy to get free.'

'Silk tightens under stress and those pearls are an expensive string, the thread is strong. No, Sarah, I was trussed like a gamecock in a basket and had to wait to be rescued.'

'I am so sorry. I can understand why you are angry,' she murmured.

'I am hardly angry about that. My friends dismissed it as a drunken, amorous romp—they just want to meet the lady involved, whom they think must be a most inventive playmate. No, what angers me is the fact that you saw fit to pay me for my *services* last night.' He gestured abruptly toward the pearls.

'I didn't! At least, they seemed like something useful to help tie you and then I thought, you have a living to make…' Her voice trailed away.

'Not as a male whore,' he said harshly.

'Oh no, never that,' she whispered. 'You did me a favor. I had no thought of payment, just a gift.' He was right, it had been insensitive, insulting. She straightened her spine. 'I apologize. I have no idea how I can make amends. I just wish I could.'

She saw his eyes close and the harsh line of his mouth relax into a rueful smile. 'I am a stiff-rumped idiot to take offense. It was a miracle you were thinking straight at all, and as you say, you thought I had a living to earn.'

'You haven't?'

Jonathan smiled, silent.

'Who are you?' He shook his head.

'That is unfair,' Sarah protested. 'You know my name now.'

He grinned. 'All part of your punishment for the offense to my pride.' The smile was positively wicked now. Something inside her tightened in fearful excitement.

'Part?'

He withdrew his hand from his pocket and there was the silk stocking, dangling from one long finger.

She edged toward the bed. 'You...you want to tie *me* up?' Her voice rose to a squeak as the excitement turned hot and lodged low, sending shocks of anticipation into the secret places that were becoming damp even as he watched her so intently. 'And make love to me? Here?'

'Mmm. If you would like me to.' Jonathan seemed so cool, but she could see the pulse hammering in his throat where his shirt lay open and his lips were parted, so very temptingly.

It was madness. They would have to be so quiet—*could* she be quiet if he touched her as he had before? Could she trust him to untie her again? But the excitement was building, coiling, making her feel different—dangerous, reckless. Jonathan had awakened something inside her that she could hardly recognize.

'Only if you promise to untie me before you leave,' she said, trying to match his teasing tone.

'I promise.' And the look in his eyes was no longer teasing, no longer hot. For a moment she saw tenderness and melted. He locked the door, then moved suddenly, like a cat, to spin her into his arms. The robe was off her shoulders, the night-gown sliding toward the floor, even as his mouth crushed down on her's and his arms lifted her, tossing her onto the bed, gasping with laughter and a delicious, fearful anticipation. 'I need another stocking.'

'Top drawer of the dresser.' She watched him tear his own clothes off as he walked across the room, his very urgency arousing her. He was so beautiful, she thought, feasting her eyes on taut buttocks and the elegant dip of his spine at the waist, the length of his legs and the definition of the muscles. Last night she had been too apprehensive to really look at him. Even his feet, with their long tendons and the flexible toes curling into the Chinese rug, were beautiful.

He came back, stocking in hand, and stood contemplating the bed head. He was already aroused, she saw with gathering excitement, as he tied one stocking to each of the top corner posts, then looped the free ends around her wrists so that she was lying back against the pillows, her arms outstretched. 'Comfortable?'

'Yes,' she admitted, wary.

'I will not take any notice of demands to stop or cries of *No!* If you want me to free you, say *Release me,* and I will, at once.'

'Promise?'

'Promise.' Jonathan strolled round to the foot of the bed and took her right foot in his hand, lifting it to his mouth. 'Are you ticklish?'

'No,' Sarah said, lying, as he began to suck her toes. *Toes? Toes were not sexual, toes were... Oh!* By the time both feet had been nibbled, sucked and licked she was in a state of bemused desperation. Was he punishing her? Was he never going to kiss her, touch her breasts, do any of those things he had done last night, or would he drive her insane just by sucking her toes and never move above her ankles?

Chapter Three

'Jonathan!'

'Yes?' He looked up, face serious, an unholy twinkle in his eyes.

'Please?' Sarah was not sure what she wanted, she just knew she needed it *now*. He grinned and began to lick upward. *Oh yes*. At last he was going to stop tormenting her and tip her over into that blissful state... He just kept going, up her thigh, lingering on her hipbone, across her belly to her naval. 'Oh.' It was nice, it was more than nice, but it wasn't *that*. The skin across her belly tightened as though to control the heat that was swirling inside her and she tilted her hips up, hoping he would take the hint. If she only had her hands free!

Then he reached her breasts and settled down, comfortably propped on one elbow, to continue tormenting her, nibbling and licking like a man with a bowl of strawberries who wanted to savor the scent and the taste for as long as possible. He reached out for something with his free hand, drew it toward her and she felt the snaking slither of the pearls, cool against her skin as they trailed over her hipbone and slid between her thighs.

Jonathan began to tweak the string and they grazed over

the sensitized soft skin, touching, just, the aching nub that she so wanted him to caress, a teasing, frustrating counterpoint to the shocks of sensation his lips and teeth were sending direct from her nipples to her groin.

She was moaning, her head restless on the pillows as she felt him sit back on his heels, one hand still trailing the pearls through the moist, swollen ache between her thighs. He was watching her, she knew it, but fear and shame had dissolved in the cauldron of sensation he was stirring up within her.

Sarah opened her eyes and looked at him, his erection straining up against his flat stomach, and realized, through her own haze of desire, just how rigidly he was controlling himself to pleasure her and how much she wanted to touch him. As he bent to flick his tongue across the track of the pearls, she felt, with an intensity that shocked her, that she wanted to caress him like that.

'Release me,' she said, wriggling back so she was half sitting against the pillows. 'Please, release me.'

As she hoped, he straddled her body, moving up the bed so he was astride her rib cage as he reached for her right wrist. His erection was right in front of her face, so close she could see a pearl of liquid at the tip. As he stretched across she raised her head and took him into her mouth and they both froze, he with a gasp of shock, she with the rush of sensation.

'Sarah!' He tried to pull away, but she closed her teeth in delicate warning and he was still again while she moved her lips, her tongue, fascinated by the taste and the texture and the effect she was having. Jonathan began to work at the knots and suddenly her hand was free and she could flatten it against the taut buttocks, holding him to her while he freed the other wrist, and then his weight shifted and she realized he was gripping the rail above her head.

He was so still, his breath rasping as she sucked, drawing her tongue up and down, loving the intimacy and the power.

She could sense, as her hands held him, the effort it was taking him not to thrust into her mouth, realized the strain she was putting him under and somehow summoned up the will to release him. He moved with the speed of a lunging swordsman, sliding down her body, crushing her under his weight, his pelvis pressing against hers, and she reacted instinctively, opening to him even as her fingers bit into his shoulders.

Jonathan found himself stretched over Sarah's body, her legs cradling him, his hips tensed to thrust. He caught himself, the effort wrenching a groan from deep in his chest. 'God!' He rolled off her, forearm flung across his eyes, fighting for control. She had trusted him and he had damn nearly...then her hand took him, sure and generous, and he turned back to caress her, shaking in her embrace as they fell into ecstasy and darkness together.

Sarah was curled against him, sleeping, he realized, as he came to himself. That had never happened to him before. His mistresses had never shown any inclination to snuggle confidingly against him, and that avoidance of feigned sentiment suited him perfectly. Caroline, his current *maîtresse,* most certainly never clung. The thought of appearing anything less than perfect sent her from the bed the moment he left it to retreat behind a screen and emerge ten or so minutes later, cool and immaculate. And by then he would be in his robe pouring champagne ready for an uninvolved exchange of civilized pleasantries. All so very sophisticated, all so very...cold.

This was not cold. Sarah's body hugged his with the trusting, innocently sensual abandon of a sleeping kitten, her breath tickling the hairs around his left nipple, her right arm flung over his rib cage, her right leg across his thighs. They were both hot and damp, sticky and tousled, and he found that strangely pleasurable.

Jonathan wondered how long he had slept, then stopped caring and rubbed his cheek against the tangle of brown curls that was all he could reach. After a moment he dropped a kiss on the crown of Sarah's head and smiled as she stirred, muttering, and caught his nipple between her lips, playing with it in her sleep. It hardened and other parts of his body began to react. Jonathan shifted a little, so she let go with a soft sound of protest and lay still again.

He had not reckoned on feeling like this when he had let his temper and his pride ride him that morning. He had spent the day tracking her down and the evening finding his way into the house. An unlocked storeroom window had given him access, then he had slipped upstairs to check each bedroom until he had found hers.

The alcove with its swathe of drapery had been perfect—perfect to wait unobserved as the maid closed the curtains across the windows, and perfect, as he had rapidly discovered, to torment him with first the scent and then the sight of Sarah.

He had closed his eyes as the maid undressed her: he had not lost all control. But his eyes might just as well have been wide open as he followed every whisper of silk, every rustle of petticoats, the sound of her sigh of relief as her stays were unlaced, the maid's comments on the pretty clocking at the ankle of her stockings.

Then there had been the soft sound of a loose nightgown falling over her head to toes that, his imagination was telling him, were bare, and the murmur of their conversation. All so intimate, so feminine, as the two young women shared their joy that the unwelcome suitor had been routed.

Sarah had not confided how she had achieved that to her maid, he noticed, realizing he would have been well served for his intrusion if he had had to spend long minutes listening to a dissection of his performance.

But that realization did nothing to dampen the heat of the anger that the discovery of the pearls had ignited. His friends' teasing had been bearable, rooted more in admiration of his prowess at finding a bedmate so inventive rather than scorn at the predicament he had found himself in. No, it was the fact that she had carelessly left him jewelry worth a considerable sum laced mockingly into his bonds.

It was not until he had seen the remorse in her wide, gray eyes and understood that she genuinely had not counted their value, had thought only of delaying him long enough to escape, that the hurt pride vanished like smoke in the wind.

Idiot, he thought now, stroking the warm, soft skin of her shoulder with his palm. Sarah was not some pouting Society beauty buying what she wanted, careless of the feelings of those she used. She was different, and he was beginning to find that very difference disturbingly appealing.

The clock struck one as he pulled the light coverlet up over their bodies and let himself drift off to sleep, his mind full of new and disconcerting possibilities, his arms full of curves and fragrance.

'Sarah.' She came up out of a dream of Jonathan to find him there, bending over her, fully dressed.

'You are real,' she observed, half-fuddled with sleep and pleasure, then smiled as his eyes crinkled with amusement at her folly. 'Of course you are. What time is it?'

'Four. I must go before the household stirs.'

She sat up, careless of the way the sheet fell to her waist, and surprised at how quickly she had become so shameless in his presence. 'You are leaving Saint's Ford, aren't you? You will not be coming back.' Of course he would not; this was merely an unusual incident for him. For her, she realized, watching his face in the candlelight, it was everything.

She had solved the problem of Sir Jeremy and paid with her heart for it.

Jonathan stroked the back of his hand down her cheek. 'Your highwayman will never come back, Sarah. Would you be glad to think that perhaps you have reformed me?'

'I do not think you were ever a very dangerous highwayman,' she observed, fighting to keep her tone light. 'So I doubt I can claim much merit for any reformation that has occurred. But yes, it is not a safe occupation for a man such as yourself: I would not like to think you might have ended on a gallows.'

'A man such as myself?' he asked, his mouth twisting into a smile that seemed to mock himself, not her.

'Honorable, kind, brave and clever,' Sarah said, wondering at Jonathan's sudden stillness.

'Thank you,' he said softly, lifting her hand and pressing his lips to her knuckles. 'You give me something to live up to, my sweet.' He was on his feet, and unlocking the door before she could say anything else. Then he paused in the open doorway before slipping like a ghost into the dark corridor and away.

'I suppose you expect me to allow you to go to that house party your school friend invited you to, despite your behavior,' Sir Hugh Tatton snapped as Sarah sat nibbling listlessly at her bread and butter ten days later.

'Jessica Gifford?' She had forgotten all about that invitation. Jessica, a firm friend despite a two-year difference in their ages, had left school to earn her own living as a governess, and then, by some miracle, had met and married Lord Standon.

'She is the Countess of Standon now, Papa. And it is Lady Dereham whose invitation it was. She is a cousin of Lord Standon's.'

'Lords, ladies—hah! Aye, and there was something smoky about that match, from what one hears,' Sir High grumbled. 'Henrietta wrote to me from London to say Standon was kicking up no end of a to-do, flaunting his new mistress all over Town, and the next thing we know he's off on the Continent marrying some governess he finds there, if you please.'

'She has obviously reformed him, Sir Hugh,' Mrs. Catchpole ventured nervously, still obviously expecting retribution for not exercising sufficient control over Sarah. 'And she must be a superior young woman if she went to Miss Fletching's Academy, as Sarah did.'

'Hah!'

'And it might be as well if dear Sarah does attend the party. There will be numerous eligible gentlemen present. Gentlemen who would be interested in making a speedy match if the dowry is right...' She let her voice trail away as Sarah felt her blushes mounting. Somehow she kept her mouth closed on the vehement rejection of any suggestion that she might try to palm off her love child on an unsuspecting husband.

'Indeed,' Sir Hugh said slowly. 'A point well made, ma'am. One trusts that there is no need for haste, but still, one cannot be too careful.'

As if I would, Sarah thought, laying her hand protectively over her belly, then realizing the hollowness of the gesture. There was no chance she was pregnant, thanks to Jonathan's care of her, but if she were, under no circumstances would she let his child grow up as any other man's. Not the child of the man she loved.

'Sarah?' Mrs. Catchpole was on her feet.

'I... I'm sorry, a crumb...' Sarah said, wildly catching at any excuse for leaping to her feet, her hands pressed to her mouth. 'Water, I'll just go and get...' She fled. *Love? I am in love? Of course I am. I am in love with an utterly unsuit-*

able man whose full name I do not know, who is never coming back and who, obviously, does not love me.

'Mary,' she said firmly, startling the maid, who was standing in the middle of her bedroom frowning at the black silk mask in her hands, 'we have to think about what to pack for Lady Standon's party. It seems I must catch myself a husband.'

'Yes, Miss Sarah. What is this? I found it at the bottom of your stocking drawer.' The maid held out the band of silk.

'A souvenir of an adventure,' Sarah said, blinking back a tear. 'One that is about to become just the memory of a dream.'

Chapter Four

'Jessica!' Careless of waiting servants or other houseguests, Sarah threw herself into her friend's arms. 'Oh, Jessica, I am so happy to see you!'

Reeling slightly from the impact, Lady Standon hugged her tight, then held her at arm's length, the better to look at her. Jessica looked radiant, Sarah thought.

'What's wrong?' She tucked Sarah's hand under her arm and drew her into the house. 'Come and meet Bel—Lady Dereham—and the others and then I'll show you your room and you can tell me all about it. Whatever it is.'

Coppergate, the Derehams' country house, was deep in the Hertfordshire countryside and had the warm feel of a home. Lady Dereham greeted her with a smile, introducing her to the other guests, who were all relaxing, comfortably informal, in the big salon. Sarah did her best to commit the names of the host of assorted Ravenhurst relatives to memory before letting Jessica whisk her away.

'So, tell me what is wrong. There are dark circles under your eyes and I would swear you have lost weight. Is it Sir Jeremy?'

Jessica curled up in the window seat and listened as Sarah paced the room recounting the tale of Sir Jeremy's infamy, her impetuous ride and her meeting with Jonathan. When Sarah got to the part where he made his outrageous suggestion to rescue her from her fiancé, Jessica clapped her hands over her mouth and stared in horrified amazement.

'Sarah! You let him deflower you?'

'No! I told you—he *almost* did.' Jessica closed her eyes for a moment. 'Jessica, I am in love with him.'

'My dear! It is impossibly romantic. Does he have a nickname for the broadsheets and ride a black stallion?'

'He has a very ugly horse and no nickname I am aware of.' Sarah sighed. 'It is mad of me even to dream. He's a gentleman gone to the bad, I think.'

'It won't do,' Jessica said with a shake of her head. 'You know that. This isn't a Minerva Press novel and he won't appear in the nick of time transformed into a duke.'

'I know.' She was resigned to it, after so many days of sighing for him.

'Well, the last thing you'll want is to be flirting with the young men at the party, that's for sure. You can always take refuge with Elinor Ravenhurst, who is very rational and regards all men as unnecessary frivolity, and Lady Maude Templeton, who declares she knows who she wants to marry but hasn't organized it yet. The poor man has no idea he is about to be organized, of course, and he is quite hopelessly ineligible.

'Falling in love is painful, but will get better in time,' Jessica murmured. 'I just hope you do not truly *love* him, because if you do, that will take a long time to heal.'

There was a difference, Sarah thought, as she went down to dinner attempting to ignore Mrs. Catchpole's prattling. Being in love or loving. Which was it? Loving implied knowing a person deeply and truly. What did she know about Jonathan?

He was intelligent and honorable, he had a sense of humor, he was forgiving, he made love like…'a devil or an angel?' she murmured, causing her chaperone to glance sharply at her.

'Sarah, this is no time for wool gathering. This is a significant opportunity for you to meet not just eligible young men, but influential hostesses. Now smile!'

'Yes, Priscilla,' Sarah said meekly to Mrs. Catchpole, pulling herself together. She owed it to her hostess to be an amiable guest, and that would not be aided by her thinking about the caress of Jonathan's mouth at her breast or paying attention to the low, demanding pulse that made her fidget and ache.

Informal Lady Dereham might be, but she arranged her dining table in accordance with precedence, and Sarah was partnered by the vicar and had, on her left side, Lieutenant Harris, a cheerful military man with a bluff sense of humor.

Her mood, when the ladies rose to leave the men to their port and politics, was therefore rather more tranquil. It would be interesting to seek out the two young ladies Jessica had mentioned. Miss Elinor Ravenhurst was easy enough to locate, a tall redhead sitting in a corner with her nose in a book and dressed in a gown of a depressing beige.

'Miss Ravenhurst? I am Sarah Tatton. I hope I do not interrupt, but Lady Standon mentioned you as someone with a very rational turn of mind and I thought I would like to speak with you.'

'Rational?' Miss Ravenhurst smiled and closed her book. 'She means that she despairs of interesting me in a young man or finding any young man prepared to take an interest in me. Are you a scholar, too, Miss Tatton?'

'No, I am not in the mood for masculine company,' Sarah confessed, sitting down.

Intelligent hazel eyes studied her. 'Either you are in retreat from an unwelcome suitor or you are in love with someone unsuitable.'

'Both,' Sarah confessed, startled.

'Then you must meet Maude.' Elinor waved her fan, a battered affair that seemed to have been sat upon, and received an answering wave from a handsome young woman chatting with three army officers.

'She will not wish to be interrupted,' Sarah began, but Lady Maude abandoned her swains with a flirtatious smile and came across.

'Maude, this is Sarah Tatton, who is unsuitably in love,' Miss Ravenhurst announced with the air of a scholar identifying an interesting specimen.

'Really?' Lady Maude sat down in a flurry of expensive silk skirts and held out her hand. 'Is it mutual?'

'No, Lady Maude. He has no idea of my feelings and I have no idea of his name, his whereabouts or anything, other than that he is entirely ineligible.'

'Call me Maude, please.' Her ladyship, dark, vivacious and enviably pretty, perched on the sofa next to Miss Ravenhurst, a contrast in styles. 'And I see you've already met Elinor, who is a lost cause as far as men are concerned, but who will talk common sense and try to persuade us from rash action. Mind you, I cannot help but believe that somewhere is exactly the right man for her, just as there is for you and for me.'

'Not rash, merely irrational, Maude,' Elinor corrected. 'A female should not be dependent upon a mere male for her every happiness.'

'I quite agree, insofar as most things are concerned. But there are areas of happiness for which one must depend upon mere males, are there not, Sarah?' Maude's wicked twinkle left no doubt which areas she was referring to and Sarah felt herself color. 'Oh, my! You blush. Is he such a great lover, this unsuitable man of yours?'

'Wonderful,' Sarah admitted, amazed that she could confide so easily. But she sensed that these two young women, so very different, would be both kind and discreet. 'I will tell you what occurred, if you promise not to say anything to anyone else.'

'We are both,' Elinor announced, leaning forward, 'agog.'

Sarah awoke the next morning feeling somewhat better. True, Jonathan was still lost to her, but she had made two new friends and had found that her old friendship with Jessica was as strong as ever. Confiding in all three of them had stilled her uncomfortably active conscience. They had reassured her that of course she should not have obliged her father and married Sir Jeremy, having discovered his unpleasant character.

When she went down to breakfast she found it an exclusively female company, for the men, Bel informed her, had all gone out to inspect the stables.

'We are having a dance this evening,' Bel announced. 'A nice, formal, *refined* dance. Everyone will have arrived by then and the men may wash off the smell of the stables and behave like civilized human beings. Discussion of politics, horses and hunting will be forbidden and no one under the age of sixty-five may play cards.'

The last thing that Sarah felt like doing was participating in a ball, but she knew what was expected of a good guest. 'Lovely! I am so glad I brought a new ball gown,' she declared brightly.

It had not occurred to Sarah, until she was standing in the doorway and watching the houseguests and the neighboring gentry mingling and laughing in the long room, that being hopelessly in love did not just entail the pain of losing the man of her dreams. It also meant that either she must remain a spinster, and childless, all her days or marry a man she did not love.

'Sarah?'

'Elinor, I am sorry, I am blocking the door. What a delightful scene, is it not?'

'Very animated,' Elinor agreed, as they entered side by side. She was dressed in gray silk with a cream lace trim, both of which colors effectively killed any glow in her cheeks. 'And noisy. However, I have a book hidden behind the sofa cushions in the retiring room, so once I have been observed treading on at least one pair of male toes, I can probably escape.'

Maude, who was, of course, surrounded by young men, waved and Sarah heard her companion sigh as they crossed to her. Feeling she had to compensate for Elinor's lack of enthusiasm, she assumed her best social smile and soon found her dance card much in demand.

When she had first come out such popularity would have thrilled her; now she felt like someone who had an antipathy to cats but who was proving irresistible to the creatures.

'No,' she said firmly to one of Lord Dereham's friends, 'Thank you, Major Piper, but I do not waltz.' Never having achieved the exalted status of holding a voucher for Almack's, Sarah had not been approved by a Patroness and knew that to waltz without such blessing would label her as fast.

So she danced the first set of country dances, then the quadrille, and wondered that she could still keep smiling and pretending to flirt when what she wanted was to be alone with a big man with smiling green eyes and a deep voice and a mouth made for sin.

The third set was a waltz so she could make her excuses

and go to where Elinor was sitting out in an alcove sipping lemonade and reading a small book behind her fan.

She had almost reached her when Bel spoke behind her. 'Miss Tatton! I believe you have no partner for the next set.'

'No, ma'am,' Sarah said, turning. 'I have not been approved to—'

The man beside Lady Dereham was tall, powerfully built, and in formal evening attire. His dark brown hair was cropped fashionably, his expression one of polite expectation. But the look in his green eyes was one of shock that matched her own and the lips of his sensual mouth were slightly parted as though on a sharp intake of breath.

'Oh, that is of no matter in a family party.' Bel dismissed the rules with a flick of her exquisite French fan. 'May I introduce the Earl of Redcliffe? He is hoping you will stand up for him for this set. Lord Redcliffe, Miss Tatton is a dear friend of Lady Standon's.'

'Miss Tatton.' His bow was immaculate, his voice deep and achingly familiar. It could not be. It was impossible that her highwayman—*her love*—was standing there in front of her, a respectable member of the aristocracy.

'Redcliffe!' It was Gareth, Lord Standon. He slapped the big man on the shoulder, then took his hand. 'You are so late I thought you weren't coming.'

'I apologize.' Jonathan shook hands with his friend. 'I had to go into Town unexpectedly. Things to arrange. But nothing would make me miss your party.' He glanced at Sarah. 'Almost nothing.'

And then the paralysis that had come over her when she had seen him began to ebb away and she realized the hot sensation that coursed through her was anger.

Chapter Five

'Thank you, *my* lord.' A fine line appeared between Bel's brows at the emphasis. 'I do not waltz.' Her voice rose, heads turned.

'Sarah—'

'I do not want to dance.' She could hear her tone becoming shrill and modulated it, forcing something close to a smile. 'Thank you.'

'Miss Tatton,' Jonathan said. 'I would not *constrain* you to anything against your will.' She felt the color rise in her cheeks. It was as though the scene in the ballroom was shifting in and out of focus and the man in front of her was alternately formally attired and standing against a background of chattering couples, and stark naked in her bedchamber, a wicked smile on his lips and her stocking dangling from his fingers.

'Let us try, shall we?' he suggested. 'You can always tell me to *release* you, should you find the experience disturbing.'

Disturbing? The heat was gathering low in her belly, she felt light-headed and breathless and *wanting,* and the anger pulsed through the arousal and the ache and she just needed to hit him and kiss him and...

Her hand was in his and she could not, without making a scene, escape. Jonathan drew her onto the floor and took her in a firm hold. 'You are doubtless as surprised as I am, to meet like this.'

'I am most certainly surprised, my lord,' she said. *Oh God, he smells the same. Leather and citrus and man.*

'My lord?' He quirked an eyebrow at her as the music began. 'What has happened to *Jonathan*?'

'I do not know. Tell me, what *has* happened to Jonathan?'

The fact that she was angry and upset and not merely shocked seemed finally to penetrate his consciousness. 'What is the matter?'

'Matter?' Somehow she managed to keep her voice down as he swept her the length of the room and round into a complicated turn at the end. She had never danced the waltz except with a dancing master; now, she realized, she was so preoccupied that she simply followed Jonathan's lead through the most difficult steps.

'You lied to me, you deceived me, you took advantage of me and you wonder why I am angry?'

'Yes,' he said bluntly, the arched dark brows lowering in answering anger. 'I never took advantage of you, I never deceived you, I never lied to you—'

'You lied by omission.' He forced her into a tight, swooping turn, her skirts swinging out, the room shifting dizzyingly about her. Sarah glimpsed Maude's face, staring. 'I thought you were a highwayman, or if not that, at least an ordinary man, a gentleman who had fallen on hard times. How could you not tell me who you were?'

Then the reason he had not, and the real reason she was so upset, hit her like a blow and she stopped dead in the middle of the floor as couples swerved to avoid them.

'But of course you could not tell me,' she whispered. 'Because if you had, you thought I would say that you had compromised me, that as a gentleman you must marry me and you would have been trapped. That is it, is it not?'

'No!' Jonathan somehow managed to keep his voice down from a bellow.

'And I suppose you laughed about it with your friends,' Sarah added. 'It was all for a bet, I presume? The highwayman act.'

'Of course it was a damn bet!' A couple gliding past stared at him. Sarah was glaring at him as if he was some kind of libertine bent on ravishment. 'And of course I said nothing about you to them. For God's sake, let's get out of this confounded dance.'

'Certainly, if only to take myself out of range of your blaspheming and bad language.' She turned on her heel and stalked off the floor, leaving him standing there, the focus of all eyes.

'I trod on her feet,' he explained to those couples within hearing and followed her, attempting to look ruefully amused when all he wanted to do was snarl.

By the time he reached the edge Sarah had vanished. Jonathan, despite his height, could see no topknot of glossy brown curls, no slender figure in almond silk. A dark-haired beauty with a heart-shaped face and an expression of exasperation appeared in front of him. He dredged into his memories of last Season. Lady Maude Templeton. 'She's gone out onto the terrace. That way.' She pointed, then walked off. Jonathan thought he heard her add, 'Men!' as she went.

Jaw set, Jonathan stalked off in the direction indicated. Idiot woman, of course he hadn't told her who he was! Couldn't she see why? And why wasn't she pleased to see him? He was pleased to see her. More than pleased. It upset his plans, but to hell with that; Sarah was here and he wanted her. After he'd boxed her ears.

The torch-lit terrace held a scattering of couples strolling and flirting. There was no sign of Sarah, but he had not expected her to stop here, in full view. He took the sweeping steps down onto the lawns and glimpsed the flutter of pale skirts in the darkness.

When he reached the same spot, treading quietly, his dancing pumps making no sound on the close-scythed turf, he could not see her. Then he realized that the shrubs that had been planted along this wing of the house had a narrow gap in them. Slipping through, he found a graveled walk between them and the house walls. Sarah had her back to one of the sloping buttresses of the old wall, her gaze fixed on a group of tumbling cherubs set amongst the greenery.

Her head came round as he stepped onto the gravel and he felt his body tighten at the sight of her wide eyes, the rise and fall of her breasts in the low-cut silk.

'Go away.' She stood her ground, chin up.

Jonathan kept walking. 'No. Why are you so angry with me?'

'I told you!'

'Did you really expect me, when we first met and we made our extraordinary decision, to whip off my mask and introduce myself as the Earl of Redcliffe? My concern was for your protection.'

'Poppycock!' Sarah snapped. 'Have you any idea how humiliated I feel? Had you no thought that this might happen if we met again? Or was it impossible to believe that humble Miss Tatton might move in the same circles as yourself?'

'Well, you hadn't up to then,' he retorted.

'No, and I imagine you are none too pleased to find I am now!' The color was flying in her cheeks, he could see angry tears sparkling, and the effort not to seize hold of her and shake her and kiss her and take her was almost overwhelming.

'It was certainly not what I planned. I intended—' He never got the words out. Sarah thumped him on the chest with her clenched fist. 'Damn it, that hurt!'

'*Good.*' She did it again. 'That's how I feel, as if someone has punched me in the chest. I *trusted* you and all the time you were just amusing yourself with some silly little gentry virgin who had got herself into a pickle.'

'Amusing myself? If I had been amusing myself, Miss Tatton, you wouldn't still be a virgin, believe me.' Jonathan grabbed her wrists before she could land another blow and yanked her hard against himself. 'If I had been *amusing myself* things might have gone rather differently.'

She glared up at him, lips parted, face flushed, the scent of hot, angry woman filling his senses and bringing with it the prickle of awareness that she was not afraid of him, not just angry with him, but that she desired him and that he wanted her. Here and now.

Sarah gasped as he pushed her back against the buttress, its slight slope bringing his weight down on her, crushing his loins against her pelvis as he spread his legs to trap her. Her wriggling thrust her against him, and he thrust back, gasping as the heat of her met the aching length of his erection, their naked flesh separated only by thin, silk breeches and the flimsy defenses of her gown.

He trapped her hands above her head, his big hand enveloping both wrists easily, and smiled down into her face, lit by the spill of light from the window above. 'Now *this* is amusing myself. Be honest, sweeting: do you want me to let you go?'

Sarah went still beneath him, her eyes searching his face, her heart beating against his shirtfront. Then her eyelids closed as though they were too heavy and she whispered, 'No.'

Shaken by her reaction, he schooled himself to be gentle,

lowering his mouth over hers, determined to coax her, but she nipped at his lower lip with sharp teeth, took his mouth with a raw need that was fueled still by anger, and his own frustration rose to meet hers and the kiss became fierce and rough and she matched him, grazing teeth, thrusting, tongues dueling, pressure and demand, with no yielding, no softness.

Beneath his weight her body bucked, not to throw him off but seeking the friction of his hardness against her soft core. His hand left her breast to pull at her skirts until his fingers touched her thigh and he could push between their straining bodies, find the hot, wet folds and part them.

Sarah went still, hanging, waiting for the touch he had taught her to expect, but he slipped one finger past the tight, desperate knot of flesh and slid it into her, gasping against her mouth at the sensation, muffling her own cry of shock and arousal as he added another finger, feeling her tighten around him instinctively.

Her reaction was so arousing he thought he would come just from that alone, and forced himself to stillness, only his mouth ravishing hers, as though to release her would be to cease to breathe. Then she whimpered against his lips and he began to thrust and she arched under him, clenching, matching his strokes until he felt the quivering desperation building, building, and took pity on her, brushing his thumb against her, one touch sending her over into shuddering collapse.

Sarah sagged, her head thrown back against the warm stone, only the weight of Jonathan's body and his grip on her wrists keeping her upright. The anger had burned away. All she knew was that the man she loved had driven her into a mindless inferno of sensation and need and the impossibly wonderful satisfaction of that need.

'Sarah,' he murmured against her neck. 'Sweetheart. Are

you all right?' He released her wrists and her hands fell to his shoulders and he stood upright, bringing her with him.

'Mmm,' she managed to murmur, every inch of her aware of him, his strength and the scent of aroused man and the hardness pressed against her.

'I didn't hurt you?' She shook her head, the world gradually stopping spinning. 'You were angry. I was, too, because you were. I didn't know you would be here, any more than you knew I would. Listen, sweet—' he cradled her against himself, rocking her gently '—this can't go on, we have to talk...to resolve this.'

'No, I don't want...' she began, trying to explain, terrified what his sense of honor might compel him to say. One moment she thought herself in love with a man who knew he could never offer for her, even should he wish to, the next she found he was a man who would feel obliged to do so. Which, her spinning brain tried to fathom, was better? Or were they both too bad to bear?

'You don't want me?' he asked softly, holding her tenderly now as though that turmoil of exciting, angry passion had never been. 'I might have something to say to that.'

'You cannot force me,' Sarah began and felt him stiffen as though she had hit him again. 'I—'

'Was that a bat?' an alarmed feminine voice demanded just the other side of the bushes. 'Because if it is, I am going right back inside, Elinor Ravenhurst. I don't care how interesting the stars are.'

Maude? Elinor?

'Don't be foolish.' That was Elinor. 'It is an old wives' tale that they get into your hair.'

'Lady Maude, Miss Ravenhurst! Have you seen Miss Tatton?' Mrs. Catchpole sounded breathless. 'I do not know where she can have got to. I am most alarmed. Lady Dereham must organize a search party.'

Jonathan appeared to be shaking, then she realized he was laughing. Sarah elbowed him sharply in the ribs.

'Oh, she's here, Mrs. Catchpole,' Elinor said blithely. 'In those bushes. It was the bats, you see. We came out to look at the stars, the three of us, and then the bats swooped down and Sarah screamed and dived into the bush.'

Jonathan reacted faster than she did, brushing down her skirts, pushing a loose curl behind her ear. 'We will speak tomorrow,' he whispered, giving her a little push.

Sarah stumbled out onto the lawn looking, she was certain, as though she had been pulled through the hedge backward, rather than having merely taken refuge in it.

'Sarah! Look at you,' Mrs. Catchpole fussed.

'We'll go to my room and tidy up.' Maude tucked her hand into Sarah's arm and whisked her away down the path toward the house, leaving the chaperone trapped by Elinor's careful explanation of how one could identify the constellation Leo.

'What is going on?' Sarah demanded as Maude shut the door and stood there beaming at her.

'It's him, isn't it? Your highwayman, only he's really Jonathan Kirkland, Lord Redcliffe. I've known him for years, so I could see he'd had a shock, and then I saw your face and the two of you were having that really splendid tiff, so we thought, Elinor and I, that we had better leave you to it, but keep an eye on you. And then Mrs. Catchpole started flapping about so we came to rescue you.' She sat down on the bed. 'But what was he doing pretending to be a highwayman?'

'It was a bet,' Sarah said as Elinor came in.

'Well, you've found each other now,' she said prosaically. 'I wonder why lovers so often have such huge rows? It seems most strange.'

'I know why *I'm* angry,' Sarah said, sitting down before her knees gave way. 'But I don't know what he has to be cross about. He didn't tell me who he was because he thinks I'd have expected him to offer for me.'

'Did he say so?' Maude began to brush the back of Sarah's dress. 'Tsk! Lichen everywhere.'

'No, but what other reason could there be for not saying, once he knew my name?'

'Have you asked him?' Elinor inquired, looking up from her notebook.

'Not exactly.' Sarah bit her lip. 'I hit him. On the chest with my fists and I shouted at him. He was quite angry.'

Maude began to giggle. 'I'm not surprised. Wait until the morning. I am sure you will both be in a better frame of mind by then.'

The morning, after a night of restless sleep disturbed by quite shocking dreams, hardly seemed more promising. The breakfast parlor was populated by heavy-eyed guests sipping coffee, while many seemed to have decided to stay in their rooms.

Jonathan was seated at the far end of the table when Sarah entered with Mrs. Catchpole. He rose with the other men, then resumed his seat with a fleeting glance in her direction.

She was still pushing her omelette listlessly around her plate half an hour later when Lady Dereham appeared at her side. 'Lord Redcliffe has asked if he might speak with you in my sitting room at your convenience.'

Sarah stared. Her chaperone sat bolt upright, looking for all the world like a pointer that has sighted game. 'Sarah, dear! We must—'

'Do not disturb yourself, ma'am. I will escort Sarah.' Bel had her out of the room before Mrs. Catchpole could react. 'You look very well, my dear. There is no need to go and primp. Here we are.' Bel opened the door, gave her a little push and closed it, leaving her alone with the Earl of Redcliffe.

'Oh.' It was not the most intelligent thing she could have found to say. Sarah bit her lip and regarded his unsmiling face.

'Sarah. I have, this morning, written to your father. I thought I should show it to you before I send it.' He held out a sheet of paper.

'Written?' She took it. The words were out of focus.

'Yes. I realize that to call would be more conventional. It was my intention to return to Saint's Ford Manor and do the thing in style, but now… Sarah, there is no way I can wait.'

'You intended to come back to me?' She stared at the firm black letters, willing them to make sense.

'Of course. I had to lose the highwayman, speak to my bankers about the settlement, have a haircut—all the things a hopeful suitor needs to do.'

'Suitor? Why?' She thrust the letter back at him. 'I cannot seem to focus.'

'Sit down then, and I will read to you.' He guided her to the sofa, then stood before the hearth and cleared his throat.

'"Sir Hugh, I write to inform you of my intention to pay my addresses to your daughter, Miss Sarah Tatton. I cannot pretend that my attachment to her was not sudden. In fact I believe it was, if not love at first sight, then most certainly love from the first moment she allowed me to press a respectful salutation upon her lips."

'You spoke?'

Sarah shook her head, dumb with delight. *Respectful salutation?* That must be the first kiss that he took when they met. He was making it sound as if he had met her for the first time here, when in fact…

'"My standing and circumstances you may ascertain from an inspection of the *Peerage*. In regard to my intentions as to settlements, I trust the enclosed papers from my lawyer will prove satisfactory…"' etc., etc.' Jonathan folded the paper.

'Well, Miss Tatton? You are, I believe, of age, which means that I need not await a response from your father but may do this now.' He went down on one knee beside her. 'Sarah.' His voice was husky and she found she could not breathe, just stare into his eyes, trapped by the intensity in them. 'I love you. I think I loved you from that first kiss. I *knew* I loved you when I felt the pain of thinking you had offered me payment for lying with you. My fault, I confess, was to go and leave you without explanation, but I did it intending to return as an entirely respectable suitor. Like an idiot I wanted to surprise you, to have everything in place, perfect. Do you forgive me?'

'Oh yes. I love you, too, you see. I don't need everything to be perfect, I just need you.' She had found her tongue, and her eyes focused clearly on his face and she reached out and cupped his cheek with a hand that was steady.

'And you will marry me?'

And instead of answering, she simply leaned forward and kissed him and never noticed until afterward that her cheeks were wet.

'Lady Redcliffe, you are blushing.' Her new husband set Sarah on her feet beside the wide bed and bent to kiss her. 'Now what, after all the things we have enjoyed together, can be making you shy now?'

'This is different,' she confessed, reaching up to undo his neckcloth.

'Yes,' Jonathan agreed, leaving her fully clothed while she undressed him and then slowly, gently, unveiling her body until they stood facing each other in the twilit room, naked. 'I love you and now you are mine.'

'I know. And you are my husband and we no longer have to be careful. Will you show me how to love you?'

And without answering with words he lifted her onto the

bed and began to woo her with lips and tongue and gentle, wicked fingers until the familiar, insistent throb took over and her head began to turn, restless on the pillow, and her own hands stopped caressing and could only hold him and he shifted his weight and lay between her thighs.

'Don't be frightened.' He moved slowly, nudging, and she smiled, heady with pleasure, tingling with anticipation.

'I'm not frightened. I just want you so much. Want you inside me, to be around you, to hold you in every way I can.' It felt strange and powerful, the inexorable, heavy pressure, but her body seemed to know what to do and was accepting him. She shifted, searching for the best position, and then he smiled and surged against her and she gasped, pain flickering past to be replaced by an overwhelming sense of completion.

Jonathan stilled above her, his eyes intense on her face. They were so closely joined that she could feel the pressure of his hipbones, the tantalizing brush and weight of his testicles, the friction of his body hair. And then, as she dared to breathe again, to relax, she could feel him inside her and realized that she could tighten around him and that when she did he groaned and closed his eyes and thrust.

She could match the surging, deep rhythm, tightening, caressing, and his eyes opened again and the look in them took her breath and she held on and let herself fly until he thrust deeper than ever with a hoarse cry and she felt him convulse inside her, spilling life and heat into her, and she let go and joined him in the velvet darkness.

Sarah came to herself to find they were wrapped together, her head on his breast, their legs twined. 'In August,' Jonathan said, his hand stroking possessively down her body, 'I asked you for the most precious thing you possessed. Thank you for giving it to me.'

'My virginity?' Sarah queried, raising herself on her elbow to smile at him.

'No.' The deep green eyes smiled back. 'Your heart, my darling.'

'How could I help it?' She bent and kissed him. 'A highwayman stole it quite away.'

* * * * *

THE PIRATICAL
MISS RAVENHURST
LOUISE ALLEN

Author Note

After five Ravenhurst love stories it is time to meet the youngest and most distant of the cousins. Clemence lives in a life of privilege and comfort at the heart of Jamaican society, until circumstances force her to make a choice – marriage to the despicable Lewis Naismith or flight.

Clemence has a plan – Ravenhursts always do – but it does not include running straight into the clutches of the most feared pirate in the Caribbean. There doesn't seem to be any way out, unless she can trust both her instincts and the enigmatic navigator Nathan Stanier.

I knew Clemence would have the courage and wits to survive on the *Sea Scorpion,* but what is a young lady to do when she is comprehensively ruined in the process.

I do hope you enjoy finding out as much as I did. I felt sad to write the last word in the chronicles of *Those Scandalous Ravenhursts*, but perhaps one day I can return to their world and explore the life and loves of some of the characters I met along the way.

For Nathan Oakman who is sure to grow up to be a hero.

Chapter One

Jamaica—June 1817

'I would sooner—'

'Sooner what?' Her uncle regarded Clemence with contempt. 'You would sooner die?'

'Sooner marry the first man I met outside the gates than *that*.' She jerked her head towards her cousin, sprawled in the window seat, his attention on the female servants in the torch-lit courtyard below.

'But you do not have any choice,' Joshua Naismith said, in the same implacably patient tone he had used to her in the six months since her father's death. 'You are my ward, you will do as I tell you.'

'My father never intended me to marry Lewis,' Clemence protested. She had been protesting with a rising sense of desperation ever since she had recovered sufficiently from her daze of mourning to comprehend that her late mother's half-brother was not the protector that her father had expected him to be when he made his will. Her respectable, conservative, rather dull Uncle Joshua was a predator, his claws reaching for her fortune.

'The intentions of the late lamented Lord Clement Ravenhurst,' Mr Naismith said, 'are of no interest to me whatsoever. The effect of his will is to place you under my control, a fitting recompense for years of listening to his idiotic political opinions and his absurd social theories.'

'My father did not believe in the institution of slavery,' Clemence retorted, angered despite her own apprehension. 'Most enlightened people feel the same. You did not have to listen to what you do not believe in—you could have attempted to counter his arguments. But then you have neither the intellectual capacity, nor the moral integrity to do so, have you, Uncle?'

'Insolent little bitch.' Lewis uncoiled himself from the seat and walked to his father's side. He frowned at her, an expression she had caught him practising in front of the mirror, no doubt in an attempt to transform his rather ordinary features into an ideal of well-bred authority. 'A pity you were not a boy—he raised you like one, he let you run wild like one and now, look at you—you might as well be one.'

Clemence hated the flush she could feel on her cheekbones, hated the fact that his words stung. It was shallow to wish she had a petite, curvaceous figure. A few months ago she had at least possessed a small bosom and the gentle swell of feminine hips, now, with the appetite of a mouse, she had lost so much weight that she might as well have been twelve again. Combined with the rangy height she had inherited from her father, Clemence was all too aware that she looked like a schoolboy dressed up to play a female role in a Shakespeare play.

Defensively her hand went to the weight of her hair, coiled and dressed simply in the heat. Its silky touch reminded her of her femininity, her one true beauty, all the colours of wheat and toffee and gilt, mixed and mingling.

'If I had been a boy, I wouldn't have to listen to your disgusting marriage plans,' she retorted. 'But you'd still be stealing my inheritance, whatever my sex, I have no doubt of that. Is money the *only* thing that is important to you?'

'We are merchants.' Uncle Joshua's high colour wattled his smooth jowls. 'We make money, we do not have it drop into our laps like your aristocratic relatives.'

'Papa was the youngest son, he worked for his fortune—'

'The youngest son of the Duke of Allington. Oh dear, what poverty, how he must have struggled.'

That was the one card she had not played in the weeks as hints had become suggestions and the suggestions, orders. 'You know my English relatives are powerful,' Clemence said. 'Do you wish to antagonise them?'

'They are a very long way away and hold no sway here in the West Indies.' Joshua's expression was smug. 'Here the ear of the Governor and one's credit with the bankers are all that matter. In time, when Lewis decides to go back to England, his marriage to you may well be of social advantage, that is true.'

'As I have no intention of marrying my cousin, he will have no advantage from me.'

'You *will* marry me.' Lewis took a long stride, seized her wrist and yanked her, off-balance, to face him. She was tall enough to stare into his eyes, refusing to flinch even as his fingers dug into the narrow bones of her wrist, although her heart seemed to bang against her ribs. 'The banns will be read for the first time next Sunday.'

'I will never consent and you cannot force me kicking and screaming to the altar—not and maintain your precious respectability.' Somehow she kept her voice steady. It was hard after nineteen years of being loved and indulged to find the strength to fight betrayal and greed, but some unexpected reserve of pride and desperation was keeping her defiant.

'True.' Her head snapped round at the smugness in her uncle's voice. Joshua smiled, confident. The chilly certainty crept over her that he had thought long and hard about this and the thought of her refusal on the altar steps did not worry him in the slightest. 'You have two choices, my dear niece. You can behave in a dutiful manner and marry Lewis when the banns have been called or he will come to your room every night until he has you with child and then, I think, you will agree.'

'And if I do not, even then?' Fainting, Clemence told herself fiercely, would not help in the slightest, even though the room swam and the temptation to just let go and slip out of this nightmare was almost overwhelming.

'There is always a market for healthy children on the islands,' Lewis said, hitching one buttock on the table edge and smiling at her. 'We will just keep going until you come to your senses.'

'You—' Clemence swallowed and tried again. 'You would sell your *own child* into slavery?'

Lewis shrugged. 'What use is an illegitimate brat? Marry me and your children will want for nothing. Refuse and what happens to them will be entirely your doing.'

'They will want for nothing save a decent father,' she snapped back, praying that her churning stomach would not betray her. 'You are a rapist, an embezzler and a blackmailer and you—' she turned furiously on her uncle '—are as bad. I cannot believe your lackwit son thought of this scheme all by himself.'

Joshua had never hit her before, no one had. Clemence did not believe the threat in her uncle's raised hand, did not flinch away until the blow caught her on the cheekbone under her right eye, spinning her off her feet to crash against the table and fall to the floor.

Somehow she managed to push herself up, then stumble to her feet, her head spinning. Joshua Naismith's voice came from a long way away, his image so shrunk he seemed to be at the wrong end of a telescope. His voice buzzed in her ears. 'Will you consent to the banns being read and agree to marry Lewis?'

'No.' *Never.*

'Then you will go to your room and stay there. Your meals will be brought to you and you will eat; your scrawny figure offends me. Lewis will visit you tomorrow. I think you are in no fit state to pay him proper heed tonight.'

Proper heed? If her cousin came within range of her and any kind of sharp weapon he would never be able to father a child again. 'Ring for Eliza,' Clemence said, lifting her hand to her throbbing face. 'I need her assistance.'

'You have a new abigail.' Joshua reached out and tugged the bell. 'That insolent girl of yours has been dismissed. Freed slaves indeed!' The woman who entered was buxom, her skin the colour of smooth coffee, her hair braided intricately. The look she shot Clemence held contempt and dislike.

'Your mistress?' She stared at Lewis. No wonder Marie Luce was looking like that: she must know the men's intentions and know that Clemence would be taking Lewis's attention away from her.

'She does as she is told,' Lewis said smoothly. 'And will be rewarded for it. Take her to her chamber, make sure she eats,' he added to the other woman. 'Lock the door and then come to my room.'

Clemence let herself be led out of the door. Here, in the long passage with its louvred windows open at each end to encourage a draught, the sound of the sea on the beach far below was a living presence. Her feet stumbled on the familiar smooth stone flags. From the white walls the darkened portraits of generations of ancestors stared blankly down, impotent to help her.

'Where is Eliza?' Thank goodness her maid was a freed woman with her own papers, not subject to the whim of the Naismiths.

Marie Luce shrugged, her dark eyes hostile as she gripped Clemence's arm, half-supporting, half-imprisoning her. 'I do not know. I do not care.' Her lilting accent made poetry out of the acid words. 'Why do you make Master Lewis angry? Marry him, then he will get you with child and forget about you.'

'I do not want him, you are welcome to him,' Clemence retorted as they reached the door of her room. 'Please fetch me some warm water to bathe my face.' The door clicked shut behind the maid and the key turned. Through the slats she could hear her heelless shoes clicking as she made her way to the back door and the kitchen wing.

Clemence sank down on the dressing-table stool, her fingers tight on the edge for support. The image that stared back at her from the mirror was not reassuring. Her right cheek was already swelling, the skin red and darkening, her eye beginning to close. It would be black tomorrow, she realised. Her left eye, wide, looked more startlingly green in contrast and her hair had slipped from its pins and lay in a heavy braid on her shoulder.

Gingerly, Clemence straightened her back, wincing at the bruises from the impact with the table. There was no padding on her bones to cushion any falls, she realised; it was mere luck she had not broken ribs. She must eat. Starving herself into a decline would not help matters, although what would?

The door opened to admit Marie Luce with one of the footmen carrying a supper tray. The man, one of the house staff she had known all her life, took a startled look at her face and then stared straight ahead, expressionless. 'Master Lewis says you are to eat,' the other woman said, putting down the water ewer she held. 'I stay until you do.'

Clemence dipped a cloth in the water and held it to her face. It stung and throbbed: she supposed she should be grateful Uncle Joshua had used his ringless right hand and the blow had not broken the skin. 'Very well.' Chicken and rice, stuffed pimentos, corn fritters, cake with syrup, milk. Her stomach roiled, but instinct told Clemence to eat, however little appetite she had and however painful it was to chew.

She knew the worst now: it was time to fight, although how, locked in her room, she had no idea. The plates scraped clean and the milk drunk, Marie Luce cleared the table and let herself out. Clemence strained to hear—the key grated in the lock. It was too much to hope that the woman would be careless about that.

She felt steadier for the food. It seemed weeks since she had eaten properly, grief turning to uneasiness, then apprehension, then fear as her uncle's domination over the household and estate and her life had tightened into a stranglehold.

It was pointless to expect help from outside; their friends and acquaintances had been told she was ill with grief, unbalanced, and the doctor had ordered complete seclusion and rest. Even her close friends Catherine Page and Laura Steeples had believed her uncle's lies and obediently kept away. She had seen their letters to him, full of shocked sympathy that she was in such a decline.

And who could she trust, in any case? She had trusted Joshua, and how wrong she had been about him!

Clemence stood and went to the full-length window, its casement open on to the fragrant heat of the night. Her father had insisted that Raven's Hold was built right on the edge of the cliff, just as the family castle in Northumberland was, and the balcony of her room jutted out into space above the sea.

When she was a child, after her mother's death, she had run wild with the sons of the local planters, borrowing their clothes, scrambling through the cane fields, hiding in the plantation buildings. Scandalised local matrons had finally persuaded her father that she should become a conformable young lady once her fourteenth birthday was past and so her days of climbing out of the window at night and up the trellis to freedom and adventures were long past.

She leaned on the balcony and smiled, her expression turning into a grimace as the bruises made themselves felt. If only it were so easy to climb away now!

But why not? Clemence straightened, tinglingly alert. If she could get out of the house, down to the harbour, then the *Raven Princess* would be there, due to sail for England with the morning light. It was the largest of her father's ships—her ships—now that pirates had captured *Raven Duchess*, the action that had precipitated her father's heart stroke and death.

But if she just ran away they would hunt her down like a fugitive slave… Clemence paced into the room, thinking furiously. Her uncle's sneer came back to her. *You would sooner die?* Let him think that, then. Somewhere, surely, were the boy's clothes she had once worn. She pulled open presses, flung up the lids of the trunks, releasing wafts of sandalwood from their interiors. Yes, here at the bottom of one full of rarely used blankets were the loose canvas breeches, the shirt and waistcoat.

She pulled off her gown and tried them on. The bottom of the trousers flapped above her ankle bones now, but the shirt and waistcoat had always been on the large side. After some thought she tore linen strips and bound her chest tightly; her bosom was unimpressive, but even so, it was better to take no chances. Clemence dug out the buckled shoes, tried them on her bare feet, then looked in the mirror. The image of a gangly youth stared back, oddly adorned by the thick braid of hair.

That was going to have to go, there was no room for regret. Clemence found the scissors, gritted her teeth and hacked. The hair went into a cloth, knotted tightly, then wrapped up into a bundle with everything she had been wearing that evening. A thought struck her and she took out the gown again to tear a thin, ragged strip from the hem. Her slippers she flung out of the window and the modest pearls and earrings she buried under the jewellery in her trinket box.

The new figure that looked back at her from the glass had ragged hair around its ears and a dramatically darkening bruise over cheek and eye. Her mind seemed to be running clearly now, as though she had pushed through a forest of fear and desperation into open air. Clemence took the pen from the standish and scrawled *I cannot bear it...* On a sheet of paper. A drop of water from the washstand was an artistic and convincing teardrop to blur the shaky signature. The ink splashed on to the dressing table, over her fingers. All the better to show agitation.

She looped the bundle on to her belt and set a stool by the balcony before scrambling up on to the rail. Perched there, she snagged the strip from her gown under a splinter, then kicked the stool over. There: the perfect picture of a desperate fall to the crashing waves below. How Uncle Joshua was going to explain that was his problem.

Now all she had to do was to ignore the lethal drop below and pray that the vines and the trellis would still hold her. Clemence reached up, set her shoe on the first, distantly remembered foothold, and swung clear of the rail.

She rapidly realised just how dangerous this was, something the child that she had been had simply not considered. And five years of ladylike behaviour, culminating in weeks spent almost ill with grief and desperation, had weakened her muscles. Her dinner lurched in her stomach and her throat went dry. Teeth gritted she climbed on, trying not to think about centipedes, spiders or any of the other interesting inhabitants of the ornamental vines she was clutching. However venomous they might be, they were not threatening to rape and rob her.

The breath sobbed in her throat, but she reached the ledge that ran around the house just beneath the eaves and began to shuffle along it, clinging to the gutters. All she had to do now was to get around the corner and she could drop on to the roof of the kitchen wing. From there it was an easy slide to the ground.

A shutter banged open just below where her heels jutted out into space. Clemence froze. 'No, I don't *want* her, how many times have I got to tell you?' It was Lewis, irritated and abrupt. 'Why would I *want* that scrawny, cantankerous little bitch? It is simply business.'

There was the sound of a woman's voice, low and seductive. Marie Luce. Lewis grunted. 'Get your clothes off, then.' Such a gallant lover, Clemence thought. Her cousin had left the shutters open, forcing her to move with exaggerated care in case her leather soles gritted on the rough stone. Then she was round, dropping on to the thick palmetto thatch, sliding down to the lean-to shed roof and clambering to the ground.

Old One-Eye, the guard dog, whined and came over stiffly to lick her hand, the links of his chain chinking. There was noise from the kitchens, the hum and chirp of insects, the chatter of a night bird. No one would hear her stealthy exit through the yard gate, despite the creaky hinge that never got oiled.

Clemence took to her heels, the bundle bouncing on her hip. Now all she had to do was to get far enough away to hide the evidence that she was still alive, and steal a horse.

It was a moonless night, the darkness of Kingston harbour thickly sprinkled with the sparks of ships' riding-lights. Clemence slid from the horse's back, slapped it on the rump and watched it gallop away, back towards the penn she had taken it from almost three hours before.

The unpaved streets were rough under her stumbling feet but she pushed on, keeping to the shadows, avoiding the clustered drinking houses and brothels that lined the way down to the harbour. It was just her luck that *Raven Princess* was moored at the furthest end, Clemence thought, dodging behind some stacked barrels to avoid a group of men approaching down the centre of the street.

And when she got there, she was not at all certain that simply marching on board and demanding to be taken to England was a sensible thing to do. Captain Moorcroft could well decide to return her to Uncle Joshua, despite the fact that the ship was hers. The rights of women was not a highly regarded principle, let alone here on Jamaica in the year 1817.

The hot air held the rich mingled odours of refuse and dense vegetation, open drains, rum, wood smoke and horse dung, but Clemence ignored the familiar stench, quickening her pace into a jog trot. The next quay was the Ravenhurst moorings and the *Raven Princess*…was gone.

She stood staring, mouth open in shock, mind blank, frantically scanning the moored ships for a sight of the black-haired, golden-crowned figurehead. *It must be here!*

'What you looking for, boy?' a voice asked from behind her.

'The *Raven Princess*,' she stammered, her voice husky with shock and disbelief.

'Sailed this evening, damn them, they finished loading early. What do you want with it?'

Clemence turned, keeping her head down so the roughly chopped hair hid her face. 'Cabin boy,' she muttered. 'Cap'n Moorcroft promised me a berth.' There were five men, hard to see against the flare of light from a big tavern, its doors wide open on to the street.

'Is that so? We could do with a cabin boy, couldn't we, lads?' the slightly built figure in the centre of the group said, his voice soft. The hairs on Clemence's nape rose. The others sniggered. 'You come along with us, lad. We'll find you a berth all right.'

'No. No, thank you.' She began to edge away.

'That's "No, thank you, Cap'n",' a tall man with a tricorne hat on his head said, stepping round to block her retreat.

'Cap'n,' she repeated obediently. 'I'll just—'

'Come with us.' The tall man gave her a shove, right up to the rest of the group. The man he called Cap'n put out a hand and laid it on her shoulder. She was close enough to see him now, narrow-faced, his bony jaw obscured by a few days' stubble, his head bare. His clothes were flamboyant, antique almost; coat tails wide, the magnificent lace at his throat, soiled. The eyes that met Clemence's were brown, flat, cold. If a lizard could speak...

'What's your name, boy?'

'Clem. Cap'n.' She tried to hold the reptilian stare, but her eyes dropped, down to where the wrist of the hand that held her was bared, the lace fallen back. There was a tattoo on the back of his hand, the tail and sting of a scorpion, its head and body vanishing into his wide-cuffed sleeve. Her vision blurred.

'Come along then, Clem.'

There was nowhere to run to and the long fingers were

biting into her collarbone. Clemence let herself be pushed towards the tavern. It was crowded, she told herself, inside she'd be able to give them the slip.

She knew what they were, and knew, too, that she would be safer by far with Uncle Joshua and Lewis than with these men. They were pirates, and the man who held her, unless scorpion tattoos were the latest fashion, was Red Matthew McTiernan.

They bundled her up the steps, across the porch and into the heat and light and noise of the tavern. She let herself be pushed along, her eyes darting about the room for an escape route as the crowd shifted uneasily to let McTiernan and his men through. This was a rough place, but the customers were reacting like foxes when the wolf arrives at the kill.

A man came forward, wiping his hands on a stained apron. 'He's over there.' He jerked his head towards a table in the far corner.

The man who sat there was alone, despite the pressure for tables. He was playing hazard, left hand against right, his attention focused on the white cubes that bounced and rolled. He was tall, rangy, carrying no surplus weight. *Built for speed, like a frigate*, Clemence thought, staring at him when she should be watching for her chance. His hair was over-long, brown with sun-bleached tips, his skin very tanned, his clothes had the look of much-worn quality.

'Stanier.'

He looked up, his eyes a startling blue against his dark skin. 'Yes?'

'They tell me you want a navigator's berth.' The man called Stanier nodded. 'Are you any good?'

'I'm the best in these seas,' he said, his lips curving into what might, charitably, be called a smile. 'But you knew that, McTiernan, or you wouldn't be here.'

The bony fingers gripping her shoulder fell away, down to rest on the hilt of the sword that hung by the captain's side. As a ripple of tension ran round the small group, Clemence eased back, poised to slide into the crowd behind.

'That's Captain McTiernan to you.'

'It is if I serve with you,' Stanier said, his tone equable. 'And I will, if it is worth my while.'

'You know what I'm offering,' McTiernan snapped.

'And I want my own cabin. And a servant.'

'What do you think you are? One of his Majesty's bleeding naval officers still? They threw you out—so don't go putting on airs and graces with me.'

Stanier smiled, his eyes cold. 'More fool them. I'm just the best navigator you'll ever see, navy or no navy.'

Now. Clemence slid one foot back, then the other, half-turned and—

'Oh, no, you don't, my lad.' The big man with the tricorne spun her round, fetching her a back-handed cuff that hit her bruised face. Blinded with the sudden pain, Clemence staggered, fell and crashed into a chair in a tangle of limbs.

She put out her right hand, grasping for something to hold on to, and found she was gripping a muscular thigh. Warm, strong—somehow, she couldn't let go.

'What have we here?' She looked up, managing to focus on the interested blue eyes that were studying her hand. She looked down as the navigator lifted it from his leg, prizing the fingers open. An ink stain ran across them. 'You can write, boy?'

'Yessir.' She nodded vehemently, wanting, in that moment, only to be with him, her hand in his. Safe. Lord, how desperate was she, that this hard man represented safety?

'Can you do your figures?' He put out one long finger and just touched the bruise on her face.

'Yessir.' She forced herself not to flinch away.

'Excellent. I'll take you as my servant, then.' Stanier got to his feet, hauling Clemence up by the collar to stand at his side. 'Any objections, gentlemen?'

Chapter Two

'That's our new cabin boy.' Nathan Stanier studied the speaker. Big, of Danish descent perhaps, incongruously pin-neat from the crown of his tricorne to the tips of his polished shoes. Cutler, the first mate, the man with the washed-out blue eyes that could have belonged to a barracuda for all the warmth and humanity they held.

'And now he's mine,' Nathan said. 'I'm sure there's some-one else in the crew who can carry your slops and warm a few hammocks.'

The lad stood passively by his side. Nathan thought he could detect a fine tremor running through him—whether it was fear or the pain from the blow to his face, he could not tell.

The boy looked too innocent to be aware of the main reason this crew wanted him on board. It was no part of his plans to act as bear-leader to dockside waifs and strays, but something was different with this lad. He must be getting soft, or perhaps it was years of looking out for midshipmen, so wet behind the ears they spent the first month crying for their mothers at night. Not that training the navy's up-and-coming officers was any longer a concern of his. Lord Phillips had seen to that, the old devil.

Cutler's eyes narrowed, his hand clenching on the hilt of his weapon. 'Let him keep the boy,' McTiernan said softly. 'I'm not one to interfere with a man's pleasures.' Someone pushed through the crowded room and murmured into the captain's ear. 'It seems the militia is about on the Spanish Town road. Time to leave, gentlemen.'

Nathan put his hand on the boy's shoulder. 'Don't even think about making a run for it,' he murmured. There was no response. Under his palm the narrow bones felt too fragile. The lad was painfully thin. 'What's your name?'

'C... Clem. Sir.' That odd, gruff little voice. Nerves, or not broken properly yet.

'How old are you?'

'Sixteen.'

Fourteen was more like it. Nathan gestured to one of the waiters and spun him a coin. 'Get my bags—and take care not to knock them.' He didn't want his instruments jarred out of true before he'd even begun. 'Have you got anything, Clem?'

A mute shake of the head, then, 'They just grabbed me, outside.' So there was probably a family somewhere, wondering what had happened to their son. Nathan shrugged mentally—no worse than the press-gang. He had more important things to be worrying about than one scruffy youth. Things like staying alive in this shark pool with all his limbs attached, making sure McTiernan continued to believe he was exactly what he said he was—right up to the point when he despatched the man to his richly deserved fate.

The boy scrambled down into the jolly boat, moving easily between the half-dozen rowers. He was used to small craft, at least. He huddled into the bows, arms wrapped tightly around himself as though somehow, in this heat, he was cold.

The rowers pulled away with a practised lack of fuss, sliding the boat through the maze of moored shipping, out almost to the Palisades. The sound of the surf breaking on the low sand-bar sheltering the harbour was loud.

He should have known that McTiernan would choose to drop anchor at the tip of the bar close to the remains of the infamous Port Royal. All that remained of the great pirate stronghold now after over a century of earthquake, hurricanes and fire was a ghost of one of the wickedest places on earth, but the huts clinging to the sand inches above the water would be the natural home for McTiernan and his crew.

It was darker now, out beyond the legitimate shipping huddled together as if for mutual protection from the sea wolves. The bulk that loomed up in front of them was showing few lights, but one flashed in response to a soft hail from the jolly boat. The *Sea Scorpion* was what he had expected: ship-rigged, not much above the size of a frigate and built for speed in this sea of shallow waters and twisting channels.

He pushed the boy towards the ladder and climbed after him. 'Wot's this?' The squat man peering at them in the light of one lantern was unmistakably the bo'sun, right down to the tarred and knotted rope starter he carried to strike any seaman he caught slacking, just as a naval bo'sun would.

'*Mr* Stanier, our new navigator, and that's his boy.' McTiernan's soft voice laid mocking emphasis on the title. 'Give him the guest cabin, seeing as how we have no visitors staying with us.'

'What does he mean, guest cabin?' Clem whispered, bemused by the captain's chuckle.

'Hostages. You need to keep them in reasonable condition—the ones you expect a great deal of money for, at any rate.' And if you didn't expect money for them, you amused yourself by hacking them to pieces until the decks ran scarlet and then fed the sharks with the remains. He thought he would refrain from explaining why McTiernan was nicknamed *Red*. Time enough for the boy to realise exactly what he had got himself into.

The cabin was a good one, almost high enough for Nathan to stand upright, with a porthole, two fixed bunks and even the luxury of a miniscule compartment containing an unlovely bucket, another porthole and a ledge for a tin basin.

Clem poked his head round the door and emerged grimacing. Amused, Nathan remarked, 'Keeping that clean is part of your job. Better than the shared heads, believe me.' It seemed the lad was finicky, despite the fact he couldn't have been used to any better at home. 'Come with me, we'll find some food, locate the salt-water pump.' He lifted the lantern and hooked it on to a peg in the central beam. Clem blinked and half-turned away. 'How did your face get in that mess?'

'My uncle hit me.' There was anger vibrating under the words; perhaps the boy wasn't as passive as he seemed.

'You stay with me, as much as possible. When you are not with me, try to stay out on the open deck, or in here; don't be alone with anyone else until we know them better. You understand?' A shake of the head. Damn, an innocent who needed things spelled out. 'There are no women on the ship. For some of the crew that's a problem and you could be the answer.'

Clemence stared at him, feeling the blood ebbing away from her face. They thought she was a boy but even then they'd... Oh, God. And then they'd find she was a girl and then... 'That's what the captain meant when he said he wouldn't deprive you of your pleasures,' she said, staring appalled at her rescuer. 'He thinks you—'

'He's wrong,' Stanier said shortly and her stomach lurched

back into place with relief. 'Lads hold no attraction for me whatsoever; you are quite safe here, Clem.'

She swallowed. That was an entirely new definition of *safe*. Whatever this man was, or was not, the fact remained that he was voluntarily sailing with one of the nastiest pirate crews in the West Indies. His calm confidence and size might provoke a desire to wrap her arms around him and hang on for grim life, but her judgement was clouded by fear, she knew that. When the rivers flooded you saw snakes and mice, cats and rats all clinging to a piece of floating vegetation, all too frightened of drowning to think of eating each other. Yet.

'Right.' She nodded firmly. *Concentrate.* She had to keep up this deception, please this man so she kept his protection—and watch like a hawk for a chance of escape.

'Are you hungry? No? Well, I am. Come along.' She followed him out, resisting the urge to hang on to his coat tails. As a child she'd had the run of her father's ships in port, sliding down companionways, hanging out of portholes, even climbing the rigging. This ship was not any different, she realised, as they made their way towards the smell of boiling meat, except that the crew were not well-disciplined employees, but dangerous, feral scum.

They located the galley mid-ship, the great boiler sitting on its platform of bricks, the cook looming out of the savoury steam, ladle in hand, meat cleaver stuck in his straining belt like a cutlass. 'You want any vittles, you'll wait to the morning.'

'I am Mr Stanier, navigator, and you will find food for my servant and me. Now.'

The man stared back, then nodded. 'Aye, sir.'

'And as we're in port, I assume you'll have had fresh provisions loaded. I'll have meat, bread, butter, cheese, fruit, ale. What's your name?'

'Street, sir.'

'Then get a move on, Street.' He looked at Clemence. 'Wake up, boy. Find a tray, platters. Look lively.'

Clemence staggered back to the cabin under the weight of a tray laden with enough food, in her opinion, for six, and dumped it on to the table that ran down the centre of their cabin. Stanier stood, stooping to look out of the porthole, while she set out the food and his platter, poured ale and then went to perch on the edge of the smaller bunk bed, built to follow the curve of the ship's side.

What was he staring at? She tried to retrieve some sense of direction and decided he was looking out at the wreckage of old Port Royal, although what there was to see there on a moonless night—

'Why aren't you eating?' He had turned and was frowning at her.

'I ate before…before I left.'

'Well, eat more, you are skin and bones.' She opened her mouth. 'That's an order. Get over here, sit down and eat.'

'This isn't the navy,' Clemence said, then bit her lip and did as she was told.

'No, that is true enough.' Stanier grinned, the first sign of any real amusement she had seen from him. It was not, now she came to think about it, a very warm smile. It exposed a set of excellent teeth and crinkled the skin at the corners of his eyes attractively enough, but the blue eyes were watchful. 'What's happened to *sir*?'

'Sorry, sir.' She slid on to the three-legged stool and tried to recall how her young male friends had behaved at table. Like a flock of gannets, mostly. 'I haven't got a knife, sir. Sorry.'

'Have you got a handkerchief?' Stanier enquired, then did smile, quite genuinely, when Clemence shook her head in puzzlement. With an effort she kept her mouth closed. When he smiled, he looked… She hauled some air down into her lungs and tried not to gawp like a complete looby. Thankfully he had his back to her, rummaging in one of the canvas kit bags piled in the corner of the cabin. He turned back, holding out a clasp knife and a spotted handkerchief. 'There.'

'Thank you.' She tucked the handkerchief in the neck of her shirt as a bib and unfolded the knife, trying not to imagine sitting next to him at a dinner party, both of them in evening dress, flirting a little. And then walking out on to the terrace and perhaps flirting a little more… Which was ridiculous. She never flirted, she had never wanted to.

'You should carry that knife all the time. Can you use it?' Stanier speared a thick slice of boiled mutton, laid it on a slab of bread and attacked it with concentration.

'On a man? Er…no.' Clemence thought about Lewis. 'But I probably could if I was frightened enough.'

'Good,' he said, swallowing and reaching for his ale. 'Go on, eat.'

'I thought I'd wait for you, sir. You're hungry.' He was eating like a man half-starved.

'I am. First food for forty-eight hours.' Stanier cut a wedge of cheese and pushed the rest towards her.

'Why, sir?' Clemence cut some and discovered that she could find a corner still to fill.

'Pockets to let,' he said frankly. 'If this hadn't come along, I'd have been forced to do an honest day's work.'

'Well, this certainly isn't one,' Clemence snapped before she could think.

'Indeed?' In the swaying lantern light the blue eyes were watchful over the rim of the horn beaker. 'You're very judgmental, young Clem.'

'Pirates killed my father, took his ship.' She ducked her head, tried to sound young and sullen. It wasn't hard.

'I see. And you ended up with Uncle who knocked you around, eh?' He leaned across the table and put his fingers under her chin, tilting her face up so he could see the bruises. 'Heard the expression about frying pans and fires, Clem?'

'Yessir.' She resisted the impulse to lean her aching face into his warm, calloused hand. It was only that she was tired and frightened and anxious and wanted someone to hold her, tell her it was all going to be all right. But of course it wasn't going to be all right and this man was not the one to turn to for comfort, either. Something stirred inside her, the faint hope that there might be someone, somewhere, she could trust one day. She was getting tired—beyond tired—and maudlin. All she could rely on was herself.

Stanier seemed to have stopped eating, at last.

'I'll take these plates back.'

'No, you won't. You're not wandering about this ship at night until you know your way around.' He took the tray from her. 'Look in that bag there, you'll find sheets.'

It was a fussy pirate who carried his clean linen with him, Clemence thought, stumbling sleepily across to open the bag. But sure enough, clean sheets there were, even if they were threadbare and darned. She covered the lumpy paliasses, flapped another sheet over the top, rolled up blankets for pillows and then shut herself into the odorous little cubicle. If she did nothing else tomorrow, she was going to find a scrubbing brush and attack this.

But privacy, even smelly privacy, would perhaps save her. She couldn't imagine how she would have survived otherwise in a ship full of men. Clemence managed to wedge open the porthole to let in the smell of the sea, then emerged. Water and washing would have to wait; all she wanted now was sleep and to wake up to find this had all been an unpleasant dream.

Could she get into bed, or would Stanier want her to do anything else? She was dithering when he came back in. 'I am not, thank God,' he remarked, 'expected to stand watch tonight. Bed, young Clem.' He regarded Clemence critically. 'No soap, no toothbrush, no clean linen, either. I'll have to see what we can find you in the morning. I don't imagine going to bed unwashed and in his shirt ever troubled a boy, though.'

'No, sir.' Clemence thought longingly of her deep tub, of Castile soap and frangipani flowers floating in the cool water. Of a clean bed and deep pillows and smiling, soft-footed servants holding out a drifting nightgown of snowy lawn.

Stanier sat down on the edge of his bunk and shed his coat, then his waistcoat and began to unbutton his shirt. The air seemed to vanish from her lungs. He was going to strip off here and now and... He stood up and she bent to pull off her shoes as though someone had tugged a string.

She risked a peek up through her fringe. He was still standing there, she could see his feet. There wasn't anything else she could take off while he was there... Belt. Yes, she could unbuckle that. Out of the corner of her eye she could see him heeling off his shoes. One foot vanished, he must have put it on the bunk to roll down his stocking. Yes. A bare foot appeared, the other vanished.

'What are you doing, boy?'

'Buckle's tight,' she mumbled.

'Need any help?'

'No!' It came out as a strangled squawk. Thank goodness, he was going into the privy cupboard. As the door closed Clemence hauled off her trousers and dived under the sheet, yanking it up over her nose.

The door creaked. He was coming out. Clemence pulled

the sheet up higher and pretended to be asleep. Drawn by some demon of curiosity, she opened her eyes a fraction and looked through her lashes. Stanier was stark naked, his breeches grasped in one hand. She bit her tongue as she stifled a gasp. He tossed the clothes on to a chair, then stood, running one hand through his hair, apparently deep in thought.

She should close her eyes, she knew that, but still she stared into the shifting shadows, mesmerised. Long legs, defined muscles, slim hips, flat stomach bisected by the arrow of hair running down from his chest. Clemence's eyes followed it, down to the impressively unequivocal evidence that she was sharing a cabin with a man. She had known that, she told herself. Of course she had. It was just seeing him like this, so close, so male, made it very difficult to breathe.

It was not as though she was ignorant, either. She had swum with her childhood playmates in the pools below the waterfalls, but this was no pre-pubescent boy. In a slave-owning society you saw naked adults, too, but you averted your eyes from the humiliating treatment of another human being. She shouldn't be staring now, but Stanier seemed so comfortable with his own body, so relaxed in his nudity, that she doubted he would dive for his breeches if he realised she was awake. Only, he did not know she was a woman, of course.

'Asleep, boy?' he asked softly.

Clemence screwed her eyes shut, mumbled and turned over, hunching her shoulders. Behind, she heard his amused chuckle. 'You'd better not snore.'

Nathan eyed the bunk. The lad had made it up tidily enough, but sleep did not beckon. In fact, he felt uncomfortably awake, which was a damnable nuisance, given that he was going to need to be alert and on his guard at daybreak to take *Sea Scorpion* out of harbour and on to whatever course McTiernan wanted. Knowing the man's reputation, he would set something tricky, as a test.

He found the thick notebook in his old leather satchel and climbed into bed with it. From the opposite bunk came the sound of soft breathing. And what the hell was he doing, acquiring someone else to take care of when he had his own skin to worry about?

Nathan set himself to study the notes he had made on the area a hundred miles around Jamaica. He had not been bragging when he had told McTiernan that he was the best navigator in these waters: he probably was. In theory.

He did not underestimate his own strengths, his depth of knowledge, his experience in most of the great oceans of the world. The problem was, the Caribbean was not one of them and he knew that two months spent weaving through their treacherous waters making endless notes was not enough. Not nearly enough. At which point he became aware of the nagging heaviness in his groin and finally realised just why he was so restless.

What the hell was that about? And why? He had more than enough on his mind to drive any thought of women from it, and in any case, he'd hardly seen a female all evening, so there should be no inconvenient image in the back of his mind to surface and tease him.

The flash of dark eyes and black hair, the remembered lush curves of his late wife, presented themselves irresistibly to his mind. Nathan shifted impatiently. He thought he had learned not to think about Julietta; besides, lust was no longer the emotion those thoughts brought with them.

The recollection of Clem's slim, ink-stained fingers gripping his thigh rose up to replace that of Julietta's hands caressing down his body. Nathan shifted abruptly in the bed in reflexive rejection. For God's sake! He was as bad as this crew, if that was the cause of his discomfort.

From across the cabin came an odd sound—Clem was grinding his teeth in his sleep. Nathan grinned, contemplating hefting a shoe at the sleeping boy. No, he could acquit himself of that particular inclination—it must simply be an odd reaction to finding himself in the most dangerous situation in all his thirty years. The thought of straightforward danger was somehow soothing. Nathan put the book under his pillow, extinguished the lantern and fell asleep.

Chapter Three

'**W**ake up!'

Clemence blinked into the gloom of the cabin, momentarily confused. Where...? Memory came back like a blow and she scrabbled at the sheet twisted around her legs. It was, thankfully, still covering her from the waist down and her shirt shrouded the rest of her.

Stanier was tucking his shirt into his breeches. She felt the colour flood up into her face at the memory of last night, then found herself watching as his bare chest vanished as he did up the buttons, long brown fingers dextrous despite his speed. As if she was not in enough trouble without finding herself physically drawn to the man! She had never felt that before, but then she had never been rescued by a tough, attractive man before either, which probably accounted for it. Whatever the explanation, it was not a comfortable sensation. Surprising areas of her insides seemed to be involved in the reaction.

'Come on, look lively!' So, now she had to get out of bed, find her breeches and get into the cubby hole, all under Stanier's, admittedly uninterested, gaze. She tugged at the shirt, which came to just above her knees, slid out from under the sheet, scooped up her trousers and edged round the table.

'You are far too thin.'

She whisked into the cupboard and shut the door. Enough light came through the porthole to see the bucket, but of course, there was still no water to wash in. 'Things were difficult since my father died,' she said through the thin panels, fumbling with the fastenings on her trousers and tightening her belt. Thinking about her father, she felt reality hit her. Pirates had taken *Raven Duchess*, killing her father as surely as if they had knifed him, and now here she was, not only in their hands, but feeling grateful to a man who was as good as one himself. She'd had some excuse last night, she had hardly been herself. Now, after a night's sleep, she should face reality.

He *was* a pirate. She had seen him accept the position with her own eyes, heard him state his terms to McTiernan. So he was just as bad as the rest of the crew and deserved a fate as severe as theirs should be. Clemence opened the door and stepped out, jaw set.

'I'm sorry about your father.' Stanier was coatless, a long jerkin, not unlike her own waistcoat, pulled on over his shirt. 'Do you know which ship it was that attacked his?'

Clemence shrugged, combing her hair into some sort of order with her fingers. They had never discovered who had been responsible. The one survivor, found clinging to a spar, was too far gone to communicate, even if his tongue had not been cut out.

Her face felt greasy, she was sticky and sweaty under the linen bindings around her chest and there was grit between her toes. 'Could have been this one for all I know,' she said, having no trouble sounding like a sulky boy.

'I hope not,' Stanier said.

'Why should you care? You're one of them,' she pointed out, too angry with him and his casual sympathy to be cautious.

'True.' She had expected anger in return, even a cuff for her insolence, but he looked merely thoughtful. 'There are degrees of piracy.'

'Like degrees of murder?' Clemence retorted. 'Anyway, you've chosen to sail with the absolute scum of the seas, so that makes it first-degree piracy.'

'You're outspoken, lad.' Stanier came round the table and took her chin in one hand, tipping up her face so he could study it. 'I wonder you dare.'

'I don't care if you *are* angry. Things can't get much worse.'

'Oh, they can, believe me,' Stanier said softly, tilting her head, his fingers hard on her jawbone. 'Is that eye paining you much?'

'Only when someone hits it,' Clemence said, contemplating struggling, then deciding it was certain to be futile. He was too close, far too close for comfort. She could smell him, his sweat. Not the rank odour of the habitually unwashed crew, but the curiously arousing scent of a man who was usually clean, but was now hot and musky from bed. Goosebumps ran up her spine.

'Well, if you want to avoid that, you can go and find me some coffee and bread.' Did he really mean it? Would he hit her if she displeased him? Of course he would, he thought her just a troublesome boy and boys were always getting beaten. 'Then bring it up on deck. It'll be dawn soon.' He picked up a telescope from the bunk and fitted it into a long pocket in his jerkin, then dropped a watch into another. 'Here, take this and remember what I said about staying out of trouble.'

Clemence caught the clasp knife that was tossed to her,

fumbling the catch. Stanier frowned, his gaze sharpening. 'It's this eye,' she said defensively, recalling her playmates' jibes that she *caught like a girl*. 'I can't see out of it properly.' Then he was gone and she could hold on to the end of the table, ridiculously shaken.

Toughen up, she told herself fiercely. *Think like a boy.* Which was easier said than done, given that all her treacherous feminine instincts were telling her quite the opposite whenever Stanier was close. The knife fastened to her belt, she made her way to the galley. Instinctively, she kept her head down, trying to make herself as small and inconspicuous as possible, until she found she was being stared at curiously. Perhaps looking like a victim was not a good idea in the middle of this crew, used to preying on the weak.

Clemence arrived at the galley, head up, shoulders back, practising a swagger. She conjured up Georgy Phillips, the leader of her gang of childhood male friends. He would love this adventure. He was welcome to it.

'Mr Street? I've come for Mr Stanier's coffee. And something to eat.' There was bacon frying, she could smell it. 'Some bacon.'

'That's for the captain.' But the cook said it amiably enough, slopping a black liquid that might have been coffee into a mug.

'But there's lots of it. And Mr Stanier's to have what he wants, the captain said so.' Street was hardly likely to check, and it seemed that Stanier had got what he'd demanded as a price to sail with them.

'Did he now?' Street shoved a piece of plank with bread on it towards her. There wouldn't be any of that once they were at sea and the land-bought supplies went stale. 'Go on, then. You want some coffee, too, boy?'

'Please, sir.' Clemence was pretty certain that the cook

didn't warrant a *sir*, but a bit of crawling did no harm. She carved off four thick slices of bread and slipped round behind the man to layer bacon between them, dribbling on the rich melted fat for good measure. Street let her take a pewter plate, then watched, a gap-toothed grin on his face, as she juggled two mugs of coffee and the food.

'Don't drop it, boy, you'll not wheedle any more out of me,' he warned.

'Nossir, thank you, sir.' Now she had to find her way on deck, up at least two companionways, with her hands full. At least they were still at anchor; she would soon have to do this sort of thing with the ship pitching and tossing.

She made it with the loss of half a mug of coffee when one hand made a grab for the food as she passed him and she had to duck and run. Muttering, she regarded her coffee-stained trousers with resignation, and climbed out of the hatch on to deck.

It was a scene of apparent chaos, but she had seen enough ships preparing to make sail to know this all had a purpose. The light was waxing now, she could see the length of the deck and the lamps were extinguished. With the plate clutched protectively close to her chest, Clemence negotiated the steep steps up to the poop deck and found Stanier deep in conversation with the tall, oddly neat man with the pale blue eyes. The one who had hit her. Mr Cutler, the first mate.

They had a chart spread out on the raised hatch cover of the stern cabin and were studying it. As Clemence came up behind them, Stanier straightened. 'I agree, that's the best course if you aren't concerned about speed.'

'Are you suggesting there's a faster way?'

Stanier extended one finger and indicated something Clemence could not see. The sight of that long digit, the one that had traced a question down her bruised cheek, made her shift uncomfortably.

'That's a dangerous passage, too big a risk.' Cutler shook his head.

'Not if you hit it at just the right time.' Stanier began to roll up the chart. 'How much speed do you need? Are you chasing something or just patrolling?'

'Best pickings have got over twelve hours' start on us, there's no catching the *Raven Princess* now.' Clemence almost dropped the food. 'But if you've got the knack of that passage, then the captain will be glad to see it.'

'That's what I thought. And it brings you out in the shelter of Lizard Island. You've got good anchorage, fresh water and command of the shipping lanes through there. And you never know, *Raven Princess* might have been delayed. Too good not to check, I'd have thought.'

Bastard! 'Your coffee, Mr Stanier.' She thrust the mug into his hand, forcing him to grasp the heated metal, and was gratified by his wince as he snatched at the handle. He deserved it. That was *her* ship he was talking about capturing. 'And some bread and bacon. Sir.'

He looked at her narrowly over the rim of the mug as he blew on his coffee. 'That all for me?'

'Yessir.'

'Take your knife and cut it up. Take half and eat it.'

'You'll spoil the brat.' The mate's lip lifted in a sneer.

'He's half-starved and no use to me unless he's fit.' Stanier gave a dismissive, one-shouldered shrug. 'Clem, eat and then go and get that cabin shipshape. You can unpack everything, just don't drop the instruments.'

Clemence found a corner on the main deck and curled up with her breakfast on top of a low stack of barrels, safely out of the way of the hurrying hands. Just when she had started liking the man, he turned out to be as bad as the rest of them. She shook her head abruptly; it was a lesson not to trust any of them. Ever.

Despite her feelings, she could still enjoy the food. The bacon was good, still warm, savoury, the bread soaked with salty grease. She scrubbed the back of her hand across her mouth, then wiped her palms on her trousers without thinking. The resulting mess—smears of ink, coffee, grease and dust—was unpleasant, but she could hardly change her clothes.

Street was surprisingly helpful when she returned her crocks. 'Ship's sail-maker's over there. Doubles as tailor, for them as wants it.' He nodded towards a man sitting cross-legged on a pile of rolled hammocks. 'Hey, Gerritty! Navigator's boy needs slops.'

The tailor squinted at Clemence. 'Look in that chest, see what'll fit,' he said through a mouthful of big needles, his accent a thick Irish brogue. 'I'm not making you anything, mind, not wasting my time on boys.'

'Thank you.' The trunk held a motley collection, some of it quality, some of it sailors' gear. Clemence had the uncomfortable feeling that most of it had been taken from captives. She found two pairs of trousers that looked as though she could take them in to fit, some shirts, a jacket and a warm knitted tunic. 'May I take these?'

'Aye.' The sail-maker produced an evil-looking knife and cut some twine. 'He any good, this new navigator?'

Clemence shrugged. 'Don't know. He only took me on yesterday. Talks like he is.' The Irishman snorted at her tone. 'Where can I get a bucket and a scrubbing brush?'

She wasn't looking forward to tackling the privy cupboard, but she wasn't prepared to live with it either. She was uncomfortably aware that if life had not favoured her with the wealth to keep servants, then she would have made a very reluctant housekeeper, but some hard cleaning was preferable to squalor, any day of the week.

It took her half an hour to locate cleaning materials, dodging some rough teasing on the way. On her way down to the cabin she collected a second lantern by the simple expedient of stealing it from another cabin, then started by washing the portholes and cleaning the lamps. She made the beds, glancing with interest at the thick leather-bound notebook under Stanier's pillow, but cautiously left it untouched, unpacked his bags and set the instruments out on the table with care.

They were shiny, complex and obviously expensive. She raised the fiddles around the sides of the table in case the instruments slid about and eyed them, fascinated. Perhaps he would show her how they worked.

The rest of his gear she stowed in the lockers. It was good quality stuff, but well worn and included, she was thankful to see, a huswif with thread and needles. At least she could alter her new clothes herself.

And that just left the privy. Clemence had an idea how to deal with that.

They were out of harbour, the island receding behind them, the breeze stiff and steady, the sun on the waves, dazzling. It was a day when it felt good to be at sea, even without the relief of having piloted the ship out under the hypercritical gaze of Cutler and Captain McTiernan, who lounged with deceptive casualness against a raised hatch cover.

'What's going on down there?' Cutler craned to see where a group were clustered round the rail, peering at something in the sea. Laughter floated up.

'I'll take a look.' Nathan stretched, glad of an excuse to

shake the tension out of his shoulders. 'I need to get my sextant, anyway.'

He assessed the mood of the group as he approached it. They were having fun, probably at someone's expense, but it was good humoured enough. 'What's up?' He shouldered his way to the rail, the hands dropping back, tugging forelocks when they saw who it was. McTiernan's crew were worryingly well disciplined.

Hell. 'Clem, what the devil are you doing?' The boy leant over the rail, a rope in his hands, the muscles on his slim forearms standing out with the effort. His trousers were filthy, he had bound the handkerchief Nathan had given him around his forehead and he looked a complete urchin with smudges on his face and grime up his arms.

Except that there was an elegance about the line of his back, the arched feet, braced on the deck, were small, the backside exposed by the shirt riding up was rounded and the skin below his collar was unexpectedly delicate.

Blinking away a sudden sensation of complete confusion, Nathan snapped, 'Clem!'

'Sorry, sir.' He was hauling at whatever it was now and it rose up suddenly, landed on the deck and showered them all with water. 'That bucket, sir. Seemed the easiest way to clean it.'

It was, certainly, a very clean bucket. Angry, for no reason he could determine, Nathan narrowed his eyes at the flushed, bruised face that met his gaze with a look of eager willingness that was surely false. Nathan had dealt with dumb insolence often enough to recognise it now.

'Look at the state of you, boy. I'll not have a servant that looks like a swine-herd.'

'I'll go and change, sir.'

The boy was angry, he realised with a jolt. Angry with him.

Was he still brooding on Nathan's role on a pirate ship? Well, he was going to have to accept it, pretty damned quickly.

'Go,' he said with a jerk of his head, not realising until Clem and the bucket had vanished that the boy had nothing to change into. But that was not his problem—navigating this ship to place it in the best possible position for some fat merchantman to sail right into its jaws was. That was his job.

When he came down to the cabin over an hour later he was hit by light, air and the tang of salt water and lye soap. The cabin was spotless, the inner door standing open on to what had been a fetid little cubby hole and was now clean and dimly lit with the light from the open porthole.

A water tub stood on the floor, his mirror and shaving tackle were on the shelf, a towel dangled from a nail and a cloth was draped decorously over the bucket.

Clem was sitting at the table with a large bodkin, some twine and a pile of newspapers. 'What are you doing now?' Nathan demanded.

In response, Clem lifted his hand. Neat squares of newspaper were threaded onto the twine. 'For the privy,' he said concisely. 'I found the newspaper by the galley range.'

'My God.' Nathan stared round a cabin that would have done a post captain proud. 'You'll make someone a wonderful wife, Clem.'

As soon as he said it he could have bitten his tongue out. The boy went scarlet, his expression horrified. 'Damn it, I was teasing, I don't mean… I don't mean what I was warning you about last night. The other men, if they see this, will just think you're a good servant.'

'Well, I did it for me, too,' Clem retorted. 'I've got to live here as well. I don't enjoy cleaning,' he added with a grimace.

'No. And you aren't used to it, either, are you?' Nathan

spun a chair round and straddled it, arms along the back as he studied the flushed and indignant face opposite him. 'When you are angry, that lilting local accent vanishes completely. You've been educated, haven't you, Clem? You're from quite a respectable family.'

'I—' There was no point in lying about it. Clemence bent her head, letting her hair fall over her face, and mumbled, 'Yes. I went to school in Spanish Town. My father was a merchant, just in a small way.'

'So the loss of your ship was a blow? Financially, I mean?'

She nodded, her mind working frantically to sort out a story that was as close to the truth as she could make it. Fewer risks of slipping up later, that way. 'My uncle took everything that was left. He claims he's looking after it, as my guardian.' Indignation made her voice shake. 'I didn't feel safe any more, so I got a berth on the *Raven Princess*, in secret. Only she sailed early.'

'Couldn't you have gone to the Governor?' Stanier asked.

'The Governor? You have no idea, have you? No idea at all what it's like being a—' She stopped, appalled at what she had almost said.

'A what, Clem?' He was watching her like a hawk, she realised, risking a glance up through the fringe of ragged hair.

'A small merchant's son. Someone with no influence. Sir,' she added, somewhat belatedly.

'I think we can drop the *sir*, in here at least. My name is Nathan.' Clemence nodded, not trusting herself to speak yet, not after that near-disaster. 'So, we know about you now. What do you make of me, Clem?'

Make of him? What should she say? That he was probably the most disturbingly male creature she had ever come across? That she probably owed him her life, but that she could not trust him one inch? That she admired his style, but despised his morals?

'I think,' she said slowly, returning with care to her island lilt, 'that you are a gentleman and I know that you were once in the navy, if what McTiernan said yesterday evening in the tavern is true. And it would seem to fit with your character.'

The unthinking natural arrogance of command, for one thing. But she couldn't put it like that. 'You are used to giving orders, your kit is very good quality, even if it is quite worn. There's a broad arrow stamped on some of the instrument cases, so they were government issue once.'

Stanier—Nathan—nodded. 'You're right, Clem.' Something inside her warmed at the praise, despite the pride that was telling her she wanted nothing from him, least of all his good opinion. 'Yes, I'm the younger son of a gentleman and, yes, I was in the navy.'

'What happened?' Intrigued now, she shook back her hair and sat up straighter, watching his face. Something shadowed, dark, moved behind those blue eyes and the lines at the corners of his mouth tightened.

'I was given the opportunity to resign.'

'Oh.' There really wasn't any tactful way of asking. 'Why?'

'A little private enterprise here, a little bloody-minded insubordination there, a duel.'

'A duel?' Clemence stared. 'I thought naval officers weren't allowed to duel.'

'Correct.' Nathan's mouth twisted into a wry smile, but the bleakness behind his eyes spoke of complex emotion.

'Did you kill him?'

He shook his head and she felt unaccountably relieved. 'No, I did not.' It would be a horrible thing to have to live with—but why should she worry about the spiritual health of a King's officer turned pirate?

'Then what happened?'

'You can imagine how well that went down with my family. It was felt that my absence would be the best way of dealing with the situation. So I found employment here and there, legal and perhaps not quite so legal, and ended up in Kingston with no ship and no money.'

'Why are you telling me all this?' she asked. Instinct told her that Nathan Stanier was a proud, private man. He could not be enjoying sharing the details of his disgrace and penury with a scrubby youth rescued from the dockside.

'They say that a man has no secrets from his valet, and you are the nearest to one of those I'm likely to have for a while. You might as well know the worst about me from the outset.' He got up in a smooth movement that seemed to mask barely controlled emotion. Shame? she wondered. Or just anger at the situation he found himself in?

She could feel herself slipping closer and closer to letting her guard down with him and that, she knew, could be fatal. 'But I knew the worst about you already,' she pointed out, hauling herself back from the brink of blurting out who, and what, she was, casting herself onto that broad chest and giving up fighting. 'I knew you have taken McTiernan's money and that makes you a pirate. I really can't think of anything worse. Can you?'

Chapter Four

Nathan spun round on his heel and stared at her. 'For a bright lad, you've a reckless tongue,' he remarked, his voice mild. His eyes, bleak, belied his tone utterly. 'Yes, I can think of worse things. Betrayal and treachery for two.' Then he laughed, sending a shiver down her spine. 'But you're right, they don't get much worse than this crew, I suspect, and now we're part of it.'

'Well, *I* didn't volunteer,' Clemence said bitterly.

'No, and I didn't save your ungrateful skin from that pack of jackals in order to get self-righteous lectures from you either, brat. So keep your lip buttoned, Clem, or I'll tan your breeches for you.'

She subsided, instantly. Let him think she was terrified of a beating; better that than have him lay hands on her. The vision of herself turned over Nathan Stanier's knee and that broad palm descending on her upturned buttocks made her go hot and cold all over. There was no way, surely, that he could fail to notice that she was a girl if that happened.

'I'll go and get our dinner, shall I?' she offered, by way of a flag of truce.

'I'm eating with the captain and Cutler.' Nathan was shrugging into his coat. Old naval respect for a captain must be engrained, Clemence thought dourly, if he felt he had to tidy himself up for that scum.

'Will they tell you where we are going?' she asked. If they docked at a harbour on one of the other islands, surely she could slip ashore?

'Hunting,' Nathan said. 'And not from a harbour, if that's what you are hoping for. McTiernan's got a hideaway, and I can show him a shortcut to get to it. Now, enough questions. Are you going to eat properly, if I'm not there to nag you?'

Disarmed by his concern, she smiled. Life was so complicated. It would be much easier if it was black and white, if he was an out-and-out villain, but he wasn't and liking, gratitude and the disconcerting tingle of desire kept undermining her certainty. 'Yes, I promise. I'm hungry after all that work.' Nathan was staring at her. 'What is it?'

'That bruise is getting worse,' he said abruptly. 'It looks… odd. You're all right otherwise? You're not seasick?'

'In this weather? No. I don't know what I would be like in a storm, though. My father used to take me on short sea journeys with him. The crews were very good, they'd let me go anywhere, even though I was a—a child,' she finished hastily.

The moment he was gone, she went to look at her reflection in his shaving mirror. Yes, her face was black, blue and purple on one side and still swollen. Her hair was lank and she plucked at it, wondering whether to wash it. It was horrible like this, but on the other hand it helped her disguise, and that was the most important thing. Clemence fished the bandana out of her back pocket and tied it round her forehead again, pulling it one way, then another for effect.

Then the irony of it struck her. Here she was, prinking and posing in front of a mirror, trying to make herself look as unfeminine and unattractive as possible, when all the time she should be on her way to England, to her aunt Amelia the Duchess of Allington, stepmother to the present duke, who was to give her some town bronze before her come-out next Season. They'd have the letter by now, telling them of her father's death, of her own *ill health*.

She should be in the luxury of her own cabin on a large merchantman, practising flirting with the officers and worrying that she did not have pretty enough gowns in her luggage.

A proper young lady in this situation should be in a state of collapse, not scrubbing out privies, swaggering about with a knife and sharing a cabin with an attractive, dangerous, good-for-nothing rogue. Depressingly, this proved she was not a proper young lady. On the other hand, if she was, she would still be in the Naismiths' power. Better to be a skinny tomboy and alive.

Clemence gave the bandana one last tweak and headed for the galley, her stomach rumbling with genuine hunger as it had not done for weeks.

Street was ladling an unpleasant-looking grey slop into four buckets. Clemence wrinkled her nose, hung back and hoped this was not dinner.

'There, that'll do for 'em.' The cook gestured to the two hands who were waiting. 'They got water?'

'Enough,' one of the men said, spitting on the deck close to Clemence's feet. 'Waste of space, the lot of them. Not worth nothing.'

'If the captain says keep 'em, we keep 'em,' Street said, his voice a warning growl. 'He's got his reasons. You check the water and let me know if they're sickening. I'm not taking a lashing for you if you let any of them die.'

'Yeah, yeah,' the man grumbled, hefting a couple of buckets and shuffling off, followed by his mate.

'Mr Street?' Clemence ventured. 'I've come for my dinner, sir.' The cook waved a bloodstained hand towards a rather more savoury-looking cauldron of stew. He seemed out of temper, but not with her, so she ventured, 'Are there prisoners on board?'

'None of your business, lad.' He swung round to glower at her. 'You keep your nose out of things that don't concern you if you want to keep a whole hide. And don't go down to the orlop deck, either. You hear?'

'Yes, Mr Street.' The orlop deck? Why mention that? It was the very lowest deck, below the waterline where the cables were stowed. There would be no cabins down there, just dark holds with bilge water, rats and darkness; it would never have occurred to her to visit it. The cook went back to wielding his meat cleaver on a leg of pork, so she took bread to sop up the stew, poured some of the thin ale into a tankard and retreated to her refuge on top of the barrels.

The stew was better than she had expected and her appetite sharper, but Clemence spooned the gravy into her mouth absently, her eyes unfocused on the expanse of blue stretching out to the horizon. If there were captives down on the orlop deck, then they would be common seamen, she assumed, otherwise, if they had any value, they would be up in a proper cabin being kept alive with some care.

And if they were seamen, then some of them might be men from *Raven Duchess*. She stared down at the planking, scrubbed white by constant holystoning, the tar bubbling between the joints in the heat. Somewhere down there below, in foul darkness, could be men in her employ, men who'd been kept prisoner for six months. Men she was responsible for.

'Then lay in the course you suggest through the channel, Mr Stanier. We'll take it at first light.' It was Captain McTiernan, Nathan at his side, Cutler behind them. All three men had their hands clasped behind their backs, just as she had seen her father pacing with his captains. It seemed impossible that pirates would behave in the same everyday way, but the more she saw, the more she realised they were not bogeymen out of a children's storybook, they were real men operating in the real world. Their work just happened to be evil.

Instinct made her wriggle down amongst the barrels as though she could hide in some crevice, then common sense stopped her. It was not safe to cringe and cower; if McTiernan saw her, he might assume she was spying on him. As they drew level she wiped her crust round the tin plate and drained her tankard with an appearance of nonchalance, despite the fact that her heart was thudding against her ribs.

McTiernan stopped, bracketed by the two men, and looked at her. Clemence stared back, trying, without much difficulty, to look suitably nervous and humble. His eyes were flat, without emotion, staring at her as though she was no more, nor less, than one of the casks. Her eyes shifted to the left. Cutler was more obviously assessing—now she knew what a lamb in the slaughterman's yard felt like. She shivered and glanced at Nathan, trying to read the message in the deep blue gaze. Warning or reassurance?

McTiernan blinked, slowly, and she half-expected to see an inner eyelid slide back into place like the lizards that scuttled up every wall in Raven's Hold. Then, without speaking, he turned. Clemence felt the breath *whoosh* out of her lungs just as there was a shout from above.

Everyone looked up. Something was falling. Wedged between the barrels, Clemence tried to wriggle away, then the tail of her shirt caught, jerking her back. She felt a sharp blow to her head and the world erupted into stars.

Minutes passed, or hours. Her head hurt. She was on her back on the deck and above her she could see the captain, staring upwards towards the mast-tops that seemed to circle dizzyingly with the ship's motion. Then someone bent over her. Nathan. The sick tension inside her relaxed; it was all right now. He was here.

'Lie still.' His hand pressed down on her shoulder and she lay back, closing her eyes. Her head hurt abominably, but the warm touch meant she was safe, she reasoned with what parts of her brain still seemed to be working. Something else, her common sense presumably, jabbed her. Nothing was all right, least of all the way she was feeling about this renegade officer.

'Is he dead?' Cutler. *If I'm dead, he'll eat me.* The words whispered in her mind; she was beginning to drift in and out of consciousness.

'No, just stunned. I'll take him below.'

'Flog the bastard.' It was McTiernan, his voice flat calm.

But I haven't done anything, she wanted to shout. *It wasn't my fault!* She shifted, trying to wriggle away, but Nathan's hand curled round and held her.

'Steady, Clem. He's angry with the hand who dropped the fid.' So that was what it was. Her memory produced the image of a heavy wooden spike. Point down it would have killed her.

'Because it hit me?' she murmured. McTiernan was this angry because a cabin boy had been hit on the head?

'No.' Her eyes opened as he knelt, slid one arm under her knees, the other under her back. 'Because it almost hit him.'

Nathan straightened with her in his arms. The world lurched, steadied, to reveal a man on the deck, cowering.

'Fifty. Now.' McTiernan turned on his heel and walked away, leaving the man screaming after him.

'All hands for punishment!' Cutler roared, making her start and try to burrow against the security of Nathan's hard chest.

'I'm taking the lad down,' he said. 'You don't need me

for this and he's no use to me unconscious. I need to check his head.'

Fifty? Fifty lashes? 'That will kill him,' Clemence managed to say. Her view, mercifully, was confined to the open neck of Nathan's shirt, the hollow at the base of his throat, the underside of his jaw. She made herself focus on the satiny texture of the skin, the few freckles, the pucker of a small scar, the way his Adam's apple moved when he swallowed.

'Oh, yes, it most certainly will. Close your eyes, lie still, I've got you.'

Oh, God. He had got her, oh, yes, indeed. The realisation of her danger thudded through her throbbing headache seconds after Clemence let her head sink gratefully on to his shoulder.

She was closer than she had ever been to Nathan and his hands seemed to be in the places that were most dangerous—the curve of her hip, her tightly strapped ribcage. She couldn't see what had happened to the hem of her long shirt that she had been using to disguise the fact that there were no bulges in her trousers where a boy ought to bulge.

'I'm all right, you can put me down.' She was ignored. Of course, Nathan Stanier took no orders from scrubby boys. He would have to set her on her feet when they got to the companionway though, she reasoned, praying he was not intending to undress her to tuck her up in bed.

But it seemed that Nathan had thought out the logistics of descending steep stairs on a pitching ship with his arms full. He swung her round and hung her over his shoulder, one arm tight around the back of her thighs as he climbed down. 'Sorry if this jars your head, but we'll be down in a minute.' And they were and she was back in his arms almost shaking with the jumble of sensations, fears, emotions that were rattling round her poor aching head.

'There.' He put her down. Clemence opened her eyes and

saw they were in their cabin. This was her bunk, thank goodness. She'd say she wanted to sleep…

But she wasn't safe, not yet. Nathan knelt in front of her, overwhelmingly big on the confined space, and tipped her forward against his chest so he could part her hair and look at her scalp.

'Skin isn't broken, but you'll have a nasty lump.' He didn't seem ready to release her, one hand flat on her back, holding her close, the other running gently through her hair, checking for lumps. Clemence let her forehead rest against his shoulder. Madness. Bliss. All her senses were full of him, his heat, the feel of him, the scent of him, the aura of strength that seemed to flow from him. She could stay like this all day. Safe. She began to drift.

'Clem?' Nathan's voice was puzzled. 'Why the devil are you trussed up like the Christmas goose?'

'Cracked ribs,' she said on a gulp, back in the real world with a vengeance. 'When my uncle hit me. I, er…fell against a table.'

'Rubbish. You'd have yelled the place down just now when I slung you over my shoulder if you'd got cracked ribs.' He slid his hands free and sat back on his heels beside the bunk. Clemence closed her eyes as though that could hide her. She wanted so much to believe he would protect her when he knew her secret, wanted so much, in the midst of this nightmare, to believe there was good in this flawed man. 'Clem, take your shirt off.'

'No.' She opened her eyes and met his, read the questions in them.

'Why not?'

There was nowhere to go, no lie she could think of, no escape. Eyes locked with his, braced for his reaction, Clemence said, 'Because I'm a girl.' And waited.

Silence, then, 'Well, thank God for that,' Nathan said.

'What?' She sat bolt upright, then clutched her head as the cabin swam around her. 'What do you mean, *thank God*?'

Nathan was looking at her with all the usual composure wiped off his face. He seemed a good five years' younger, grinning with what had to be relief. 'Because my body was telling me there was a woman around,' he confessed, running a hand through his hair. 'I kept finding myself staring at you, but I didn't know why. The relief of finding that my dissipated way of life hasn't left me lusting after cabin boys is considerable, believe me. What's your real name?'

'Clemence.' The release of tension on finding that he had not become a slavering monster bent on rapine turned into temper. It was that, or tears. 'And the relief might be considerable for you, but now I am sharing a cabin with a man who knows I am a woman and whose body is most certainly interested in that fact—a piece of information I could well do without, believe me! Forgive me, but *I* was much happier when you were simply confused and uncomfortable.'

'So, you think I am more likely to ravish Clemence than Clem, do you?' He rocked back on his heels and stood up, hands on hips, looking down at her.

She had made him angry again. Clemence lay down cautiously, too dizzy to stay sitting up. 'No, I don't think that. My cousin was going to force me every night until he got me with child and I had to agree to marry him. I may not know you, but I do understand that *you* don't treat people like that. But this...' she waved a hand around the confines of the cabin, the closeness of him, the privy cupboard '...this is not very *comfortable*. Not for a woman alone with a man she doesn't know.'

You wouldn't mistreat people you know as individuals, that is, she qualified to herself. Putting a pirate ship in the way of capturing and plundering merchant vessels and killing their crews, that was another matter. You couldn't tell that sort of thing about people just by looking at them, it seemed.

'My God.' He sat down on the nearest chair. 'No wonder you ran away. Which of them hit you?'

'My uncle. Why?'

'For future reference,' Nathan said grimly. 'This cousin of yours—he didn't—'

'No. I'm too scrawny to interest him at the moment. He was going to fatten me up.' Nathan's growl sent a shiver of pleasure down her spine at the thought of Lewis walking into the cabin and coming up against that formidable pair of fists. 'Are you going to tell anyone about me?'

'Hell, no! If you were in danger when they thought you a boy, you wouldn't be safe for one minute if they knew you are a woman.' He pulled out a chair and sat down out of reach of her, whether for his peace of mind or hers, she couldn't tell. 'How old are you?'

'Nineteen. Twenty in two months' time.'

Nathan's eyebrows went up and he raked one long-fingered hand back through his hair again, reducing it to a boyish tangle. Clemence resisted the urge to get up and comb it straight. 'This gets worse and worse.'

'Why?'

'*Why?* I thought you were fourteen, a child. Now I know you're not—' He stopped, frowning. 'We need to think about the practicalities of this.'

'There aren't any, not really.' Clemence sat up against the hard bulkhead with some caution. 'There's the closet, thank goodness, and now you know who I am I can just ask for privacy when I need it.'

'When are your courses due?' he asked, in such a matter-of-fact manner that she answered him before she had time to be embarrassed.

'Three weeks.' Goodness, she hadn't thought of that.

'Good.' Nathan was pretending to pay careful attention to a knot-hole in the table. 'You are doing very well with the way you move. I guess you know some young lads?'

'I used to run wild with them until I was fourteen,' she confessed. 'What is that noise?' There were no live pigs on board, surely?

'A man screaming,' Nathan said, getting up and slamming both portholes shut. 'Try not to listen.'

'It's him, isn't it? The man who dropped the fid.' Suddenly it was all too much. Somehow she had managed to endure Uncle Joshua's threats, Cousin Lewis's plans for her. She had acted with determination and escaped, stolen a horse without a qualm, kept her head when McTiernan and his men had seized her, coped with two days on a pirate ship and now…

Clemence dragged her sleeve across her eyes and sniffed, trying to hold back the tears.

'Stop it, crying isn't going to help him,' Nathan said abruptly.

'They are killing him by inches, torturing him,' she retorted. 'Can't you do anything?'

'No.'

She half-turned, hunching her shoulder towards him. Of course he was right, there was nothing to be done. It was just that she expected him to work miracles. Oh, damn! Why had he discovered she was female? It weakened her; she was turning to him for help he couldn't give and which she shouldn't expect. The moment she'd decided to escape from Raven's Hold she had taken her own destiny into her hands, however feeble they might prove to be, and now she was reacting like Miss Clemence Ravenhurst, sheltered young lady.

'Clem. *Clemence.*' She shook her head, fighting to try to regain her composure and her independence. 'Oh, come here.' Nathan sat down on the bunk and pulled her rigidly resisting body into his arms. He pressed her unbruised cheek against his chest, muffling her ear into his shirt, and held his palm to the other side of her head so that all she could hear was his heartbeat, the sound of his breathing and the turmoil of her own thoughts.

'Clemence,' he repeated, his voice a rumble in her ear. 'That's an unusual name. But I've heard it before, not all that long ago, either. Can't think where, though.'

'You've had a few other things on your mind,' she suggested, trying to drag her imagination away from what was happening on deck.

Nathan gave a snort of laughter, stirring her hair. 'Yes, just a few.' His hold on her tightened, not unpleasantly. He felt very strong. It was a novelty, being held by a man other than Papa. He'd been one for rapid bear-hugs, her father, impetuous lifts so her feet left the floor as he twirled her round. 'How did you get this thin, Clem? I'd better keep calling you Clem, less risk of a slip.'

'Yes,' she agreed, her lips touching the soft linen of his coarse white shirt as she spoke. A fraction of an inch away was the heat of his skin; she could almost taste it. 'I was always slender. When my father died I didn't feel much like eating; then, when I realised what Uncle Joshua was doing, my appetite vanished all together.' She shivered and felt Nathan's hand caress gently down her swollen cheek.

'They made me eat the night I escaped. Apparently I was so skinny it would be unpleasant for Cousin Lewis to bed with me. He said I was like a boy.' Nathan stiffened and muttered something, but all she could hear was that low growl again. 'That's what gave me the idea. I still had the clothes from when I used to run wild as a child with the local planters' sons.'

'How did you get out?' He was talking to distract her, she thought, grateful for the attempt.

'The house is on a cliff and my room has a balcony over-hanging the sea. I wrote a despairing note to make them think I had thrown myself over and I climbed up the creepers from the balcony, along the ledge just below the roof and then slid down some other roofs. I stole a horse from one of the penns about two miles away.' Nathan made an interrogative noise. 'You'd say farm, I suppose. Or agricultural estate. I threw my clothes and my plait of hair away far from the house. They'll think I'm dead, I hope.'

Clemence felt him lift his head. 'It's over.'

That poor man. He had probably done many awful things himself in the past, but he deserved a fair trial for his crimes, some dignity, not a brutal death for a tiny mistake.

Nathan didn't free her and she did not try to duck out of his embrace. It was an illusion, she knew, but even the illusion of safety, of someone who cared, was enough just now. She felt her body softening, relaxing into his. 'You've got guts. What did you hope to do?' he asked.

'Stow away, get to another island, find work.' The lie slid easily over her tongue without her having to think. However good he was being to her now, if he knew she was a Raven-hurst, guessed at the power and the wealth of her relatives, then she became not a stray he had rescued, but thousands of pounds' worth of hostage.

'And what do you want to do now?' he asked.

'Have a bath,' Clemence answered fervently.

Nathan chuckled, opened his arms and let her sit back upright. 'We could both do with that,' he agreed. Free of his embrace, she could study him. His eyes were not just blue, she realised. There was a golden ring round the iris and tiny flecks of black. As he watched her they seemed to grow darker, more intense. 'I'll have to see what I can organise. It'll be cold water, though.'

She nodded, hardly hearing what he was saying, her eyes searching his face for something she could not define. It felt as though he was still holding her, as though the blow to her head had shifted her thoughts and her perceptions. He knew she was a woman now, and somehow that made her see him differently also.

'Nathan…' Clemence touched his arm, not certain what she was asking, and then he was pulling her into his arms and his mouth took her lips and she knew.

Chapter Five

How had he not realised immediately that Clem was a woman? Every instinct he possessed had been trying to tell him, and a life of near misses had taught him to listen to his instincts. He had been focused on getting into the crew of the *Sea Scorpion* and staying alive while he did so. Perhaps his brain had more sense than his instincts and put survival over sex.

Nathan held himself still, caressing her mouth with his as though she were made of eggshell porcelain. Oh, yes, not a girl but a woman. Young, yes, untouched certainly, but everything that was feminine in her had been in her eyes as she looked at him a moment ago, just as every male impulse was telling him to claim her now.

It was a long time since he had felt like this about a woman. Seven years, in fact. *But that was in another country, and besides, the wench is dead.* He shook himself; now was not the time to be thinking of those dark dramas and the poetry into which he had plunged in the aftermath of the scandal on Minorca.

She was transforming under his hands, that thin body curving into him, her boyish gestures becoming languid and feminine. The strong part of him, the code of honour he had been brought up in, the naval discipline that had formed him and had all but broken him, were enough to stop the animal within from pressing her back on to the hard bunk and taking her, but they were not enough to stop him kissing, holding, inhaling the female scent of her skin. In the brutal masculine world in which he was trapped, that scent was like everything civilised and beautiful.

If he tried to take her now, he probably could. Not because she was wanton, but because she was frightened and he represented all she had of safety. He sensed that in her near collapse into tears and could only admire the way she had summoned up her courage to keep fighting. That alone was enough to restrain him, he realised, sliding his tongue between her lips, sweeping it around to taste her, tease the sensitive tissue. Clem gave a little gasp, her breath hitching, and he lifted his mouth away.

Too much, too soon. *She is so fragile*, Nathan thought, as he ran his thumb gently under the downswept lashes that shielded those big green eyes and feathered her undamaged cheek. Despite her height, her bones felt slender; despite her deceptively boyish appearance, the high cheekbones and pointed chin had a charm that spoke of delicacy.

He couldn't imagine the courage it had taken for her to escape the way she had, the guts she needed to cope and adapt to finding herself here on what must seem a ship from hell.

'I think that cold bath is probably a good thing for any number of reasons,' he said, finding his voice oddly husky.

'I—' She opened her eyes and looked at him. 'What happened?'

'I kissed you.'

'I know that.' She gave him a look part-exasperation, part-amusement, wholly female. 'Why? I mean, why did you stop?'

'Because I shouldn't have started and, having started, I knew damn well I shouldn't continue. I don't seduce virgins, Clem.' *Although one once seduced me.* And now he really had opened a Pandora's box of troubles for himself. He didn't need his imagination any longer to guess how she would be in his arms, he knew. He needed no fantasy to conjure up the sweet softness of her mouth or the taste of her.

Nathan stood up and went to sit on the far side of the table. No reason to let her see just how aroused that insane kiss had made him.

'Thank you,' she said politely, making him smile despite himself. 'But you shouldn't take all the blame. I enjoyed it and I feel better for you holding me. I've missed being hugged,' she added, rather forlornly.

Oh, God! There was nothing he would like more than to hug her. And kiss her. And take off those boy's clothes and unwrap the binding around her small breasts and kiss the soft, compressed curves beneath. And lay her back on that hard bunk and—

'I must go up on deck. I'll tell them I want a tub sent down and some water and they are to be quiet about it because you are very sick from that blow to your head.'

He stood looking down at Clem, fighting the urge to grab her, bundle her into a boat and get away. Which was impossible. There were things he had to do and no one girl was going to prevent him doing them.

Clemence. He said the name in his mind, savouring the sound of it, a sort of fruity sweet tang of a name. Tart and challenging, yet mellow, too. She nodded, watching him. She was thinking hard, he could tell, but those thoughts were hidden. She had learned well in those nightmare weeks at the mercy of her relatives.

'I'll get into bed, pull up the blanket and pretend to be

dozing. When they've gone I'll wedge the latch before I take my bath.'

That did it. The image of Clem standing up, slowly pulling off that shirt, unbinding her breasts, stepping shivering into cold water, her nipples puckering, was so vivid Nathan drew in a deep, racking breath. Her eyes slid down his body, stopped, widened. 'Good idea. I'll knock when I come back.'

Clemence sat staring at the back of the cabin door for some minutes after it had shut abruptly behind Nathan. So, not only was she sharing a cabin with a man she desired and who had discovered she was a woman, but a man who was showing unmistakable evidence of the fact that he desired her, too.

She understood the theory of lovemaking, naturally. But she had never observed the—her mind scrabbled rather wildly for a word—the *mechanism* before. And she had produced that effect on him. The feeling of gratification was something to be ashamed of, she told herself severely.

What would she have done if Nathan had done more than kiss her? Protest or yield? She had a sinking feeling that she would have yielded. No, worse, she would have positively incited him. She had seen those sculpted muscles; now she wanted to caress them.

Shame, confusion, arousal were all uncomfortable internal sensations when you had just had a nasty thump on the head. Clemence slid down under the blanket, pulled it high over her ears and closed her eyes, thankful to be still for a while. If she could slip into sleep, she could pretend *this* was the dream.

The sound of voices, the rattle of the door opening, jerked her out of her doze, rigid under the blanket. It seemed a very slight barricade. There was a thump on the floor, some more banging about, then the door closed again. Cautiously Clemence sat up. There was a small half-barrel on the floor, just big enough for a person to sit in with their knees drawn up, and two big buckets of water and a jug.

She slipped out of bed and wedged the latch on the door with her knife, then went to dip a finger in the water containers. The buckets were salt, but the jug was fresh for her face and hair. A rummage through Nathan's kit bag produced a new block of green soap. She sniffed. Olive oil. On the side were imprinted the words *Savon de Marseilles*. And there was a luxuriously large sponge as well. French olive-oil soap and sponges? Had he been in the Mediterranean recently? She sensed there was a lot he had not told her.

Clemence stripped, sighing with relief as the linen strips uncoiled from around her ribs. She ran her hands over her torso, massaging the ridges where the bandages had cut into her skin. Nathan's hands had rested there, and there—and just there.

She stepped into the tub, shivered and hunkered down, gasping as the cold water covered her belly. Her head throbbed; the strange new pulse between her thighs throbbed, too, despite the chill of the water, and she realised the fear that had been ever present in the pit of her stomach for days had gone at last.

There was no logical explanation—it was dangerous folly not to be frightened. Clemence reached for the block of soap and began to work up a lather.

Nathan tapped on the door, wondering at the apprehension that gripped him. What was he going to find inside? His imagination reacted luridly to months of enforced celibacy at sea; it suddenly seemed a long time since he had left England and paid off his mistress. The remembered sweetness of Clemence in his arms conjured up the vision of a slender, naked woman, dripping with water, a nymph uncoiling herself from her tiny pool. The reality, when the door opened, was Clem, wet hair tousled, cheeks glowing and exuding a healthy, and less than erotic, smell of olive-oil soap.

In her clean second-hand clothes she looked the perfect well-scrubbed youth until she met his eye and blushed, rosily. Heat washed through his body and he gritted his teeth. 'Better?'

'Yes, much, much better, thank you. I found some birch-bark powder in your medical kit and that helped my headache, and the bliss of being clean, I cannot describe.' She gave a complicated little wriggle of sensual satisfaction, causing his loins to tighten painfully, and smiled. 'It is horrible being dirty; I don't know why it is so difficult to get boys to wash. Surely no one is willingly dirty?'

Nathan found he was not up to discussing any subject touching Clemence and the removal of clothes. She followed his eyes to the tub of dirty water, perhaps assuming his silence was irritation. 'Sorry, I was just trying to work out how to empty it.'

'I'll use the empty bucket and bail it out through the port-hole.' He tossed his waistcoat on to the bunk and rolled up his sleeves. 'You've been very thrifty with the water.'

She was looking at his bare forearms. Nathan watched his own muscles bunch as he hefted the bucket and found, to his inner amusement, that he was endeavouring to make as light work of the task as possible. *Poseur*, he mocked himself. *Showing off like a cock with a new hen.* He remembered the *frisson* of pleasure when he had sensed Julietta's eyes on him in his uniform, the temptation to swagger to impress her.

'There isn't much space in the tub,' Clemence pointed

out, jerking him back to the present. 'And there'll be even less room for you.'

Nathan chucked a pail full of water out of the porthole, his mind distractingly full of the image of Clemence curled up in the tub. 'You'll have to scrub my back, then, if I can't reach,' he said, half-joking.

'I suppose I could,' she said doubtfully. 'With my eyes closed, of course. Have you a back brush?'

'No. I was teasing you.' She smiled at him, unexpectedly, and he found himself grinning back. 'Are you usually this calm about things, Clem? I would have thought you fully justified if you were throwing hysterics by now.'

'It wouldn't do any good, would it?' she pointed out, folding discarded clothes with a housewifely air that contrasted ludicrously with her appearance.

'I wish my father was alive and I was at home with him, or, if that cannot happen, I wish my uncle and cousin were the men Papa believed them to be. Or, worst come to worst, I wish I had stowed away on a nice merchantman and was now having tea in the captain's wife's cabin. But if wishes were horses, beggars would ride and having hysterics would not be pleasant for you.'

'That's considerate of you.' Nathan poured clean water into the tub and began to unbutton his shirt.

'It is in my interests not to alienate you,' Clemence pointed out, all of a sudden as cool and sharp as fresh lemonade. She sat down on her bunk, curled her legs under her and faced the wall.

'What's the matter?' Nathan asked, his fingers stilling on the horn buttons.

'I do not want to have to go into the privy cupboard while you have your bath.'

'Oh. Yes, of course.' He would have stripped off without

a second thought, Nathan realised; he was so focused on not pulling her into his arms that he was forgetting all the other ways he could shock or alarm her.

The shock of the cold water as he crouched down was a blessed relief for a moment, then the absence of the nagging tension in his groin was replaced by the sobering reality of protecting a young woman on the *Sea Scorpion*. Clemence would be safer in a dockside brothel—at least she could climb out of a window.

Nathan shook his head in admiration as he scrubbed soap into his torso. Out of a window overhanging the sea, up creepers, along a roof, stealing a horse… Now that was a woman with courage and brains. He had been brought up to regard the ideal woman as frail, clinging and charmingly reliant upon a man's every word. And he had found himself one who apparently embodied all of those attributes combined with the exotic looks of half-Greek parentage. The only fault his mother would have found with her—at first—was her lack of money.

They had all been well-dowered young ladies, the candidates for his hand that his mother had paraded before him. She always managed to completely ignore the fact that, however worthy her late husband's breeding might be, he had gambled all the money away and that their elder son had to manage a household with the parsimony of a miser. The need for Nathan to marry money was not spelled out, but he was always aware that if he did not, then he could expect to exist upon what the navy provided.

So, the daughters of well-off squires, the granddaughters of merchants, the youngest child of younger sons of the minor aristocracy were all considered—provided they brought money with them. And, while most of them seemed pleased at the thought of a tall naval officer with a baron for a brother, Nathan had found the entire process distasteful. His mother, he was well aware, had made a *suitable* match to a man she despised. His brother Daniel had wed the sour-faced youngest daughter of an earl because of her breeding and her dowry—substantial, Nathan had always assumed, because of the need to get her off her family's hands. Neither gave him any desire to marry for money.

So he had married for love. More fool he.

Now, of course, any of those well-dowered damsels would flee screaming if they found themselves alone with him. Nathan grimaced and stood up, slopping water everywhere, and began to wash his hair. Too much to hope that Clemence had left him any fresh water, he reached for the jug and found it half-full.

'Admirable woman,' he said, pouring it in a luxurious stream over his head. 'All this fresh water left.'

'I don't need much now my hair is short,' she said, her shoulders still firmly turned away from him.

'Was it very long?' Nathan stepped out, splashed through the puddles and found a linen towel.

'To my waist,' she said with a sigh. 'My only beauty.'

'Your what?' Nathan balanced, one foot wrapped in the towel as he dried his toes, and stared at the back of her head and the damp mop of hair that, when dry, was all the colours of pulled taffy. 'That I cannot believe.'

'I am not fishing for compliments,' Clemence said, apparently resigned to her looks. 'I know I am too tall, too slim and my face has too many angles. My papa used to say that I was as flat as a kipper in front, but I've never seen a kipper, so I don't know.'

Nathan swallowed. This was more information than he felt able to cope with, even after a cold bath. The memory of her body moulding into his came back. Even with her bosom bound, he knew perfectly well that kippers were not that shape.

'You've lived on Jamaica all your life, then?' he asked, pulling on his loosest trousers and snatching at an innocuous topic of conversation.

'Yes. Papa and Mama came out here just after they were married. Papa was a younger son, like you.' She sighed. 'Mama died ten years ago of the yellow fever.'

'It isn't a very healthy climate,' Nathan said sympathetically, finding a clean shirt.

'I know. But I don't seem to catch things, perhaps because I was born out here. Have you finished?'

Clemence was getting a crick in her back from sitting hunched up and her imagination was uncomfortably exercised by the knowledge of what was going on behind her, her ears following every splash, the sound of Nathan working up a lather on bare skin, his sigh of pleasure when he tipped the fresh water over his head, the flap of his shirt as he shook it out.

'Yes, I'm finished.'

She swung her bare feet off the bunk and grimaced as they hit a puddle. The floor of the neat cabin was awash with more water than she believed had been brought in, there were wet towels on the chairs, dirty clothing discarded into the wet.

'Tsk!' She stood regarding it, hands on hips.

'You sound like my mother,' Nathan said, standing unrepentant in the middle of the damp disorder.

'Why are men so messy?' Clemence demanded. 'Women aren't messy; at least, I'm not.' She bent to pick up a towel and started to mop at a puddle. 'Mind you, that's easy to say when one has servants, I suppose.'

'Do you keep slaves?'

'No! Papa never did, we don't agree with it. And since the

trade was abolished ten years ago, he was campaigning to abolish keeping slaves, too. But, of course, the planters say it is uneconomic to grow sugar using waged labourers and the Americans rely on slave labour as well, so our planters say it is uneconomic to change because of the competition. It was easier for us, being merchants, to stick to our principles. Uncle Joshua and Cousin Lewis,' she added with a grimace, 'are planters.'

'I'd like to meet those two,' Nathan remarked. She saw his fist clench against his thigh and once again entertained the fantasy of it lifting Lewis off the floor with a solid punch to his insipient double chin.

'I hope I never see them again. Are all those clothes dirty? Only I'll use them to mop up with if I'm going to have to wash them anyway.'

Nathan started to scoop dirty water out of the tub. 'You shouldn't have to clean and wash for me.'

'I'm your cabin boy, remember? And I don't expect there's a fat, cheerful washerwoman on board, now is there?'

'No. How's your head?'

'All right, unless I touch it.' In fact, strangely, she felt better than she had for days. Food and fresh air must be helping, but perhaps it was also the stimulus of taking events into her own hands. From somewhere her courage had returned; however awful this was, at least she was no longer a passive victim. And Nathan knowing she was a woman was not awful at all, although it should be.

It was not going to end happily, this odd relationship with a gentleman gone to the bad. Of course, if this was a sensation novel, she would redeem him by the end of the last chapter and they would sail off into the sunset together to a life of idyllic, romantic love on some enchanted island. Kept alive, presumably, by tropical fruits, fish and the odd shipwreck. But how did you redeem a pirate?

Clemence rolled her eyes at her own folly. She could just imagine Nathan's reaction to her sitting him down and questioning his motives, suggesting he ought to reform because, basically, he was a good man. He had told her about his fall from grace with the navy, the downhill path that had brought him here. His heart wasn't in it, she was sure, but he was not going to admit that to her.

And did she want to sail off with him? Of course she didn't, she was destined for London, a Season and a gentleman of impeccable breeding, wealth, manners and prospects. Miss Ravenhurst could set her sights just as high as she pleased, she thought, finding them resting speculatively on one well-muscled back just in front of her. And she was independent enough to do just as she wanted.

But now she was a laundry maid, not a lady, and likely to be for the foreseeable future. She began to scoop up sodden washing. That olive-oil soap seemed to lather fairly well in salt water and Mr Street would tell her where to hang the laundry to dry.

The door banged back, making her start and drop the clothes. Peering up through the table legs as she crouched to pick them up, Clemence saw the figure in the door. Mc-Tiernan.

'The wind's picked up,' he said abruptly to Nathan, ignoring her. 'You'll take us through the passage tonight, Stanier.'

She saw Nathan's bare feet flex on the deck, as though adjusting his stance for action, but all he said was, 'That's a tricky passage in daylight, let alone in the dark.'

'There's a moon. You're supposed to be the best, Stanier. We touch anything, I'll have you keelhauled.'

'When was the last time *Sea Scorpion* had her bottom

scraped?' Nathan asked, as though the question of being dragged under the barnacle-encrusted belly of the ship was an interesting academic point.

'It's overdue,' the captain said as he turned on his heel, leaving them in silence.

'How many times have you done that passage?' Clemence asked as casually as she could.

'Never.' He began to gather up instruments, polishing the lenses of his sextant. 'I've heard about it, I've studied the charts, that's all.'

'Oh. Mr Cutler will help, won't he?' she worried, throwing the wet bundle into a corner and fetching his notebook and the roll of charts, her stomach swooping with apprehension.

'I don't think our first mate likes me much.' Nathan squinted at a pencil point and reached for his knife to whittle it. 'I think Mr Cutler would be quite happy if we nudged a head of coral or a nice sharp rock. Not enough to do any damage, you understand, just enough to upset the captain.'

'Can I help?' She had no idea how, and anyway, he'd just dismiss the offer. She was a girl, after all, men didn't accept help from women, not when it really mattered.

Nathan looked up, his blue eyes hard and steady, studying her as he had that night in the tavern. 'Yes, you can.' He nodded towards the bunk. 'Get some rest now, it's going to be a long night. I'll come for you.'

Clemence finished tidying up, a tight knot of anticipation and apprehension in her stomach. Nathan wanted her help, he didn't just dismiss her or belittle her. His eyes searched hers so intently and he seemed to find something there; she had no idea what.

Obedient, she lay down on her bunk and closed her eyes, but it was a long time before she slept.

Chapter Six

Clemence stood a pace behind Nathan, clutched the sextant and shivered. The evening air was not cold, far from it, but the sense of menace hung like a chill fog around the poop deck.

'Well?' She forced herself not to cringe closer to Nathan as McTiernan swung round. 'What are we waiting for? Enter the channel.'

'When the moon is up,' Nathan said, a statement, not a request. 'We'll beat up and down here until it is.'

McTiernan's eyes narrowed, but he nodded abruptly to the steersman. 'As Mr Stanier orders.'

The atmosphere had changed from merely frightening to something else entirely. The pirates were hunting, she realised, the scent of blood was in their nostrils and the channel was the equivalent of a track through the forest that would lead them to their prey.

She watched Nathan's supple back as he bent over the chart spread out on the hatch, wondering how he managed to look so relaxed and confident under such pressure. It was, she thought, remembering that first startling glimpse of him naked, a beautiful back, unblemished golden skin over long, strong muscles.

'You, boy. Fetch coffee.' Cutler's voice, as precise as his clothing, made her jump. Setting the sextant down carefully by Nathan's right hand, she turned to obey.

'And a lantern, Clem,' Nathan added.

It filled the time, getting the coffee for the men on the poop deck, finding a lantern, but not enough. What if they did hit a rock or a reef? What if the *Sea Scorpion* was holed and there were men, as she suspected, captive down in the dark hell of the orlop deck?

She wished she'd mentioned them to Nathan, but now was not the time. Slowly the moon rose, then, at last, the sea was washed with silver. The land, the forest tumbling down to the sands, was stark black and white and, between two headlands, a ribbon of water marked the treacherous shortcut to Lizard Island.

'Two points round,' Nathan said to the man at the wheel, and it seemed that at least half a dozen people let out pent-up breath. 'I suggest you reef more sail, Mr Cutler. I need control, not speed now.

'Clem, get up to the bows with the leadsman. He'll call depth and what's coming up on the lead, but I want you to scrape some off and bring it to me, every cast. Run.'

The mate on the *Raven Duchess* had shown her how to cast the lead when she was young, although she had never had the strength to make the throw that sent the weight on its knotted cord out ahead, and she knew how the hollow in the end was filled with tallow to pick up whatever was on the sea bed.

The hand was swinging and casting now, counting out as the knots flew past his fingers, then shouting the result as the line went slack. He hauled the lead up, dripping.

'I've got to take some of the bottom for Mr Stanier,' Clemence said, pulling out her knife and scraping off the coarse sand that clung to the tallow. She ran back as the man cast again, her hand spread palm-up in the lantern-light for Nathan to study.

She was shaking. He took her wrist in one warm hand to raise it closer and his thumb caressed briefly over the delicate skin of her inner wrist. 'Black sand and no shell.' He picked up the notebook and made a note. 'Again. Run.'

Back and forth, back and forth, for what seemed like hours. The leadsman's monotonous chant was the loudest noise on deck and her palm grew sore from rubbing off sand and shell. There was hardly time to watch Nathan as she wanted to, his face rapt and remote as he studied chart and notes, the outline of the dark land and the set of the sails. He sent a hand forward to climb out along the bowsprit to watch ahead for the tell-tale foam of waves breaking over almost submerged rocks, but the real danger, she knew, were the heads of coral that lurked unseen just under the surface, ready to rip the bottom out of a ship.

The islands on either side grew closer and closer as they crept along on reefed sails. Cutler put two men on the wheel. No one was speaking now, except the leadsman and the watchers.

Then Nathan picked up a telescope, strode to the side, caught hold of the rigging and began to climb until he reached just below the yards, hooked one arm into the ropes and leaned out, his eyes fixed on the sea ahead.

'He'd better know what he's doing,' a soft voice said in Clemence's ear. McTiernan. The hair on her neck stood up as he laid a hand on her shoulder.

'He does, Cap'n,' she said stoutly, staring up at the dark figure silhouetted against the sky, and found she believed it. There was a call from the bows. 'I've got to go, sir. The leadsman.'

She wriggled out from under his hand and scurried off as Nathan began to call down course corrections to the wheel. What sort of captain put his whole ship at risk, just to test out one man? *An insane one*, the voice in her head said. It was almost as though McTiernan saw Nathan as a threat.

'No bottom!' the leadsman sang out, pulling up a clean weight, and she relaxed a little, leaning against the rail while he prepared to cast again. Nathan was coming down the rigging now, moving like a shadow to jump on to the deck and go back to stand beside the captain.

Yes, no wonder McTiernan was wary of him—they both had an intangible natural authority, a charisma. Cutler could dominate, but she couldn't imagine him leading, whereas McTiernan had the mesmeric quality of a snake and Nathan simply exuded the confidence that what he said, went.

He had found the deep channel, it seemed, the lead kept coming up clean, or with white sand at depth, and on the last call he brought her back to stand by his side.

'All right, Clem?' She nodded. 'Enjoying yourself?'

Enjoying myself? Is he mad? We're on a pirate ship captained by a homicidal maniac, sailing through a dangerous channel he's never sailed before in the dead of night and he asks me if I'm enjoying myself? 'Yes,' Clemence said, realising it was true. For the moment she was one of this crew, with a role to play—that was part of it. And she was close to Nathan, watching him work, and that, overwhelmingly, was the whole of it.

'Good. Pass me the sextant, will you, and find something to take notes.' He began to take star sights, calling out figures for her to write in columns.

'Where did you get your education, boy?' Cutler, bent over to look, far too close at her shoulder.

'School, sir. Spanish Town, before we lost our money, sir.'

'Clem, those figures.' Nathan put down the instrument and jerked his head. She came to stand at his side, holding the notebook flat while he ran his finger down the column. 'Good, you've a clear script, boy.'

'How much longer?' she ventured, wanting to slip her hand into his, whether in gratitude at the praise or for giving her an excuse to move away from Cutler, or simply to touch him, she was not sure. But it was not hard, in this company, to resist the urge.

'Soon.' As he said it, the hand in the crow's nest shouted down.

'Open water dead ahead!'

'I suggest we drop anchor, Captain.' Nathan made a mark on the chart and turned it towards the man. 'It will be dark soon, with moonset. I imagine you do not want to be in open water when the sun comes up, not without a chance to reconnoitre first. We won't be the only craft seeking shelter in this group of islands.'

'Aye.' McTiernan looked down at the map, then up at Nathan. 'It seems you're as good as you say.' He nodded sharply. 'Make it so, Mr Cutler.' Nathan snapped his fingers at Clemence and began to roll up his charts. She hurried to pick up the sextant and telescope, stuffing the notebook into the pocket in her waistcoat tails. 'Where the hell do you think you're going, Mr Stanier?'

'To correct this chart and then to sleep, Captain.' His voice was level, but Clemence caught the challenge under it and her heart began to pound. He waited, a long few seconds until McTiernan nodded again, before he deigned to explain. 'If we need to bolt back up this channel in a hurry, I want this chart accurate, because it most certainly isn't now.'

They were almost at the hatch before the captain spoke. 'Five bells, Mr Stanier.'

'Aye, aye, sir.'

Clemence padded after Nathan, her arms full, yawning hugely, excitement and relived tension bubbling inside her. Inside the cabin she put her load on the table and turned, unable to suppress the broad smile that seemed to crack her face.

'You were wonderful! So cool with that vulture watching every move, I couldn't believe it. And there was so much wrong with the chart, I saw all those marks you were making, all the errors you found.' She stared at him, admiration and something else she could not quite identify animating her. 'It was *marvellous*.'

'It was a bloody miracle.' Nathan leaned back against the door and let his head rest against the panels, eyes closed. 'I never, ever, want to have to do something like that again, so long as I live.'

'But you made it look so easy,' Clemence protested. He was tired, that was all, she told herself. All her security rested on this man being invincible. Nathan opened his eyes, met hers and then held out his right hand; it was shaking very slightly. He dropped his gaze to it, staring until the tremor stopped.

'That, Clemence, is the trick. Never, ever, let them see you feel fear, never, in action, let yourself believe you are afraid.'

'*You* get scared?' she asked, disbelieving.

'Only a fool does not feel fear. Listen to it, hear what the warning is, do what you can to prepare for the dangers and then, when it is time to act, put the fear aside.'

'I thought I was weak, being frightened,' she admitted.

'No, sensible. And human.' He had closed his eyes again,

leaning back against the door as though too weary to move to the chair.

Clemence went and wrapped her arms around his waist, laid her cheek on his chest and hugged, hard.

'Ough!' Nathan huffed, half-laughing. 'What are you doing?' He made no move to escape her embrace, rather seemed to relax into it.

'Hugging you. You need a hug. You deserve a hug—I don't expect you get many.' His chest moved, he was laughing, silently. Clemence felt her cheeks getting hot. 'I don't mean *that*; the sort of hugs you pay for. I mean friendly hugs.' She unwrapped her arms and pulled out a chair, tugging at his sleeve. 'Sit down, you are far too big to haul about. I suppose you'll insist on doing that chart before you'll sleep. I'll go and get some coffee.'

When she got back with a beaker of the thick black liquid he was dead to the world, his head on his folded arms, the pencil fallen from his hand, his hair in his eyes.

Clemence set down the beaker and moved the pencil, resisting the impulse to smooth back the thick hair, play with the sun-bleached tips. Best to let him sleep. She climbed on to her bunk and sat watching him, feeling again the strapping of muscle over his ribs, the long back muscles where her palms had pressed, the heat of his tired body.

Flawed, complex, beautiful, dangerously enigmatic. She was very much afraid that she was... Her lids drooped.

'Clem!' Nathan's hand fell from her shoulder as she woke with a start. 'Time to wake up, nearly five bells.'

Her neck had a crick in it and she felt hot and sweaty. 'Oh.' She stretched. 'Have you been to bed?'

'No, I slept for half an hour, drank my nice cold coffee

and altered the chart.' He jerked his head towards the privy door. 'I've finished with the cupboard.'

Last night's moment of vulnerability had gone. This morning Nathan was all business, making notes, sorting through the rolls of charts, his hands rock-steady. Clemence took herself off to the cupboard and emerged, ten minutes later, considerably more awake.

'Nathan?'

'Mmm?'

'Did you know there are prisoners on board?'

'No.' He put down a pair of dividers and stared at her. 'Where?'

'Down on the orlop deck.' She explained what she had heard and seen.

'But McTiernan doesn't take ordinary seamen, he slaughters the lot.'

'I know. So why does he want these? And some of them may be from my father's ship. I can't leave them down there.'

'Oh, yes, you can. Unless you want to join them, that is.'

'Nathan, please.' She dragged a chair up and sat down, knee to knee, her voice wheedling. 'You can do something, surely?'

'Don't you dare try that wide-eyed stuff on me, Clem,' he warned. 'It irritates the hell out of me at the best of times and, just now, it's damned dangerous.'

'Sorry.' She didn't know what had come over her. Normally that sort of eyelash fluttering, *Oh, Mr Stanier, you are wonderful, won't you do it for me?* irritated her, too, when she'd seen other young women trying it on men.

Clemence knew she was hopeless at flirting; she always had been, feeling a complete idiot making eyes at boys she'd known all her life and pretending to be five foot one and a fragile little bloom when she was nothing of the kind. Attempting to deploy her inept feminine wiles on Nathan Stanier was madness. Feeling as she did about him was even madder.

'I'll see what I can find out,' he conceded. 'Come on, breakfast time.'

Street was frying yams when they made their way to the galley, the savoury smell making Clemence's mouth water with longing. Nathan raided the skillet of bacon, peering into the pots that bubbled, their contents sloshing back and forth with the motion of the ship as they slid between the restraining bars on the range.

'That's surely not our dinner, is it?' He dipped a cautious finger into one pot.

'Nah, that swill's for the cargo.' Street grinned.

'You are not much concerned with keeping them alive, then?' Nathan sucked his finger clean, grimacing.

'Not what you'd call a high-value cargo, field hands,' Street remarked. 'But I keep them alive, as much as food and water will do.'

'It's slaves down there, then?' Nathan queried, pouring himself thin ale and draining the tankard.

'They will be, by the time we get them to St Martin. The French'll buy anything, they're that short since the Peace, what with the trade being outlawed.'

'So captive merchant crews are sold to the French islands and just conveniently vanish into the upland plantations out of reach of any English help? Good business idea.'

Clemence was positively hissing with indignation by the time she and Nathan found a deserted piece of deck to lean against the rail and eat.

'The bastard! I'd like to—'

'Quiet! At least we know he wants them kept alive. If

they're worth money, they've a good chance of getting off this ship. I was worried he was keeping them for sport—shark bait or something.' Nathan tossed a piece of bacon rind over the side as though to make his point.

'What? He wouldn't? Alive, you mean?'

'He would and he does. He's got a very strange idea of entertainment, has our captain. He isn't called *Red* because of his taste in spotted kerchiefs, it's because blood's red and he likes it. Lots of it.'

'You…you're frightening me,' Clemence managed to say around the constriction in her throat. She didn't want him to treat her like a sheltered little girl, but like a grown woman. On the other hand, there were some details she could very well do without.

'Good. Be very frightened—you are less likely to do anything foolish.'

'I'd heard he had a dreadful reputation, but I didn't know he was like that.' She shuddered. But she couldn't just let men she knew be sold off as slaves. She would have to think of something.

'Mr Stanier!' The light was breaking through, chasing the night back into deep pools of shadow either side of the channel. Ahead, in the open sea, a brisk breeze was making white horses on the wavelets.

'Coming, sir.' Nathan pushed his ale into Clemence's hands. 'Now, things get lively.'

Nathan studied the open waters of the Windward Passage as *Sea Scorpion* slipped out of the channel and turned starboard to the sheltered deep anchorage between Lizard Island and, at their back, the scatter of islands they had picked their way through the night before. Ahead was the major route for shipping between Hispaniola and Cuba and topsails were distantly visible. Closer to the island the white lateen sails of fishing boats dotted the sea—small fry, safe from the big shark.

He turned on his heel, seeming to glance casually over the forested slopes and rock-strewn beaches behind them. Somewhere, if things had gone to plan, spy glasses were watching them and messages were being sent to a middling-sized merchant vessel with a conveniently damaged mast. It would come limping out of shelter, like a bird with a broken wing, right under the nose of the *Sea Scorpion*—and McTiernan would not be able to resist.

'You seem pleased with life, Mr Stanier.'

'Who wouldn't smile at a morning like this, Mr Cutler?' On his other side he sensed Clem stiffening, but she neither pressed closer to him nor moved away. She was scared of Cutler, but she had guts.

'Drop anchor!' There was a roar as the pinions were knocked out and the chain rushed free, the anchor dropping through clear water to the sand beneath, then a few moments of peace again until the bo'sun began ordering the hands to their morning chores.

'You're not expecting any business along yet?'

'No.' Cutler was looking up into the rigging, his eyes checking, evaluating every knot and sheet. 'Those fat lazy merchantmen won't stir themselves for a while yet.'

Beside him Clem gave a muffled snort and Nathan kicked her lightly on the ankle in warning; the last thing they needed was her giving Cutler a lecture on the superiority of merchantmen over pirate vessels.

A jolly boat was swung out with water casks to fill at the stream that burst out of the forest on to the beach in a miniature waterfall. Even without the telescope he could make out the spreading pool beneath the fall. 'Imagine swimming in that,' Clem said wistfully.

Nathan looked at her. Leaning with elbows on the rail, chin in hand, rear end stuck out, she was lost in a daydream. With no difficulty at all he joined her in it. Somehow he had no trouble at all imagining Clemence naked, slipping like a fish through the water, coming up to the surface laughing, her hands full of shells, walking towards him, small high breasts covered in sun-reflecting droplets...

He looked again and hissed, 'Stand up straight and pull your shirt down.'

She jumped to obey, startled question in her eyes.

'You might be too thin,' he muttered in her ear, 'but no lad has got a backside like that!' *Oh, God, and now that was in his head, too, pert and rounded, just asking to be cupped in his palms like a ripe peach.*

She went pink, but looked pleased. 'Really? That's good. I must be putting weight on.'

Women! 'It is no such—'

'Sail ho!' The cry from the masthead had everyone turning towards the rail. There, emerging slowly from behind the headland, was a small merchantman, sail drooping, mast oddly angled, crew swarming over the rigging in frantic activity.

'Raise the anchor!' Cutler roared and the bo'sun came at the run, starter in hand, shoving and bullying the hands into place around the capstan. Men were climbing the rigging, making for their designated places on the yards ready to lower the sail, and the lids of sea chests crashed open as the crew left on deck armed themselves.

'Get below.' Nathan pushed Clem towards the companionway.

'No!' She dug in her heels, then saw the look on his face. 'I'll go down before we close with them,' she promised.

'Do that. This is going to be a hot fight.'

'How do you know?' Clem demanded, half-running to keep up with him as he made for the nearest arms' chest to find a cutlass. 'It's a small ship.'

'Instinct,' he lied, mentally kicking himself for the slip.

'But they aren't heavily armed,' she continued to speculate.

'Spare me your views on marine strategy,' Nathan said coldly, desperate to stop her talking.

'Sorry.' She subsided, shooting him a side-long look from under her lashes that was pure feminine speculation.

The anchor was up, the sails crashing down, beginning to fill as the hands scrambled back to the deck. Nathan tried the edge on the cutlass with his thumb and studied the men on the poop deck. Just behind the steersman, that was the place.

Sea Scorpion began to move, nosing out towards the sea and its victim. 'Hoist the bones,' Cutler yelled and a man ran to the main mast and began to lash an odd bundle to it.

'What's that?' Beside him Clem craned to see.

'The skull and cross-bones,' Nathan said grimly, watching it jerk up to the foremast.

'But…that's not a flag. Those are real…' Clem turned away, her face white as she saw the gulls swoop to feast on the remains that still clung to the pathetic relics.

'I told you, our captain has a novel sense of humour.' To say nothing of a unique personal style. The merchantman had seen them now. Its few gun ports dropped open; across the water there was the sound of shouted orders, the rumble of gun carriages. The armament looked pitifully small, but that was all to the good, Nathan thought. They didn't want a long-distance gun battle, they needed hand-to-hand fighting if the trap was to be sprung on the *Sea Scorpion*.

Beside him Clemence gasped. 'They are running out their guns—what if we're hit? The men down below won't have a chance.'

'Nothing we can do. Clem, be quiet—'

There was a shout from the crow's nest. 'Cap'n! Big merchantman, just coming into sight off the starboard bow!'

There was a rush for the rail, telescopes trained beyond the stricken ship. Minutes passed, then, 'It's the *Raven Princess*, Cap'n!'

Chapter Seven

'**Y**es!' For the first time Nathan saw McTiernan animated.
The captain slammed his clenched fist into the other palm.
'Leave this one, it isn't going far.' He turned to the wheelman,
firing rapid orders as Cutler shouted up to the sail handlers.

Sea Scorpion swung round, away from her crippled victim towards the richly tempting prize of a great ocean-going
craft bound for London. 'Hell!' Nathan let the one word escape, then shut his lips tight. The rat had so nearly walked
into the trap and now, whiskers twitching, it was off after a
bigger, tastier piece of cheese and there was absolutely nothing he could do about it.

'No, oh, no.' Clem's whisper cut through his own furious
thoughts. 'Not the *Raven Princess*.'

'Why not?'

'I… I know the captain, some of the crew. That was the
ship I was making for when McTiernan stopped me.'

It must be the thought of what would have happened to
her as a member of a captured crew that was making her so
distressed. She was going to cry in a minute, he could see
her full lower lip begin to tremble.

'Clem,' he hissed, 'if you can't control yourself, you'll have to go below. There is nothing either of us can do about this.'

'Why should you want to?' she spat at him, her face contorted with anger. 'You're one of them, you'll share the killing and the booty and the plunder and I expect you'll want me to wash the blood off your clothes when you come back from getting it.'

'Clem, shut up.' He took her arm and shook her. 'You are attracting attention.'

'I will not stand by and—' His hand over her mouth cut off the threat. Nathan wrapped his other arm around her waist and hoisted her off her feet, kicking and struggling. Her buttocks squirmed against his groin, sending desire lancing through him, deepening his anger. His entire strategy was going to hell in a handcart and this damned woman, who hadn't the sense to be terrified, was going to give it a final shove off the cliff if he couldn't shut her up.

'What the devil are you about, Mr Stanier?' Cutler shouted down from the rail of the poop deck.

'He's frightened, Mr Cutler, but he won't go down. He'll be a damn nuisance under our feet, I'll dump him in the cabin and be right back.'

Ruthless, Nathan slung Clem over his shoulder with considerably less care than he had shown the day before and got her, struggling and cursing at him, down the companionway.

'Will you shut up, Clem?'

'Put me down!' She fetched him a painful thump in the kidneys with a clenched fist. Nathan dropped her on to her feet and pushed her back against a bulkhead, keeping one hand pressed to her shoulder to hold her still. The deck around them was deserted, everyone was either above decks or at the guns.

'There, you are down.' She glared at him, hands fisted on her hips. 'Now, show some sense and *shut up.*'

'There was no need to manhandle me.' She pushed the hair out of her eyes and tugged at her shirt tails.

'There was every need.' She wriggled and he brought up his other hand and pinned her against the wood. Even under the strapping he could see the rise and fall of her bosom, catch her feminine scent, hot, furious, heady.

'You *pirate*, you bully, you—' The injustice, even though she had no way of knowing the truth, was the final straw. Wrestling with her had stimulated an erection that ached, his hands could feel her heat, he could hear her panting breaths, his nostrils were full of her.

Nathan took a step forward and kissed her hard on the mouth with none of the delicacy and restraint he had used before and with the full force of his angry frustration behind it.

Clemence's gasp of shock was swallowed up by the fierce open-mouthed kiss. She grabbed his wrists, but she might as well have been wrestling with the capstan bars. Something slid through her, a strange mixture of anger and triumph that she had provoked him into this violent acceptance of her femininity.

But the anger was winning—the logical emotion, the wise one. She jerked up one knee and he moved in like a swordsman, almost as though he had expected it, turning her aggressive gesture into weakness as she found him between her thighs, his whole body pressed against her, the heat of his erection searing against her belly.

His tongue was in her mouth, thrusting. Clemence closed her teeth and he jerked back and looked down at her, his face stark. 'Clemence—*hell.*'

Panting, she stared at him from a distance of perhaps six

inches. He looked shaken, yet still angry. *He should be grovelling at my feet.* Nathan met her stormy gaze and something deep in those blue eyes stirred, despite the expression on his face. He desired her, it was not just anger at her outburst.

Before she could think, Clemence let go of his wrists and seized his head, dragged it down to her lips again, clung for a few dizzying moments and then pulled free.

'Are you sorry? I should hope so,' she said shakily. 'So…so am I. Sorry.' Slowly he lifted his hands away from her shoulders and she stared back at him, each of them cautious, as if they were two wrestlers not knowing if the other truly had called *quits*. 'May I come back on deck? I won't say anything, I promise.' There was nothing she could do, except watch and pray that *Raven Princess* could outrun them. And if the worst happened, then it was her duty to stand and watch it, not cower in her cabin with her head under the pillow.

'Clemence, what just happened was madness.' Nathan touched her swollen lower lip with the back of his fingers.

'Well, it wasn't very sensible,' she agreed shakily, 'but I think we can forgive ourselves, because otherwise we are going to have to spend some very long, silent hours in that cabin.' He was still looking grim, but that produced a reluctant grin.

'Come on, then. Hell, your mouth is swollen. You look as though you've been kissed hard.' Clemence narrowed her eyes at him. Nathan shrugged, his smile twisting wryly, raised his wrist to his mouth and bit with a grimace. Blood welled from the puncture and he smeared it onto her lip and down her chin. 'There. Look cowed, I've cuffed you, cut the inside of your lip.'

'All right.' Feeling quite adequately cowed, and more than a little confused, Clemence dug a bandana out of her pocket and held it to the side of her mouth, bracing herself for their reappearance on deck and Cutler's hard stare.

But there was no need to fear they were of the slightest interest to anyone; as they reached the rail there was a shout from above. 'Frigate!'

McTiernan froze, then a stream of low-voiced invective hissed from between his clenched teeth. Most of the words meant nothing to Clemence, but the sheer malevolence of it chilled her to the bone.

Beautiful, sunlit, the white sails of the distant naval ship strained in the wind, bringing her into a direct line between hunter and hunted. Clemence thought she had never seen anything more wonderful in her life.

'There's time to take the smaller ship.' Her jaw dropped as Nathan called up to McTiernan. He began to climb to the poop deck. 'We could board her, grab any portable valuables. Cut and run.'

Nathan? Clemence stared, disbelieving, as the men talked. Yes, she could accept, just, that he was the navigator, that when they went into action he would take part, but that he would deliberately incite McTiernan to take a helpless ship shocked her to the core.

'No, that bastard will see us, the visibility is too good. Mr Cutler, take us back behind Lizard Island and into the pool, we'll skulk like curs until that damn King's ship's gone and then...' he showed his stained teeth in a humourless grin '... then we'll take the next thing that shows a bowsprit, and God have mercy on them, because I won't.'

Clemence did not need any instructions to stay out of the way. She retreated to her perch amongst the casks and watched, blank-eyed, as the ship turned tail back into the shelter of Lizard Island. The watering crew were waiting on the beach, but the *Sea Scorpion* kept going. Surely McTiernan was not going to abandon his own men and a valuable jolly boat?

Puzzlement broke through her misery as she saw the topsails were being reefed in, then the mainsail. Boats were lowered, lines thrown out to them. As *Sea Scorpion*'s speed dropped to a glide, the boats took up the slack and began to steer her towards what seemed to be sheer cliff. Men in two of the boats that were not towing rowed right up to the tumbling vegetation and she realised that they were pulling back a screen of greenery to reveal the tight mouth of an entrance.

Slowed to walking pace now, the ship slid forward, her shadow black on the white sand, fish shoals darting away as though at the approach of a giant predator. They were through the screen, into an almost circular sea pool. Clemence had seen inlets like this before, caused when the roofs of caves collapsed; she'd even swum in one in the days before she had become a virtual prisoner, a million years ago.

So, this was McTiernan's secret hideaway and, thanks to Nathan showing him the shortcut through the sea passage, he was now even closer to Kingston harbour and had an ideal route to surprise the rich merchantmen leaving it.

The jolly boat with the water casks came through the gap in the wake of the flotilla of rowing boats, and the screen of creepers was hauled back into place. It was perfect, Clemence realised, standing up on the casks to look around. There was even a beach at the far end big enough for some shacks. Used, no doubt, for storing plunder. The only thing it was lacking was a source of fresh water, hence the laborious business of filling the casks from the waterfall further along the beach.

The anchor chain roared out through the hawsehole and *Sea Scorpion* came to rest, bobbing grotesquely in its idyllic setting like its namesake in the middle of an exquisite Meissen bowl.

'There you are.' It was Nathan, hands on hips, eyes screwed up against the sun dazzle.

'How could you?' she hissed.

He leaned in close with a jerk of his head to bring her hunkering down so he could murmur in her ear. 'Would you believe to try to delay us for the frigate to arrive?' he enquired.

'And risk capture yourself? How naïve do you think I am?' Nathan opened his mouth to speak. 'No, don't answer that.'

'Which?' He raised one eyebrow, infuriating her further. 'The answers are—possibly, but it might be a profitable risk to take for the reward and, no, not naïve, just somewhat sheltered from this sort of thing.'

'What sort of thing? Double-dealing, back-stabbing, money-grubbing treachery? I thought you disapproved of betrayal and disloyalty.'

'I do, when I'm dealing with human beings with some basic moral sense. This lot are fair game.' There was the sound of footsteps on the boards. Nathan drew back and added, at a normal volume, 'And next time, do what you're told, when you're told, or you'll get more than a cuff in the mouth. Understand?'

Over his shoulder Cutler loomed. 'Yessir, Mr Stanier,' Clemence said, nodding frantically and holding the kerchief to her mouth. 'Sorry, sir.'

'Let me know when you get tired of the brat, Stanier,' Cutler said, his gaze sliding over Clemence. 'I'm sure we'll find a use for him.'

'Not while I've a pile of washing needing doing,' Nathan said easily. 'Shift yourself, Clem, I want that cabin shipshape when I come down.'

Escaping below decks was a relief, even with a pile of dirty clothes to wash in the hot seawater she dipped from the cook's big cauldron. He made no fuss about her taking fresh for rinsing either, with the supply now easily replenished.

Clemence scrubbed and wrung and dipped, regarding her wrinkled fingers with something like dismay. Her skin was becoming tanned, her fingernails chipped, the soft palms a thing of the past. How pampered she had been, she realised, pushing sweaty hair back from her forehead and attacking her stained trousers.

She had supervised the household, studied her Spanish and French and her music, written to friends and relatives, shopped—and thought herself busy. The promised London Season would have been nothing but shopping and pleasure with only one task before her, the finding of a suitable husband.

Well, she wasn't going to find one now, even if she emerged alive and unscathed from this adventure. Clemence sat back on her heels, jolted by the thought. She had been so set on escaping from the Naismiths that the consequences had simply not occurred to her.

She had never found a gentleman on Jamaica who stirred more than a flutter in her heart and she had cherished no particular daydream of the one she would find in London, but it was a shock to realise that no gentleman was going to want her now, virgin or not.

And the fact that the only man who did stir her was Nathan Stanier was not much consolation, either. She had a lowering thought that the effect he had on her was purely physical, which probably showed she was wanton, and the notion that she was falling in love with him was simply the product of enforced intimacy, gratitude that he had saved her and the disturbing effect of whatever it was that seemed to spark between them.

Just sex, Clemence thought gloomily, sucking the finger

she had rubbed raw in an attempt to get the coffee stains out of her shirt. It certainly was for him. All she was to Nathan Stanier was an inconvenient stray who brought the added complication—to one who had at least been brought up as a gentleman—that if he made love to her he would probably feel guilty about it afterwards.

She ought to feel guilty just thinking about sex, she knew that. Well-bred young women had to pretend they knew nothing about it and did not want to know either. The first was nonsense, of course. You couldn't live on a tropical island, surrounded by burgeoning fertility, hot nights and the amazingly lax morals of a good part of the European population without grasping rather more than the essentials.

As for the second unspoken rule, well, she had never wanted a man before, so the subject had been of academic interest up to now. There had been Mr Benson, of course, whose classically handsome profile had troubled her dreams a little for a week or two, and the oddly flustered feeling that the attempts at flirtation of some of the bolder naval officers provoked, but that was all.

So this almost constant awareness of her own body, the slightly breathless feeling of anticipation the entire time, the embarrassingly persistent pulse that made her want to squeeze her legs together in a vain attempt to calm it, those were all Nathan Stanier's doing. Those two kisses, one so gentle, one so angry, had completely undone her, plunged her into a state where all she wanted was to have him make love to her. Completely. After all, if she survived this she was going to be ruined. She might as well get some benefit out of it…

'Penny for them?'

The bar of soap shot out of her clutching fingers and skidded across the cabin. Clemence twisted round with a muffled shriek, lost her balance and sat down in a puddle. Nathan, just inside the door, regarded her with that infuriating eyebrow raised and an expression on his face that convinced her that she must look a complete idiot. A completely undesirable idiot.

Her face, of course, would be scarlet, what with lust and embarrassment and the heat and the steam from the hot water. Her hair, she could feel, was hanging in lank rats' tails, she had washerwoman's fingers—and it was all his fault.

Clemence counted to ten, in Spanish, backwards, thought, *Imagine you're at dinner at the King's House with the Governor*, and managed not to shriek at him. 'I am hot, I am tired, I am upset and I have about a hundredweight of wet washing to wring out,' she articulated with dangerous calm and produced a small tight smile that had the desired effect of lowering that eyebrow.

'Right.' He came fully into the cabin, shut the door and retrieved the soap from under her bunk. 'Let's tackle the easy things first. I'll wring. Do you know where you can hang these out?'

'Mr Street showed me, between decks, forr'ard of the sailmaker's station.' This was the man she was having utterly improper fantasies about and here they were, discussing the laundry. Something of the trouble in her thoughts must have been reflected on her face because, as Nathan heaved the tub of wet clothes on to the table, he regarded her quizzically.

'I was thinking about what is going to happen to me if I ever manage to get out of this,' she admitted.

'We'll think of something.' He began to twist the sopping garments, the tendons on his wrists standing out sharply. Clemence watched the play of muscles under the thin linen sleeves. Those were the hands that had pinned her to the bulkhead a short while ago, had made her feel helpless and powerful, both at the same time. She wanted to feel them on her again, wanted to try his strength, stroke his naked skin, lick the paler skin just below the lobe of his ear...

'Put them in here.' She snatched up the empty water pail and put it on the table, almost hopping from foot to foot in her anxiety to be out of the cabin. It was suddenly too small. Or perhaps he was too big.

Nathan was still there when she returned, only now he was stuffing things into the big leather satchel. 'Where are you going?' He wasn't leaving, surely?

'I told McTiernan I want to go along to the headland, get height and take bearings. I thought we could deal with some of your other woes while we were at it.' He was going to make love to her? There was silence while she stared at him, feeling the blood ebb and flow under her skin. 'Clem? You don't mind a walk, do you? You said you were feeling hot and tired—the exercise will do you good.'

'Right, yes, exercise, of course,' she gabbled. He wasn't a mind reader, the words *Take Me* were not emblazoned on her forehead, he was talking about her complaints, not her fantasies. Clemence struggled for some poise. 'Can I help with anything?'

'Go to the galley, get something to take with us to eat.' He tossed her another satchel. 'I'll see you on deck in a minute.'

One of the hands rowed them across to the huts on the beach and pointed out the path through the trees that led to the stream. 'Looks as though it will be a gentle slope until then,' Nathan said, swinging the bulky satchel over his shoulder. 'Then it will be a stiffer climb to the headland. Can you manage?'

Clemence nodded, following at his heels. Already, just

being clear of the ship, she was feeling better. She looked back, catching a glimpse of it through the trees as it rode at anchor: black, waiting, sinister. Down in the deepest, darkest part men were huddled in abject misery, dying perhaps. She felt so helpless.

'Forget the ship for a while.' Nathan was looking back over his shoulder.

Clemence nodded and ran to catch up; until she could think of something positive to do, it was futile to keep worrying at the problem. They walked in single file, silent, for perhaps half an hour until the sound of falling water drew them to the stream. It fell over a waterfall into a deep pool that, in turn, drained through the trees, over the cliff and into the pool they had seen on the beach.

It was a magic place, sunlight filtering through the leaves, the cool water cupped in a ring of rocks, the foaming lace of the waterfall. They stood looking at it, side by side, then Nathan said, 'You could swim when we come back down. It is safe up here, not like the beach pool.'

It made Clemence feel better just thinking about it. 'I could?'

'I'd stand guard.' Nathan turned away and began to strike off up a steeper path.

Goodness, he's fit, Clemence thought, aware that she was puffing as she climbed in the wake of his long stride. Weeks of enforced inaction inside, hardly any food, the immobility of grief, had taken their toll on someone used to walking and riding every day.

Nathan stopped and waited for her as the forest gave way to the bare slopes above. 'Here.' He held out his hand and Clemence put hers into it. 'I used to be able to walk for miles,' she lamented, allowing herself to be towed up a steep bit. 'And I rode every day. And only a few years ago I was climbing trees and playing in the cane fields and now I'm panting over one little hill.'

'Not so little. Look.' Nathan released her hand as he gestured and she realised they had climbed to the top of Lizard Island. The sea spread out in front of them, islets dotted like spilled beads on crushed blue velvet. The frigate had come up with the damaged merchantman and even without the telescope Clemence could see the activity as sailors from the warship helped the crew with the rigging.

'They'll be safely on their way soon,' she commented, pointing. 'And they'll tell the frigate which way we went as well.'

'They won't find us, not unless we signal,' Nathan broke off, looking thoughtful. 'Fire would do it, but there's no point up here, that wouldn't pinpoint anything and I presume you'd have a fixed objection to setting the *Sea Scorpion* on fire.'

'With the holds full of trapped men? Yes, I would!' She sat down on a smooth boulder and regarded him. 'Would you really betray McTiernan and the crew?'

'For the bounty on their heads? Yes. I could do with the money.' Nathan had the glass to his eye, scanning not just the sea, but sweeping round to the larger island behind them and the wooded slopes falling away from their viewpoint.

'That seems...'

'Risky?' He lowered the glass and studied her face. Clemence knew she was frowning.

'Well, yes, that of course, McTiernan would have your liver. But you signed up with them.'

'Honour amongst thieves? You think I should be loyal to that crew of murderous vagabonds?'

'I know it sounds wrong.' She struggled with it some more. 'It is just that two wrongs don't make a right.'

'So loyalty is an absolute virtue and, having joined the

pirates, I must remain one? My shipmates, right or wrong?'
Nathan rested one hip on a rock in front of her. 'You are a
severe moralist, Clem.'

'Oh, no, never that!' Clemence protested. 'I don't want
to judge.'

'But you are judging me?'

'Yes,' she conceded miserably confused. 'I know I am.'
She hated the moral ambiguity, *his* moral ambiguity. Why
couldn't he be a hero, purer than pure? How could she be
trembling on the brink of falling in love with a man like him?

Chapter Eight

'So, you can't trust a pirate turncoat?' Nathan enquired.

'I shouldn't. But I do about some things.' She scuffed the gritty soil under her toe. 'I trust you not to betray me, even when I do foolish things.'

'Yes, you can rely on me for that. But you couldn't trust me not to kiss you,' he pointed out.

'I wanted you to,' she said baldly, still staring at her toes. 'Both times. And you stopped at a kiss. Thank goodness,' she added hastily.

'You are a virgin, Clemence,' he said, his voice harsh. 'I am—I *was*—a gentleman. I told you, I do not seduce virgins.'

'No. Of course not.' When she dared to look up again, Nathan was on his feet, using the rock as a rest while he made notes. 'Can I help?'

'No, thank you,' he said absently, squinting at the horizon and then looking back at his notes. 'Why not lay out the food and we'll eat? Have a look over there—' He waved towards an outcrop of tumbled rocks. 'There might be a good view on the other side of those. I'll be along in a minute.'

Clemence gathered up her satchel and made for the rocks.

She had been wondering how to discreetly slip away and find a rock to shelter behind to make herself comfortable; Nathan was being very tactful.

As Clemence disappeared around the heap of rocks Nathan pulled a mirror, the size of his palm, from his pocket and angled it to the sun, moving it in a jerky rhythm. 'Look this way, damn you,' he muttered. The frigate still rode beside the merchantman, its flag hoists inactive. Somewhere out on that blue expanse was the fishing boat that had been dogging their steps and had signalled ahead when they entered the channel last night. It was gratifying that they had second-guessed McTiernan's movements, set the first decoy up at the right place.

Appear to leave, stay close, use second decoy, he signalled, over and over. Finally a dark dot appeared against the white canvas, struggling up towards the to'gallants. He put the mirror back in his pocket and raised the telescope.

Acknowledged. Stand by. Two days. Two more days eyeball to eyeball with McTiernan and Cutler. This had better be worth it, although just at the moment he was coming to the conclusion that simply getting out with a whole skin was the most he could hope for. A whole skin and Clemence.

Nathan scrubbed a hand through his hair. It was bad enough having those clear eyes judging him for being a pirate, let alone a turncoat pirate. The temptation to justify himself to her was strong, but if she knew the truth it would only put her in more danger than she was already. He would just have to add her disapproval to the other burdens of the situation.

With the telescope tucked under his arm, Nathan went to see what she had managed to find for their picnic. 'A whole chicken? How in Hades did you manage that?' It was small and scrawny, but even so, a chicken was a chicken.

'I snivelled a bit. Said you'd hit me and I wanted something to put you in a good mood,' she confessed with a grin. 'Mr Street had just fished three birds out of the pot. He said I had probably deserved a good thrashing because all boys were the spawn of the devil, but he was smiling, so I grabbed a chicken and a loaf and some of the butter and things.' She gestured at the spread.

'You'd make a very promising conman, young Clem.' Nathan hunkered down and began to tear the fowl apart. 'What would Miss Clemence be doing now, assuming your uncle hadn't turned out to be such a villain?'

'Oh, managing the household, sewing, meeting friends. I've got a nice garden.' Something about the way she was so focused on the food and so off-hand with her brief description made him suspicious.

'Courting a handsome local lad?'

'No!' That was very vehement. 'I know them all too well— it would be like courting my own brother.'

'Dashing naval officers, then?' Nathan settled down, propped himself on one elbow, and began to gnaw at a chicken leg. 'I hear the uniform attracts the ladies.' *I know damn well it does—that and a fat purse of prize money.*

'Don't you know from your own experience?' she asked, looking up, her eyes very green in the sunlight. The scruffy urchin had vanished and in his place was a young lady regarding him from beneath haughtily lifted eyebrows.

'I was at sea a lot of the time,' he said, treading cautiously, unsure whether she was testing his story or simply showing feminine curiosity about the women in his life.

'Oh, yes, I recall you telling me about your career. You obviously had far more exciting things to be doing than courting gentlewomen.' Clemence lobbed a chicken bone over one shoulder into the undergrowth, the young lady vanishing again. 'No, I never found the naval officers very tempting, either. They were so determined to see how far their flirtations would get them before they could escape again to their ships, leaving a trail of broken hearts in their wake.'

'Did you go to receptions at the King's House?'

'Oh, yes.' Clemence spread butter on a crust with a lavish hand. 'Goodness, I'm so hungry—it must be the sea air.' She tucked a lock of hair back behind her ear and waved the crust for emphasis. 'I don't know about England, but here virtually the entire white population is on visiting terms and is invited to receptions by the Governor.

'Society is so small that the social divisions almost disappear. Visiting ladies always say that balls and routs are complete romps and turn up their noses at us when they find themselves sitting next to an attorney or a shopkeeper at a dinner party, but it would be ridiculous if society were confined to a handful of leading planters and the richest merchants.'

'So, no young man to deliver you back to,' Nathan mused, realising he was not finding that thought displeasing.

'It is a trifle premature to think about getting back safe to Kingston, is it not?' Clemence asked.

'Perhaps. I like to plan ahead. What's your surname, Clemence?' he asked, realising that she had never told him. Now why not?

'Browne.' The response was so quick, he should not have been suspicious, but there was something about the way she held his eyes, as though daring him to challenge her, that told him she was lying. No, she did not trust him, not wholly. Sensible woman.

He nodded and she leaned against a rock, apparently sated,

and tipped her face up to the sun. The shaggy hair fell back, giving Nathan a clear sight of her face. The swelling had gone down, the bruises were turning yellow. Soon the disfigurement would be gone, any lingering traces disguised by a healthy tan. How easy would it be to hide the fact that she was a girl when that happened?

Two days to survive before this all came to a head. Nathan shifted uncomfortably. Lying around felt wrong, even though there was nothing he could do now. He had gone into this deception knowing there was a good chance he would not come out of it. At the time, the gains had seemed worth the risk and he had always been ready to play the odds, especially when he did not much care about his own skin. Now he was responsible for Clemence and there was no one he could rely on to protect her if the worst happened. He had to stay alive—which might not be something he had much control over.

Although there were the men in the hold. Would they be in any condition to fight if he could free them? It would shorten the odds, although the timing would be critical.

'You look grim,' Clemence observed, head on one side. 'And tired. Are you sleeping at night?'

'Yes, I'm sleeping.' And dreaming. His dreams seemed to be full of smoke and blood and the rattle of that disgusting bundle of rotting bones at the masthead. He woke every time feeling as though he'd just fought a ship action. It was curiously pleasant to have someone to worry about him.

'Good.' Clemence closed her eyes again and he sat and watched while she dropped off. Her mouth opened a little, her breath came in foolish whiffles and her long limbs relaxed into an endearing, graceful sprawl. Nathan wanted to crawl over, put his head in her lap and sleep, too, perhaps to wake and find she was stroking his hair. Instead, he sat up and thought, long and hard.

Clemence woke, feeling warm and relaxed and safe. Her eyes were closed, but she could feel Nathan watching her, those deep blue eyes resting on her face. Why did she have to meet him when she was looking absolutely at her worst? Hair hacked off, face black and blue, what small curves she had ruthlessly suppressed, nothing but a scruffy urchin.

He had kissed her twice, and had managed to restrain his passionate impulses very effectively. What would he think of her if he could see her all dressed up, her hair grown again, her bruises gone? Nothing, probably, just that here was another young lady. And if Miss Clemence Ravenhurst met Mr Nathan Stanier on Jamaica, she assumed he'd be in shackles and on his way to the gallows and in no state to flirt.

On that disturbing thought she opened her eyes wide. Nathan smiled at her sleepily. Whatever happened, she had to make sure he did not get caught if, by some miracle, they got safe back to Kingston. He probably had some gallant notion of delivering her to the Governor; she would have to stop that. He might think he was looking after her, but she suspected it might work both ways.

'I think I can swim now without sinking,' she announced, gathering up the remains of the food.

'How long has it been since you have swum?' he asked, stopping to help her down the steep part again.

'Just before my father died,' she confessed, amused to see that he looked faintly shocked and, perhaps, intrigued. 'There are lots of bathing pools on the island and many ladies swim. You have to be careful around the swamps, of course, because of the unhealthy airs, but the fast-flowing streams are safe.'

A little *frisson* ran through her. Nathan was studiously

not commenting, which meant, perhaps, that his imagination was running riot, a fact that ought to embarrass her, but did not. It seemed that being kidnapped by pirates resulted in a deplorable lowering of one's sensibilities.

'Ladies swim in England, don't they?' she asked. 'In the sea, at any rate. I've heard about bathing machines.'

Nathan gave a snort of laughter. 'Yes, they swim—or at least, immerse themselves in the sea. They wear strange flannel bathing dresses and are guarded by fierce women with arms like blacksmiths whose job is to dunk them right under.'

'What on earth for? It sounds horrible.' And wet flannel. Ugh. The joy of swimming was to be naked, to feel the water slide like silk over your limbs, to hang, suspended like a bird, weightless.

'Because one does not swim for pleasure in England, one does it for one's health.'

'I'm sure the men don't put on strange flannel garments and submit to being dunked,' Clemence retorted. 'I'm sure you swim naked where you want to and it is up to the ladies to keep out of the way.'

Was it her imagination or was the back of Nathan's neck becoming flushed? It was probably just the heat—surely she wasn't embarrassing him? As they reached the pool, he turned aside. 'I'll sit here on this log and keep an eye on the path up from the cove,' he said, to her ears sounding somehow constrained as he stood with his back to her and the water. 'There are towels in my pack.'

'Thank you.' Touched by his thoughtfulness Clemence reached out, then pulled her hand back. He might misinterpret her action and imagine she wanted…something. She caught herself up, turned her hand towards the satchel and pulled out a thin linen towel. He would be correct—she *did* want him and he was being gentlemanly about his needs, so provocation was not the action of a lady.

She looked down at her filthy feet as she heeled off her shoes and chuckled. Those weren't the feet of a lady, either, or the hands. The sight of her masculine attire draped on the bushes would doubtless give her unknown Aunt Amelia in London hysterics, and as for the tale of what had happened in the last few months—well, she couldn't imagine beginning to try to explain that to a well-bred society lady.

The water was cool to a cautious toe. Clemence sat on a rock and slipped in before she could think about it, vanishing straight down into the depths. She surfaced with a strangled shriek.

'Clemence! Are you all right?' She pushed the dripping hair back from her face with both hands and hung there, treading water and looking up. Nathan, knife in hand, was poised on the brink of the pool above her.

'Yes, sorry I startled you. I'm fine, but it is deep and cold and I jumped right in.' After that first searching look, he was now staring firmly ahead into the bushes on the far side. Clemence glanced down at herself. Here in the shade all she could see though the greenish water was the pale shimmer of her body. Possibly, from above, she was rather more revealed, but that was all the more reason for them both to be on the same level.

'Why don't you swim, too? It is so refreshing once you are in.'

'Is it deep right across?' he asked, still not looking down.

'Yes, very. We could stay back to back, that would be perfectly proper,' she coaxed. And cold water was very dampening to male passion, she had heard, so he would not have to exert any will-power. Making that as an additional argument might not be a good idea, so she contented herself with paddling off under an overhanging fern to allow him to undress in privacy.

'Close your eyes.' Clemence squeezed them shut, then opened them just a crack in time to see Nathan's naked body slice through the surface in a shallow dive.

He surfaced, hair otter-sleek to his head. 'It's freezing, woman!' But he was grinning as he sent a great splash of water towards her with a sweep of his arm. So much for modestly swimming back to back.

Clemence ducked and swam underwater across the pool, glimpsing the pale length of his body through the green haze, then popped up behind him. 'Not if you move about,' she called, turning on to her back and kicking up a shower of spray to cascade on to his head. Nathan dived like a dolphin, arching up, leaving her with a startling image of fluid body, taut buttocks and long legs, then the surface of the pool was empty except for her and the spreading rings of ripples.

'Nathan?' she queried foolishly into the sudden silence, as something seized her ankles and she was pulled down by ruthless hands. Clemence shut her mouth just in time, kicked and they released her, only to fasten on her waist and propel her up, breaking the surface and tossing her into the air.

She landed with a huge splash, flailing and laughing and spouting water. 'Wretch!'

'That's for luring me into your freezing pool.' He swam lazily towards the little waterfall and levered himself up on braced forearms, twisting to sit on a concealed ledge just under the surface, the cascade breaking over his head and shoulders so he was almost lost in foam. He looked, Clemence thought, like a water god waiting to surprise travellers or perhaps to pounce lustfully on a passing nymph.

She was the nearest thing to a nymph available, she speculated, paddling gently on the spot, watching Nathan who, with closed eyes, was luxuriating in the pounding massage of the water on his shoulders. There was a clump of lily-like blooms growing beside her sheltering fern, the flower trumpets a rich amber yellow with nodding dark-brown stamens. Clemence reached up and broke one off, then tucked it behind her ear.

With her bruised face she would look ridiculous, she was quite certain, but it might make Nathan smile; somehow, his pleasure had become important to her. She swam slowly out into the middle of the pool and waited for him to open his eyes. When he did, he just stared. Her heart sank; he was not amused, merely baffled by her behaviour.

'Clemence,' he managed after a long minute, probably at a loss for anything nice to say.

'I know, I look an idiot, I was just thinking you look like a water god and you ought to have a nymph and I was trying to appear more nymph-like because I thought that would amuse you, but obviously I don't and you aren't...' She was babbling. Slowly her voice trailed away, the heat of her blushes burning her cheeks.

Nathan simply slid into the water and took two long overarm strokes to reach her. He put one hand either side of her waist, Clemence lifted her hands to his shoulders and they hung together in the green water, a foot apart, staring into each other's eyes.

'Yes,' he said slowly. 'That's what you are, a water spirit with your big green eyes and those fey looks and your long, graceful limbs made for slipping through clear water.'

'Me?' The word came out on a gasp. He was so close she could feel his body heat through the water. She could see down below the surface, down to the dark hair on his chest, narrowing to where she dared not let her gaze follow. Under her palms she could feel the bunch and flex of muscles as he trod water, supporting her, and the ripples their floating bodies made washed against her skin like the touch of a thousand caressing fingers.

'Yes, you,' Nathan said. He did not seem to have the same inhibitions about looking down through the water as she had. 'And I can't recall who you said likened your figure to a kipper, but all I can say is, they have been eating some very odd fish.'

'I'm flat...'

'You shouldn't listen to other people.'

'Just to you?'

'Yes, I know what I'm talking about. You have curves in all the right places, Clemence.' His hands slid down to her hips and then back to her waist.

'But—' She stared down at her chest, biting her lip. Their bodies glimmered pale as ivory through the greenish water as though seen through thick old glass. Oddly, there did seem to be rather more bosom than she had possessed when she'd fled Raven's Hold.

'And you have the loveliest breasts. Perfect.' Before she could flutter her feet and propel herself away, his right hand came up, cupped, just below her left breast. He did not touch her, yet the upward pressure on the water seemed to support the flesh, caress it. The nipple stiffened betrayingly. 'Perfect,' Nathan repeated. Then he was swimming away from her to the bank.

Confused, delighted, aroused and painfully shy, Clemence turned, thankful for the cool water against her hot cheeks as she heard Nathan splashing as he got out of the pool behind her.

There were the sounds of him moving away, then she sensed she was alone. *Perfect?* He thought her body was perfect? It must be a long time indeed since he had lain with a woman if that was what he thought, Clemence told herself. On the other hand, men did seem to be able to get physically excited by *anything* female, which was very odd of them.

Take Cousin Lewis, for example, she mused, as she climbed out of the water and reached for the towel. He had made it very clear he thought her unattractive and yet he was also supremely confident that he could have sex with her and leave her with child, even though he had a beautiful and passionate mistress under the same roof.

She towelled herself, then wrapped the linen strips tight around her breasts again. She was beginning to hate the hot restrictive feeling, so much worse than the carefully structured support of light stays. But Nathan was right; for some reason, perhaps the food and fresh air and exercise, her small curves were coming back and she could not risk discovery for the sake of comfort.

'Are you decent?' He sounded as detached as if they had just been for a country walk with a chaperon, not swimming naked in a tropical pool.

'Perfectly,' Clemence assured him, managing to sound equally genteel. 'I wish I'd brought a comb, though.'

'Here.' Nathan produced a battered bone comb from the depths of a waistcoat pocket, eyeing her critically as she raked it through her hair.

Clemence shook her head to produce a tousled look and squinted at him through her damp fringe. 'My hair was my only beauty; I used to be able to comb it out almost down to my waist. Cutting it off hurt, but at the time I'd have shaved my head if it got me out of there.'

'Is that what they told you? That your hair was your only beauty?' Nathan shook his head. 'Obviously big green eyes like forest pools are two a penny on Jamaica. Come on, nymph, or the captain will have us holystoning the decks as punishment for being late back.'

Clemence found she was grinning foolishly as she followed Nathan's wide shoulders down the path. He thought her eyes were beautiful, he thought her figure was beautiful, he thought... She let herself slip into a daydream where her hair had miraculously grown again and Nathan was no navy renegade turned pirate, but instead appeared in elegant full-dress naval uniform to claim her hand, rescued her from the Naismiths, swept her off to his bedchamber...

'What's the matter?'

'Um?'

He was looking back over his shoulder at her. 'You sighed.'

'Oh. I suppose I'm tired, a little. Don't take any notice.'

Because I certainly cannot! Miracles do not happen, dreams do not come true and reality is just that. Real.

As she thought it, they came out of the trees and there, before them, was the hidden harbour, the *Sea Scorpion* in its lair at the centre. Quiet, malevolent and deadly. Clemence stared, all her sensual daydreams shrivelling like a love letter thrown on to hot coals. Here was her reality.

Chapter Nine

'**W**ell?' McTiernan was there as they climbed the ladder up to the main deck. Clemence clenched her hands on the wooden rungs, her head just below the soles of Nathan's shoes as the cold voice sliced away what remained of the warm glow inside her. 'What did you see?'

Nathan finished his climb, swung his leg over the side and dropped to the deck before he answered, turning away with McTiernan and leaving her to scramble up unaided and mercifully unregarded.

'The frigate's still there, helping the merchantman with its rigging. It's got no boats out, they haven't swung their cutter over to go exploring. My guess is that they think we're long gone.' Nathan produced his notebook, opening it up to show something to the captain.

'Those two islets? Yes, what about them?'

'From up high you can see there's a shallow sand-bar between them, but you can't detect it on the surface and the Admiralty charts don't show it, either. No rocks or coral heads and there's deep water either side. If we can get our angle of attack right, we ought to be able to drive a ship on to that and board it at our leisure. No need to pound it to bits and you can kedge it off again undamaged when you are ready.'

'Show me on the chart.' Clemence went and leaned on the mast on the far side, pretending to pick her teeth with a wood splinter. 'Aye...' McTiernan was nodding, she could see his shadow '...now that's a nice, tidy scheme, Mr Stanier.'

'I suggest you get skiffs out, harry the ship from both sides to drive it, otherwise there's too much sea for it to escape into,' Nathan continued.

Sick, Clemence pushed away from the mast and went to the galley which seemed, just now, like sanctuary. And she had started to believe that Nathan was a good man at heart, that he might be on the side of the angels—even if only for the thought of the reward.

McTiernan might be a pirate, but at least he wasn't two-faced. Nathan had absolutely no need to have put that strategy to the captain. McTiernan would have been quite happy with a report on the frigate. His only motive could have been to ingratiate himself, and, presumably, to share in the plunder until such time he could find an opportunity to betray this ship with some chance of escaping with a whole skin.

How could her instincts be so at fault? How could she have this bone-deep certainty that he was not all he seemed, when every time she let herself believe in him, he did something that proved her wrong?

'Look where you're going, boy!' She skipped back just in time to avoid the two men with the slop buckets of swill for the prisoners below. One of them dropped a cloth holding ship's biscuits and swore.

'I'll bring them, you've got your hands full.' She snatched up the bundle and fell in behind them, heart thudding. Now she would discover where the men were kept, perhaps see the door opened, catch a glimpse so she could assess their condition.

Down they went, down again, the decks becoming lower, the light from lanterns less bright, the stench of the bilges stronger. Finally the men grounded their pails and one lifted a key on a chain from a hook.

'What the—?' The foul language swept over Clemence, made worse somehow by the icy calm with which the rant was delivered.

'I was just helping, Cap'n,' she stammered when McTiernan was finally silent. Behind him, on the lowest step of the companionway, she could see Nathan's shadowy form.

'If I catch you down here again, brat, I'll have the flesh off your back. You hear me?'

'Yessir.'

'And that goes for anyone I don't tell to come here. Anyone. Is *that* clear?'

'Yessir.'

'Then get the hell out of here.' She tried to slide past him, but he lashed out at her as she did so, sending her into the bulkhead as though she weighed nothing. Clemence bounced off and into Nathan who grabbed her, none too gently.

He shoved her on to the steps. 'Idiot boy.' Clemence stumbled up, her head spinning, until they reached the deck where their cabin was. Nathan took her ear and dragged her towards it, keeping up a stream of angry reproof. 'You do as the captain says, always, do you hear me? Or you'll feel my fist even before he gets to you.'

The shove he gave her sent her sprawling onto his bunk as he slammed the door. Clemence tried to rub as many painful spots as she could at once—ear, head, shoulder—and glowered at Nathan.

'Ow!'

'Serves you right.' He leaned back against the door panels and regarded her with a look that held everything of the angry ship's officer and absolutely nothing of the tender man from the pool. 'Just what did you hope to achieve with that ridiculous start?'

'To see how the men were secured, whether they were chained up or free inside the hold, how many there are and if I knew any of them.'

'That *would* have been helpful if they recognised you— *good day, Miss Clemence,*' Nathan mimicked savagely. 'Even the dimmest member of the crew is going to suspect something if their captives started falling on your neck with happy cries of recognition.'

'It was so dark down there, you could hardly see, and anyway, they would never dream it was me,' she retorted. 'If we get into a fight, I was going to slip down and let them out. At best, they could attack the crew, at worst they wouldn't be trapped down there if we are holed.'

'Brilliant,' Nathan said.

'Thank you.' *At last, he realises that I am capable of doing something to help.*

'Brilliant, if you want to end up dead,' he continued grimly, 'You are not dealing with your uncle here, you are dealing with a murderous, insane, cunning, suspicious brute and you will give me your word you will not set foot on any deck below this one.'

'No.' Clemence rubbed her ear resentfully. 'You hurt me.'

'It had to look real. Swear, Clemence, or I'll lock you in this cabin for the duration.'

She had never broken a promise in her life. Oaths were sacred, but was a promise to a renegade binding? Was her conscience worth more than the lives below deck?

'I promise,' she said. *I promise to let those men out, I promise to do everything in my power to sink this ship.*

Nathan had obviously dealt with equivocal promises before. 'What, exactly, do you promise?'

'I promise not to go down to the orlop deck again,' she said between gritted teeth.

'Good, now stay here out of McTiernan's sight until he finds someone else to divert his attention.' He went out, closing the door behind him with such deliberate care that he may as well have slammed it.

'Yes, Lieutenant, or Captain or whatever you were, Stanier,' Clemence said mutinously to the empty air. 'Whatever you say, *sir.*' It did not help that she knew, deep down under her simmering frustration and anxiety, that he was only trying to protect her. She rubbed her ear again, wincing as she circled her shoulder to ease the bruises where McTiernan had flung her against the bulkhead, and made a conscious effort not to sulk.

Nathan leaned on the rail of the poop deck and watched Clemence seated below on an upturned bucket, peeling sweet potatoes for the next day by the light of a lantern. When he had let her out of the cabin, judging McTiernan's mood to have lifted a trifle, she was silent, stiff-shouldered, but not, thank God, prone to pouting.

She seemed to feel safe with the cook, so he did not interfere when she went to the galley and offered her services. At least he could keep an eye on her and she had stopped rubbing her sore ear. He felt bad about that, but he could hardly have taken her by the hand and led her off under McTiernan's bloodshot gaze. The urge to tell her who he was, what he was about, was an almost physical pressure that had to be resisted for her own safety. Clemence, when her emotions were engaged, was not the best actress in the world.

'We'll skulk for one more day,' the captain was saying to the first mate and the bo'sun. 'Let that bloody frigate get well away, then at first light the day after tomorrow we'll slip out and see what we can catch. Mr Stanier, show them your trap.'

Nathan turned to the chart and began to explain. When he looked back, Clemence and her bucket of potatoes had gone. With any luck she'd be asleep when he went down.

'You'll take the second watch, Mr Stanier.'

'Aye, aye, sir.' Time to snatch some sleep himself, in that case. Nathan touched two fingers to the brim of the wide straw hat he wore, noting inwardly how deeply the habits of respect to a captain were ingrained, and made for the cabin, collecting a mug of the well-stewed coffee from the galley stove as he passed.

'Good lad of yours, Mr Stanier.' Street loomed out of the shadows.

'He is that, most of the time. Boys will be boys.' Nathan eyed the big cook. He was a rogue, but not, he judged, a vicious one. 'Keep an eye out for him for me, eh? If we get into a scrap and I'm...not around.'

'Aye.' Street nodded, impassive. 'I'll do that.'

That was probably all he could do in the way of insurance. Nathan opened the door softly on to the dark cabin, noting the hump in the opposite bunk that was Clemence's sleeping form. He took off his shoes, unbuckled his sword belt and lay down, silent in the stillness so as not to wake her.

Then the quality of that stillness hit him and he held his breath. No one was breathing. When he pulled back the bedding he found not a young woman, but a roll of blankets. He did not waste any time swearing. There was only one place she could be, in defiance of her promises.

He did not take a lantern, feeling his way through the shadows, down past the gun deck with the occupied hammocks swinging to the motion of the ship and small groups of men dicing in pools of candlelight, down like a silent wraith into the stinking darkness of the orlop.

Only it was not dark. There was a figure holding a half-shuttered lantern, hand raised to the keys on their hook. As his heel hit the deck she swung round with a gasp and the keys dropped.

'You little fool.' He went down on one knee to retrieve the keys. 'I trusted you. Why is it impossible for a woman to keep her word?'

'This is more important,' she hissed back, her face white in the lamplight. He must have scared the wits out of her. 'This is my duty. Let me open the door and see who is in there, speak to them.'

'Duty!' He got to his feet. He knew where duty got you. 'Get back up. *Now.*'

They both heard the sound of feet on the deck over their heads at the same instant, saw the spill of light from a lantern. He had never hit a woman in his life, had never dreamed that he would. Nathan clenched his fist and caught Clemence a neat uppercut under her chin. She went down like a stone. He had just enough time to push her under the steps before McTiernan and Cutler appeared in the hatchway above.

'Well, well, well. What have we here, Mr Cutler?' The drawl sent a cold finger down Nathan's spine, his hand closed on empty air where his sword should be.

'It seems we have a navigator who doesn't obey orders, Captain,' the first mate answered, his eyes sliding warily over Nathan. 'You want to explain what you are doing here, Mr Stanier?'

'Curiosity.' Nathan hung the key back on its hook.

'Curiosity flayed the cat,' McTiernan said, coming slowly down the steps, his eyes never leaving Nathan's face. '*With* the cat.' He smiled thinly at his nasty pun. 'I don't make idle threats, Mr Stanier.'

'I imagine not.' Nathan felt relief that his voice was steady. His stomach churned. Out of the corner of his eye he saw Clemence stir and willed her to be still.

'A dozen?' Cutler suggested, something like a smile creasing the corner of his mouth.

'Eight,' McTiernan corrected. 'I want him on his feet in thirty-six hours. We'll have it done now; call all hands and tell the bo'sun.'

'With your permission, I'll stop off at my cabin and change,' Nathan drawled. 'This is a decent pair of trousers, I don't want to get blood on them.'

'…blood on them.' Clemence managed to focus her spinning brain and process the words that she had been hearing for the past few moments. *Blood.* They were going to flog Nathan. She had got him killed.

Three pairs of feet climbed the wooden steps over her head. Clemence dragged herself out and managed, using her hands, to climb after them. Her jaw throbbed, her ears were ringing, but that was as nothing compared to the utter terror gripping her. She saw Nathan move away from the others, go towards their cabin. At least they had not tied his hands. Could he get through a porthole? No, too small.

'Nathan.' He was stripping off his trousers as she hurtled into the cabin, breathless with fear. He dropped them on the floor and pulled on a pair of old loose canvas ones, not bothering to tuck the shirt back.

'Are you all right?' He pulled her towards him, his hands

firm on her bruised jaw as he explored it with calloused fingers. 'I didn't have time to argue with you.'

She ignored the question, jerking her chin out of his grip. 'Nathan, tell them it was me, that you were only following me.' She hung on his arm as he turned to the door.

'Clemence, if they take you to flog you they will find you're a girl, then they'll rape you.'

The cabin spun round her. 'I know, but it was my fault, I broke my promise, you can't be flogged for something I did.'

'And if they try to rape you,' Nathan continued inexorably, 'I'll have to try to stop them and they'll kill me. Eight lashes will not kill me. Now, do you want to get me killed in order to salve your conscience?'

'No! Nathan, I'm so sorry…' Eight lashes with a cat-o'-nine-tails. She couldn't even begin to imagine the pain, then she remembered the screams of the man who had dropped the fid from the mast and the room went dark.

'Listen.' Nathan had her by the shoulders, shaking her. 'You can't faint on me, you must not cry. Do you hear me? If you do, you'll give yourself away and this is for nothing.' She nodded, her eyes locked with his, something of his strength seeping in to give her courage. 'Come on, let's get it over with.'

Silent, feeling as though her blood was congealing in her veins, Clemence followed him. He must feel fear, and yet he did not show it. She could never put this right, but at least she could make sure it didn't get any worse, she resolved. She would be quiet, she would not weep and she would look after him when it was all over. He might, she supposed, forgive her one day. She thought she could never forgive herself.

Blinking, she stumbled out on to the lamplit deck, the hands all crowded round, the babble of excited voices. Nathan pushed her towards someone and a meaty hand took her shoulder and pulled her back behind him. Street.

'No. I've got to watch,' she stammered. 'My fault.' Listening to it happen would be even worse, she sensed. The cook shrugged, but let her stand in front of him. Nathan had tossed his shirt aside and stood, in front of one of the hatch grills that had been upended, bare feet braced on the scrubbed white planks. The bo'sun came forward with lashings, tied his wrists and ankles so he was spread-eagled against the frame, his face turned from her.

The man walked back, picked up a bag and drew the cat-o'-nine-tails from it, running his fingers through the knotted strings to shake out the tangles. Clemence's stomach clenched. She forced her eyes wide.

The crew fell silent, waiting. Their faces, she saw, were not showing any pleasure at this spectacle. Nathan was liked, or, at least, respected, and they knew that with this captain it could be their turn next. The first lash landed with a noise that made her flinch back against Street's great belly. He put one hand on each shoulder and held her. 'Steady, lad.'

Two. Three. The blood was running now. Four. Five. So much for Cutler's nice white deck, Clemence thought wildly. Nathan was silent, still, braced for the next blow, the muscles of his back and shoulders rigid and stark in the light. Six. He sagged, then recovered. Seven. She realised she was praying, her lips moving silently, although she hardly knew what she was asking for. This time he hung from his bonds, unmoving.

'*Thank you, God,*' she murmured, realising what she had been asking for. He had fainted.

Eight.

Street pushed her to one side and strode forward, catching Nathan's limp body as the lashings were cut. He slung him over one shoulder as if he was a side of beef and stomped back to the companionway. 'Bring water, boy. Salt and fresh.'

It took a moment to make her legs work. Clemence felt as though she were watching someone else through a thick pane of glass. Water splashed everywhere as she filled buckets, hands shaking. 'Here, I'll take those.' It was Gerritty, the sail-maker, taking a bucket and thrusting a bundle of soft rags into her hand. 'You'll need these.'

'Thank you.' She followed him down. There was no doctor on board. What should she do? What did you do for a man whose back was cut to ribbons?

She pushed past the men, stripping back the blanket on Nathan's bunk, taking away the pillow. 'Put him here.'

The big man laid the limp body face down, grunted and went out. 'Salt water first, while he's out of it,' the sail-maker advised. 'Cleans it out. Then the fresh.'

Street came back and thrust a bottle into her hand. 'Here, brandy.' That appeared to be all the advice she was going to get.

The door closed behind them, leaving Clemence on her knees beside the bunk. Acting on instinct, she fumbled under Nathan's heavy body for the fastenings on his trousers, then pulled them down, leaving him naked on the bed. It never occurred to her to feel any embarrassment. Keeping him as comfortable as possible was all that mattered.

She rolled towels and pushed them along his sides and flanks, then started to wipe the blood off all the undamaged skin. She draped another sheet over him from the waist down, then made herself really look at his back for the first time.

It was as though someone had been tracing the pattern for a crazy patchwork quilt on his back in red ink, careless of how it ran. Salt water, Gerritty had said, and quickly, before he began to come round. Sponging, rinsing, she worked doggedly, not realising she was crying until something tickled the sore point of her chin and she rubbed the back of her hand across it.

There. She looked doubtfully at her still-bleeding handiwork. Now fresh water. And then what? Should it be bandaged, or left to the air? At least there were no flying insects here.

In the end she wrung out a large piece of soft clean cotton cloth and draped it over the wounds, then went to mix birch-bark powder into a mug of water. With nothing left to do, she went back to sit by his head to wait.

She wanted to put her hand over his as it lay lax on the pillow, but somehow she felt she had forfeited the right to touch him like that, even when he was unconscious.

The long hiss of indrawn breath had her alert in an instant. 'Nathan?'

His lips moved. Lip-reading, she came to the conclusion it was curses. She reached for the mug, then realised he could not drink in that position. 'I'll be back, just one moment.'

'Mr Street!'

The cook turned from his game of cards. 'Aye, lad? How's he doing?'

'He can't drink lying on his stomach. Have you got a clay pipe? A new one?'

He got up and lifted a long churchwarden pipe from a rack on the wall, its stem a good foot long, and knocked the bowl off with a sharp blow on the tabletop. 'That's good thinking, boy. He's come round, then?'

'Just. He's swearing a lot.'

'That'll do him good. You all right, Clem?'

'Yessir, thank you.' She could have hugged him, grease and all.

* * *

Nathan was moving his head, restless, when she got back. 'Clem?'

'I'm here.' She restrained the impulse to ask how it felt, how he was, all the other useless, automatic questions. Instead she dipped one end of the pipe stem in the mug of birch-bark powder and water and sucked until she could taste the bitter liquid in her mouth. She turned his head gently on the pillow and slid the stem into his mouth. 'Suck.' He grimaced, twisting away, but she held his head firmly. 'That's an order, Mr Stanier,' she said, making her shaking voice hard. Nathan gave a small gasp that she realised with surprise was a laugh, and did as she said.

When the liquid was almost gone she trickled brandy into the mug, sighing with relief when he slid back into unconsciousness again. Then she sat down on the deck by his shoulder, rested her head back against its hard edge and settled down to wait.

Now, with nothing to do but think, it was hard not to slip into complete despair. She was falling in love with Nathan Stanier; she could no longer delude herself that it was gratitude or desire or infatuation. And something was telling her to ignore the evidence of his presence on this ship and trust him with the rest of her life, if he wanted her.

But now she had broken her word to him and he had been punished, brutally, for her defiance. He might have desired her, he was too much a gentleman to stop protecting her, but he was never, after this, going to love her.

Chapter Ten

'Clemence?'

She was awake and twisting round on her knees in an instant. 'Yes? Nathan, what do you need?' His forehead was hot and sweaty under her palm, the cloth over his back darkly stained in the lantern light. 'Something to drink? Try more of this, there's brandy and water and the bark powder.'

He sucked greedily and his voice, when he spoke again, was stronger. 'What's on my back?'

'A damp cloth. I washed the wounds in salt water, then fresh, and covered them.'

'Good. There's a jar of salve in my pack. Green salve.'

Clemence found it, sniffed. 'It smells very odd.'

'It will help the healing and stop the cloth from sticking.' He lay still while she lifted the cloth away. 'How does it look?' He was by far the calmer of the two of them; she could hardly stop her hands from shaking.

'Um.' *Dreadful.* 'There's some swelling. It has stopped bleeding.' *More or less.* 'Do I spread the salve on the cloth?' The thought of having to touch that raw flesh, cause even more pain, made her dizzy.

'Yes.' There was silence while she worked at the table, trying to spread the evil-smelling stuff as evenly as possible. Then she lifted it by two corners and came back to the bed. 'Clemence, are you crying?'

'Yes,' she admitted.

'It stings when you drip.' Again that impossible hint of a laugh.

'Sorry.' She laid the cloth back in place, trying to ignore the indrawn hiss of breath. Then she sat down again, close to his head so he did not have to move to see where she was. 'I'm so sorry.'

'More salt water, good for it.' He had closed his eyes again.

'I mean I am sorry for this. For breaking my promise, for doing this to you.' She grabbed one of the cloths and blew her nose, furious with herself for showing her emotions. Nathan did not need tears and self-recrimination. He needed calm and sleep. She dipped a cloth in cold water and began to bathe his forehead.

'You did what you thought was right. You didn't ask me to get involved.'

'But I knew I could rely on you,' she admitted. 'I doubt I'd have had the nerve to do it at all without knowing that.' He seemed to have forgiven her—she could hardly believe it.

'You trust me, then?' Nathan's eyelids parted to reveal a glimmer of deep blue.

'With my life.'

He murmured something else that she could not catch. But he had drifted off again.

At some point she must have dozed and slid down to curl up on the floor, Clemence realised, waking to find herself stiff and cramped. She rolled over and sat up, wincing at the discomfort in her jaw and the aches in her joints, blinking at the light coming in through the porthole. It was morning. The bunk above her was empty. 'Nathan!'

'Here.' He came out of the privy cupboard, the sheet swathed round his hips.

Furious with relief and anxiety, Clemence scrambled to her feet, scolding like a fishwife. 'What do you think you are doing? How do you expect to get better? Get back to bed this instant!'

Under his tan he was flushed and he was moving like an old man in the grip of arthritis, but Nathan made it to a chair and sat down. 'There are some things a man cannot do lying on his front,' he pointed out, ignoring her *tsk!* of exasperation. 'And I need to keep moving.'

'Why?' Clemence demanded baldly, moving behind him to peer at the cloth.

'Because I need to be on deck and I can't navigate the ship flat on my stomach.'

'Why have you got to be there? I'll tell Captain McTiernan that you have a fever—which you have, don't try and deny it—and are in no fit state to help him harry any shipping tomorrow. It is his fault. If the man wasn't insane, he wouldn't flog valuable officers.'

'You'll explain that to him, will you? And after he picks you up and drops you overboard for insolence, who is going to bandage my back and get me my breakfast?'

'You should be lying down, resting. *Please*, Nathan.'

In answer he placed his elbows on the table and leaned forward, letting his forearms take the weight. 'Like this, I am resting. I need to eat and drink and the fever will go down. If you bandage my back, the salve will work. Believe me, I know what I'm doing.' He sounded as though he was hanging on to his patience by a thread, but she was too worried to heed that.

'How do you know? You've never been flogged before, I've seen your back.'

'But I've seen men flogged.'

Clemence backed away and sat down, hard, on his bunk. She found she was shaking her head.

'Please will you bandage my back?' he asked. 'And bring me food and help me get back up on deck?'

'Why should I?' she whispered.

'Because this is painful and I need the help? Because I'll feel better for eating?' he suggested. 'Because if I'm on deck at least we'll know what is going on? Because if I'm mobile there is some hope of getting those men below out of there?'

Clemence bit her lip. If he was lying down, he would be resting. Conventional wisdom said that you starved fevers. If he was not navigating, perhaps McTiernan would not make such a good job of hunting his prey.

'Because you trust me?' Nathan asked softly.

With my life. But not with head and not with my heart, oh, no. Not with those. 'Very well.' Clemence found the spare set of clean linen strips she had made to bind her own chest.

He sat up gingerly as she approached and raised his arms, making beads of sweat start on his forehead. But he sat still, with an effort she could feel vibrating through her fingers as she wrapped the bandages round, bringing a pass up over each shoulder to keep the strapping in place so she did not have to make them too tight.

'Thank you.' He leaned back on to his forearms. Clemence went in search of food, coffee and the strangely comforting bulk of Mr Street.

Nathan set himself to ignore the exhausting pain in his back and thought about Clemence. Tomorrow, if everything went according to plan, he would take the *Sea Scorpion* into a trap. If he survived the resulting action and if the ship was captured and if he got Clemence off safely— He stopped, contemplating that long list of *ifs*. Assume all that. Then he would take her back to Jamaica and do something about her uncle and cousin. And then what?

This adventure would have ruined her, he knew that. It made not a jot of difference whether he seduced her or not, the assumption would be that she was no longer a respectable marital proposition.

He didn't give a damn about that. All he knew was that he wanted her, physically and, increasingly, for all sorts of other reasons as well, the overriding one of which was the strong need he felt to protect her. And now marriage was the only thing that would save her from whatever fate awaited the ruined orphan daughters of small merchants within a claustrophobic island community.

Would she have him? She was as stubborn as a mule. She said that she trusted him, although he doubted that trust was wholehearted—she was too intelligent for that. How was she going to react to the extent of his deception and what he must tell her about his past life? And then, if he persuaded her to say *yes*, others would most certainly have something to say about such a match. His mother, for one, the rumour-mongers for another. For himself, he didn't care. He was never going to fall in love again, that was over and done with; marriage to Clemence would do very well. But could she cope with the reality of life with him?

She was very young, very inexperienced in the hard realities of life away from her comfortable middle-class existence. If she married him, her world would be turned on its head yet again. Would that be better than the alternative? It had to be. Although, looked at from the viewpoint of this cabin, at this moment, he was not much of a catch; his prospects just now appeared negligible.

Nathan shifted in his seat and swore. The pain was going to be better tomorrow, he knew. Agony though it had been, eight lashes got nowhere near the dreadful damage a prolonged flogging would inflict.

He was going to have to get up again in a minute and move around. By tomorrow, he had to be at least fit enough to keep on his feet, hold a pistol and look after Clemence or all of this agonising over her future would be pointless.

Gritting his teeth, he stood and moved to where she had folded his clothes so neatly. It made him smile, the way she attacked the hated task of keeping the cabin clean and tidy and the rueful way she acknowledged that she had been fortunate in the past to have had servants. She didn't grumble about her changed circumstances, just coerced the dirt and disorder into submission and got on with the next thing. He wanted, Nathan realised, to pamper her and shower her with luxury and that was ridiculous. She would not be the woman he thought she was, if she would find that kind of existence acceptable, even assuming he could afford it.

No, marriage to him would be hard work and something utterly different from anything Clemence was used to. She was so very young, ten years younger than he. Was he being fair to even think of asking her? Probably not, but that was not going to stop him, if he survived. Fairness didn't come into it; making the best of a bad situation and doing his duty to look after her was all that mattered.

He sat down to put on his shirt, relieved to find that he was not as weak as he feared. The widespread damage to his back was painful, but it did not, from that number of lashes, have the deep impact a sword or bullet wound had, shocking the entire system and costing pints of blood. Already the green salve that he had purchased from a herbalist when he had been briefly stationed on Corfu was working its magic. It was going to be a while before he slept on his back though, he thought, pushing his feet into his shoes and standing with caution to buckle his sword belt low on his hips so it did not chafe.

Clemence found him as he made it to the deck and stood catching his breath. 'You idiot!' she hissed, stabbing him in the chest with one very sharp finger. 'What are you doing? You told me you were resting.'

'You are behaving like a nagging wife,' he murmured, observing with interest the way she coloured up. Interesting that she should react so. Was it possible that she had been thinking of herself in those terms?

She dropped her hand and glared, shrugging, a sulky boy again for the onlookers. 'You'll bleed on your shirt and I'll have to wash it again,' she said.

'Cheeky brat,' he said with a simulacrum of irritation. 'Go and get me some food.' He resisted the temptation to follow her with his eyes as she left, focusing instead on the challenge of negotiating the ladder to the poop deck, with McTiernan waiting at the top of them.

'You're a hard man, Stanier,' the captain observed when he joined him at the wheel. 'Perhaps I should have added a few more lashes.'

'There's just so much I can take of staring at my cabin walls.' Nathan almost shrugged, then thought better of it. Exercise was one thing, violently agitating his back muscles, another. He hitched a hip on to the hatch cover. 'What's the plan for tomorrow?'

'One of the skiffs has just come in.' McTiernan jerked his head towards the little craft bobbing alongside. The crew were furling the lateen sail and securing the lines. 'There's a nice little merchantman making ready to sail with a most interesting cargo.' Nathan raised an eyebrow. 'Chests—and an armed escort at the dockside.'

'Bullion?'

'Could be. All very secretive, the idiots. If they'd taken no precautions, they wouldn't have stood out.' Nathan suppressed a grin. *Bluff and double bluff.* 'If the winds hold as they are, it will be passing tomorrow before noon. We'll get the skiffs out and the lugger with a couple of light guns on it to herd it back towards your sand-bar.' He ran a cold eye down Nathan's carefully still body. 'You up to the chase?'

Nathan contemplated the likely results of saying *no.* 'Aye, Captain.' Down on the deck he could see Clemence balancing his meal in one hand with two tankards gripped in the other and exchanging mild insults with two of the hands. 'I'll get some food,' he observed, concentrating on not wincing as he stood up. She was getting too confident, he worried, then saw her put the food down on a barrel and swing up into the rigging, climbing like a monkey to the first spar, apparently just for the hell of it. No, perhaps she was right. Who would suspect a merchant's daughter could be capable of scrambling about twenty foot above deck?

'Get down here, Clem!' Clemence peered down through the lattice of rigging at Nathan's upturned face. He wasn't going to let her fuss over him, that was plain. She began to descend, revelling in the freedom that climbing gave her. Her muscles were working again, she had an appetite, she felt fit and happy and terrified, all at once, and the source of that happiness was standing eating the cheese she'd brought him, a scowl on his face.

Nathan was only pretending to be angry, she was almost certain. Sometimes she thought that she was beginning to understand him, could read the expression in his eyes. And then he reacted in a way that surprised her, or the amusement turned to something still and secretive and she realised she didn't know him at all. And although he knew her lethally dangerous secret, she was convinced that he was confiding in her only what was absolutely unavoidable.

She dropped to the deck and trotted over. 'Sorry.'

'No, you are not.' He pushed the food towards her and shifted his position as if getting comfortable.

Instinctively Clemence followed his gaze around. Yes, there was no one within earshot. 'What is it?'

'I don't know whether I'll get another chance to talk to you—McTiernan is planning and we could be on deck all night. Tomorrow there will be a fight. They've spotted the ship they want, and very tempting it is, too. We'll drive it on to the sand-bar and then the plan is to board it.'

'Yes?'

'But the crew of the merchantman will board us instead and when that happens I want you to get down to the orlop and let those men out. Tell them that the navy is up top and show them the weapon chests on the gun deck—and then get into the cabin and stay there. Do you understand?'

'The navy? How do you know?' Understanding and an enormous sense of relief flooded through her. 'You've planned this all along, haven't you? The crippled merchantman...that was a trap that went wrong. You aren't just an opportunist, seeing if you can find a way to get a reward if the chance arises, are you?'

'No. You'll do as I say?'

She ignored the question. 'Who are you?'

He met her eyes, his shuttered. 'Nathan Stanier.'

'You are still in the navy, aren't you?' *Please say yes, please tell me that I can believe in you.*

'I'm working with them. I've told you all you need to know.' He hesitated. 'If anything happens and I'm...not around, go to Street. He's the best of a bad bunch.'

The cold seemed to sink down from the crown of her head to her toes, despite the heat. 'You mean, if you are killed?'

'It is going to get confused. I might not be in the right place at the right time, that's all.'

'How can you fight with your back in that state?' she asked through tight lips.

'I shall endeavour to use a pistol and not engage in any strenuous hand-to-hand combat,' Nathan said lightly, as though they were discussing a friendly fencing match and not a pitched battle with murderous pirates.

'Nathan.' She had to say this now, in this moment of stillness before the storm, or she might never have the opportunity to say it again. Something in her tone reached him, his eyes narrowed on her face. 'Nathan, I am sorry I did not trust you at first. I do now.' Somehow, she couldn't say the other thing, utter the three words that filled her heart. She did not have the courage.

But he knew there was something behind her sudden admission, even if he did not understand it. He kept his face under control with an effort that was visible to her, but Clemence had no way of telling what emotion he was concealing.

'Clemence, you are very young,' he began and her heart sank. 'What you think about me is...confused.'

'I had to start growing up extremely fast the day my father died,' she countered. 'I know what I feel. It took me some time to trust you—and you didn't help!—but I liked you, almost from the start.'

'We have been thrown together, intimately. You have come to rely on me. It is not so very surprising that you think you may—' He searched for a phrase. 'That you have come to like me more than is wise,' he persisted patiently.

He did guess she felt more than liking for him. A wave of humiliating heat swept over her. Perhaps he even thought she had formed a *tendre* for him. 'I didn't say I liked you too well,' she said with an attempt at hauteur, but knowing that she was blushing furiously. 'Goodness, I know you are a rogue, navy or not, and your life must be full of loose women. I'm not such an idiot that I'd think you *wanted* me, or anything like that.' *Oh, Lord, how did I get into this muddle?* 'You think I'm an annoying brat, even if you do want to kiss me occasionally, but I expect that's just being male.' She stopped. 'I just wanted you to know I do trust you.'

'I see.' Nathan studied her flushed face. 'What has changed?'

'I don't know. I shouldn't trust you, even now. You won't tell me what you really are.'

He grimaced. 'I tell you what it is safe for you to know. And you are right, men want to kiss pretty girls, it is one of the failings of the sex. And I think you are a handful, although I don't think I'd describe you as a brat. You don't have to make declarations of trust, Clem, I'll do my best to get you out of this, and, when I do, we'll see what the Governor can do to make things right.'

She shook her head, not at all comforted by the thought of the Governor's assistance.

'Try not to worry—if he cannot hush this up, then I'll marry you. I don't think I'm much of a bargain, but marriage to me is probably better than life as a ruined woman.'

'Marry you?' A bucket of cold sea water wouldn't be much more of a slap in the face. Clemence bit her lip and struggled to preserve some dignity after that comprehensively well-meaning and damning proposal. She had told him she trusted him, against reason, and he thought she was asking him to take care of her when all this was over. And, of course, that meant marriage, so the wretched man was being noble about it.

'Thank you, Mr Stanier, but no. I doubt a young lady could expect a less romantic offer of marriage. I told you that I trusted you, not that I was looking for a husband. Please be assured that I will not put you to the trouble; I would walk the streets of Kingston, rather, than marry a man like you.'

'Clemence, damn it—'

She ducked away from his outstretched hand. 'Excuse me, I'll just go and check I know where all the weapon chests are below deck.' *And find a corner in the dark to have a good weep.*

'Clem!'

She ran. Behind her she heard McTiernan. 'Mr Stanier! When you have quite finished failing to control that boy, perhaps you would be so good as to join us?'

Chapter Eleven

Nathan was still cursing himself hours later when he went down to the cabin to snatch a few hours' sleep. The pain in his back as he eased cautiously down to lie on his stomach on the bunk was an almost welcome distraction. From across the cabin came the sound of Clemence attempting to breathe as though she were asleep and not lying there confused and wounded by his tactlessness.

A demon of temptation whispered that he should go over there, take her in his arms and make love to her. His conscience told him that doing that could only make things worse; besides, he was in no fit state to make love to a virgin as she deserved to be loved. Which thought produced the inevitably uncomfortable result.

Damn, there went any hope of sleep. The one thing he had been resolved upon was that he must protect her, not hurt her, and instead he had leapt to conclusions and in trying to reassure her he had managed to both wound her and shatter the confidence between them. And come daybreak she was going to need that confidence.

The fact that her violent repudiation of his proposal made

him not irritated, or relieved, but disappointed, was not lost on him. If she were not having unwise feelings, then he most certainly was. But increasingly the idea of marriage to Clemence, young as she was, ignorant, too, of the realities of life to a man who made his living at sea, was becoming strangely tempting.

He lay, dozing fitfully, part of his mind noting the ship's bell counting the hours, vividly aware of the pattern of Clemence's breathing as she finally slept.

When a thin light began to show through the porthole he got to his feet, methodically working the protesting muscles, wincing as the healing lash marks stuck to the bandages.

It was better than he had feared and once the action began he would not be so aware of it. He'd fought with a bullet in his upper arm and a sabre slash down his thigh before now. Nathan laid out his pistols on the table and quietly began to strip them down and clean them. More than his life was going to depend on them today.

When he could not leave it any longer, he went to her bunk and laid the back of his hand against her cheek. 'Clemence.'

'Mmm?' She turned her face against his hand like a cat, a smile curving her lips, eyes closed. Nathan saw the exact moment when she recalled where she was and what had happened yesterday. He took his hand away and turned back to the table, unwilling to see her eyes on him, for her to see him lift his own hand against his cheek for a fleeting moment.

'Time to get up. Stay near the head of the companionway and then, when we're about to grapple her, go down to the orlop.' He wanted to say *take care*, for all the good it did, but his voice seemed to be failing him and he needed to be out of there.

The door handle was in his grasp when she spoke. 'I just want to say, I *do* trust you. And, good luck, Nathan.'

He should turn, talk to her, but he found he could not. Something was tight in his throat—it felt, impossibly, like his heart. Somehow he got the door open. 'Thank you.'

Superstition maintained that when something was going absolutely to plan, then disaster could not be far away. By that reckoning, he was in for a bad time, Nathan decided, watching the merchantman *Bonny Lass* tack and turn ahead of them, harried by the light guns of the skiff blocking the open sea. The gap between the islets beckoned, temptingly. Unless they had a man in the top-mast crow's nest, then they would never see the danger shimmering beneath the waves, not if they were the ship McTiernan believed them to be.

Closer and closer they drew, gaining on their prey. 'Terrible sail handling,' Cutler remarked as *Bonny Lass* lost more way.

'Panicking,' Nathan suggested, one wary eye out for Clemence, loitering by the dark mouth of the companionway. *Don't overdo it*, he thought urgently as though he could reach James Melville, his old friend, captaining the decoy in his shirt-sleeves with no gold lace to betray his true identity.

Long minutes passed as the two ships closed. He could see them in his mind's eye as though from the peak of Lizard Island, two elegant toys skimming across the green-blue ocean without a hint of the carnage that was about to be unleashed.

Bonny Lass slid into the trap. Nathan felt himself hold his breath. Had he miscalculated? Was the smaller ship going to clear the sand-bar? And then it struck as though it had hit a wall and *Sea Scorpion*, responding to the helm, swung round to come up alongside it.

Nathan spun on his heel; the mouth of the companion-way was empty. Clemence had gone. He drew his pistol and turned back, one target in mind, but McTiernan was already down the steps, dodging amidst the mêlée. Cursing, Nathan followed Cutler, searching for a clear shot.

Clemence was buffeted by the men running up from the gun deck to join the hand-to-hand fighting above. That one last glimpse she had of Nathan, pistol in hand, seemed burned into her mind as she stumbled down, snatching a lantern as she went.

The key was still on its hook and behind the closed door she could hear shouts. As she tried to unlock the door something heavy hit the inside, sending the key tumbling from her fingers. Doggedly she tried again and it came open, bringing with it the men who had been trying to break it down.

One of them lunged for her throat. 'Johnnie Wright! It's me, Clemence Ravenhurst!'

She hardly recognised him. The mate of the *Raven Duchess*, his face white and pinched, his eyes wild, stared at her, hands still raised. 'Miss Clemence?'

'Yes. No time to explain, Johnnie—we're alongside a naval vessel. Can any of you fight? I know where there are weapons.'

'Aye, we can fight, can't we, lads?' There was a roar from behind him, then they were tumbling out of the hold, bearded, stinking, out for blood. Clemence turned and ran up the companionway, her scarecrow army at her heels.

'Here.' She gestured at the open weapon chests. *'Hurry!'*

They stampeded past her up to the noise of shouting, shots, the grinding of the two ships against each other. Panting, Clemence pulled her knife out of its sheath and followed.

She couldn't see Nathan, but she could see McTiernan,

Cutler at his side, fighting surrounded by bodies. There were blue naval uniforms, officers fighting hand to hand, seamen she didn't recognise who must be part of the decoy's crew. Splinters flew up from the deck at her feet and she saw marines in the rigging, firing down. A hand descended, pulled her back through a door.

Street wiped blood off his meat cleaver and showed his teeth. 'Your Mr Stanier's not what he seems, boy. Told me to look out for you. You reckon I ought to heed him?'

'He'll help you, if you do,' Clemence promised, craning to see past the cook's bulk. 'He said you're the best of the bunch. You can't want to follow a man like McTiernan, surely?'

'He's my captain, I don't turn my coat, leastways, not while the bastard's alive and breathing.'

A shadow fell across the doorway, a sailor, pistol in hand, the barrel pointing directly at Clemence. Trapped against the stove, she threw up her hands in a pointless gesture of defence; after all this, she was going to die here, now. It seemed impossible to feel such terror and still be conscious. She wanted to live, she wanted Nathan and now it was all going to end in noise and blood and smashed bone and agony—

The gun went off, the sound loud in the confined space, her heart seemed to stop, beside her an earthenware pot shattered. He had missed. In the second it took her to realise she was still alive, Street raised his hand wrapped around a long-barrelled pistol. The man took the shot in the face, falling back, dead before he hit the deck as Clemence, sickened, reeled back with a sob of terror, her vision filled with the image of what the bullet had done to human features. That had been a man. That had almost been her.

Then there was a scream, lost in a tremendous crashing, the sun vanished and the whole mainmast of the decoy ship began to fall. Clemence ducked away from Street's hand, dived through the door and saw Nathan in the stern as the mast came down between them.

Clemence's slight figure was lost in the descending mass of spars and canvas. Nathan began to move forward, parrying a descending sword. 'Hulme!' he shouted into the face of the lieutenant wielding the weapon.

The man pulled the stroke. 'Sir!'

'Pass the word, there are captives from the hold fighting on our side.' He raised his pistol, fired and a man about to stab a midshipman fell off the rail with a scream. 'I'm going forward.'

'You're going to hell.' It was Cutler, blood dripping down his face, his cutlass in his fist. 'You bloody spy.' He gestured with one hand, beckoning Nathan forward like an alley bruiser with a victim. 'Come on and die, Stanier.'

Nathan had no loaded weapons left, his cutlass had broken off five minutes before as he sliced at a pirate and hit a cannon on the down stroke.

'Sir!' Hulme was holding out his own sword.

'Thanks, but I've no time for this.' The dagger came out of its sheath as though it were oiled and his eyes were still locked with the first mate's when the blade thudded into the man's chest.

Nathan yanked it out and was running before the big body collapsed on to the deck, dodging through the knots of fighting men. The fallen mast blocked one end of the deck from the other as effectively as a wall—a shifting, treacherous wall full of traps and tangles. He turned aside, swung out into the rigging and began to climb.

The pain flashing across his back was like fire as he reached and stretched but he kept going, heading for the ropes dangling from the first spar. He couldn't see Clemence, but he could see McTiernan, cold as ice, his blade cutting down men all around him.

Then a scarecrow of a man pushed his way through to confront the captain. What he was yelling, Nathan couldn't hear as he climbed, bullets flying past his ears, but he saw the contemptuous ease with which McTiernan felled him with a sideways sweep of his cutlass, raised the weapon for the death blow.

And out of the smoke and confusion Clemence appeared, a broken spar in her hands. She swung it, even as Nathan shouted her name, and McTiernan's blade stuck into the wood. The man yanked it towards him and she went with it, into his lethal embrace.

He was still below the dangling rope. Nathan jumped, reaching with a yell of pain as the wounds on his back split open, but he had it, swinging across the barrier of the fallen mast. At the height of the swing he let go and hit *Sea Scorpion*'s limp foresail, one hand scrabbling for a handhold, the other slicing into the canvas with his dagger. The weapon held him for a moment and then began to cut down. All he could do was hang on, trying to control his descent with his feet as he slid towards the deck.

Below him was a blur of movement, but he could hear Clemence screaming defiance at McTiernan, and then he saw her, her hands locked around the man's sword hand with desperate strength, while he shook her back and forth like a terrier with a rat.

Nathan landed, staggering, behind them and launched himself at McTiernan's back just as the man swung Clemence round, taking Nathan off his feet. He seized her as he fell. 'Let go!' She fell with him and he dragged her up and behind him, turning to face the pirate with the realisation that the only weapon he held was one small dagger and the man was too close for a throw.

'I'm going to slice you open and drag your guts out in front of your eyes,' McTiernan hissed, lowering his cutlass to weave a dizzying pattern.

'Clemence, run.'

'No.' She edged further round and he realised that she was effectively trapped. If McTiernan took him, she had no escape.

The man lunged, the point of the weapon slicing through his shirt, across his belly like a whiplash. Nathan recoiled back, shifting his balance, searching for an opening, aware that if he had to, he could take the blade in his body to give Clemence a chance to get free.

'Stanier!' It was Melville.

Nathan looked up in time to catch the thrown sword and drive McTiernan back with one slashing stroke. He took Clemence's arm and almost hurled her through the opening.

'Melville! Catch!' There was no time for more as McTiernan leapt forward with a roar, Nathan's foot slid on the blood-soaked deck and he went down, flat on his back.

'Nathan!' Clemence bit, screamed, struggled, but the burly man in the blue uniform simply wrapped his arms round her, hauled her to the side and thrust her at a marine.

'Get him below. Guard him.'

She did not make it easy, and the marine, confused about exactly who he had got hold of, was not gentle. There was a sickening moment when she hung over the gap between the two ships as they ground together and then more hands took her, bundled her below, thrust her into a cabin. She heard the lock turn and hurled herself at the door, hammering at the panels. 'Nathan!'

The explosion hit her before she heard it. A great blow, like a hurricane striking, then the side of the cabin blew in, at first very slowly, as if in a dream, and then, as the noise came, with a thundering crash. Something hit her head, she was aware she was falling, then, nothing.

'Miss Clemence! Miss Clemence, wake up do, miss!'

Eliza? She must have overslept; Papa would be impatient if she was late for breakfast. Clemence made an effort, then realised that the drum beat thudding through her was a monumental headache.

'Eliza?' She managed to open her eyes a crack. There was the familiar face of her maid, her face contorted with worry. Perhaps she was ill. But she was never ill. Something was wrong.

'Miss Clemence, there's so much trouble and grief, you must wake up!' Yes, something was wrong. Uncle had dismissed Eliza. Papa was dead. Nathan was—

'Nathan?' Hands took her shoulders as she sat up, pillows were heaped behind her. 'Where am I?' This wasn't her bedchamber, this wasn't the cabin.

'The hospital, Miss Clemence. And there's a guard outside and they do say you were one of the pirates' women, and it's only because you are a female that you aren't in the gaol with the rest of them that got captured.'

'I'm not,' she managed, before Eliza held water to her lips. 'What happened? Is the *Sea Scorpion* taken?'

'Sunk, Miss Clemence, and most of that crew of scum with her, two days ago. I'm working for Mrs Hemingford now and she does charitable work in the women's wards once a week and I saw you being carried in, yesterday.' Eliza, her dark face anxious, shook her head. 'I didn't think it was wise to say I recognised you, not with Mr Naismith about. I don't trust him, the way he made me go without letting me see you. I knew you'd speak to me first if you wanted to dismiss me.' She helped Clemence drink again. 'I said I'd like to come down and help some more, and Mrs Hemingford, she's a good Christian woman, she said I could.'

Clemence struggled to absorb it all. Nathan was either dead or in prison. If he was free, he'd have looked for her. Now she would have to look for him. She tried to ignore the clammy feeling of fear in the pit of her stomach and looked down at her body. Her bindings and all her clothes had gone and she was clad in a coarse cotton nightgown.

'Eliza, can you get me clothes? I must wash and dress and go to the Governor.'

'How are you going to get out, Miss Clemence?' Then the maid grinned and got to her feet. 'I know, don't you fret, I'll not be long.'

Somehow Clemence managed to keep calm until Eliza returned half an hour later. 'It's not decent, her in those men's clothes,' Clemence heard her saying to someone outside. 'You let us in and we'll have her looking like a God-fearing woman, at least.'

The lanky white woman with her hair in a turban was carrying a bundle on her shoulder while Eliza lugged in a pail of water. 'My friend Susan,' she said with a jerk of her head to her silent companion. 'Can you get up and washed, Miss Clemence?' She began to rip the sheet into strips. 'These'll do nicely to tie up poor Susan.'

Comprehension of what Eliza intended swept over her, propelling her out of bed despite her headache and her shaky limbs. 'Oh, thank you! I'll do my best to repay you, just as soon as I can.'

'That's all right, miss.' The other woman smiled. 'Eliza

here's done me no end of favours these last few weeks, with my children being so sick. Don't you worry about me none.' She was shedding her clothing down to her shift as she spoke, and after a hasty wash Clemence dressed herself.

Skirts and stays and stockings felt very strange after days in trousers. She wrapped her head in the turban while Eliza tied up Susan on the bed, pushing a handkerchief carefully into her mouth as a gag. 'You start thrashing around and kicking in ten minutes,' she said. 'Look odd if you don't. Pretend we hit you on the head.'

With the bundle of clothes on her shoulder, Clemence walked past the dozing guard, down the long shady corridor and out into the sunshine. The ground beneath her feet seemed to shift uneasily. 'I haven't got my land legs back yet,' she said, holding on to Eliza's arm. 'How are we going to get inland to the King's House?'

'No need.' The maid guided her around a pothole. 'He's down for the trials, wants to preside over the hangings, so they say. Here we are.'

Gaining admission to the Governor's town residence dressed as a washerwoman was not easy until the disturbance Clemence was creating brought out Mr Turpin, the Governor's confidential secretary.

'Miss Ravenhurst! We thought you were dead!' He stood staring at her over his spectacles as though he had seen a ghost. 'Come in, come in, the Governor will be most happy and relieved to see you.'

He ushered them into a reception room and went out, only to return a few minutes later. 'Well, this is providential,' he said mysteriously, opening a door and showing Clemence through. It closed sharply behind her, leaving Eliza on the other side. The Governor stood up from behind his desk, as did two gentlemen who had been sitting with him.

'Clemence,' said her uncle's reproachful voice. 'You poor misguided child, thank God you are safe.'

Chapter Twelve

'No!' The shock was like a blow. All that had happened, all the danger and for *nothing*. She was back in this man's power. Clemence turned to the Governor, desperate to find the right words. 'They are trying to take my inheritance, force me to marry—don't let them—'

'My dear Miss Ravenhurst, please.' The Governor held up his hands. 'No hysterics, I beseech you. Your poor uncle has been with me time and again since your disappearance and a more concerned relative you could not hope to see. I am sincerely sorry that you have chosen to distress him so.'

'*What?*'

'The shame of it, your Excellency,' Uncle Joshua lamented. 'You may well understand that we gave out that she was dead rather than admit that the poor, wanton creature had run off with a lover.'

'I did not! I ran away from you.' Clemence stabbed a finger at the Naismiths. 'And I was captured by pirates—'

'Dear Heaven! The abandoned female in boy's clothing taken on the *Sea Scorpion*. Thank God your poor father was spared this news.' The Governor regarded her with horrified fascination.

'The shame!' Uncle Joshua moaned. 'I had no idea she had sunk so low. We will take her home. Even now, Lewis may do the noble thing for the sake of the family name and wed her.'

'No!' Clemence made a break for the door, but her cousin was before her, scooping her up in his arms. He was stronger than she would ever have guessed, or perhaps she was weaker. Kicking and fighting, Clemence found herself being carried through the house and out of the back door.

The yard was full of men, marines in their scarlet, some naval officers and, chained together in the middle, a huddle of familiar figures. Street, Gerritty the Irish sail-maker, half a dozen of the hands. Next to the cook, a bandage around his head, his shirt in bloodstained tatters, was Nathan.

Nathan had seen her, thank God, for she had no idea whether to shout his name would make things better or worse. Almost sick with relief that he was alive, Clemence began to struggle as hard as she could manage, creating as much disturbance as she could. When it came to the reckoning, no one was ever going to say she had gone with the Naismiths willingly, but when she craned back over Lewis's shoulder, no one had moved to help her.

They were all staring, guards and prisoners alike, and as the turban fell off her cropped head she saw the recognition on the men's faces. Nathan, his eyes blazing, mouthed something. *I'll come for you*—is that what he had said? But how could he? The very fact that he was there with the captives showed his gamble of turning informer had not paid off and her desperate hope that he was still a naval officer had been just wishful thinking.

The yard gate slammed behind them, the big carriage was standing waiting. Lewis flung her into the carriage and climbed in after her before she could reach the handle and get out the other side. 'Sit still or I'll tie your hands,' he snapped.

'You can't get away with this.'

Her uncle settled himself comfortably opposite them, folded his hands across his belly and beamed at her. 'You have behaved like a mad whore in front of the Governor, his confidential secretary and an assortment of naval officers. Really, Clemence, I could not have hoped for better. No one will now question your seclusion at Raven's Hold and all will honour Lewis for his selfless sacrifice for the family name when he eventually weds you.

'Of course,' he added thoughtfully, 'we'll need to make certain you aren't breeding a pirate brat first.'

Clemence opened her mouth in furious denial and then shut it again. If she did not tell them she was still a virgin, then that would keep Lewis from her bed for a few weeks, at least. It wouldn't be much of a reprieve. Marie Luce, like all the female staff, would know her cycle as well as she did herself, but if she was not free within two weeks she could abandon hope.

No, never that. She would never give up, even if they hanged Nathan, even if Lewis forced himself on her; one day she was going to bring them to justice.

Clemence gave a little sigh and slumped into a feigned faint. She had to think, to shut their hateful faces out of her mind. But all that filled it was the image of Nathan, battered, bloody, chained. *I love you, I love you.* She reached out with her will, trying to touch his consciousness, but nothing came back to her, there was no feeling of connection. She had lost him.

To her surprise, the Naismiths took her to her own room. Her thoughts must have shown on her face, for Lewis strode across and turned the key in the doors to the balcony.

'The trellis and the climbers will be gone by nightfall,' he informed her, putting the key into his pocket. 'Then you may take the air again.'

'You aren't worried that I might throw myself over in truth?' Clemence enquired bitterly from the chair where the coachman had deposited her.

'That would be a tragedy, of course. And we would be subject to society's reproaches for not having understood just how demented you had become,' her uncle agreed. 'But our grief would be assuaged by our thankfulness that you had made a will in our favour, weeks before this madness came upon you.'

'I made no will,' Clemence said slowly, cold fingers running up and down her spine.

'You sign so many papers, my dear.' Joshua went to give the balcony doors a precautionary shake. 'And you have such a nice, clear signature.' He ran his eye over her, his mouth compressing in irritation. 'Now, turn yourself into something resembling a gentlewoman.' He turned to Marie Luce, who had slipped in behind them and was waiting silently, hands folded. 'How long before we can be certain she's not breeding?'

'Best say four weeks, master, to be certain sure. She'll look like a lady again by then.'

'See to it.' Joshua stalked out, Lewis at his heels, already discussing business matters, already dismissing her as yet another tiresome problem solved.

Ignoring Marie Luce, Clemence got to her feet and walked to stand in front of the long pier glass. The woman that stared back at her looked as though she had escaped from Bedlam, filthy, tattered, sunburned, her hair a ragged thatch, her eyes wild. The bruises on her face had gone, only to be replaced by a fresh crop of scrapes, and there were scratches all over her hands and arms.

No one was going to take her seriously while she looked like this, Clemence realised. She had no idea how she was going to escape, but when she did, she was going to be Miss Ravenhurst, granddaughter of the Duke of Allington, and someone was going to have to take her very seriously indeed.

'Fetch me hot water, creams, someone who can dress hair,' she said to Marie Luce, who stood watching her with an expression of smug insolence on her face. 'Or do you want me to tell Mr Lewis that you are jealous and do not want to help me look like a lady again?'

That at least wiped the smile off the woman's face, but it was a petty victory. It did not give her the key to the door or news of Nathan, yet defiance made her feel stronger, kept the lethally sapping despair at bay.

Clemence made herself bathe, used every one of the aids to beauty a young lady was permitted, had her ragged hair transformed into a smart, if eccentric, crop and forced down a large supper while behind the shutters there was the noise of men tearing down the trellis and the climbers, her staircase to freedom.

Then, alone at last, she sat straightening hairpins and trying to recall everything she had ever read in sensation novels about picking locks, ready for the small hours when she could try to open the door. It shouldn't be hard, she comforted herself. In such a hot climate internal doors and their locks were lightweight and the household relied for security on external watchmen and bars on the windows.

Raven's Hold had fallen silent by degrees until all she could hear was the chirp of crickets, distant dogs barking and the sea below. Clemence knelt down, took her strongest hairpin and began to probe the lock.

The thud from the balcony was so sudden in the silence that the pin jerked in her hand, scoring a deep scratch into the polished wood. Clemence scrambled to her feet as, with a rending noise, something was forced into the lock and the double doors burst open to reveal a tall figure.

He stepped into the room, his eyes fixed on her, and for a blank moment she stared back. 'Nathan?'

'Clemence?' He sounded even more stunned than she felt. 'My God, you look—' He broke off. 'You look like a lady.'

'And you look like a gentleman,' she replied, finding her feet rooted to the ground with shock. A somewhat dishevelled one as a result of whatever acrobatics it had taken to arrive on her balcony, it was true, but a gentleman none the less with cropped hair, clean shaven, in fresh linen and well-cut breeches. 'You're free,' she added, inanely. 'I thought they were going to hang you.'

She still could not move, half-convinced he was an illusion, but he recovered from his shock sooner than she and came across the room to take her in his arms and she knew he was no phantom. She hugged him tightly, then remembered, as her hands felt the strapping beneath his shirt, that he was hurt.

'Nathan, your back, I'm sorry...'

'Shh.' He pulled her back against him and she let him hold her, her hands sliding down to rest at his waist. 'It will all be well now.'

It seemed, resting her head against his chest, that it might be, because he was alive and here.

'What were you doing?' he asked.

'Picking the lock so I could get out and rescue you,' she admitted. 'It sounds very easy in Minerva Press novels.'

'I see.' He was shaking somewhat; she had the lowering suspicion that he was laughing, but she had no intention of letting go to find out. 'And having picked the lock, how did the rest of the plan go?'

'I wasn't wasting time planning. I needed to get away from them first, then I could think. Find my maid Eliza, that was the first step.'

'She's waiting for you.'

That did bring her out of her daze. 'Eliza? How?'

'Let's get out of here—there's too much to tell you.' He hunkered down and studied the lock.

'But how did you get in here?' Clemence ran to the balcony. There was a grappling hook biting into the carved stone and a rope dangled down into the darkness. 'Who is on the other end of that rope?' she asked, coming back into the room, all too aware of Lewis's room and his open windows.

'Street, one bemused midshipman and the crew of the frigate *Orion*'s jolly boat.'

'Street!' He merely nodded, his concentration on the lock. 'And you are navy? Truly?'

The door clicked open and Nathan got to his feet. 'Captain Nathan Stanier, at your service, Miss Clemence.' The relief took the strength out of her legs. Clemence sat down with a bump on the nearest chest. 'Come on, we haven't got time for sitting about.' He snuffed all but one candle and took that to the balcony, shielding it and uncovering it with his hand before blowing it out. 'Right, now we've got to get to that cove quarter of a mile along to the east and I think we can relax.'

Clemence pulled herself together and pushed the questions that were clamouring for answers to the back of her mind. 'This way. If we go out of the dining-room windows on to the veranda and then along to the kitchen yard, we'll miss the watchman at the gate.'

Nathan followed her, soft-footed on the wide polished boards as she led him through the rooms, as familiar as the palm of her own hand in the darkness. The loose window latch opened easily and then they were out into the fragrant, sound-filled night.

Old One-Eye gave a soft *wuff* of greeting as he scented her and came padding across, the links of his chain rattling. 'Damn,' Nathan murmured beside her and she saw his hand go to his knife.

'No!' she hissed back. 'And I'm taking him with me; he's old, I'm not leaving him with them.'

'We can't take a geriatric guard dog in a jolly boat,' Nathan protested as she fumbled for the catch on the dog's heavy studded collar, but she just tugged One-Eye towards the gate and he followed, muttering. She thought she heard *totty-headed woman*, but she couldn't swear to it, and anyway, he sounded amused.

The cove was a favourite picnic spot and Clemence did not need the occasional flash of a shielded lantern ahead to follow the path through the brush and down the cliff path to the beach. One-Eye, who seemed to take this unorthodox walk in his stride, growled low in his throat as figures appeared out of the darkness and the shape of the beached boat became clear.

'Quiet, One-Eye. Friends,' Clemence ordered, although as one of the silhouettes turned into the unmistakable bulk of Street, she was not so sure.

'You all right, Clem?' he asked, his voice grumbling out of the darkness.

'Yes, thank you. But what are you doing here?'

'Joined the navy, haven't I?' he said. 'Mr Stanier said I'd got a choice, that or the gallows, seeing as how I looked after you.'

'Better get in the boat, sir.' A young man, she assumed
the bemused midshipman of Nathan's description, was edging them towards the water. 'Er, are we taking the hound,
ma'am?' What he thought of being sent out with a pirate ship's
cook on a clandestine mission on English soil, to rescue a
woman and an elderly dog, she could not imagine.

'Certainly we are.'

Only one sailor was bitten, and the midshipman drenched,
getting the very reluctant animal into the boat, and Nathan's
shoulders against hers were rigid with what she could only
assume was suppressed laughter, but they were at sea at last.

'Where are we going? To the Governor?'

Clemence let herself lean into Nathan's side and he put his
arm around her, no doubt an action harmful to naval discipline, but he did not appear to care.

'No. I fear his mind is unlikely to be elastic on the subject of young women who run away from their guardians.
I'm quite certain we can convince him in time, but tonight
I think you rest, then we can assemble our case and I'll deal
with him tomorrow with you safely out of the way.'

'Very well.' It was sensible, although her fantasy of confronting Uncle Joshua in front of the island's Council, finger
pointing dramatically at the miscreant, was too satisfying to
easily give up.

'Captain Melville has a house in Kingston that we've been
using as a base. We'll go there—no one knows that the navy
is the tenant.'

'Spying,' Clemence murmured, almost asleep. 'I knew
you were a shady character.'

She woke up as Nathan handed her out of the boat to Street,
who seemed more than a little put about to have an armful
of young woman who sounded like the boy Clem, but who

was clad in fine lawns and silk ribbons. Clemence found herself bundled back into Nathan's arms with unseemly haste.

'I can walk,' she protested, wide awake.

'Quicker like this.' Nathan strode off, with Street and the dog at his heels, leaving the boat party to row back out to where she assumed the frigate must be anchored. They were in the streets of middling houses in the west end of town, dwellings hanging on to respectability by their fingernails, an area where the shabby-genteel residents kept themselves to themselves.

Nathan turned into a passageway, then into a yard. The back door opened with alacrity and there was Eliza. 'Oh, Miss Clemence! He's got you safe. Oh, thank you, sir!' She flung the door wide and ushered them in. 'And One-Eye. Who's a good dog, then?' She made a fuss of the hound, who leaned panting against her leg before turning to glower at Street, lurking uncomfortably in the doorway. 'And you, you great lummox—what are you doing here?'

'Bodyguard,' he growled.

Nathan set Clemence on her feet. 'Eliza, you'll show Miss Clemence to her room.' He looked at her. 'You'll want to sleep.'

'I couldn't sleep a wink,' Clemence said. 'Not until I find out what has happened. And, Eliza, you should get to bed.'

'I'll just show you your room, Miss Clemence,' the maid began.

'It is all right, Mr—I mean, Captain Stanier can show me.' There was a gasp from the maid. 'Eliza, I've been sharing his cabin for nights, it is all right.'

Without waiting she turned and climbed the stairs. After a moment she heard footsteps behind her and smiled. Thank goodness, she had been afraid he was going to treat her like a society lady the moment they were free.

'The door on the right.' It was a simple room, but clean and the wide bed with its white mosquito net sat serenely in the middle of an expanse of polished floor.

'Oh, a real bed. Bliss.'

'Then sleep.' Nathan was standing in the doorway, watching her.

'No. Not until we talk.' She held out a hand and he came in and took one of the rattan chairs. Clemence curled up in the other, noticing with a pang of anxiety that he stayed sitting upright, not letting his back touch the chair. 'Tell me who you are and how the men from the hold are.'

'We've lost some of them, but the survivors are, on the whole, all right, although some have fevers and all are badly malnourished. There are eight of your men safe. As for me, I am part of a mission to eradicate pirates in the Caribbean.' Nathan steepled his fingers and looked as though he were about to present a formal report. 'We deprived McTiernan of his navigator in a brothel about a week before he took me on; it took a while to spread the rumours about me, enough for him to get interested, but not suspicious.'

'The *Orion* is your ship?' She imagined the elegant, white-sailed frigate, Nathan on the quarterdeck.

'No, Melville's. I haven't a ship at the moment, I was detached for the mission. You can guess the rest—the disabled merchantman was the first intended honey-trap. When that didn't work, we set up the sand-bar trap with a supposedly secret bullion ship as bait.'

'How did you communicate?' Clemence watched him, noticing the cut in his hairline, bruises on his cheek, the edge of a bandage showing beneath one cuff.

'It was pre-arranged, most of it. Contingency plans for every eventuality we could think of. I knew about the sand-bar, I only pretended to find it when we were up on the headland. While you were setting out the food, I was signalling with a mirror.'

'It all seems very efficient,' Clemence observed, wondering as she looked at him now, with his austere manner and his spare reporting, how she could ever have thought him a suspicious rogue. 'I must have been a nuisance. Why didn't you tell me the truth?'

'I wanted you to react to things as naturally as possible.' He shrugged. 'And instinct told me that the less you knew, the safer you were.'

'I see. And when I saw you this afternoon?'

'Yesterday by now, I would guess.' He glanced at the clock. 'Yesterday I had been helping salvage what we could of *Sea Scorpion*, searching for survivors, which was why I looked as I did. I wasn't chained in the middle of those men, but I was talking to them, trying to sort out the ones it was safe to try and have reprieved. There are some good seamen amongst them.'

'And when you saw me?'

'I did not know what was going on, the Governor's men were armed. I couldn't risk shooting starting. When Eliza came tumbling out into the yard after you, I got the whole story out of her.'

'So what was I doing in the hospital?'

'That was a mistake, no one knew who you were. Melville just grabbed you when I threw you at him, and anyway, he got knocked unconscious when that cannon went off and I didn't speak to him again until after I had seen you.'

It seemed that all she had to concern herself about was her own future. 'It is all under control, then? All shipshape and navy fashion?' He nodded, smiling, and got to his feet. 'And what about me?'

'I'll talk to lawyers tomorrow, and then the Governor.

We'll get your inheritance back, Clemence, never fear. We'll find you somewhere to stay safely until it is all over.'

She stood up. 'And when it is?'

'I meant it, Clemence. With the best will in the world, I don't think your reputation is going to survive this scandal. We'll go back to England and I will marry you.'

'Out of the goodness of your heart?' she enquired, trying to keep the bitter edge out of the question. No, it would not happen. He was going to put all this into the hands of lawyers, sail off and leave her, and she would never see him again. Because marrying a man who proposed to you out of decency and kindness was impossible, even if—especially if—you loved him.

'Because I would like to.' He frowned at her as though the sincerity in his own voice had taken him by surprise. 'Clemence, you have come to matter to me. You know I desire you, that has never been in doubt. I'm too old for you, of course—'

'Nonsense!' The protest was jerked out of her before she realised how betraying it was. Nathan looked down into her face and took her hands.

'Ten years and a great deal of experience older than you, sweetheart.'

'I don't consider that,' she murmured, suddenly shy. 'Isn't there anyone else?'

'No one, I swear. England will be difficult, I know, but you will come to like it, make friends. Won't you take pity on me?'

'Take pity on *you*? Your friends will say you are the one to be pitied for marrying a ruined woman who had been on a pirate ship.'

'No, my friends will love you.'

And will you love me? she wondered, her hands curling into his. Would he learn to love her? She would make him a good wife and perhaps he would, in time. She had never been able to envisage the man she would marry; now, here was one she desired, one she liked and she loved. It seemed he shared the desire and the liking. Was that enough? It was more than many couples had, she knew.

'If... Yes. Yes, I will marry you,' she said, suddenly as dizzy as if she had thrown herself from the peak of the mainmast.

Chapter Thirteen

'Clemence.' It was a sigh, and on the breath Nathan kissed her, his mouth certain, his grasp that of a man claiming what was his. Passive, unsure of what he expected, she let him explore her mouth, his lips shifting over hers, his tongue fretting over the join of her lips until she parted shyly for him. And then that shaft of desire pierced her, just as it had when they had kissed in anger and passion on the ship and she opened for him, drew him in, tasted and savoured and arched herself against the maleness that was going to be hers.

His hands cupped her behind, lifting her to him on tip-toe so she was in no doubt of how aroused he was as he shifted against her, setting up a rhythm that made her moan against his mouth.

Her hands went to his head, her palms tingling with the friction of his unfamiliar, short hair, traced down the tendons of his neck, then up, skimmed lightly, tenderly, over the wound on his forehead, found the strong whorl of his ear and played for a moment with the lobe, wondering hazily at her own desire to take it between her teeth and nip. There was so much to learn and Nathan was going to teach her and the lick of fearful anticipation only added a delicious edge to that thought.

The half-awakened sensuality Nathan had stirred in her, her own imaginings, the heat and strength and sureness of him were coming together to transform her body that she thought she knew so well into an aching, urgent, desperate thing of liquid heat and tingling nerves. And this, this dizzying sensation, she knew was only the beginning.

Slowly, he lowered her so her feet were flat on the ground and freed her mouth. Clemence opened her eyes and found his, looking as dazed as she felt.

'I think,' Nathan managed, sounding like a man who had been running, 'that we may find we are very compatible in bed.'

'Isn't it always like that?' Her fingers had curled around his forearms, seemingly of their own volition, but he did not seem in any hurry to move away.

'Not in my experience,' he confessed. 'Clemence, I must go.'

'Must you?' she murmured, unable to free either her hands or her eyes.

'If I do not go now, I will not be able to.'

'Then stay.' The blue of his eyes darkened, whether with doubt or desire she was not sure. 'Nathan, we are going to be married and I do not want to be alone tonight.' She managed a smile, a quite successful one under the circumstances, she thought. 'I am used to sleeping with you now.'

The way her lower lip quivered into a smile undid him. It was all there in that smile and in her green eyes, locked with his. Innocent passion, trust, the need for comfort. Who was he protecting by rejecting her, leaving her to face her memories alone while he walked off to his room in the smug certainty that he had done the right thing, the virtuous thing?

Nathan wrestled with the doubt that he was justifying doing what his own desires were clamouring for. He had got the strength to walk away, he decided. If he wanted to.

He freed her hands from their grip on his arms and went to the door. 'Good night,' Clemence whispered behind him.

'I hope so,' he said, turning the key in the lock and coming back to her, seeing her face light up. 'A very good night, I hope.'

The sudden doubt flickered behind her eyes. 'I don't know what to do. I'm afraid you'll be disappointed.'

'Well, fortunately I do know, and I do not think you could disappoint me, Clemence.' It was more his fear of disappointing her, Nathan thought wryly, finding the buttons either side of the waist of her gown. One virgin in a personal history of long periods of abstinence at sea interspersed with intense relationships with expensive, but highly skilled *chères amies*. And that virgin, his wife, had been a confident, passionate little temptress without, he was convinced, a nerve in her body.

And not one woman before had looked at him with such trusting expectation, which only made the pressure worse. *Slowly*, he told himself, easing the gown from her shoulders, bending to kiss the tender skin exposed just above the small breasts her corset lifted to him, like a gift.

She gave a little gasp and managed to find room to begin unbuttoning his shirt. Then she found the bandaging beneath and remembered, pulling her hands away. 'Nathan, I'm sorry, I forgot your back. How could I have been so thoughtless? Forgive me.' She tried to edge away, but he held her, his palms cupping her shoulders.

'I will be fine, Clemence, I promise. Look.' He shrugged out of his shirt, turning to show her. 'See, no more bleeding.'

'And there's a cut on your arm, and your stomach and bruises. Nathan, you should be in bed, resting, not—'

'Not making love to a beautiful woman?' He smiled at her blush and the definite shake of her head in denial of the compliment. 'Isn't the warrior deserving of a reward?'

The look she gave him in response to that question was pure Clem, but she stood still for him to unlace her corset, standing in her shift and stockings, her hands clasped shyly as though afraid to touch him now. 'The mosquitoes are getting bad,' she murmured 'Perhaps we should get under the net?'

Fighting one's way under a mosquito net, working all round trying to tuck it under the mattress from inside, and then pursuing the one buzzing menace that had managed to get in with them, might not have been the most erotic prelude to lovemaking, but it broke down the last vestiges of reserve.

Clemence came into his embrace willingly as he lay back on the soft white covers and curled up, her head on his shoulder. *Let her set the pace*, his instinct told him, *let her relax*.

'Oh, the bliss of a proper bed,' she sighed, her exploring fingers wrecking havoc with his pulse rate as she stroked the skin exposed by the bandages over his shoulders.

'Your uncle certainly gave you a beautiful bedchamber,' Nathan remarked, set on talking until she was at ease. Discussing furniture seemed as good a way as any to keep his own arousal in check. He ran his fingertip along the upper edge of her shift, watching the betraying little peak of her nipple hardening beneath the fine lawn. 'And the house was far finer than I had expected, from what you had told me about him.'

'But Raven's Hold is my house,' she said, lifting her hand and stroking lightly over his evening beard, her fingertips running along the edge of his jaw in a way that made him shiver. 'Uncle Joshua and Lewis moved in when Papa died and just took over.'

'Raven's Hold?' Memory was stirring, claws of apprehension tightening in his gut. He knew he had heard her name before.

'Called after the family castle in Northumberland,' she was saying, now seemingly engrossed in tracing the line of his collarbone.

Nathan jolted up on his elbows, forcing her to roll onto her back. 'Clemence, what is your surname?'

'I told you, Browne.' She was teasing him.

'No, your real name.' Something in his tone reached her and she sat up, her eyes puzzled and wary.

'Ravenhurst.'

Nathan closed his eyes for a moment. 'The Duke of Allington is your cousin?'

'Yes,' she said smiling. 'Do you know him? I haven't met any of my cousins. I was going to London for next year's Season when Papa died. But I'll meet them now we are going to England.'

'I met *Lord* Standon and *Lady* Dereham, whose husband is an old friend, in London when I was on leave, before I sailed for the West Indies. They were expecting *Lord* Sebastian Ravenhurst and his wife, the *Grand Duchess* Eva, to join them in a few weeks. I have not met the *Duke*, no, nor your uncle the *bishop* nor any of the rest of them—they were presumably too busy occupying their niche at the pinnacle of society at the time.'

'Nathan? You are angry—what is it?'

'I told you who I am—were you not listening? I am the younger son of an impoverished baron. I am a career naval officer with no land of my own, no prospect of a title and advancement other than what I can earn myself in a dangerous profession. I thought you were the daughter of a modestly well-off merchant and that, by offering you marriage, I would save you from the consequences of the situation you found yourself in, that the life I could give you would not be materially worse than you were used to.'

'Yes, but I would not be worse off! You are saving my reputation, you are taking care of me and we have my inheritance—when the lawyers manage to untangle it.'

Nathan sat up, trying not to wince at the strain on his back. Ignoring wounds when sexually aroused was one thing—now every laceration and bruise seemed to be alive and protesting. 'Just what, exactly, does your inheritance consist of?'

'Six merchantmen—it was seven before *Raven Duchess* was taken.' She began to count them off on her fingers. '*Princess*, *Lady*, *Baroness*, *Marchioness*, *Belle Dame* and *Countess*. Then there are the warehouses, Raven's Hold, the house in Spanish Town and three penns, all with free labour, two in Port Royal parish and one in St Andrew. They supply food for the household really, not income.' She was studying his face now, her expression anxious. 'And the investments, of course.'

'Of course,' Nathan echoed. 'The investments. Clemence, listen to me. You do not need to marry me, all you need to do is to arrive in London, put yourself under the protection of the Ravenhursts and everything will be all right. They'll send out lawyers who will eat the Naismiths alive and so cow the Governor that not a whisper of this will escape—their influence in society is such that your name will be completely untarnished.'

'But, I would *like* to marry you, Nathan.'

'You said yourself that there was no one to whom you were attracted on the island, so no wonder you are willing to marry me now. When you get to London you will have the choice of every eligible man in society. You do not need to throw yourself away on me,' he added harshly.

'But I wouldn't be! How could I throw myself away on a good, courageous, honourable man?'

He hugged those words to himself for a second, then put them away somewhere to recollect when she was gone. 'Because you can do better,' he said harshly.

'Nathan—' Whatever it was she had been about to say was cut off. Clemence shook her head, as though arguing with herself.

'Clemence, I have only the money that I earn myself— my pay and prize money. I was, seven years ago, so well off from prize money that I felt it safe to take a wife.'

'A wife? You have been married?'

He nodded. 'She is dead. I did not take enough care of her. And she was very expensive—the money is gone.' There, now she knew.

'Did you love her?'

'Yes.'

'So you are a widower, you can marry again.'

'I am trailing the scandal of her death,' he said tersely and something in her expression showed she recalled a conversation they had had before.

'The duel you fought?'

'With the man who intended to become her lover,' he said, heedless of the blow to his pride that admission caused. 'You see how desirable I am? If we lived quietly, that would hardly matter, but you have a position in society. I do not relish taking on the mantle of the fortune hunter who brought about the downfall of yet another well-bred virgin.'

'So you do not wish to marry me at all, really?' Clemence slid back so she was against one of the bedposts. 'You were just doing the honourable thing to save my reputation.'

She waved a hand at the rumpled white bedding. 'And I suppose, at least, once you had taught me to be less ignorant, you would not have minded bedding the wife you took out of kindness.'

Nathan wanted to protest, to tell her he wanted, not just to bed her, but to discover her in his bed every day. That far from forcing himself to do the honourable thing, he now found he was having to use all his will-power not to act dishonourably and take her, here and now, and keep her. Because Clemence Ravenhurst had got under his skin and into his heart in a way that he had thought would never happen to him again. If he were not careful, he would find himself fancying that he was in love with her and that was only a delusion, for that part of him was dead.

'You are too young,' he tried. 'If you had more experience of the world, you would understand...'

'I am too young, too rich and too well connected. I see,' Clemence said, her voice flat. 'What it boils down to is that you do not care to face my relatives and risk what they might say of you. What I am, as a person, does not count in this equation. Very well, I understand that a man's honour is a very touchy and particular thing. And I am so very sorry about your wife. Please...' she gestured towards the door '...please do not let me keep you from your rest.'

'Clemence.' They stared at each other. He was exasperated with himself for his inability to explain this without hurting her, and under that he found he was hurting, too, far more than he would have believed possible for a man whose emotions had been cauterized seven years before. And Clemence, he knew perfectly well, was as upset as he, for her own reasons.

She had been through enough. She did not deserve to find herself persuaded into marriage with a man she had come to trust and depend on, have her innocence disturbed by his lovemaking and then to be told she was alone after all, except for her important relatives, far away. Yes, of course she wanted to cling to him and the security that marriage, however inappropriate, would give her.

'Nathan, please will you get off my bed and out of my bedroom? As it appears that I am not about to lose my virginity tonight, I would rather like to get some sleep.'

In the face of that, there was not much else to do than fight his way out of the mosquito netting, find his shirt and shoes and remove himself. He sincerely hoped she was going to get more sleep than he expected to.

It was all too much to take in, but one thing was clear: he had loved his wife and he blamed himself for her death.

She had to be thankful they had not made love, Clemence told herself, staring at the indentation Nathan's long body had made in the bedding. She was rich, she was eligible, she was well connected and those three highly desirable characteristics were enough to drive away the man she was in love with. *Loved*, she corrected herself.

The marriage would not have taken place, of course; he would have discovered her name before that. She recalled, with a stab of guilt, that on the ship she had deliberately not told him who she was, afraid the temptation of such a hostage would be too much for the rogue she suspected he might be.

What had just happened proved he was every bit as honourable as she could have hoped—and that very honour was stopping him marrying her. That and the fact that he did not love her, of course. It was important to remember that, to remember that he had offered only to protect her because, otherwise, surely he would have made that declaration?

He had loved his wife. Did he love her still? Was the bitterness in his voice for her, for himself or for the man with whom he had fought that duel? What had happened to provoke that calamity?

And what would Nathan have done if that conversation about Raven's Hold had taken place after they had made love, not before? Would he have married her then?

A high-pitched buzzing at last stirred her from her position against the bedpost. It took ten minutes to tuck in the net and to hunt the mosquito, by which time she was beyond tiredness, beyond even feeling miserable. Taking her remaining clothing off was too much trouble. Clemence curled up in the middle of the bed and sank into sleep.

'Miss Clemence?' It was Eliza. 'It is eight o'clock. The gentlemen say they are sorry not to let you sleep longer, but they need to speak with you. They say, will you take breakfast with them?'

This time Clemence had no trouble recalling where she was and why. She sat up, pushing her short hair back from her face, thankfully aware that a few hours' sleep had restored her body and her wits to something like normal.

Inside there was a dull ache of loss, but there was a bitter energy, too. She could not rely on anyone but herself, it seemed. So be it.

She had only yesterday's muslin to dress in, with salt-water stains around the hem and the marks of One-Eye's affectionate slobbering on the skirts. That would need to be remedied and she would need to borrow the money, somehow, to send Eliza out shopping for her.

Three men in naval uniform rose as she entered the shabby dining parlour at the front of the house. Nathan, a burly captain she seemed to recognise from somewhere and a tall lieutenant with a wide smile that suited his chubby face. Her eyes on the captain, Clemence made a slight curtsy. 'Gentlemen.'

She saw him glance at Nathan, then he seemed to realise he was being asked to take command of the introductions. 'Captain James Melville of the *Orion* at your service, ma'am. This is Lieutenant Conroy. Captain Stanier you already know.'

'Good morning.' Clemence shook hands, forcing herself to allow her fingers to rest in Nathan's grasp for a reasonable length of time. She sat beside Captain Melville, Mr Conroy opposite her and Nathan at the foot of the table, and managed a social smile. 'I must thank you, Captain, for sending your men and the midshipman to rescue me last night.'

'The least we could do, Miss Ravenhurst.' Eliza came in with platters of fruit and meats and Melville broke off while she set out the food and put the tea and coffee pots by Clemence's right hand.

'Miss Ravenhurst, we have been joined by two other frigates and a cutter bearing orders for *Orion* to sail for England as soon as I have been able to hand over command of this operation to the senior officer commanding. Captain Stanier has apprised me of the deplorable actions of your uncle and I can only agree with him that the resources of the Ravenhursts would best bring this matter to a speedy conclusion. It is also of the first consideration to remove you from any danger and I understand that the Governor may take some persuading of this.' He drank coffee, watching her over the rim of the cup to gauge her reaction. Clemence nodded.

'It appears to us, therefore, that the sooner you can be united with your family in London, the better, ma'am.'

'Indeed. If it had not been for my father's death I would have sailed some weeks ago for a long-planned visit.' Clemence ate, her attention on Melville. That way, despite her internal agitation, she could at least try to ignore Nathan's silent presence at the end of the table.

'It seems impossible to secure you passage on a merchant-man, given the delicacy of your situation here.' Melville passed her fruit and began to peel himself a pawpaw. 'How soon could you and your maid be ready to sail on the *Orion*?'

'On the frigate? I—' Clemence made herself focus. 'I do not know if Eliza will wish to make such a journey, she is a free woman; in fact, I do not know how she is able to be here, for she has another employer now.'

'She tells me she has resigned her position and is willing to sail with you,' Melville said. 'What else is required?'

'Clothes—every necessity, in fact,' Clemence admitted. 'And I have no money, I will need to borrow from somewhere before Eliza can shop for me.'

'That we can take care of.' Melville waved the difficulty away. 'Conroy, you accompany Miss Ravenhurst's maid—we do not want to place her in any difficulty if the Naismiths see her and realise what she is about.'

'And we need to lay a land mine under the Naismiths,' Nathan said, making her jump. 'I suggest that while Eliza and Conroy are out, you, Miss Ravenhurst, write an account of all their actions following the death of your father, including their most recent imprisonment of you. Melville and Conroy will witness it and we will leave it with our agent here against the time the Ravenhursts' lawyers take action.'

'Thank you,' she said, finding that she could meet his gaze and smile, after all. This was the man with whom she had nearly lain last night, this tall, distinguished, serious-looking officer. It did not seem possible. And then he smiled and she saw the rogue with the dice sitting in the dockside tavern who had made her feel safe in the middle of terror. The man whose look made her tremble and ache.

'It will give you considerable satisfaction to be able to continue the campaign against the pirates with more ships, I imagine, Captain Stanier,' she observed in her best drawing-room manner, accepting his empty cup to refill it.

'It would do, Miss Ravenhurst, if I were not to be returning on the *Orion*,' Nathan said, reaching with both hands to catch the cup as it slipped out of her suddenly nerveless fingers.

Chapter Fourteen

'Miss Ravenhurst, are you faint?' Both Conroy and Melville were on their feet, looking at her anxiously. 'You have gone quite pale,' the captain continued, reaching for the bell.

'No, not at all. I thought I saw a centipede, over there, by the sideboard,' she improvised. 'They are venomous, you know. But I think I was mistaken.'

Nathan's hands were still cupped around hers. 'Nothing spilled,' he observed, lowering them after a moment.

'No, indeed, not even milk,' she joked, managing a smile for her own feeble wit. Nathan, on the *Orion*? To be with him on a frigate for six, perhaps eight weeks? She would not have to say goodbye to him for ever in a day or two—yet the painful pleasure of being close to him could only make that eventual parting worse.

And the intimacy of their shared danger and deception aboard the *Sea Scorpion*, living with him, so closely—there would be none of that. Instead she would be under the scrutiny of others the entire time, having to treat him just as she would any of the other officers.

'Are you sorry to be leaving the Jamaica station?' she asked, handing him back his filled cup. 'Do you know where you will be posted next? Or are you not to speak of such secrets?'

'I must await their lordships' command,' Nathan said, so lightly that she suspected he was as uneasy about this development as she was. No wonder—he must have thought the difficulties she had brought him would be over within days.

'You will excuse us, Miss Ravenhurst?' Melville was on his feet. 'Conroy will wait until your maid is ready to go out, but Stanier and I have to go on board. We will leave you to compose your statement in peace.'

'Yes, of course.' Clemence watched them go out, then heard the lieutenant talking to Eliza in the kitchen. She tried to think of all the things she would need for two months at sea, heading into a cooler climate. It would still be summer in England, late August perhaps, when they landed, but she had heard too many of her father's tales of English summers to place any confidence in being able to manage with light lawns and fine silks until she could replenish her wardrobe.

And where would the Ravenhursts be? she wondered. In England, so she understood, no one of fashion would remain in London during the summer. What would summer fashions in England be like? Would Nathan like her in a modish gown, perhaps following the latest French trend? Would he visit her, perhaps strolling beside some landscaped lake in a verdant English park, while the breeze blew cool and the flowers bloomed on the banks?

'Shall we make a list, Miss Clemence?'

'Oh, Eliza, you made me jump.' *And just in time, too. Of course he will not visit, he would not expect the exalted Ravenhursts to invite him. But he says he knows Cousin Gareth...* 'I was wondering what on earth we will need, because it will be perhaps two months at sea and then English weather. You'll need warmer things, too, and clothes for wet weather.'

Eliza was bustling around, finding ink and paper, looking remarkably cheerful for someone about to be uprooted and sent across the oceans at about two days' notice. 'Are you sure you don't mind coming with me?'

The maid smiled. 'Oh, no, Miss Clemence. I never thought I'd get such a chance. What an adventure!'

When she and Lieutenant Conroy finally left, the house seemed eerily quiet save for the rumbling snores of One-Eye stretched in unaccustomed comfort on the hearth rug. The men had gone off, apparently without any fear that the Naismiths might find her. And of course, they were quite right and she was being foolish. She took up a penknife and began to sharpen her nib, telling herself firmly that day-dreams about Nathan were equally foolish.

The sound of footsteps in the hallway had her on her feet, the little knife clenched in her hand as the door opened. 'Street!' The cook looked abashed.

'Sorry, Miss Clemence, I just came in to see if you was all right.'

'I... I'm fine, thank you. I didn't realise you were here, that's all.'

'Wondering if you can trust me, miss?' He cocked an eyebrow at her, more like his old self despite the absence of his bloodstained apron and villainous meat cleaver. 'I'm Mr Stanier's man now. Saved my neck, he did. And you're his lady.' He grinned and it was as if she was back in the galley again. 'Never thought young Clem would scrub up so well, miss, begging your pardon.'

'Thank you, Street. But I'm not Captain Stanier's lady, you know.'

'What? Won't he marry you? That's bad, that is. He ought to—'

'No, indeed, Street.' The big man looked ready to march

off and lecture Nathan on his responsibilities. 'There's absolutely no need for him to and I'm going to my relatives in England and they'll look after me.'

'If you say so, miss. I still think...' In the face of her complete lack of response his voice trailed off. He looked at the hound, feet twitching as it chased rabbits in its sleep. 'What you going to do with that when we sail, miss?'

'He's coming, too,' Clemence said firmly, wondering how hard it would be to convince Captain Melville to house a large, elderly and, it had to be admitted, smelly hound in his smart frigate.

The unfortunate Lieutenant Conroy escorted Eliza round every lady's emporium in Kingston in an effort to spread her purchases and not cause gossip. Then, when he finally delivered her and a carriage-load of parcels back to the house, he found himself conscripted along with Street to wash One-Eye.

'Street and I have tried,' Clemence explained. 'But it needs another man to get him into the hip bath.'

'I can see that, ma'am,' he said, rolling up his sleeves as One-Eye curled back a lip from the opposite side of the yard.

'If I hold his collar, he won't bite, but even Street couldn't lift him when he struggled.' She pushed the hair off her damp forehead while Eliza, clucking, went for another bucket of hot water, the tussle so far having emptied the bath.

'Right,' Conroy announced, advancing on the hound. 'I've fought pirates and lived, I can do this.'

Twenty minutes later the four humans were soaked and faintly hysterical with laughter while One-Eye, a paler shade of brown than Clemence could ever recall seeing him, was sulking in the scullery.

'Oh, dear, look at you, Lieutenant!' Clemence handed him

a towel while Eliza and Street carried the bath back inside. 'And you haven't got a clean shirt with you. Never mind, we'll sit here in the sunshine and dry off.'

'Miss Ravenhurst.'

There was no reason why she should feel guilty to be discovered, flushed and smiling, sitting next to a good-looking young man in a sopping wet shirt that clung in a most becoming manner to his torso. Indeed, there was nothing in Nathan's tone or expression to make her feel so. But it did.

It appeared to work powerfully on Conroy, too, who was on his feet, reaching for his coat, despite the state of his shirt.

'Sir! Bathing the dog, sir.'

'Indeed? That required both of you to get in the bath with it?'

Clemence glared, embarrassed, cross with herself for being so, and with Nathan for making her feel that way. 'Yes. Actually, it required four of us to get completely soaked, but at least I will not be taking a dirty dog on to Captain Melville's frigate.'

'Or at all, I imagine.'

'One-Eye goes, or I do not.' The old hound and Eliza were all she could take of Jamaica into her new life and she wanted them both, she realised.

'I'll be getting back to the ship, ma'am, if you don't need me any more?' If a naval officer could be said to sidle out of a gate, the lieutenant was managing it now.

'Thank you so much, Mr Conroy,' Clemence said with warmth. 'I am sure Mr Stanier will be joining you directly.'

Nathan waited until the other man was out of earshot, his arms folded across his chest. 'You are not Clem now, you must not indulge in that sort of behaviour.'

'What sort?' Clemence folded her own arms just as assertively. 'If Eliza and I had been bathing the dog with only

Street to help us, you wouldn't have said a thing. Simply because Mr Conroy is an attractive man, you react like my brother. Well, you are not.'

'I am well aware of that! Clemence, you have your reputation to think of now.'

'Nonsense,' she snapped. 'I can dress as a boy, run away to join the pirates and sleep for *nights* with a man and yet my smart relatives can magic all that away, according to you. I am sure mixed dog washing can be excused as a very minor sin for the rich, well-connected Miss Ravenhurst.'

'Just because I will not marry you does not mean you have to start flirting with every young man you come into contact with! Wait until you get to London and the chaperonage of one of your aunts, at least.'

Clemence was not quite certain which part of that comprehensively inflammatory statement she most took exception to. She closed the four-foot gap between them, index finger extended. 'If you are suggesting that I am *flirting* with Lieutenant Conroy—' *prod* '—because my nose is out of joint—' *prod* '—because you will not marry me, Nathan Stanier—' *prod* '—then you have a more swollen head than I could have imagined!'

He grabbed her hand and held it an inch away from his chest. 'I am suggesting that you are unused to not getting your own way, Miss Ravenhurst, and that you want to show me that you do not care that I am taking a more mature view of this.'

'Mature?' Clemence drew in a long, shuddering breath. 'We are back to my age again, are we? Might I point out that a mature response on your part would be to ignore a perfectly normal episode of domestic life and avoid embarrassing poor Mr Conroy.' Nathan's face darkened in a most satisfactory manner, so she cast around for oil to throw on the flames.

'Of course, I appreciate that your temper will be uncertain this morning after last night's frustrations.'

'Frustrations?' The blue eyes glittered dangerously. 'Allow me to demonstrate what frustration involves, Miss Ravenhurst.'

The yard was neglected, like the house, but at one time someone had constructed an arbour, screened with climbers. They were overgrown now and the seat within was rickety with age. It creaked ominously under their weight as Nathan scooped Clemence up and threw himself down on it, holding her across his knee with one hand despite her furious wriggling.

He is trying to frighten me for my own good, she thought, suddenly still, suddenly understanding. *But I am not frightened and I want him to want me, want him to understand what he is giving up.*

Her mouth was open under his as he thrust into the moist, soft interior and she let him, passive for a moment while she learned the rhythm, then her tongue joined his, touched, probed, fenced and her body curled against his, finding the places where they fitted together, feeling his erection under the curve of her buttocks, wriggling against it in wanton invitation.

Everything that his gentle caresses of the night before had aroused sprang into hot, urgent life again. Nathan growled, freeing her mouth, bending his head to see what he was doing as his free hand pulled down the loose neck of her damp muslin gown so that the newly burgeoning curves of her breasts were exposed to his gaze and his hot, avid mouth.

They ached and tingled and seemed to grow as he licked and nibbled and then his thumb rubbed under the corset edge and found her nipple and she arched, panting, her head thrown back on his shoulder, utterly unable to do anything but surrender to the impossible pleasure.

And then he stopped. He pulled up her gown, tied the ribbons, got to his feet and placed her on to the seat, then stood there regarding her as though absolutely nothing at all out of the ordinary had happened in the last few crowded minutes.

Nathan's breathing was fast; she could see the rise and fall of his chest under the shirt ruffle, the vein in his temple standing out, but his voice was controlled and his bow, immaculate.

'That, Clemence, is what frustration feels like. I am but a short walk from the highly skilled means of relieving it, just as I was last night. You, I regret, must learn the consequences of teasing a man, and especially, of teasing me.'

'You...' At least days on the *Sea Scorpion* had enriched her vocabulary; she searched for the worst word she could recall.

'Tsk.' He shook his head in reproof. 'Ladies do not swear. Good day, Clemence. We will come to collect you and your baggage tomorrow morning at six.'

'...bastard,' she finished in a whisper as he picked up his cocked hat and strode out of the gate. He would not hear her, but she felt better for it. Her body was on fire with new confusing sensations, her pulse was all over the place; if he had intended to utterly wreck her composure, he had succeeded a thousand-fold.

'Eliza!'

'Yes, Miss Clemence?' the maid called from the door.

'A cold bath, if you please. I have become intolerably overheated.' And then, to crown it, to be told he had gone to a brothel after leaving her bed and was going to one now! She hoped he had his pocket picked and his boots stolen and drank bad rum and felt like hell in the morning. Because that was how she felt now.

'Miss Clemence? You're crying, Miss Clemence.' Eliza was patting her hand.

'Only because I am so angry with that wretched man, Eliza, that's all.' But anger had never made her cry before. Never.

Nathan strode along the harbour front, his expression enough to send anyone in his path diving to the side. How that outburst over Conroy had happened he had no very clear idea. Of course Clemence was not flirting with the lieutenant, let alone contemplating any more shocking behaviour. They were two attractive young people who had been having strenuous fun in the company of a perfectly respectable lady's maid and one disreputable ex-pirate.

But the sight of her in that light muslin gown, wet and clinging to those lovely long legs, the way it had draped, tantalising, at the junction of her thighs, the way her breasts, sweet as apples, had curved above the demure neck of that gown, had driven him insane. The fact that he could tell, even if she was too innocent to realise, that Conroy had been equally inflamed by the sight had been the final straw.

The man had been behaving perfectly properly, he had no doubt. Conroy was a gentleman. And, damn it, so was he and a gentleman had needs and he was going to find that high-class brothel that Melville had recommended. His conscience stirred at the recollection of Clemence's face when he had taunted her with the implication that he had gone there last night.

He wished now, as he stood in front of the shady porch, the white muslin curtain blowing in the breeze and the scent of flowers drifting from the garden behind the high fence, that he had done. Which saint had said it was better to marry than to burn? He couldn't recall, but he was certainly burning and here was the remedy.

Half an hour later, reclining in a hammock in that fragrant, shady garden, a glass of planter's punch to hand and a pair of very lovely ladybirds slipping slices of fruit between his lips, he ruefully concluded that the flames might be doused a little by alcohol, but they were certainly not extinguished.

Confronted by Madame's selection of highly skilled girls, he had realised that he did not want any of them. None of them was tall and slender and green eyed. None of them looked at him with a clear, innocent gaze that seemed to go right inside him and turn his brain to mush. His body wanted them, it would be impossible to deny the very visible evidence of that, but however willing the flesh, the spirit was decidedly disinclined.

'Thank you, Madame,' he had said, looking out at the hammock swinging between two breadfruit trees. 'But I am hot, tired and in need of little refreshment, that is all.'

And now he was comfortable, cool, refreshed and feeling every bit the bastard Clemence had called him. But short of going back and making love to her—after which he would have effectively tied her to him—there was nothing to be done about it. Nathan closed his eyes and wondered just how many weeks it was going to take to get back to England and safety.

Chapter Fifteen

'I really do appreciate you taking my dog as well, Captain Melville.' One-Eye settled, hackles raised, into a corner of the cabin, showing none of the becoming gratitude his mistress was attempting to convey. The three sailors it had taken to get him up the gangplank had retired, grinning. She must remember to tip them later.

Captain Melville, with only the faintest suggestion of gritted teeth, waved away the remark. 'Not at all, ma'am. Captain Stanier has explained that you are very attached to the animal and that, given that this is the first time you have been from home, it is important that you retain your, er...pet.'

'Indeed?' Clemence slid a sideways glance towards Nathan, who was further down the same deck, directing sweating sailors loading cannon balls. 'How very thoughtful of Captain Stanier,' she said sweetly, 'but I know I am depriving one of your officers of his cabin. Who should I thank for this comfort?'

She had a very good idea, having seen a valise with the initials R.C. being carried out. She and Robert Conroy had rapidly progressed to first names as they'd struggled with the wet dog yesterday.

'Mr Conroy, Miss Ravenhurst. He takes the Third's berth and so on.'

'And some poor midshipman ends up in a cupboard?' Clemence said with a smile. 'What happened to the Second Lieutenant?'

'He has given up his cabin next door to Captain Stanier.'

That was useful to know; she must remember to be very discreet in what she said to Eliza. And it was distinctly disquieting to think of Nathan sleeping only the thickness of the thin partition away. They had exchanged the minimum number of polite phrases that morning. He showed no signs of suffering from an evening of dissipation, from which she could only conclude that either he had not indulged in one or had a remarkably hard head. Or had been otherwise engaged than in heavy drinking.

Whatever he had been doing, she had most certainly not forgiven him for yesterday afternoon and he showed no signs of remorse, so the sensible thing would be to stop thinking about him. Or at least, to try, which was not easy when her body still appeared to be remembering the whole incident in graphic detail. Clemence put her new reticule on the lower bunk and surveyed her new home.

This was, in fact, an inferior cabin to the one she and Nathan had shared, less than half the size with the two bunks one above the other and only a flap-down table. And no privy cupboard, either; they would have to improvise with a chamber pot and a corner-curtain. Nor was there a porthole; their only ventilation came from louvres in the door. This was home for possibly two months; it was a good thing they had so little luggage.

Eliza was already putting things away as the captain took himself off with a bow and an invitation to dine with him and his officers that evening.

'Under there, dog.' The maid pointed to the space beneath the lower bunk, but One-Eye simply ignored her.

'I think we'll have to chain him up outside the door,' Clemence said, popping her head outside. 'There's a hook.'

'Fred says he'll take him for walks and deal with that sort of thing.' Eliza stood in the middle of the small space, a pile of underthings in her hands, turning round and round as she tried to find somewhere to put them.

'Fred?'

'Street.' Eliza looked decidedly self-conscious. 'These will have to stay in the bags under the bunk, that's all,' she pronounced.

'Eliza?' The only response was a wiggle of her hips as the maid got down on hands and knees. 'Are you and Street walking out?'

'He should be so lucky,' the maid remarked, straightening up. 'I've only just met him. Still, he's a fine figure of a man.'

'He is certainly that.' If one judged by sheer expanse. No doubt a responsible mistress would forbid her maidservant from associating with a man of bad character—even if he had recently reformed. But this was hardly a normal situation. Clemence tried to imagine arriving at whichever stately home was the Dowager Duchess of Allington's current residence and introducing herself with her entourage of one mulatto maid, one ex-pirate, one decrepit hound and one small trunk.

For the first time Clemence started to wonder just what this unknown relative might be like and just how different life as one of the Ravenhurst clan would be from the one she was used to. The apprehension was almost enough to displace the dull ache of unhappiness about Nathan. But not quite.

But still, unpacking and making the best they could of their new quarters did pass the two hours before Midshipman Andrews presented himself with the captain's compliments and the suggestions that Miss Ravenhurst might wish to see the departure from on deck.

'You must never go on to the poop deck where the officers are without an express invitation,' Clemence warned Eliza. 'And we must do our best to stay well clear of the men working and not wander about the ship.'

'Don't see how we're going to get any fresh air, then,' the maid grumbled, clambering up the companionway. 'This thing goes up and down a lot.'

'It will be worse when we are at sea, so you must grow accustomed. But we can certainly take exercise; I'll ask the captain at dinner where we may place chairs and where we may promenade,' Clemence said soothingly, hoping that Eliza would prove immune to seasickness. A reproachful bark sent her back to untie One-Eye's leash. 'And as for you, behave yourself!'

She had seen the island so often from on board a ship that she had not expected it to be any different this time. But somehow the vista of hills and mountains, the buildings on shore, the jumble of shipping in the harbour seemed like a painting, something unreal and distant. This was no longer home.

Clemence stood, one hand gripping the rail, one tight on the hound's leash, and stared, trying to fix the scene in her memory along with the smells that the soft off-shore breeze brought across the water. A hand removed the leash from her hand and replaced it with a large handkerchief before she was even aware that silent tears were rolling down her checks.

'You will come back one day,' Nathan said, looking not at her but at the island.

'I know.' Clemence dried her eyes, but held on to the white

linen. 'It is just that I cannot imagine what I am going to or what my new family is like or what they will think of me.'

'They are good people, the ones I know,' he said. 'People with a strong sense of family who will love you because you are theirs and then, once they know you, because you are you.'

'Oh!' Charmed out of all self-consciousness, Clemence turned to face him. 'Oh, thank you.' She smiled and for a moment the blue eyes that smiled back into hers held the expression she had surprised in them sometimes aboard the *Sea Scorpion*, the look that had lingered on her face as they hung together in the cool waters of the pool. And then the shutters came down and it was the polite smile of a gentleman who had offered a minor compliment to a lady.

'It is merely the truth,' Nathan said, handed back One-Eye and walked abruptly away towards the poop.

By the time Clemence's eyes were focusing properly again, the ship was sailing east along the coast and Nathan was nowhere to be seen.

After two weeks out at sea life had settled into a routine. To Clemence it sometimes felt as though this was real life and everything else was a dream. She and Eliza had made themselves as comfortable as they could in their cabin and Eliza, at least, now knew the ship from stem to stern thanks to Street and his excuses of either needing to take One-Eye for a walk, or asking advice on his mending or cajoling the maid into joining him and the ship's cook in the galley.

'I hope he intends to make an honest woman of you,' Clemence said severely one morning after Eliza had come back to the cabin in the small hours.

'He will, if I'll take him,' Eliza had chuckled, her fingers busy whipping a hem.

The awning that the men had rigged over the chairs, table and hammocks that had colonised the 'ladies' corner' of the main deck flapped idly in the light breeze. Clemence fanned herself and rocked in her hammock, too idle to sew or read one of the books she had borrowed from the officers.

The Straits of Florida were proving hot and humid and they were experiencing an uncomfortable combination of heavy squalls interspersed with virtual calms and the officers, Nathan included, appeared to be able to think of nothing other than navigation.

They all made polite conversation at dinner, of course, scrupulously avoiding matters relating to the running of the ship, but Clemence never lingered, certain they greeted the sight of her retreating back with relief so they could relax and get back to talking of naval matters.

She adjusted her pillow now and tipped her straw hat over her nose, secure in the knowledge that she could peep through the gaps in the coarse weave and scrutinise the comings and goings on the poop deck unseen.

Nathan was up there now, in deep conversation with the officers on watch as usual. He was so scrupulously polite and reserved in her company that anyone who did not know would assume he had never met her until she had boarded the *Orion*. She had hoped, for the first week, that he would think better of his attitude towards marriage, but the respectful way she was treated by his fellow officers only confirmed what he had said—as a Ravenhurst, it would take more than an adventure on a pirate ship to ruin her standing.

And the more she thought about his late wife, the more convinced she became that he still loved her. There was more behind his refusal to wed her than the fear of being thought a fortune hunter, Clemence was certain. She was certain, too, that if she could only get close to him again he might come to realise that, precious though his lost love was, there was another waiting for him, one that was alive and warm and wanted him.

But a frontal approach was not going to work, he was armoured against that, she told herself, lying awake at night and hearing him moving around in his cabin. But what would happen if she waited until all was still and then slipped next door and into his bed? One night she had got as far as putting one foot out from under the sheet and then had snatched it back with the thought of just how humiliating it would be when he rejected her again.

As she thought about it the bo'sun appeared, the two youngest midshipmen at his heels. 'Sir, I've got Mr Markham and Mr Stills for their navigation lesson, like you said, sir. I'll be more than grateful if you can get these two sorted, they're beyond my powers.'

Nathan came down the steps. 'I gather that you two are finding your mathematical studies a challenge.' There was an exchange of sheepish looks and two nods. 'Right, well, take your notebooks and the theodolites over there and we'll see if we can keep this vessel off the Grand Bahama.'

The bo'sun knuckled his forehead and took himself off, the boys ran to do as they were bid. And Clemence, still watching furtively, saw Nathan stretch his shoulders and flex his back with a grimace that spoke of more than stiffness. His back must be healed by now, surely, but the skin must be taut and tender.

Concerned, Clemence swung her legs out of the hammock and stood up. The hound opened his eye and looked hopeful. 'Oh, come on, then. I'll just take a stroll along the deck,' she said, waving Eliza back to her sewing. 'Where's Street?'

'In the galley, I dare say, that's where he usually is.' Eliza bit off her thread and folded the petticoat. 'I'll just have all these finished by the time we get to England,' she grumbled. 'And then you'll be wearing them three at once on account of the snow.'

'Not in early September, surely?' Clemence queried, watching Nathan's progress along the deck to the waiting boys. No, he wasn't moving as well as he had before the flogging.

By the time she drew level with the hatch cover that Nathan was using as his makeshift classroom, one midshipman was being put through his paces with the theodolite while the other stared glumly at a page covered in figures.

'Difficult?' Clemence queried softly, peering over the boy's shoulder while One-Eye sat down panting beside them.

'Yes, ma'am,' he admitted glumly. 'There's something wrong, but I can't see what.'

'It's Mr Stills, isn't it? I'm very interested,' she offered. 'Why don't you work down the page explaining it to me and perhaps you'll spot the problem?' She leaned over the notebook. 'Come along, start at the top.'

She knew exactly when Nathan realised she was there and what she was doing; she felt his gaze on her like a physical weight, but she kept her head bent over the book, her finger tracing slowly along the lines of figures.

'I don't understand this,' she prompted.

'That's the angle of the headland to the bows,' Stills began confidently, 'and you have to take it away from this one and that—'

'Doesn't make sense,' Clemence finished for him, running her finger back. 'Where is the error, do you think?'

A moment's heavy breathing and Stills pointed triumphantly. 'There, ma'am, I added it twice.'

'Well done, Mr Stills,' Clemence praised. 'I think it all makes sense now, don't you?'

'Which is more than it does to me, Miss Ravenhurst,' Nathan said, coming up to stand between them and placing one hand on each shoulder. Clemence made herself relax and resisted the temptation to sway towards him. 'You are fortunate, Mr Stills. Miss Ravenhurst is a better mathematician than you, but better yet, she can read your appalling handwriting. It is no wonder you make mistakes. You may write out *Thank you, Miss Ravenhurst* fifty times in your best hand in your own time.'

'Sir!'

Clemence smiled at the unfortunate youth. 'Excuse me, gentlemen.' She strolled on, feeling the three pairs of masculine eyes resting on her as she unfurled her parasol, raised it and gave it a coquettish twirl. Nathan had not seemed angered by her interruption of his lesson, but it was a very small step towards re-establishing their easy relationship.

Street was at home in the steamy confines of the galley, swapping Creole recipes for Mediterranean specialities with the ship's cook.

'Street, may I have a word?'

'You shouldn't be down here, Miss Clemence.' He wiped his hands on his apron and came out on deck with her, slyly passing a bone to the dog as he did so. 'What can I do, ma'am?'

'Have you seen Mr Stanier's back, Street?' she asked without preamble. 'He doesn't look comfortable to me and it's more than three weeks.'

'No, ma'am, not without his shirt, I haven't. Needs oiling, I'll be bound—a massage to get the skin supple again.'

'What with? Goose grease?'

'There'll be palm oil in the galley.' Street went back inside and reappeared with a jug. 'Thought so.'

'Then you'd better have a word with him,' Clemence said. 'And massage his back tonight.'

'Me, ma'am? With these hands?' He spread his great calloused paws out, palm up. 'I'd take the new skin off, not make it better. You should do it, ma'am.'

'Me? Street, that would hardly be proper.'

He gave her a quizzical look. 'That's out of the question, then. You won't want to do anything that wasn't proper, Miss Clemence, now would you?'

'You—' She subsided, knowing full well that Street's suggestion was exactly what she wanted to do. 'Thank you, I'll see what I can think of,' she temporised, taking the jug and calling One-Eye to heel.

Nathan was sharing watches, although he could have simply sat back and become a passenger. But it was not his nature to be idle and it gave him far too much time for thought. And with Clemence swaying in her hammock by day and gracing the wardroom or the captain's cabin in the evening, he needed all the distraction he could get.

He had thought her attractive before, despite bruises, cropped hair and with her natural curves lost to grief and poor diet. Now with rest and air and good feeding she was blossoming, her hair growing into waves and curls, her figure becoming what it was meant to be.

She would never be buxom like Julietta with her lushness, but that was part of the problem, how very unlike his late wife she was. There was nothing about Clemence that reminded him of that turmoil of infatuation, love and hate.

A book fell to the floor, knocked by his coat as he eased it off. Damn, but he was feeling clumsy. Nathan untied his stock and began unbuttoning his shirt, conscious of the sensitivity of the skin as the cotton fabric moved across it. It was healed, but stiff and tender, and the continuing nagging discomfort was almost as tiring as the pain had been.

He threw the shirt on a chair and kicked his shoes across the room, followed by his stockings, hearing in his mind Clem's *Tsk!* of irritation at his untidiness. She was so close, only a thin bulkhead away. He spread his hand on the wood at the point where he guessed her bunk would be, imagining her lying in a thin nightgown, sheet discarded in the steamy heat, the perspiration dewing her brow and making that thick, short hair curl into sensual disorder.

God, but he missed her. Those brief moments when she had strolled along and helped Stills with his calculations and he had found an excuse to touch her, stand close enough to inhale her unique scent; those stood out like one coloured woodcut amidst a book full of black and white.

He tried to tell himself that, even if there were not the disparity in their fortunes, he was still not the man for her. Clemence needed love, even if she might think she was willing to settle for a marriage of convenience and friendship touched with desire. And he was not at all certain that he even understood what love was any more.

The draught of air across his back and a sharp indrawn breath were the only warning he had that he was not alone. Nathan stood very still as the door clicked shut. It was her, no one else would have entered without knocking or speaking, no one else brought the faint sensual drift of frangipani and roses on the hot air.

'Oh, your beautiful back,' she breathed in distress.

Nathan took a deep breath, telling himself that it was all to the good if she found his scars repellent, and turned.

Clemence was standing there, not in the thin nightrail of his imaginings but a most proper wrapper concealing her from chin to toe. He let out the breath, then almost choked as he saw the bare toes peeping from under the frilled hem.

'Clemence, what are you doing here?'

'Your back needs oiling, it will help relax the scarring and make it more comfortable.' She put down a jug on the table beside his logs and began to roll up her sleeves. 'Lie down.'

'What!' In the nick of time Nathan recalled the thinness of the walls and got the volume down to a hiss. 'You cannot come in here with me half-naked and massage my back!'

'But I can't do it when you've got your shirt on,' she said in the voice of someone humouring a fractious child. 'It will do it good.'

He knew it would, he could feel the cool slide of oil across the tender skin even as she spoke. 'I am sure you are correct, but you aren't going to do it.'

'I am.' In the lantern light Clemence looked very determined. She held up her hands. 'See? Smooth. Smoother than anyone else's on board. It is important for your work that you are fit—don't be a prude, Nathan.'

A prude? He had never felt less prudish in his life, which was half the problem. 'Very well, then.' He drew his belt through the trouser loops with a crack of leather and tossed it on to his shirt, then lay down on his bunk, buried his face in his arms and surrendered to whatever she wanted to do to him.

Chapter Sixteen

Nathan lay trying to follow Clemence's actions with his hearing alone. There was a rustle of fabric, over by the chair. Her wrapper? Then the soft pad of her bare feet back towards him, the sound as she put the jug on the floor beside the bunk. At least it was narrow; that would restrict her reach somewhat.

Then there was pressure alongside his right thigh, then the left, and weight came down on his buttocks. 'Clemence!' Nathan tried to buck her off, but she came down with both palms flat on his shoulder blades, flattening him back to the bed.

'Lie still, this is the only way I can do this properly.' He wriggled. 'I can't be too heavy.'

With a faint groan Nathan surrendered. At least the tickle of fabric at the top of his trousers told him that she was still wearing something, which was a mercy.

Then she bent down to pick up the jug and her weight shifted and her thighs tightened to help her balance and he realised that there was nothing merciful about this whatsoever.

'The oil might feel cool,' she warned. It dribbled into the small of his back, making him draw in a reflexive breath and shiver with sensual anticipation. 'Sorry.'

He did not feel up to explaining that this was already verging on more pleasure than he felt capable of taking. In an effort to control his own reactions he said harshly, 'I wonder you care to look at my back, much less touch it.'

'They are honourable scars,' Clemence said softly, putting the heels of both hands into the small of his back and pressing lightly as they slid upwards. 'How could I be repelled by them? I know how much courage they represent.'

It silenced him, humbled him, too. 'Clemence—'

'Shh. Just relax.'

It seemed impossible. How could a man relax with that soft feminine weight pressing his loins into the firm mattress, shifting and clinging as she worked? Her hands were firm and gentle and she seemed to understand exactly how much pressure to apply to the new skin, just where the underlying bruising was still tender.

Gradually he found he was drifting, the rhythm of her hands and the shifting balance of her body almost mesmeric. The noises of the ship working around them faded and he slid into something that was not sleep—a trance, perhaps.

This was sensual in a way he could not have imagined contact with a woman could be. Clemence was not teasing or enticing, she had no intention of using this as a prelude to lovemaking, she was too much of an innocent for those sort of games. She was doing this for him in the same way as she had tended to him after the flogging.

Under her hands his back muscles relaxed as they had not since the moment he had realised that the punishment was inevitable. As the oil sank into his skin the soreness vanished and all that was left was a heightened sensitivity, a feeling of dreamlike power, the fantasy that they were part of one another.

Her hands slowed, slid up either side of his spine in one

long sweep, then moved down until they were on the mattress, on either side. She bent forward and Nathan hung there in his sensual trance as her nipples brushed his back through the soft lawn of her gown and her breath feathered the nape of his neck.

'Are you asleep?' she whispered.

No. No, I want to roll over and take you in my arms and make love to you until you faint with pleasure, that was the honest answer. With will-power he did not know had, Nathan lay still, breathing deeply. After a moment she smiled, her mouth so close to his skin that he could feel the change in her breathing, then she straightened up and climbed carefully off his shattered body.

As the door closed softly behind her Nathan lay still, eyes closed on reality, and let himself drift into fantasy, just for once, just for that night.

'You going to get up, Mr Stanier, sir?' There was a thump and the sounds of clothes being shaken out. 'Only it's eight bells and the Bahama Keys are fine on the port bow.'

Nathan blinked and saw the bulk of Street, moving around the cabin like a pantomime housemaid. There was a tray on the fold-down table with what looked like bread and coffee. 'Your back looks better,' he added, picking up the oil jug and heading for the door. He sounded not one whit surprised.

'Street!' Nathan twisted round and sat up. *Damn it, it* was *better.*

'Yessir?' The ex-pirate was not cut out for looking innocent.

'What do you know about that?' He pointed at the jug.

'If a certain party were to have asked me for some oil for your back, sir, I'm sure I'd have forgotten about it this morning. Amazing how stuff gets left lying around, isn't it?'

He went out, hands full, leaving the door to swing behind him.

Nathan turned the chair to face the table and began to eat, his mind spinning. It seemed he was forgiven and Clemence would tolerate his company once more, a dangerous indulgence, but an irresistible one. The click of claws was all the warning he got before a wet nose nudged sharply into his ribs, effectively focusing everything on the fact that one large dog was after his breakfast.

'Miss Eliza!'

'Yes, Mr Stanier, sir?' The lilting island accent came from right behind him.

'Get this hound out of here.' He did not turn round, realising his shirt had vanished along with Street.

'Yes, sir. My,' she remarked to an accompaniment of claws being dragged across the deck, 'you've a fine set of muscles, sir, that you have. Enough to dazzle a lady. Pity to waste that, I'd say.'

When he swung round she was gone, the door latch falling.

'Oh, there he is! Bad dog, running off!' Clemence looked up from her book as Eliza dragged a reluctant One-Eye on deck. 'Where was he?'

The maid tied the leash to a ring on the rail and flopped down in the shade. 'Phew, I thought it would be nice and breezy on a ship.' She waved an embroidery pattern to and fro in front of her face. 'He was in Mr Stanier's cabin trying to steal some breakfast. Sitting there with no shirt on, Mr Stanier was; he's a fine figure of a man, I'll say that. I'll wager he strips well.'

'Eliza!' Clemence hissed, blushing all over at the thought of just how well. 'Someone will hear you.'

'And what if they do? There's nothing wrong with my

eyes, or yours, either, Miss Clemence. Why aren't you marrying the man?'

'Because he says he's not good enough for me,' Clemence confessed. 'Apparently my having a duke for a cousin and owning a small fleet of merchantmen would make him a fortune hunter.' She sighed. 'And he's still in love with his late wife.'

'Man's a fool, then.'

'Eliza, that isn't fair. I think his scruples are honourable, if infuriating, and as for his wife, I think it is very romantic— or, at least, I would do if it wasn't for the fact it affects me.'

'So you want him, then?' Eliza picked up some of the endless hemming, but left it lying on her lap. Her brown eyes were wide with curiosity and concern.

'Being a normal female in full possession of my faculties,' Clemence said tartly, 'yes, I do.'

'What are you going to do about it?'

'Short of alienating all my relatives and giving away all my money, there isn't a lot I can do,' Clemence said, staring out to sea.

'You in love with him, Miss Clemence?'

'Yes,' she confessed. Eliza opened her mouth to speak. 'And, no, don't ask why I don't tell him. Even if could bring myself to be so brassy, all it would achieve would be to make him feel sorry for me.'

They relapsed into thoughtful silence, Clemence pretending to read a very dull book of sermons the Third Lieutenant had offered her, Eliza idly basting the hem of a shift. One-Eye barked a greeting and a long shadow fell over them.

'Ladies.'

'Mr Stanier.' Clemence schooled her expression into one of polite greeting and tried not to remember the feel of Nathan's body gripped between her thighs, the heat of his skin under her palms, the strange feeling of power when he had lain quiescent under her.

'May I join you? I find myself at leisure for an hour or two. With these light airs we will be tacking back and forth for a tiresome while longer, I fear.'

'Please.' The ship's carpenter had rigged them up a table and an awning as well as fetching up chairs and the hammock.

Nathan dropped into one of the low chairs and stretched out his legs. He had shed his uniform coat for a light linen one and he had a wide-brimmed hat like the planters wore on his head. 'My back is very much better this morning, Miss Ravenhurst.' Clemence saw Eliza's sharp gaze focus on their faces.

'My suggestion that an oil massage would help proved successful?' she enquired as though her own hands had been nowhere near either back or oil.

'Miraculous,' Nathan said, his lids lowered so she could not see what was going on in those blue eyes. 'Extremely therapeutic. In fact, I can safely say I have never felt anything like it.'

'Will it be necessary to repeat it?' she asked, attempting to sound nonchalant.

'It would perhaps not be wise.' And then he did look fully at her and the heat blazed like firelight behind sapphires and the breath caught in her throat.

'Eliza, I think this would be a good time to give One-Eye some exercise,' Clemence announced.

'Yes, Miss Clemence,' Eliza said primly, folding her work and getting up. 'Come on, lazy hound, let's see what Street's got in the galley for you.' As she passed behind Nathan she caught Clemence's eye and pursed her lips in an exaggerated kiss.

'Clemence? What has occurred to put you to the blush?'

'Eliza, drat the woman,' she confessed. 'She reads more into what I did last night than...'

'I read only kindness,' Nathan said softly. 'And, considering recent events between us, considerable powers of forgiveness and trust.'

'If we are speaking of forgiveness, I can still not forget how you came to be injured in the first place,' Clemence protested. 'And as for you refusing to marry me, I suppose I can accept that your scruples are honourable, although I find them misguided. If I had known about your wife, how you feel about her still, then of course, I would have refused immediately.'

'How I feel?' he queried, frowning at her.

'You told me you loved her. And there was such emotion on your face when you spoke of her. You fought a duel over her, put your career at hazard to defend her honour—you do not need to explain any more, and I should not be intruding into those feelings in any case. I would not want to be a second wife under those circumstances, to know that my husband could not help but compare me to his first wife.'

After a moment he said, 'You are right, my feelings for you are very different from what I now feel for Julietta.' Clemence felt the cramping misery inside at the shadow that passed over his face as he spoke.

'Well,' she said with an attempt at lightness, 'we may be friends again, may we not?' There were weeks still to go, days to become accustomed to being with him and knowing that now she could never become any closer, figure any larger in his life.

'Friends?' Nathan reached out and lifted her hand, which lightly clasped the edge of the hammock. 'Yes, we may be friends.' The kiss he dropped on her fingertips was feather-light, but Clemence felt it as though it had caressed her lips. Then he picked up her book and grimaced at the open page and the moment had passed.

'You are enjoying this?'

'No, it is deadly dull, but Mr Jones gave it to me and I do not like to hurt his feelings. I thought I could read one sermon at least and then discuss it with him at dinner.'

'The trials and tribulations of being a well brought-up young lady,' Nathan teased, settling back in his chair and tipping his hat over his eyes.

'I am sure my manners will fall far short of what is expected in English society,' Clemence worried.

'You will enchant them with your freshness. Anything that is different to prevailing manners in Jamaica you will quickly learn; besides, your relatives are sure to be in the country or at the seaside, so you will have plenty of time before you have to worry about the rigours of the Season.'

'Will you go to sea again soon?' she asked, endeavouring quite successfully not to sound wistful. Nathan must never guess how she truly felt about him.

'I would hope to. I have no desire to languish on half-pay.'

'No, indeed not. I imagine that must be most frustrating. And I suppose, too, that with the end of hostilities there must be fewer opportunities.'

'Yes,' he agreed, his mouth set, and she mentally kicked herself for tactlessness.

'Papa wished to go into the navy. He was the youngest son, so that was quite acceptable. But then they found his eyesight was so very poor he was ineligible.'

'Is that why he became a merchant and built his fleet?'

'I suppose so—he did love the sea,' Clemence mused. 'Personally I am becoming thoroughly bored with it and this intolerable dawdling progress.'

'Don't wish yourself a storm.' Nathan pushed back his hat and got to his feet. 'The wind is changing now—can you feel it? We'll be clear of the Straits soon and into the Atlantic and all its swells and winds. Then we'll see how bored you are! And cold,' he added, pausing by the hammock and running the back of his hand fleetingly up her bare arm, sending delicious shivers down her spine. 'You will disappear under layers of everything you possess.'

'Forty-two days out,' Clemence observed, looking up from the diary she was keeping of the journey. 'Is it always this slow?'

'No.' Nathan glanced up from his own notes. 'We've had more contrary winds than I would have expected. Are you warm enough? I fear we will have to move our customary morning journal meeting inside soon.' From the day after what Clemence always thought of as their truce, they had been meeting in the morning to write their journals. It was companionable, yet entirely proper, and gradually she sensed that both of them had relaxed into friendship. Nathan was careful not to touch her and she resisted any inclination to flirt. It answered very well in daylight, but at night she still ached for him, lying awake listening to the sounds of him moving about in his cabin, trying to imagine what he was doing.

'Oh, no, I enjoy this.' Clemence smiled over the top of the warm scarf Midshipman Stills had bashfully offered her when he overheard her commenting on the cold.

'Three weeks perhaps, sooner with any luck,' Nathan added, looking up at the mainmast and then down to his notebook. 'We're a good two hundred miles off the Newfoundland Banks now.' Clemence glanced across to see what he was doing and smiled at the sketch of one of the hands clinging on like a monkey that he had achieved with only a few pencil lines.

'That's good.' Her own journal was so scrupulously devoid of any personal remarks or feelings that she could have heard it read at Sunday service from the poop deck without blushing and Nathan appeared as unconcerned about her reading his.

'Midshipmen are taught to sketch as part of the training.' He looked across at her, grinned and executed a swift carica-ture of her bundled up in her scarf and borrowed pea jacket. *I wish I could draw*, Clemence thought. *When we part, I will have nothing tangible to remember him by.*

'What is the first thing you are going to do when you land?' Nathan asked.

'Buy warm clothes! And then find out where Aunt Ame-lia is.'

'Which one is she? I lose track of your vast clan.'

'Lord Sebastian and Lady Dereham's mother. I have been studying the family tree in an effort to learn them all—I just hope I meet them one at a time or I will be quite over-whelmed.'

'You will cope,' Nathan said easily, closing his notebook and getting to his feet. 'I have every confidence that next Season you will be the toast of London society.'

'Oh, good.' Clemence sighed inaudibly as he smiled and left her. 'I cannot wait.'

Chapter Seventeen

'Land ho!'

'Eliza! Eliza, wake up!' Clemence scrambled off the bunk, thrust her feet into her slippers and pulled on her wrapper. 'Land!'

There was the sound of feet outside as those with cabins on their deck ran to see.

'It's the middle of the night,' Eliza complained sleepily, opening her eyes. 'Miss Clemence!' She sat bolt upright. 'You cannot go out like that—look at you.'

'Oh, bother it.' Clemence snatched up a scarf and wrapped it around her neck. 'It cannot be that cold, close to land; it is early September, after all.'

'I mean you aren't decent—' Eliza's voice vanished as Clemence ran up the companionway into the early morning light. And there it was, land at last, low wooded cliffs, rolling hills, the line of grey that seemed to be an endless shingle bar.

She clung to the rail, staring across the grey water to her new home. No scents reached her nostrils, no vivid colours broke the tranquillity of grey and brown and muted green. Would the people be as cool and muted, too?

'Welcome to England. We are off Weymouth, not so very far from Portsmouth now,' said Nathan's voice in her ear. She turned against the rail and found him close, shrugging out of his heavy coat. 'Here, put this on. You'll catch your death and you'll corrupt the innocent midshipmen before their time otherwise.'

Smiling, Clemence did as he said and found herself enclosed in warm, Nathan-scented wool. For a moment it befuddled her half-sleepy senses and she found herself looking up into his face, smiling, her face unguarded, the carefully polite smiles of friendship forgotten. 'Thank you.'

'I had made myself ignore what a kissable mouth you have,' he said, pulling her gently into a secluded corner. 'But we are nearly there now. What harm can one English kiss do?'

An English kiss, from Nathan, was, if anything, more inflammatory than a Jamaican one, perhaps because of the contrast between the cool air brushing her face and the heat of his body and his mouth. Or perhaps it was the effect of weeks of living so close to him and behaving with utter propriety.

Her lips parted and he took her mouth with the same implacable gentleness that she had learned to expect as she wrapped her arms around his neck and the coat slid unheeded to the deck.

This was the last time he would kiss her, her last chance to fill her senses and her memory with the feel and scent and taste of him before he became unobtainable, the man she would measure all the others against. The one they would never match.

His eyes were dark and hazed as he lifted his mouth from hers and stood looking into her face. 'It has not gone away, then, that connection when we touch,' he said, his voice husky.

'No.' *Does it not tell you something?* she wanted to ask

him, but that was impossible without saying that she loved him, spoiling their last hours together with regret and embarrassment and pity. Instead she smiled and lifted her hand and touched his lips lightly, then bent to pick up the coat. 'Take this, I must go below.' And she ducked under his arm and down the steps before the tears had a chance to show.

That was a mistake, Nathan told himself, shrugging back into the coat and not even attempting to pretend to himself that he was not burying his nose in the lapels to drink in the perfume of sleepy woman. A mistake and an indulgence, but also another memory of Clemence that he could store and bring out on some long, lonely watch to warm himself with.

He was conscious of another, bulkier figure close by and turned to see Melville leaning on the rail beside him, his telescope on the small sailing boat beating out to meet them. 'That's flying the ensign, they'll have been on watch for us from the harbour battery and will be bringing orders, I've no doubt.'

'I thought you were making for Portsmouth.' Nathan realised he had thought no further ahead than landfall. His own orders were to report to the Admiralty in Whitehall.

'Aye. I hope they haven't changed that and we've got to beat round to Chatham.'

The lieutenant scrambling on board with the oilcloth-wrapped packet of orders saluted smartly. 'The admiral's compliments, Captain Melville. If you would be so good as to proceed to Chatham with all speed.'

Melville caught Nathan's eye, but made no comment other than to thank the man and take the orders. Clemence, Eliza at her side, came back up on deck. The maid looked miserable, hunched in her layers of clothes as her eyes fixed hopefully on the shore, and Clemence looked paler, more weary than she had when she had left him just a little while before. As Nathan watched, Clemence put her arm around Eliza's shoulders and hugged her to her side.

'Are you both all right?' he asked.

'Tired and cold and impatient,' Clemence admitted with a rueful smile. 'Seeing land and not being able to disembark brings it home how long we have been on this ship.'

And now they would have the delay while they sailed along the entire south coast, round into the Thames estuary. He walked back to Melville. 'We could put the women off here, send them back in the boat with the lieutenant.'

'What, by themselves?' Melville looked across. 'Although they do look as though they would like to get ashore, I must admit.'

'I'll go with them. I can find them a respectable lodging, discover where Miss Ravenhurst's aunt is, send her off in a hired chaise and post up to London myself. My orders are to report to the Admiralty, not stick to the *Orion*.'

'True enough. And you won't be much later, if at all, that way. Lieutenant! Hold hard there.' He strode away across the deck, leaving Nathan to speak to Clemence.

'Would you like to go ashore here at Weymouth, now?'

'Now?' Clemence blinked at him.

'It is that or stay on board until we reach Chatham. Better to land now.' She was looking doubtful, daunted no doubt by the thought of coping alone in a strange country. 'I'll come, too,' he added. 'I can find you lodgings and organise a post chaise to take you to your aunt.'

'But your orders?'

'This will probably be faster,' he said. 'The roads are a little different from what you are used to and I can be in London in hours from here.'

'Then if it is not an inconvenience to you, I would be most

grateful, thank you.' She said it with cool good manners, a remote young lady, no longer the warm soft creature, half-tumbled from sleep, responsive in his arms. She was wise, no doubt, to distance herself like this. When he had kissed her, when she had responded to him, they had expected to be parted within hours. Now it could be a day or two.

'You had better hurry and pack, I'll send some men down to carry your things on deck.' Even Eliza roused herself at that, hurrying below to leave him to explain to the lieutenant that he was returning with three passengers, a pile of luggage and a cantankerous old hound.

Nathan stood for a minute, contemplating what he had just let himself in for. But she was tired and anxious and needed to be with her new family; to make her endure any more time, within sight of land yet in limbo, was too cruel. He just needed to extend the self-control he had been exercising for a little longer. No doubt it was good for his soul, Nathan thought with a wry smile as he followed the women and went to fetch his belongings.

Clemence clutched the rail of the skiff with one hand and her hat with the other and squinted against the stiff breeze. 'What a fabulous beach!' Golden sand arced around a wide bay before the coast lifted into cliffs and the wide expanse was dotted with figures and strange small huts.

'See the bathing machines?' Nathan stood at her elbow, his fingers clenched in One-Eye's collar. 'You could go for a swim.'

'No, thank you! I can recall everything you told me about flannel bathing dresses and large women who dunk you under.' And although the beach might be golden, the sea was grey and cold and there were no palm trees waving in a warm breeze. She shivered. This cool foreign land was home now so she'd better get used to it.

They were into the harbour channel now, steep slopes crowned with fortifications to the left, the busy quayside to the right. Clemence craned to see while Eliza at her side was wide-eyed. 'It's so different, Miss Clemence, so square and grey.'

Nathan was talking to the lieutenant who had brought the orders out to them. 'The Golden Lion? Remember, I have ladies with me—is it respectable?'

'Eminently, the senior officers always lodge there with their wives. And you can hire post chaises from them.'

Clemence felt she should take a hand in the decisions being made, assert herself and not rely upon Nathan. Soon, very soon, he would be gone and she must learn to manage. 'That sounds perfectly satisfactory, thank you.' Then a thought struck her. 'Nathan,' she whispered. 'I have no money!'

'Here.' He opened his pocket book and handed her some unfamiliar bank notes. 'This is the change from the one hundred guineas Melville drew against our official expenses. I am sure your aunt will be able to arrange to have it repaid to him.'

'Thank you.' She took the money and folded it carefully into her reticule, relieved that she was not having to borrow it from Nathan. How expensive would the inn be and how long would they have to stay? What if…? Clemence drew a deep steadying breath and told herself to stop worrying. She could cope, of course she could.

The Golden Lion proved comfortable, if rather dark and overpowering with thick hangings and a heavily be-curtained bed. 'It all smells odd,' Eliza complained as they set out on foot for Harvey's Library and Reading Rooms where the porter had assured Nathan they would find all the news-sheets they could possibly want.

'Shh, and don't stare so,' Clemence chided.

'They are all staring at us,' the maid retorted.

It was hardly surprising, Clemence thought. A young lady bundled into layers of decidedly unfashionable garments, attended by a maid in a colourful head-wrap and escorted by a naval officer and a vast man with an ancient and belligerent hound on a leash. Yes, they certainly stood out amongst the crowds going about their business and the fashionable strollers who sauntered down the pavements closer to the centre of the town.

'Here we are,' Nathan said, sounding as nearly rattled as she could recall hearing him. 'You wait outside, Street.' Under the eye of a matron with a vast bonnet and an eye glass, he swept them into the entrance of Harvey's Library.

An attendant showed them into the newspaper reading room, found them a table and chairs and brought them the *Morning Post* and *The Times* from the beginning of June.

Clemence applied herself to scanning the columns in search of any reference to the Ravenhursts, but it was hard to ignore some of the other news.

'It says here,' she reported, 'that Mr Kemble remains at Stanmore Priory under the severe visitation of what Dr Johnson styles *arthritic tyranny*, vulgarly called the gout. Poor man, having that printed. And there is famine in Transylvania, wherever that is.'

'I have found a list of the prices at the Pantheon Linen Warehouse,' Eliza contributed. 'Coloured dresses for only seventeen shillings and six pence.' She frowned. 'Is that expensive?'

'I have no idea,' Nathan said repressively. 'Concentrate, or we will be here all day.'

They had arrived at the first week in July before Clemence found it. 'Here! *It is understood that Lord Standon daily expects a most fashionable house party to assemble at his country seat in Hampshire, the distinguished company of Lord Standon's illustrious relatives to include, it is rumoured, Lord Sebastian Ravenhurst and the Grand Duchess of Maubourg.* Thank goodness.' Although a house party did sound somewhat daunting.

Nathan was already on his feet, checking the *Peerage*. 'Long Martin Court, principal seat of the Earls of Standon. And it is not far from Romsey, which means I can escort you and then take the chaise on to London.'

'I had better write.'

'You would arrive on the heels of the letter if we leave first thing tomorrow,' Nathan said, unfolding a map he had found on the shelves. 'Look, we are here, there is Romsey. Now we know where you are going and when, would you like to look at the shops?'

What she wanted was to retreat to her fusty, dark room and panic quietly about her arrival at Long Martin Court. It was almost worrying enough to distract her from the dull ache inside at the prospect of parting from Nathan for ever. Clemence fixed a smile on her face. 'That would be delightful.'

It was seven years since he had been shopping with a lady, Nathan realised, watching the tension gradually fade from Clemence's face as she browsed amongst the shops lining the more fashionable streets. He wanted to take her somewhere quiet and hold her, stroke those lines creasing her brow until they vanished, kiss her until the worry disappeared from her green eyes.

With Julietta all his energies had been devoted to keeping her out of the scrapes her impulsive nature sent her tumbling into. Emptying his wallet as she shopped had been one way of doing that, even if the silks and taffetas, the pearls and bangles, had all been deployed to attract attention and aid her in flirting with any man who paid her heed. He closed his eyes for a moment against the pain. That was all she had ever meant to do: flirt. And yet it had killed her.

But Clemence did not flirt and she did not once open her reticule, although he saw her lips curve at the sight of a shop window full of nonsensically pretty hats and look wistfully at a display of fans and shawls. He wanted to buy it all for her, see her eyes light up and hear her laugh. But he should not give her something as intimate as a garment, he knew that.

Eliza had found a shop full of small antiquities, old paintings, statues and trays of second-hand knick-knacks. She rummaged enthusiastically while the shopkeeper stared at her dark skin and her colourful head-wrap.

To distract himself from watching Clemence, Nathan picked up fans from a shelf, almost at random. One small one caught his eye. Painted with a group of young women in the centre, it was surrounded in verses in French. It wasn't new—in fact, it was slightly scuffed—but it intrigued him. The women were taking papers from cherubs who appeared to be operating some kind of lottery or lucky dip. It was hard to read in the subdued light as he skimmed the words, then he saw the name in the last verse. Clémence.

'I'll take this.' The shopkeeper wrapped it for him and he thrust it into his breast pocket as the two women tore themselves away from the trinkets and came to join him. 'Finished?'

'Yes, thank you. You must be so bored.' Clemence smiled up at him. 'Should we go back to the inn?'

'I think so. I will hire a chaise for tomorrow.'

She grew quieter and quieter as they neared the inn and

Nathan found himself suddenly devoid of conversation. 'You'll take dinner in the private parlour?' She nodded. 'I will not join you. I have business to attend to.' He stopped at the door. 'I will send a note with the time for us to leave.'

'Yes, of course,' Clemence said politely, her eyes troubled. His memory brought back the look in them when he had refused to marry her. He felt, obscurely, that he had let her down, and yet, surely by now she knew he had made the right decision? 'We will be ready.'

Almost there, he thought as he strode off down St Edmund's Street towards his non-existent business. *Almost free of the need to watch every thought and every word. Almost time for the safety of loneliness and of not having to worry about another human being.* Because that was all it was, all it could be, this odd ache inside him. He had missed feminine company and Clemence was such an original female it was hard not to be attracted by her. He had been trained to care for those under his command and he supposed that was why he felt such a need to protect her. And he wanted to make love to her and that, of course, was impossible. So the sooner he could return to his bachelor existence, the better.

It had been easier to sleep in the cramped cabin, Clemence concluded after a restless night in the high bed, alternately stifled and cold. Everything seemed to be moving still, yet the familiar shipboard noises had been replaced by cartwheels on cobbles, shouts from the harbour, heavy feet on the landing outside and heavy snores from the chamber next door.

Nathan did not snore. Clemence rolled over and buried her head under a pillow, but all that the comparative peace provided was more tranquillity in which to think and to worry.

Somehow she would get through the meeting with her family, she knew that, despite her anxious anticipation. But what then? They would expect her to become part of their world, to take her place in society and to find a husband. And how could she when the only man she loved didn't want to marry her?

Those days together on the *Orion* had given her a glimpse of what their life together could be, the companionship, the shared amusements, the spark of temper and the fun of making up. Everything, that is, except the nights spent in each other's arms. Her body ached as she let herself remember the feel of those slim hips between her thighs as she had massaged his back, the ripple of muscle under the palms, the spring of his hair, the scent of hot masculinity.

Stubborn, stubborn man! And yet, now, she could understand his scruples. And it was not as though he loved her, after all. He knew she was safe now so he had no need to fight for her.

Clemence screwed her eyes tightly shut and refused to let herself cry.

Chapter Eighteen

'We have arrived.'

The chaise swung through between tall gate posts. Clemence caught a glimpse of a quaint cottage and a man holding the gate, then they were into parkland, great sweeping grasslands dotted with trees, the glint of distant water, a small temple artfully placed on a mound. Elegant, artificial and yet deeply satisfying.

'What are those odd cattle?' Eliza pointed.

'Deer.' She knew that, she had seen pictures. Clemence tightened her grip on her reticule, her elbow rubbing against Nathan's. A hired chaise was hardly big enough for a hound and four people, not when one of them was Street. Street, Nathan had decreed, was staying with her, although in what capacity he had not said. Her imagination baulked at the thought of the ex-pirate in footman's livery.

The carriage drive seemed endless, but at last they came to a halt and Nathan opened the door and handed her down. 'Courage,' he murmured as he offered her his arm. 'You faced down Red Matthew McTiernan, one duchess will be child's play.'

The footman who answered the door was too well trained

to express surprise to find himself confronted by an unexpected member of his master's family on the arm of a naval officer, although his eyes widened at the sight of their entourage, one of whom was snarling at a peacock. The butler, materialising as they entered, was above showing even that degree of surprise and ushered Clemence and Nathan into a salon. 'Your staff will be comfortable in the servants' hall, sir. I will ascertain if her Grace is receiving.'

'Clemence! My dear child, I had no idea!' The human whirlwind who appeared five minutes later, sweeping past the butler, clasped Clemence to her bosom and kissed her on both cheeks. 'You poor lamb, I was devastated to hear about your papa and then your uncle said you were unwell—we had no thought you might be able to make the journey.'

Clemence found herself seated beside the lady she supposed must be her aunt. She was tall, although not as tall as Clemence, dark haired, long nosed and remarkably handsome. At first glance she seemed daunting, but there was humour in her large blue eyes and kindness in the clasp of her hands around Clemence's own cold ones.

'I was not unwell, ma'am. My uncle Naismith is determined on seizing my inheritance by forcing me to marry my cousin Lewis. I ran away,' she added, then ran out of words. There ought to be some way to gently lead up to what had happened, but it escaped her.

The duchess raised her eyebrows, took a deep breath, then turned her eyes on Nathan. 'With this gentleman?'

'Captain Nathan Stanier, your Grace. Royal Navy. Miss Ravenhurst's fight took her into the hands of a pirate crew of which I was, at that time, the navigator.'

'On a naval mission, I trust? Your present occupation does not represent a sudden change of heart?' Despite her sharp words, her expression as she turned back to Clemence was gentle. 'My dear, I am sure you would like to tell me all about this alone in my boudoir.'

'No, thank you, ma'am. There is nothing I cannot discuss in front of Captain Stanier. I was disguised as a boy. There was a battle and it was all very unpleasant. But, through it all, Captain Stanier knew and protected me. He was hurt because of me. Nothing…untoward occurred.' At least her aunt was not having hysterics, or had shown her the door or any of the other unpleasant scenarios that had been running through her mind.

'Call me Aunt Amelia, child.' The duchess squeezed her hands. 'You will want to rest a while and take some tea. Captain, may I trouble you to pull the bell? Thank you. Ah, Andrewes, please will you show Miss Ravenhurst to the Blue suite and send my woman to her. And a tea tray.'

'Aunt Amelia—' She was being got out of the way while her aunt interrogated Nathan, which was unfair. She should stay and defend him.

'I will just have a word with Captain Stanier, my dear,' the duchess continued, confirming her fears. 'I will come and see you shortly.'

Nathan met her eyes and mouthed, *Go*, so Clemence got to her feet, bemused. She could hardly cling to his coat and insist on staying.

'Perhaps you had better say goodbye now,' her aunt added with finality.

Clemence swallowed. She had not expected the parting to be so sudden and she had no words beyond, 'Thank you, Na… Captain.' He was studying her, like a painter looking at a subject before he laid chalk to paper. She tried again. 'You saved my life, at no little risk to your own. I thank you and I wish you well. Goodbye.'

'It was a pleasure to be of service, Miss Ravenhurst.' He reached into his coat and pulled out a slender package. 'A trifle. A keepsake. I saw your name on it, but I have not stopped to translate it, I fear.'

He bowed, she curtsied and took it, an unimportant thing when all she wanted was him, and then she was walking away from the man she had thought, for a few blissful moments, would be her destiny.

'Well, Captain Stanier?'

Despite the distinct feeling that he was up before the admiral on charges, Nathan felt a twinge of appreciation. The duchess was formidably unshaken by the unexpected arrival of her niece and, he could see, was more than capable of looking after Clemence.

'There is no doubt, your Grace, that Miss Ravenhurst is quite comprehensively compromised. She has spent nights in my cabin, during only one of which was I fooled into thinking she was male. But I can give you my word that, although she has been exposed to violence that no young woman should ever see, her virtue has not been outraged.'

'You relieve my mind,' she said drily. 'But as you say, my niece is compromised. It does not occur to you to offer her the protection of your name?'

'It did. That was my intention—before I knew who she was. I am unequal to one of her birth or her fortune. I am the younger son of the third Baron Howarth and I live on my pay. When I prevailed upon Clemence to tell me her name, I realised that the power of the Ravenhurst family would both protect her good name and effectively crush her uncle and his schemes. She has no need to marry me—she may marry who she chooses, as high as she chooses.'

'That is true.' The duchess sat studying him. Nathan

looked stolidly back at her. If she thought she was going to push him into babbling on, she was mistaken. 'What do you know about her uncle?' she asked at length.

'That when Clemence ran away her face was swollen from the blow he had dealt her because she had refused his son. Their intention was for the young man to come to her bed and force her until she was with child. They assumed this would compel her to give in for the sake of the baby, thus giving them permanent control of her fortune.'

He had thought he could get through this without emotion, but it was an effort to control the anger in his voice. The duchess's eyes widened in shock, but she did not speak. 'The navy has legal representation on Jamaica. We have left a deposition with them against the time when you wish to act.'

'Then I must thank you, Captain Stanier. It seems Clemence owes you her life—I am not sure how we may repay that debt.' He made an abrupt gesture of rejection and she nodded. A perceptive woman with more sensibility than her forthright appearance had led him to expect. 'What are your plans now?'

'To report to the Admiralty as soon as I reach London. The post chaise is waiting.'

'Then all I can do is thank you.' The duchess rose and held out her hand. He bowed over it and turned. 'Tell me, Captain Stanier,' she said softly as he was halfway to the door, 'do you love her?'

It halted him in mid-stride, the truth of it like a blow. Nathan stood, his back to the tall woman, staring into the glass that hung on the wall, reflecting his image and hers into the overmantel glass and back again. He saw his own face, endlessly repeated and the sudden shock of knowledge on it, and he saw, too, the pity on hers.

In front of him the door handle turned and the door opened a fraction. It was Clemence, he knew it by instinct. She had not wanted to abandon him to her aunt's questions; now she had come back to defend him.

'Do I love Clemence?' he repeated, his voice clear and cool, his intent driving the words through the wooden panels as though they were a rapier thrust. The door stopped opening. 'No,' he lied, shocked at how the word hurt. 'No, but I would have done my duty by her if that was the right thing, naturally. I confess, it is a relief not to have to take that step. I have been married once, your Grace. I have no desire to be burdened with a second wife, however sweet and young.'

The gasp was so soft he hardly heard it—perhaps he imagined it. He felt as though he had hit her. By why should he feel so badly? She did not love him, even if she felt friendship, gratitude and perhaps, still, some half-aroused desire. At worst, she had formed a *tendre* for him and that would soon vanish in the admiration and attention of a dozen young aspirants for her hand and heart. The door closed softly. *Click.* There, it was finished.

'Good day, your Grace.'

The hall was empty when he stepped out into it, although the butler appeared with the usual supernatural efficiency of his kind, Nathan's hat and gloves in hand. 'I have found accommodation for Miss Ravenhurst's maid and *man*.'

'Personal cook and bodyguard,' Nathan explained, finding some faint amusement at the expression that crossed the butler's face.

'As you say, sir. Doubtless we can outfit him suitably. The hound is in the stables.'

But not for long, I'll warrant. 'Thank you.' There was nothing for it now but to walk out of the wide front doors and get into the chaise and drive back to London and to duty and the whims of their lordships of the Admiralty and to learn to pretend that the last three months had not happened. To come to terms with the fact that his feelings for Clemence Ravenhurst were not simply liking and friendship and desire, but love. Thank God he would never have to see her again.

Clemence stood on the landing, a foot back from the balustrade, and watched Nathan's back until the doors closed, something hot and painful lodged in her chest. What had she thought, what had she dreamed? Surely not that he would change his mind at the last moment, ignore the wealth and magnificence of her cousin's home, the dignity and station of her aunt and discover that he loved her after all?

Yes, of course that was what she had dreamed. A fantasy of Nathan on his knees, clasping her hands, telling her he could not live without her and his scruples were as nothing compared to the force of his love and adoration for her.

So, now she knew. He would have done his duty and she was sweet and young. But it was a relief not to have to marry her, he had said, with the air of a man explaining why a horse was not of the right conformation to suit him.

Something was hurting her hand. She looked down to find it clenched around the slim hard package he had given her. Clemence retraced her steps to the bedchamber that had been allotted to her and sat down at the dressing table to unwrap it.

It was a fan. Not new, slightly scuffed, with plain sticks and a printed design on one side. Feeling as though she was watching someone else through a window, Clemence opened it and studied the design. Six young women clustered around a table on which stood a revolving drum and above their heads little Cupids fluttered, taking papers from the drum and giving them to the girls. The verses were in French, the print small. Clemence began to read. It was, it seemed, a lottery for a lover.

> Here is Love, putting the charms
> Of all these beauties to the test.
> The prizes, he has promised, will be
> The true qualities of men…
> A constant friend, a faithful husband,
> Are both a lottery.

It was horribly apposite. Clemence made herself continue to translate. Isis, despairing, had drawn a blank, Aglaé a man with no merit; Aglaure, though, was more fortunate, winning a man both constant and handsome. Mélise finds she has a man with three good qualities—he will be generous, handsome and sensitive. Clemence began to see the pattern: the next girl would win a man with four virtues and, indeed, Aline's lover was destined be a man with wit, beauty, good heart and fidelity.

> And finally, there remains but one.
> It is for the lovely Clémence.

That was what Nathan had meant—he had seen her name. She read on, the fragile object trembling in her hand.

> Her destiny is wonderful, but rare.
> It surpasses all her hopes.
> A stout heart, a quick mind,
> Virtue, courage and a handsome form.
> Her lover is blessed with them all.
> She has won the fivefold prize.

He had not translated it, she had to believe him. He would not be so cruel. He had bought the pretty thing for her simply because of her name upon it, never guessing the irony. Clémence's promised lover was everything Nathan was in her mind, everything she loved him for.

She closed the fan until all she was holding was the slender length of it between its polished brown guard sticks. Her hands closed on it, tightened. It would break so easily, just like her heart.

After a long while she laid it down and drew a silk handkerchief from her reticule, wrapped the fan in it with care and slid open the drawer beneath the dressing-table mirror. It fitted as though it had been made for it, just as Nathan had been made for her. Clemence slid the drawer shut, consigning it to darkness.

When both Eliza and a housemaid with the tea tray arrived she was standing by the window looking out over the sweeping lawns that ran down to a lake. Several couples were strolling in the sunlight, a boy was throwing a ball to a tall man and two nursemaids followed on behind, their arms full of squirming bundles.

She turned, eyes dry and aching, and smiled at Eliza. 'I expect those are some of my cousins down there. What a lot of people to get to know.'

'A good thing, a big family,' Eliza observed, hands folded primly in front of her crisp white apron. The minute the other maid had gone she threw up her hands, dignity forgotten. 'This place is huge, Miss Clemence! A palace! The King's House on Jamaica is nothing to this—and the *staff*. My knees are knocking, they're so grand, believe me. And they stare so.'

'They are not used to seeing many people of colour,' Clemence explained. 'They do not mean any harm by it and you will all soon become accustomed to each other. How is Street getting on?'

'That butler, Mr Andrewes, has taken him off to find him what he says are suitable clothes. And poor old One-Eye is chained up in the stables, though Fred says he'll look after him.'

'You are one of the upper servants here,' Clemence warned her. 'But I am a very junior member of the family and you will take my precedence. Do you understand? I am sure the housekeeper will explain how to go on.'

'Yes, Miss Clemence. I'll unpack your things.' She turned to the trunk, but Clemence heard her murmur, 'An upper servant! Me!'

Clemence had not realised how tensely she had been awaiting her aunt's questions until the tap on the door brought her to her feet.

'Are you rested, my dear?'

'Yes, Aunt Amelia. This is a very lovely room, thank you.'

'You must thank Jessica, your cousin Standon's wife, as she is your hostess. But that can wait until dinner time. If you can spare your maid now, perhaps we should talk.'

It was quite plainly an order, however pleasantly put. 'Yes, Aunt Amelia. Eliza, you may leave us now.' She sat down, hands folded, trying to remember her deportment lessons.

Her aunt regarded her steadily. 'Can you tell me what has happened, from the time your papa died? Is that possible without distressing you too much?'

'Yes, I can do that, ma'am.' Clemence took a deep breath and began, in as orderly and dispassionate manner as she could, to set out what had happened to her ever since the news of the loss of *Raven Duchess* had reached them and her world had fallen apart. She told the older woman everything except the intimate passages with Nathan—those she could hardly bear to think of, let alone speak about.

There was silence when she reached the end of her narrative, then the duchess gave a little sigh. 'That is a terrible story. You have been very brave, my dear. Now, are you quite certain that nothing has occurred that you have been unable to tell me of?'

Her meaning was quite clear to Clemence. She felt the colour mounting in her cheeks, but she said quite steadily, 'Did you not believe Captain Stanier?'

'Yes, I did. No, I mean was there anything that happened that you were not able to confide in him?'

'No.' Clemence was beyond feeling shy about discussing this. 'Cousin Lewis found me too scrawny to attract him unless he absolutely had to bed me and no one on the ship knew my sex.'

'Good. Then that is one less thing to worry about,' her aunt said briskly. Clemence relaxed, forgetting she was facing an experienced questioner. 'Are you in love with him?' the duchess asked casually.

'Y— No! Good heavens! No, of course not.' Was she believed? The duchess was far too skilled at hiding her feelings for her to tell.

'Excellent, although you do surprise me—he is a most attractive young man.' The duchess's mouth curved into a positively wicked smile. 'But there are other handsome men out there and ones with titles and fortunes beside. So all we need to do now is to provide you with a fitting wardrobe and to introduce you to society. You will need to tell Mr Wallingford, our solicitor, all about your inheritance and he will make sure the Naismiths are dealt with.'

'Good,' Clemence said with some feeling, wishing it were possible to send both father and son to sea with Red Matthew McTiernan for a few months. Keelhauling was too good for them.

'And now, my dear, it is time for you to change for dinner while I tell you all about your new family.'

Chapter Nineteen

Nathan stood in the waiting room outside the admiral's office in no very compliant frame of mind. His nerves felt raw since he had left Hampshire and distance did not seem to help. If anything, the more time he had to think about Clemence and the awful truth that he had fallen in love with her, the worse he felt.

He had risen through the navy, always accepting his orders without question, even when they had seemed eccentric and inexplicable. Now he found himself resentful and ready to argue. They had sent him out to Jamaica to fight pirates; he had done so—with some success, if he said so himself— and now they were hauling him back before they even knew how he had prospered.

If they had left him where he was, he would never have realised he was in love with Clemence. He could be happily hunting buccaneers at this very moment, if they had just left him be. The admiral's secretary opened the door. 'Captain Stanier?'

'Sir.' He arrived on the rug in front of the desk, saluted and stared stonily at the weather-beaten and irascible face glowering back.

'What's the matter with you, Stanier? Unhappy because we've called you back? Hah.'

'I am entirely at your lordship's disposal. Sir.'

'You most certainly are. What do you think we sent you out there for?'

'To fight pirates, my lord.'

The admiral narrowed his eyes, unable to fault the tone or the words. 'I recall at the time telling you to assess the situation and develop a strategy to fight pirates.'

'My lord.' And what the hell did they think he and Melville had been doing?

'So you've had a look. Tell me what needs doing. And stand at ease, man, you look as if you've a poker up your breeches.'

'I was about to send despatches, my lord.'

'Not good enough. I need you to convince their lordships of the need to put more resources out there because I'm damned if I can. This needs stamping out, once and for all before these freebooters and scum become useful allies for our late colonists. And I don't trust those Americans an inch—too much competition for trade in that area, however friendly they seem to be.

'We didn't deal effectively with the Barbary pirates and they are still a thorn in the flesh of every law-abiding merchantman in the Mediterranean. You've been out to the West Indies, you've seen the situation, now I want you to work on a strategy and we'll get the ships and money we need.'

Nathan felt himself relax. That at least sounded logical. 'And then I can go back out there?'

'Yes, you and Melville. I need you both to meet with Commodore Lord Hoste. You know where his office is? Well, get yourself along there and get organised.' He waved a hand in dismissal. 'And, Stanier—he'll need a vice-commodore to take control out there. Do you understand what I am saying?'

'But Melville—'

'Melville is a good fighting captain. You are that and a strategist as well.'

Feeling somewhat as though he had been hit over the head, Nathan found Lord Hoste's office. *Vice-commodore?*

Melville was already there, both men bent over charts, a secretary scribbling in the background. Hoste, an elegant man in his early forties who cultivated a deceptive manner of caring for little except the cut of his coat and the mix of his snuff, raised a languid brow at Nathan's arrival.

'How long do you need to get yourself equipped for two weeks in the country, Stanier?'

'My lord?'

'I was promised to a house party; you had better both come, too, because I'm damned if I'm going to stick in London, it's as dead as a graveyard and as stuffy as hell. We can work there as well as here. A couple of extra men are always welcome at these affairs and we'll have every excuse for shutting ourselves away when they want us to listen to some simpering ingénue thumping the piano, eh?'

'Your hostess—'

'Done, sorted, all agreed.' He waved a hand towards the secretary. 'Tompion's coming, too, with his cipher books and the charts and so forth. Can you be ready by Tuesday?'

Two days? 'Yes, my lord.'

His brother Daniel's valet could drag his stuff out of storage and beat the moths out of it, he supposed. It wouldn't take more than a day to replenish his stocks of linen and call on his bootmaker. His brother was still at the town house, pleased to see him and confiding wearily that staying put throughout the summer was the cheapest option. 'Priscilla's gone off with the children to stay with her mother at Worthing,' Lord Howarth had said with the air of a man off the leash. 'Too unfashionable to stay in town at this time of year. Don't like to argue with her, not now. She's increasing. Again.'

The downing of a number of bumpers of strong drink to celebrate the forthcoming arrival of another little Stanier would doubtless help him pass this evening, at least. Nathan pulled his attention back to the charts spread out on the wide map table and joined with Melville in deciding exactly what they needed to take with them. His mood had changed. If he really had got that coveted promotion, a challenging mission, then soon, surely, that dull internal ache would disappear and he would find his old self-sufficiency again?

'Will you tell me more about the pirates, Cousin Clemence? Please?' The eleven-year-old Grand Duke of Maubourg presented himself in front of Clemence's wicker chair, hair in his eyes, a scrape on his cheek and mud all round the bottoms of his trousers. He seemed to be enjoying his English summer holiday as much as his parents must savour their regular escapes from court life at Maubourg.

His stepfather, her cousin Lord Sebastian Ravenhurst, sprawled on a rug at the duchess's feet, having informed his mother that Freddie had exhausted him. His unsympathetic parent merely dumped his baby daughter on his admirably flat stomach and laughed.

'Don't plague Cousin Clemence,' he said now. 'She wants a rest, too.'

That was true. A morning of exploring the gardens with Lady Standon—Cousin Jessica—who was interested in which exotic species she might import for her glass houses, a close interrogation from Mr Ravenhurst—antiquarian and collector, Cousin Theo—on the use of mahogany in furniture in the West Indies, and a spirited game of bat and ball with Freddie, his stepfather and Lord Dereham—Cousin Ashe—

had left her glad to sit down and finally warm enough to shed one of the cashmere shawls she was wrapped in.

Clemence thought she was getting a grip on who was who, who was married to which cousin and what had been happening in their lives lately, but it was making her head spin.

Freddie was still looking hopeful. He had the great brown eyes of his mother, Eva, and, like the grand duchess, was skilled at looking innocent and appealing when it suited him.

'Go and talk to Street,' she suggested with a sudden flash of inspiration. 'He used to be a pirate.'

'No!' The brown eyes grew huge and Freddie turned to gaze in awe at Street, who stood on the edge of the lawn, arms folded, One-Eye sitting at his feet. Clemence was not certain what he thought he was guarding her against, but she found his stolid bulk curiously comforting and Jessica was deeply impressed with the Creole recipes he had introduced to the cook.

'But yes. Although you had better ask your mama first.' Eva might take a poor view of her only son being sent to play with a pirate.

'You could take the boat out on the lake,' Eva said serenely, fanning herself against the heat of what everyone assured Clemence was a hot September day.

'But—'

'Freddie swims very well,' his doting mama assured her. 'But no cutlasses!' she called after her son as Freddie took to his heels.

It occurred to Clemence that she should have asked her hostess first before introducing a pirate into the household. 'I should have told you all about Street sooner,' she confessed. 'I hope no one minds? Only he saved my life, and he is quite reformed.' She crossed her fingers.

'I thought Captain Stanier had done that.' Jessica sat up, pushing her wide-brimmed hat back from her face.

'He did, several times. But Street saved me from being shot in the galley when there was the battle with the navy.' She woke up every night, shuddering with terror at the memory of those moments when she had been convinced she was going to die, hearing the explosion of the shot, seeing the eyes of the man and his extended arm as he took aim.

Oddly the nightmares had only begun since Nathan had left, almost as though the knowledge of his nearness had kept them at bay. She wondered, when she braced herself to think about it, whether it was the fact that Nathan had not been there when it happened that made it so frightening in retrospect. Last night had been the worst yet. She had woken to find herself drenched with sweat, Eliza's arms around her, trying to shake her out of the nightmare.

'We have some naval guests arriving soon,' Jessica continued as they all watched Street settling to the oars with Freddie in the bows, his arms clasped round One-Eye's neck. 'Perhaps we had better forget Street's former employment while they are here.'

'Navy in the plural, my dear?' Gareth, Lord Standon, passed her a glass of lemonade. 'I thought it was just George Hoste we were expecting today. Oh, and that idiot Polkington and his sisters.'

'He might be an idiot—he is certainly the world's worst gossip—but I feel sorry for the girls.'

'You should have invited some more bachelors, in that case.' Gareth lay back in his chair. 'There is Harris coming this afternoon and the curate will be at dinner, but we've three young ladies to be entertained.'

'I certainly don't need any bachelors,' Clemence said hastily.

'Nonsense, all unmarried girls need bachelors to practise on. That was what was missing from my life and look what happened to me as a result,' Jessica observed, exchanging a smile with her husband that curled Clemence's toes in her slippers. 'Anyway,' she continued. 'Hoste is unwed, although he is a lost cause—far too indolent for marriage—but the other two may be single for all I know.'

'Surely you know who you invited, dear,' the duchess observed.

'Hoste is in the middle of some urgent navy business and asked if he could bring them,' Jessica said vaguely. 'Oh, look! The hound has jumped in after the ducks. And Freddie has fallen overboard. And there goes Street.'

Quite who was rescuing who, it was difficult to tell. The lake was not deep, but it was muddy and full of weed and the boy and the man were laughing too hard to swim properly and One-Eye was enjoying himself trying to catch ducks, and the rowing boat had overturned and by the time an elegant carriage with a crest on the door drew up the butler was forced to escort the occupants to the lakeside and a scene of chaos.

The entire house party was gathered by the water, shouting encouragement as Street waded to the bank, Freddie over one shoulder and pond weed draped like a collapsing wig about his ears. One-Eye heaved himself out, his jaws full of a struggling duck, and shook himself violently all over the onlookers.

Amidst shrieks from the ladies he gave a muffled bark and galloped off. Clemence turned with the others to see Andrewes leading three naval officers down the slope towards them. Tail wagging frantically, One-Eye bounded up to the one on the right and deposited the duck at his feet. The bird flapped off, quacking hysterically.

I am going to faint, Clemence thought as her vision darkened and her head began to spin. It couldn't be Nathan—she was hallucinating.

'Clemence?' It was Cousin Bel, Lady Dereham. She slipped a hand under her arm. 'Are you all right, my dear?'

'Yes, just a moment's dizziness. So foolish—I think I must have turned too quickly, made my head spin.' *It is Nathan. He isn't looking this way, he hasn't seen me.* Was it possible to escape? But there was nowhere to go, no ship in harbour. She saw now that the other officer was Captain Melville, and the tall man who was kissing Jessica on both cheeks must be Lord Hoste.

There was no escape, but at least she could hide away until she had regained some composure. The Ravenhursts *en masse*, even without the drama of a soaking wet child and an uncontrollable dog, were more than adequate cover.

Clemence smiled at Bel, skirted round behind Theo and his wife, Elinor, who were in animated conversation with Eden Ravenhurst and his pretty new wife, Lady Maude, and slid thankfully into the cover of the shrubbery. It was not until she reached the sanctuary of the terrace and risked a backwards glance that she saw that Nathan had turned and was looking up the slope directly at her. She jumped over the sill of the long window and ran through the dining hall as though McTiernan and Cutler were at her heels.

'I was just admiring this prospect of the house,' Nathan said to his hostess in apology for his distraction. 'Charming.' Clemence had vanished, leaving him with the haunting image of her white face. She did not want to see him, then—hardly surprising, given that she had heard his dismissive words to her aunt.

It had taken him until Guildford to emerge from the animated discussion he was having with Melville about the risks

and benefits of setting up a spying network across the islands
and to realise that the road was looking worryingly familiar.

'Where are we going, my lord? In the hurry to get ready,
it did not occur to me to ask.'

'Hmm?' Lord Hoste emerged from his perusal of the *Gentleman's Magazine*. 'Standon's place, near Romsey. Damn
good food.'

'Excellent,' Nathan had responded hollowly, earning himself a puzzled stare from Melville. Now James was looking
at him with dawning comprehension as he was introduced
to one Ravenhurst after the other.

'Where's Miss Ravenhurst?' he asked, sidling up to Nathan when attention turned to removing the pond weed from
Street and Freddie and sending them back to the house.

'Gone inside.'

'Don't blame her,' Melville remarked with feeling. 'I
should imagine the last thing she wants is to see us again,
reminding her of the whole bloody nightmare.'

There was that, of course, Nathan pondered as they walked
back to the house. Was he simply being a coxcomb, fancying that Clemence had a *tendre* for him and was upset on
that score, when more likely he was simply the unpleasant
reminder to her of terror and danger? Whichever it was, he
had no wish to cause her pain. Somehow he had to stay as far
from her for this interminable fortnight as he could.

'Is the company complete, ma'am?' he asked Lady Standon as they passed into the hall to be shown to their rooms.

'Only one party to come—and here they are,' Jessica said
cheerfully as the footman threw open the doors to admit a
small, thin man with the air of having a quizzing glass permanently poised and two plain young women.

'Polkington,' Nathan said. It needed only that—the witness to the tragic and shocking last days of his marriage on

Corfu, the man with the sharpest nose for gossip in Europe, here under the same roof as Clemence. And also, if he could just drag his mind away from his emotions and think about his career for a moment, in a position to remind his distinguished superior officer of the scandalous and illegal duel he had fought.

'You know each other?' Delighted at this serendipitous circumstance Jessica was bringing him forward as she greeted her guests. 'Mr Polkington! I do trust the journey went well? Here is Captain Stanier, whom I believe you know, just arrived also. Miss Polkington, Miss Jane...' She abandoned him for the two young women.

'Stanier.' They exchanged nods. Up came the quizzing glass. 'You are just back from the West Indies, I believe? My correspondents tell me of the most exciting occurrences taking place—pirates, scandals...'

'Your correspondents are most assiduous. I have scarcely got back myself. Pirates, I have to confess to, in plenty. But scandal?' he drawled, sounding bored. Surely, he could not have heard anything about Clemence?

'My dear man, do not alarm yourself. I have just had the most titillating letter from my second cousin in the Governor's staff, but where a lady is concerned my lips are sealed. Especially a lady with such illustrious relatives.' Polkington seemed to be hugging the delicious secret to himself. Nathan remembered his technique—nothing overt, never that, but hints and teasing and an air of mystery that could blow the slightest glance into a full-scale love affair or one angry word into a blood feud.

'You are wise,' Nathan remarked. 'I have never seen a more formidable collection of cousins. I would be most wary of giving offence to any lady in this household.'

Polkington pursed his lips and produced his high-pitched

titter. 'Oh, yes, indeed. I believe you are not the only gentleman present given to duelling, Captain Stanier.'

'If looks could kill,' James Melville commented in Nathan's ear as he watched Polkington being ushered upstairs with his sisters, 'that man would be writhing on the floor at your feet. I never thought to see him here. An unpleasant reminder of Corfu.'

'He has got wind of some scandal in Jamaica. I have just pointed out to him the likely consequence of distressing any lady under the collective protection of the Ravenhurst menfolk.'

'What? If you didn't run him through first?' His friend jerked his head towards one of the panelled doors leading off the hall. 'Standon has handed over the keys of the library to Hoste. Tompion is setting it up as an office for us. I would go and freshen up, he's expecting us down here in half an hour—the man's a glutton for work.' He grinned. 'Still, if it'll stop you getting into a fight...'

'I don't duel,' Nathan said harshly. 'Not any longer.'

'I was thinking of a clenched fist, myself,' Melville countered. 'I can't see you waiting for a Ravenhurst to happen along if Miss Clemence requires your protection.' He strode off and was through the study door before Nathan could think of an answer. *Damn it*, he thought, following the footman who was waiting patiently beside his luggage. *Am I that transparent?*

Chapter Twenty

Clemence managed to avoid Nathan for the entire evening.
The reception rooms were numerous and interconnecting,
so it was as simple matter, by keeping her wits about her, to
slip from one to the other, to take refuge behind a bank of
hot-house blooms or to dodge out of an open window on to
the terrace and in through another, the moment one sighted
a golden-brown head of hair or the blue cloth and gold braid
of dress uniform.

She had discovered from Jessica why he was there, had to
accept he had had no foreknowledge of it, nor could he have
avoided it. It felt as though she was in a nightmare, wanting
to go to him, forbidden to do so by every instinct of self-pres-
ervation. The rooms were crowded by evening guests come
for dinner so she had to concentrate on making conversation
with a string of strangers and near-strangers as well as keeping an eye out for Nathan.

She had found a secluded sofa and was catching her breath
when a thin man she had been introduced to earlier appeared
holding two glasses of wine. Pollington? No, Polkington. She
made an effort, sat up straighter and smiled.

'Miss Ravenhurst. May I join you?'

'Of course. Thank you.' There was nowhere to put a wine glass, so it seemed churlish to refuse the one he pressed into her hand.

'And how are you finding our English weather after Jamaica?' he enquired.

'A little chilly, sir. I will soon become accustomed.'

'As will the gallant Captain Stanier.'

'And Captain Melville,' she added.

'Of course. You knew them both on the island?'

'A little.' Clemence shrugged negligently and took a sip of wine. 'I came back on Captain Melville's frigate, the *Orion*.'

'So I hear.' Somehow Mr Polkington gave the impression of hearing a great deal. 'So very fortunate that that dreadful business on Corfu did not break Captain Stanier. Such a loss to the service that would have been.'

Don't ask! 'Oh? What a charming gown your sister is wearing.'

'And a tragedy, too.' Mr Polkington sighed. 'Such a pretty young woman, the late Mrs Stanier.'

Clemence took a mouthful of wine and fought temptation. 'I believe so.' She could feel her will-power slipping away. 'I know nothing about it, of course.'

'No? Well, it was a whirlwind romance, of course. Lovely young woman—half-Greek, you know.'

'I didn't,' Clemence murmured.

'Black hair, flashing eyes, figure of Aphrodite. Such a mistake for young officers to marry, I always think. I said so to my friend the Governor at the time, but there—Stanier was swept off his feet, I do believe.'

'Indeed?'

'And such a lively girl, Julietta. No harm in her—I will never believe otherwise—but lively, you know, lively.'

'A flirt?' Clemence suggested, drawn in despite herself.

'That's it in a nutshell.' Polkington smiled benevolently, while his black eyes were fixed on her like a robin that had spotted a worm.

He is trying to provoke a reaction, she thought, schooling her expression to one of polite interest. *He has heard something about us.* 'Oh, Lady Maude is waving to me, will you excuse me, Mr Polkington?'

Lady Maude was nowhere to be seen, but her's had been the first name to come into Clemence's head. She hurried across the room and out into a antechamber, glancing back to make sure Polkington had stayed where he was.

'Ough!'

'Oh, I am so sorry, I wasn't looking— Nathan!'

'Clemence.' He glanced over her shoulder back into the main room. 'Have you been talking to Polkington?'

'He has been talking to me, rather. Odious, insinuating man.'

'He has a cousin in the Governor's household, it would appear. But he is too wary of the Ravenhursts to do more than poke and pry.'

It felt so temptingly good to be close to him again. Clemence allowed herself to be drawn into the anteroom and seated on a sofa. 'A glass of wine?'

'No, thank you. And he hardly mentioned Jamaica to me.' As soon as she said it his lips tightened and she could have kicked herself for her lack of tact.

'So, he was gossiping about me instead?'

This was not how she had imagined being with Nathan again. 'Yes.'

'About Corfu?'

'Yes.'

'Then I had better tell you the truth.'

'It is none of my business,' Clemence interjected.

'No?' Just what did he mean by that cool monosyllable? 'I will tell you anyway. I prefer my friends to know the facts, not to listen to Polkington's gossip. What has he said?'

'That your wife's name was Julietta, that she was half-Greek and very lovely and, er...lively.'

'That is all true, at least.' Nathan leaned back, his long legs crossed, his arm casually along the back of the sofa as they sat turned to face each other. To an onlooker he must seem entirely relaxed, but Clemence knew him too well to be deceived. There was a tautness about his jaw and the smile on his lips did not reach his eyes.

'I thought I was in love with her—so did half the gentlemen on the island. Her father was a prosperous local merchant married to an Englishwoman of some style and education. I proposed one heady, moonlit evening and she accepted me. Her father—no fool—encouraged a rapid wedding and there we were, two virtual strangers learning to live together.'

'And she was not as you had thought?' Clemence asked carefully. She had thought that hearing about his lost love would hurt her, but instead all she felt was sorrow for the newlyweds, so evidently heading for disaster.

'Neither of us was what the other had expected. She thought she was getting a doting, fun-loving and indulgent husband. I thought I was gaining domestic bliss and set about reforming myself—doubtless into a stolid prig. She carried on flirting, perfectly harmlessly, I can see now. I became the heavy husband, forbidding her to enjoy herself, in effect. One night she slipped away to a party I had said we were not going to attend. When I arrived, fuming, she was on the balcony with my friend Lieutenant Fellowes.'

'Oh, Lord.' Clemence realised she had extended a hand to his and drew it back sharply. 'What were they doing?'

'Nothing so very bad. He had plucked a flower and was

fixing it at the bosom of her dress which, Julietta being Julietta, was held up more by will-power than by anything else. I hit Adrian, he accused me of slandering my own wife—and the next thing we knew we were facing each other at dawn in a field with a pair of pistols.' Nathan's eyes were unfocused as though he were looking back down the years.

'You didn't kill him, though? You told me you hadn't?'

'I had told you I had duelled? I had forgotten that. I obviously told young Clem altogether too much.' He smiled at her, back from the past, and something warm and vulnerable uncurled inside her and dared to hope for a second. 'I just caught him on the shoulder, a flesh wound—which you may choose to believe, or not, is what I intended. He missed me. And then we looked at each other and realised what a pair of bloody fools we both were and shook hands and went and had breakfast by way of the doctor's house.'

'Thank goodness,' Clemence murmured. 'But wasn't duelling forbidden?'

'Of course. But Adrian insisted to anyone who would listen that it had all been an accident while we were having a shooting competition to try out his new pistols. The authorities might have taken a harder line—no one really believed a word of it—but by then Julietta was dead.'

He made to get to his feet as if suddenly he could not manage to tell this story any longer. Clemence reached out again and this time curled her fingers into his hand. 'No, Nathan, please tell me the rest.' He sat back again.

'She knew about the duel, of course. Whether she thought I would be killed or whether she feared my anger if I survived, I have no idea. I was not very understanding when I left her that morning. But she rode, by herself, to her father's estate in the countryside and on the way there was an accident of some kind. They found her in the road, the horse by her side. Her neck was broken.'

'Oh, no,' Clemence breathed. 'You loved her and you had not even had the chance to say goodbye to her. And to face that in the midst of the scandal after the duel.' She bit down on her lip to steady the quiver in her voice. 'It must have been hell.'

Her hand was still in his. He sat looking down at it for a while in silence, playing with the seams of her glove. 'No, I didn't love her, I realised that too late. That was almost the worst thing of all, the knowledge that if I had had more sense, more self-control, I would never have got us into that situation. I should have waited, seen it was just infatuation, and she would have been safe.'

'How old were you?' she asked abruptly, startling him into looking up at her.

'Twenty-three. She was nineteen.'

'And you blame yourself, with the wisdom of your current age and experience, for the folly of a young man? I am nineteen, like she was—no, I quite forgot it, but I have had a birthday, I am twenty.' Fancy forgetting a birthday! But she had other things on her mind at the time... 'Women mature more quickly than men in matters of the emotions. She should have known she was not in love with you, too.'

'You think you can tell?' His blue eyes were hard and bitter.

'Oh, yes,' Clemence said, releasing his hand and getting to her feet in a swirl of skirts. 'I know perfectly well when I am in love with a man.' Where the courage to utter the words had come from, she had no idea. They stared at each other as he got slowly to his feet. 'It was a tragedy. I am so sorry it seems to have convinced you that it would be folly to risk your heart again.'

'There you are, Miss Ravenhurst. I am to take you in to dinner.' Captain Melville looked from one face to the other. 'Have I interrupted something?'

'Merely Miss Ravenhurst chiding me for taking lessons from past history,' Nathan said. He seemed rather white, but perhaps it was simply her own perceptions that were awry. She was certainly feeling somewhat light-headed.

'Learning from history? Why, that is an excellent precept, I would have thought, Miss Ravenhurst.'

'It is,' Clemence agreed, laying her hand on his proffered forearm. 'Provided one is certain that the circumstances are exactly the same in both cases.'

How she was going to eat anything with her heart apparently lodged in her throat, she had no idea, she thought, smiling at the gentleman on her left-hand side as Captain Melville seated her. What had come over her? She had as good as told Nathan that she loved him. It must have been the selfish relief of discovering that he did not love his wife, and never had.

Her neighbour was addressing her. Clemence struggled to recall his name. Mr… Wallingford, that was it. The lawyer that Cousin Sebastian had summoned from London to help deal with the Naismiths. They were to have a meeting tomorrow, Sebastian had informed her.

'Yes, I am finding it rather cool in England,' she agreed. It was the standard first question from everyone she met. She could easily manage such a predictable exchange with her mind on something else, and now it was working furiously on the conundrum of Nathan.

He felt something for her, she was certain, although he was most certainly hiding it well. And that was doubtless because of her relatives and her money. There was nothing she could do about disowning the connection with the Raven-hursts, Clemence thought, nor would she want to. She looked up and down the long table and felt the glow of knowing that these people were her blood kin and had accepted her with warmth and uncritical affection.

But she could do something about her money. She slid a sidelong glance at the lawyer—he looked like a man of intelligence and cunning. Just what she needed if she was going to take a huge risk with her future.

What the hell was that about? Nathan tried to watch Clemence while maintaining a flow of polite chit-chat with the lady on his right whose name he had already completely forgotten.

Was he going mad, or had Clemence just as good as told him she was in love with him? What else could she have meant? He spooned soup, laughed at some feeble *on-dit* and took too deep a swallow of wine while he wrestled with the mystery of Clemence's feelings.

He had been so sure that all she had felt for him was a mild *tendre*, the natural result of having been forced to rely on him for her life and of having been propelled into quite shocking intimacy with him. That they were physically attracted, there could be no doubt, but physical attraction, as he knew only too well, was not the same as love.

She was too young to know her own mind, to understand her emotions; he had believed that—and she had just thrown the notion back in his face. Could it simply be pique because he had refused to marry her and had told her aunt he was not in love with her? No. Not Clemence. She didn't sulk, she wasn't petty and she would not play games like that with him.

The footmen came forward to clear the soup bowls. Nathan sat back in his chair, looked down the table again and caught her gaze, clear and green and open. He swallowed, hard, against the lump in his throat and realised, shocked, that his eyes were moist. She loved him. *She loved him.*

And then he saw Lord Sebastian Ravenhurst, his hooded eyes resting on his cousin's face, and the lump turned to lead. She could love him until the stars fell, but that did not make him any more suitable a husband for the wealthy Miss Ravenhurst, with the whole of society spread out at the toes of her pretty new slippers for her to explore. They might love, and she might deem the world well lost for it, but it was his duty to do the right thing.

'Mr Theo Ravenhurst thinks we might dance after dinner,' the plain brunette on his left remarked. 'Do you dance, Captain Stanier?'

'With reluctance, Miss Polkington.' She pouted. 'Not from lack of admiration of my partners,' he added hastily. 'More to spare them from having their toes crushed.' She giggled and began to chatter about past balls and parties. Nathan ate his duck and contemplated an evening torturing himself by watching Clemence dance.

He could imagine her feet in those bronze kid slippers twinkling beneath the modish quilted hem of her skirt. Perhaps there would be a flash of silk-stockinged ankle. Her shoulders would gleam even more in the candlelight as her skin warmed with the exertion and her small breasts would rise and fall with her breathing.

And he would be in severe need of a cold plunge in the lake in a minute if he didn't control his imagination. Nathan spread his napkin strategically across his lap and attempted to recall the unerotic image of Clem's grubby bare feet protruding from the bottom of flapping canvas trousers. It did not help.

But at least inconvenient arousal, however uncomfortable, did not threaten the pain of unrequited love. He had known he had to accept it for himself, but to believe that might Clemence feel the same way was agony.

By the end of the meal Nathan was convinced he would rather be boarding a heavily defended pirate ship than facing an evening of dancing.

'Do you think Hoste is going to want to work on?' he asked Melville.

'You sound as if you wish he will!' His friend nodded towards the group of guests clustered around Lady Standon. There was his senior officer, joining in with the persuasion to have the long drawing-room carpet rolled up. 'I'm looking forward to an impromptu hop.'

'I'm going to have a strategic sprain,' Nathan said dourly, making his way to the side of the room and favouring his right foot.

'You have hurt your ankle, Captain?' It was the curate, bright-eyed with sympathy, his hands full of sheet music.

'An old weakness.'

'Could you turn the music for me if you are not to dance?' Taking silence for consent, the other man led the way to the piano. 'I do not dance myself, you understand, but rational exercise in a respectable setting such as this is most acceptable, I feel.'

He prosed on, leaving Nathan stranded by the side of the piano, attempting to ignore Melville's unsympathetic grin. Lady Standon came over.

'Mr Danvers, so good of you to play. I am going to teach the company a new round dance and what we need is a nice strong rhythm—ah, yes, this will do nicely. Strongly marked, mind! But I will walk them through it without music first.'

Lady Standon clapped her hands. 'Please, take a partner

and form a big circle, facing in. I am going to teach you *La Pistole*, it is new from France.'

Nathan watched, half an ear on the instructions, while the couples turned to face each other, walked back and then together, linked hands and circled... Clemence was smiling up at Eden Ravenhurst, her theatre-manager cousin, one of the less reputable Ravenhursts. How lovely she looked with him, his height balancing hers, her unconventional looks, piquant in contrast to his conventional handsomeness.

They were all making some gesture with their hands that made her frown, fleetingly, then circling again and beginning again with the partner behind them.

'Ingenious,' Mr Danvers remarked. 'Very simple and they are constantly changing partners. Most amusing.' At Lady Standon's gesture he struck up the music and the couples began their measure.

Clemence had still not regained her smile. Back and forth, join hands and circle, back again. What was there to frown about? Then everyone raised their right hands like children playing at shooting, aimed at their partners and stamped their feet hard. *Bang!* Around the circle, dancers were laughing, clutching their hands to their breasts and circling to face their new partner to start again.

She was no longer in profile, now he could see her full face and she had gone pale. Lord Hoste raised his hand, aimed—*bang!* Clemence broke out of the circle and ran.

Nathan took a dozen long strides to where the commodore was turning to follow her. No one else seemed to see anything amiss. 'Leave her to me, sir,' he snapped and was past and out of the room before the older man could respond.

Clemence had not gone far, only through the small salon and out on to the terrace where she was standing quite still, her back to him. She had her arms crossed tightly and was clasping her elbows as though to hold herself together. Her shoulders were quivering. She did not move as the heels of his shoes struck on the stone flags.

'Sweetheart?' He pulled her against his chest, and she came as rigid as a board, her arms still tightly locked. 'What is it? I'm here.'

'You weren't,' she said, her voice choked. 'You weren't there.'

'You wanted me to dance with you?' This seemed a violent reaction for such a cause and not at all like her.

'No! You weren't there when he was going to shoot me. I was going to die and then Street shot him in the face and he died instead and I saw—' Her voice choked off into silence.

Appalled, Nathan gathered her tightly into his embrace and held on. She didn't seem to be weeping. After a moment he ventured, 'When?'

'Just before the mast came down.' She gave a little shudder and he felt her shoulders relax. 'I dream about it, you see,' Clemence said into his shirt front. 'Not before, but ever since you left me here. I don't dream about anything else, just that. I think it's because you were there for everything else.'

Nathan rubbed his cheek against the soft curls on her crown. *He hadn't been there.* And now Clemence, his brave Clemence, who had fought McTiernan, climbed from her balcony to freedom, defied her scheming, evil family, was reduced to running away from a romping dance with friends in the safety of the English countryside.

'I'm so sorry,' he murmured. 'So sorry.'

'No.' She shook her head, the curls moving back and forth on the starched folds of his neckcloth. 'You gave me Street. He shot the man and then you came for me. It is my fault I am so foolish.'

'Oh, no, not foolish, sweetheart.' He rocked her against the warmth of her body. 'Just tried beyond your strength.'

She had needed him. His absence gave her nightmares. She had looked him in the eye and told him, with some emphasis, that she knew when she was in love with a man. But she had never been in love or formed an attachment, she had told him that, too. His head was spinning.

'Clemence.' He tipped up her face. She had stopped shuddering and her eyes were dry. 'Clemence…' He wanted to say it—the temptation to say those three words and see the reflection of her feelings in her eyes was almost overwhelming. 'Clemence.' Somehow he managed to clench his teeth and be silent. It was harder than it had been to walk with composure to be flogged, to stand here, silent, when the woman he loved was in his arms, waiting.

And then she smiled faintly and lifted her hand to his cheek, running the back of it down and along his jaw. 'It's all right,' she murmured. 'It will be all right.'

How could it be? He frowned down at her, not at all comforted by the sadness in her candid eyes or the calm resignation in her voice.

'Ahem.' They both turned. Lord Hoste was standing, a cloak over his arm, regarding them somewhat quizzically from the window. 'You aunt feared you may be finding the night air chill, Miss Ravenhurst.' He held out the cloak and she went out of Nathan's arms towards him.

'Thank you, my lord.' Clemence allowed him to drape it around her shoulders and then, without a backward glance, stepped over the low sill and was gone.

'Snuff?' Lord Hoste produced an enamel box and flicked it open with his thumbnail. 'I think this might be an opportune time for a quiet talk, Stanier.'

Chapter Twenty-One

'That young man is in love with you,' the duchess remarked, taking a sip of chocolate.

They were seated in the first-floor bow-window embrasure of the duchess's apartment, having breakfast tête à tête and somewhat later than the rest of the guests. Clemence was heavy-eyed after a troubled night's sleep. The nightmare had not come, but her dreams had seemed full of Nathan. 'He is?' she managed, wincing at the inadequacy of the response.

Her aunt regarded her severely over the rim of the cup. 'Do not be coy with me, Clemence.'

'I *think* he is. But he doesn't think he is good enough for me.'

'You could do better,' the duchess remarked dispassionately. In a shaft of morning sunlight the three naval officers, Tompion the secretary on their heels, paced back and forth along the Rose Garden terrace, hands behind backs, as though on the poop deck.

'Only in worldly ways,' Clemence retorted, then subsided at her aunt's smile.

'Indeed. Don't you want a title?' Clemence shook her head. 'Or a great deal of money?'

'I have quite a lot of money, that's the problem—or a big part of it. He doesn't wish to figure as a fortune hunter. I had an idea about that.' The duchess's eyebrows rose. 'I don't intend giving it away, or gambling it or anything foolish. I am going to speak to Mr Wallingford the lawyer this morning, with Cousin Sebastian. They will advise me.' The energy that speaking about her idea had produced ebbed away again. She shrugged. 'At least I can guard against fortune hunters in the future.' Her eyes followed the three men who had come to an abrupt halt. Captain Melville was shaking Nathan by the hand. 'I wonder what that is about.'

'Doubtless Captain Stanier has had a brilliant idea for dealing with the pirates. He will be back at sea soon, no doubt.'

'No doubt,' Clemence agreed, biting her lip. 'Aunt Amelia. You very kindly invited me for the Season, and I expect it is going to take some months to work matters out and deal with my uncle. But in the spring, I would like to go back to Jamaica.'

'Alone?' The duchess's fine brows rose.

'I will find a companion. I am going to run the business.' She wiped her fingers on her napkin, surprised at how comforting that declaration felt, now she had made it. 'I am enjoying England and London will be a great treat,' she added, politely. 'But Jamaica is my home.' If she had to nurse a broken heart, home was a far better place to do it than a chilly foreign land.

'I see. You believe that despite your scheme for removing your wealth as an obstacle, you will not secure an offer from your gallant captain?'

'No, not now. There was a moment last night—if he had been going to speak, then surely it would have been then. It seemed I tempted fate to believe that somehow it would all come right.' Clemence shrugged again, struggling against gloom again. 'I only really believe it at three in the morning.'

'Compromising yourself will not help,' the duchess mused, earning a startled glance from Clemence. 'There is nothing worse you can do that has not already happened.' Clemence felt herself go scarlet and opened her mouth in protest. 'Well, you know what I mean! Proposing to the man will only have him reiterating all those noble sentiments. You will just have to shock him. I don't suppose Street could turn pirate again and kidnap you for ransom?'

'He wouldn't dare.' Clemence smiled at the thought. 'Eliza would give him the rough edge of her tongue. Oh, look, there they go now, walking the dog.'

'That is one expression for it,' her aunt remarked tartly as the three figures vanished into the deep shade of the shrubbery.

'They will get married soon,' Clemence assured her, making a mental note to speak to Street, very firmly, on the subject.

'So I should hope. Now then, do you intend telling me what sent you flying from the drawing room last night?'

'I do not know whether you would wish to hear, Aunt Amelia. It is something that happened on board the pirate ship. Something very…unpleasant.'

'I have nerves of steel,' the duchess said, pouring herself another cup of chocolate. 'Come along.'

'Very well.' Perhaps talking about it would help chase the nightmare away. 'I told you that Nathan had managed to send the *Sea Scorpion* after the decoy ship and when they came alongside there was a battle with men boarding and hand-to-hand fighting? Nathan had sent me below to free the merchant sailors locked in the hold and when I came up again he was fighting. I found myself with Street. A sailor came in with a pistol, he raised it and aimed it at my head.'

'Oh, my goodness, the dance!'

'Yes. It went off and for a moment I thought I was dead, but he missed me and Street shot him. In the face.'

'Right in front of you,' the duchess said faintly. 'I can imagine what that must have been like, coming on top of fearing that you were about to die yourself. But that fat rascal saved your life.'

'Yes, ma'am. Then, when Nathan left me here, I started to dream about it. Horrible nightmares. Poor Eliza tries to wake me, but she finds it hard.'

'You know, deep in your mind, that you are safe when he is near? Yes, I can see the logic in that, although it never occurred to me that nightmares might have a basis in logic.' She tossed her napkin on to the table, her face sombre. 'Leave speaking to Street about your maid to me. It is not something that an unmarried girl should have to deal with.'

A footman came in. 'Lord Sebastian's compliments, Miss Ravenhurst, and he and Mr Wallingford will await your convenience in the library at ten.'

'Thank you.' Clemence stood up and squared her shoulders. Time to think about those hideous months after her father had died. Time to set the wheels of justice in motion. That at least she could achieve.

Two hours later Sebastian was looking grimly satisfied and Clemence felt drained. Mr Wallingford, who must, she thought wearily, be the human equivalent of a terrier crossed with a mole, tapped his piles of notes into a neat stack and beamed. He had burrowed after every detail and, having found it, dragged it out for inspection and shook it vigorously to see if anything else fell out. He appeared to find the process extremely stimulating.

'Oh, very nice. We have him, we have him. He won't be able to wiggle out of this.'

'But he says he can forge my signature,' Clemence fretted.

'Nothing a smart young lawyer can't deal with—and I have just the man in my offices. He'll have the help of the naval representative out there, I understand—and the Governor will be receiving a communication from the highest level, informing him that he is to throw Naismith to the wolves. In the form—' he smirked '—of my Mr Gorridge.'

'He'll most certainly have that,' Sebastian confirmed. He got up and poured three glasses of madeira, surprising Clemence by handing her one. 'You need it. Now. This scheme of yours about your money—are you certain? You cannot undo it.'

'I know.' Clemence sipped her wine. 'I expect to go back to Jamaica as soon as this is settled and to run the business. I do not wish to attract fortune hunters. This idea is for my own protection as much as anything.'

'You do not expect to marry here in England?' Sebastian asked, his dark gaze resting thoughtfully on her face. 'I thought perhaps that this was to facilitate—'

'No. I do not expect it.' There had been the faint recollection of her dream, like a wisp of smoke when she awoke. A dream of the pool in the forest, of her being in Nathan's arms and gold rings glinting through the water. The ghost of the dream had lingered all morning. Now it faded and left her. There was nothing like the down-to-earth realism of a lawyer to snuff out foolish fantasy and as they had talked she had let go of it as though she had felt Nathan's hand slip from hers.

Nathan had had every opportunity to tell her he loved her last night on the terrace, she told herself, and he had not. Now she felt certain that he never would. She hated his honour for keeping them apart. She admired him for possessing it. With it, they could never be together—without it, he would not be the man she loved.

Clemence saw virtually nothing of Nathan all day. Either the weather was warmer than it had been, or she was becoming used to the English climate, Clemence thought, as Jessica made the unusual suggestion of an alfresco dinner.

Rugs were spread on the grass below the terrace, tables and chairs brought out and dotted about and Cook and her minions began to set long tables as a buffet.

Lady Maude appointed herself chief floral arranger and bore Clemence off, armed with baskets and small shears to raid the long borders. 'Are you going to marry Captain Stanier?' she enquired, handing Clemence some foliage sprays.

'I— No.' Clemence was taken aback by the frontal attack. 'Why would you imagine I should?'

Maude chuckled. 'I am not very long married. I see the way he looks at you and the way you look at him and the way you both carefully don't look at the same time.'

'Oh.' Clemence looked warily at Maude as she sat down in an arbour and patted the seat next to her.

'And?'

'I love him. I think he may—does—love me. But...'

'You're a Ravenhurst. Probably a rich one. He is *just* a career naval officer.' Maude threw up her hands. 'Men and their honour! Eden is illegitimate. Did you know that?'

'I gathered,' Clemence said carefully.

'As much pride as a porcupine has prickles, that man. I had to take drastic action in the end and tell him if he couldn't see the difference between pride and honour then I didn't want to marry him anyway.'

'Goodness.'

'I threw him out of my bedroom—' She saw Clemence's dropped jaw and grinned. 'I was ill in bed, he was pacing the corridor outside,' she explained.

'Well, I thought I had an idea to deal with the money, but I still can't see how I am going to attack that conviction he has that I am destined for better things just because I am a Ravenhurst. I hoped, just for a few moments, last night. But he did not speak.'

'Hmm. Well, I have to say, that your Captain Stanier may not be a Ravenhurst, but he is certainly worth fighting for.'

'If I can only find weapons it is fair to fight with,' Clemence murmured, half to herself.

'You will, and the Ravenhursts will help, you'll see. Now, let's get these flowers back.'

Clemence surprised herself by enjoying the meal. Her cousin Elinor, a redoubtable bluestocking, kept her laughing with tall tales of the adventures that had marked her courtship with Theo Ravenhurst. 'You should write sensation novels for the Minerva Press,' Clemence said after a lurid description of being chained up in a rat-infested dungeon with Theo and a jug of poison for company.

'Every word of it is true.' Theo came back with a platter of fruit and lowered himself onto the rug between the two women. 'Word of a Ravenhurst. I had a dull and blameless life until I fell in with this woman.'

'Liar.' It was Sebastian, Nathan at his side. Clemence felt her colour rising and made rather a business of making room on the rug. 'Theo, you should know, Cousin Clemence, is the scapegrace of the family. We are deeply grateful to Elinor for his reform.'

'I may have reformed him,' Elinor said with a twinkle, 'but

he has absolutely corrupted me as far as spending money on clothes is concerned. I used to be completely unconcerned about gowns,' she explained to Clemence. 'If a sack had been decent covering, I would have been satisfied with that. But now! I am so looking forward to shopping with you in town.'

'You may be disappointed,' Sebastian observed, peeling an apple. 'Clemence is intending to return to Jamaica after the Season.'

'What?' Nathan, who had been lounging almost out of her sight behind Sebastian, sat up with a jerk. 'Going back to Jamaica?'

'Yes. I intend to run the business.' For some reason her lips felt stiff.

'Oh, well done!' Elinor clapped her hands. 'How enterprising of you. But what if you become betrothed during the Season?'

'I have no expectation of doing so,' Clemence made herself say. 'Nor any desire, either.'

'I used to think that,' Elinor said comfortably. 'I was quite resigned to my studies and being a support to Mama with hers. And then along came Theo—and here we are.' She smiled, no doubt intending to be encouraging. 'You wait and see. I am sure there is someone just right for you.'

'Possibly Miss Ravenhurst believes she has already met that person and they are unsuitable,' Nathan suggested. He passed the plate with the apple Sebastian had peeled and sliced to the ladies, his hand quite steady.

'How perceptive of you, Captain Stanier,' Clemence said, taking a piece of fruit and biting into it. 'I have and, although I think him perfectly suitable, the gentleman in question has scruples that it appears he is unwilling to overcome.'

'Then he does not love you enough, I fear,' said Theo sympathetically.

'It may be that, of course,' Clemence agreed, selecting another slice. 'I tell myself I would be better off forgetting him, but I have no idea how one goes about that.'

'Painfully,' Nathan said, getting to his feet and walking away.

'Oh!' Elinor put down her glass and stared after him. 'It's him? I am so sorry, I had no idea. I am quite ready to sink, of all the tactless…'

'That's both of us,' Theo said, scrubbing his hand back through his hair. 'Sorry.'

'It's all right,' Clemence said with a sigh. 'Actually, it is quite a relief to talk about it.'

'Er—Sebastian and I will go,' Theo said, beginning to rise.

'No, please, if it doesn't embarrass you. I would rather like a masculine point of view.' Theo subsided. 'Nathan was going to marry me, because I had been compromised. That was before he realised he loved me, I think. But when he found out who I was, and realised that the family was more than sufficient to protect me from scandal, he withdrew.'

'Why?' Elinor wrapped her arms round her bent knees, propped her chin on top and regarded Clemence earnestly, as though she was one of her Greek inscriptions.

'The scandal in Minorca when his wife died and he fought a duel,' Clemence explained. 'Then, my money—he has only what he earns as a captain.'

'How much is that?' Theo asked. He rolled over on to his stomach and propped his chin in his hands.

'About £450 a year,' Clemence said. Theo winced. 'I asked Captain Melville. Then there's prize money—which could be about the same, could be thousands—but that is complete chance. And, on top of the duel and the money, he thinks I should be looking for an earl or something and marrying *properly*, as befits a Ravenhurst. He thinks that the world is my oyster and that if he married me, it would be wrong.'

'Idiot.' Elinor.

'Very proper sentiments.' Sebastian.

'Both those,' Theo observed. 'The family is all right though, isn't it, Seb?'

'Oh, yes.' Her cousin nodded. 'I have had Captain Stanier investigated from his bank account to the contents of his handkerchief drawer.'

'You've what?' Clemence glared.

'You're a Ravenhurst.' Theo grinned. 'No one breathes on you without Sebastian knowing.'

'Pity I didn't think to extend that to Jamaica when your father died,' Sebastian remarked. 'You were compromised, no getting around that. Do you want me to become the head of the family in Charles's absence and demand that he does the decent thing?'

The thought of Sebastian, or his half-brother the duke, demanding that Nathan marry her, made her blood run cold. 'No! Please, don't do that. Nathan *is* doing the decent thing, according to his conscience.'

'I am baffled,' Elinor admitted. 'I don't suppose Eva could create him Admiral of the Maubourg fleet, could she?'

'Maubourg, you idiot,' her loving husband reminded her, 'has no coast, no navy and a lake with rowing boats.'

'Drat.'

'Who is an idiot?' It was Eva, languidly graceful as ever. She sank down on to the rug and smiled at her family. 'Theo?' Her cousin grinned, balled up a napkin and threw it at her.

Clemence couldn't help smiling. They were all so happy, all so convinced that love would find a way because, for them, it had. She unfurled the old French fan Nathan had given her and looked at the fat little Cupids flying around delivering their prizes of love to the waiting girls. Far from being Clémence with her paragon of a lover, it seemed she was Isis, the one whose lot was to have no lover at all. *Adieu toute espérance*, she read. Farewell all hope.

'Miss Clemence?' Eliza folded her silk shawl away in tissue and turned, biting her lower lip.

'Yes?' It wasn't like Eliza to be so hesitant.

'We were wondering—Fred and me—if we could have a talk with you.'

'Now? At this hour?' The house party had lingered long into the evening on the lawn, the servants lighting citronella candles to keep the insects at bay, and now she was tired.

'Her Grace had a word.' Eliza shifted her feet. 'Its made him a bit edgy, if you see what I mean.'

'Not really, but I suppose I can talk to him now. Is he waiting in the sitting room?'

The single ladies had a room close to their chambers. Sighing for the peace and solitude of her bed, Clemence followed the maid along the corridor. Street was standing in the middle of the boudoir, eyeing the spindly chairs nervously. One-Eye, who knew perfectly well he was not allowed upstairs, was attempting to hide behind a footstool.

'Bad dog,' Clemence said automatically and he wriggled over on his belly, tongue lolling. 'Well, Street?'

'Her Grace said I ought to be making an honest woman of Eliza and I suppose I ought,' he admitted, shuffling his feet.

'What does Eliza think about it?'

'I'll take him,' the maid said grudgingly. Clemence looked from one to the other. The expressions on their faces said it all—the reluctant words meant nothing.

'That's all very well,' she said briskly, sitting down. 'But how are you going to support her?'

'I mean to open an inn,' the big man said. 'A proper country one on a post road with food they'll remember and good ale.'

'That sounds a good plan,' Clemence agreed. But Street was off in a world of his own. 'I'm sure you and Eliza will be very happy.'

'I used to dream about that, you know,' he confided. 'I'd stand there in my galley, stirring the pots and I'd think, *What you wants, Fred Street, is a cosy inn with a big fire in the winter.* Seems a miracle that you were in that very same galley, Miss Clemence. And I thought you was just a scruffy lad! Do you remember that galley?'

'Yes, of course—'

'Wasn't much, but it was mine. In good order, I kept it, didn't I?'

'Yes, well, I'll—'

'All gone now, down to Davy Jones's locker.' He sighed gustily. 'I'll never forget it, that last day. I'll wager you won't, either, Miss Clemence.'

'No, and—'

'I told Eliza, I did, how you almost got killed. He was a mean-looking devil, that sailor with the pistol. I thought you was a goner, Miss Clemence, I did really. He was pointing that thing at you, and I couldn't get to my gun in time.'

Under her hand, One-Eye gave a startled *yip* and Clemence forced her fingers open.

'Miracle he missed you, miracle. And then I shot him. Nasty mess that, extraordinary what a bullet in the head—'

'Fred! That's enough.'

Clemence blinked; Eliza was shaking her elbow. 'Are you all right, Miss Clemence? Fred shouldn't have talked about that, how you almost got killed. It'll bring it all back, that will.'

'We will discuss this in the morning. But I wish you both

to be very happy.' Swallowing, Clemence made her way back to her room. The floor seemed to be pitching like the deck of the ship under her feet. Behind her she heard Eliza berating One-Eye.

'Leave him, he can stay with me.' The thought of company felt good. She did not want to ask Eliza to sleep in her room; she strongly suspected she wanted to creep off and join Street in whichever attic fastness he had been allocated. Now all she had to do was to manage to forget the images Street had conjured up, not think about Nathan at all and she might have a good night's sleep. Pigs, Clemence concluded with resignation, might fly.

Chapter Twenty-Two

The urgent knocking on his door had Nathan out of bed and reaching for his sword before he opened his eyes. Then he realised where he was, dragged on the silk dressing gown that was thrown over the foot of the bed and opened the door.

'Street? What the hell are you doing here? What's the time?'

'Two, Cap'n.' The big man, incongruous in flowing night-shirt and bare feet, stood clutching a chamber stick. 'Eliza said to get you, it's Miss Clemence, sir.'

'Tell me,' Nathan snapped, his stomach sinking in a sudden swoop of fear.

'It's a nightmare, Eliza says. She can usually wake her up, but this time she can't and she's frightened.'

Nathan began to stride down the corridor. 'Send Eliza to wake the duchess.'

'She says it is you she needs, Cap'n. Miss Clemence is calling for you something pitiful.'

The room, when he reached it, was lit by four branches of candles. Eliza was leaning over the bed, shaking Clemence, who was tossing and turning, her face flushed and feverish, her hair damp. The bedclothes had been thrown back by her thrashing limbs and her nightgown was twisted around her knees. The old hound was standing on the other side, whining anxiously.

'Nathan? Please, where's Nathan?' Clemence was muttering, her voice hoarse.

'Oh, thank God, sir. She can't call out any more, her poor throat.' Eliza straightened up and as she released her hold on Clemence's shoulders, she began to toss and turn.

'Clemence?' Eliza stepped aside and he took her place. 'Clemence? Hush, I'm here now.' She seized his hand, her eyes still tight shut. Behind him the door clicked. Nathan glanced back—Street and Eliza had gone. Puzzled, but too worried about Clemence to pursue it, he got on to the bed, gathered her into his arms and began to rock her gently, talking all the time.

'I'm here, it's Nathan, you're in England, in bed. One-Eye's here, too, you're safe, no one will hurt you. I'm holding you. My love, I've got you safe.' The painful pleasure of saying it—*my love*—hit him in the gut and he tightened his hold. 'Clemence, my love, wake up, sweetheart, wake up.'

Nothing mattered now, not his honour, not his scruples, nothing, so long as she woke and felt safe. He slid down the bed, pulling her against the length of him, drowning in the scent and feel of her. 'Shh, Clemence. I'm here, I love you, you're safe.'

I love you. Nathan's voice penetrated the smoke and the screams and the noise and suddenly they had vanished and the light against her screwed-up eyelids was different and she was being held tightly against what felt and smelled wonderfully like Nathan's body.

'Nathan?'

'Open your eyes.'

Obedient, she did so and found she was in bed and that Nathan's head was on the pillow beside her, turned so he could look into her eyes.

'There, you are safe back. It was a nightmare, Clemence. Not real.' He was stroking her hair, smiling at her.

'Have I been ill?' She felt weak, as though in the aftermath of a fever. 'My throat hurts.'

'It was a very bad dream. Eliza could not wake you. You had shouted until your voice cracked and thrashed around until you were almost exhausted. Here, can you sit up?'

He helped her until she could sit up next to him, their backs propped against pillows, then held out a glass. 'This smells like barley water, it was on the nightstand. Try to drink.'

She sipped and her spinning head settled and the nightmare evaporated and all that was left was the man next to her on the big bed, smiling at her, his eyes anxious.

'When I woke up, you were saying—'

'I was saying I loved you. I thought I should not tell you, but I find I am too selfish not to let you know how I feel, even if it changes nothing. I should not be here, not now you are awake. I'll ask Eliza to call the duchess.' He began to turn, to get up.

'No!' She fastened her fingers on his wrist. 'Things have changed, everything has changed.'

'Not really.' But he lay back against the pillows, his shoulder carefully not touching hers.

'We know how we feel about each other,' she said. 'Shh! Let me finish. I know you are not in love with Julietta, perhaps never were. You know I am going back to Jamaica and have no intention of settling in England, finding a husband here.'

'It seems I misjudged you. You know your own mind after all if you really mean that,' he said, his fingers toying with the fringed sash of his dressing gown. 'Then you will go back to Jamaica to your inheritance, a wealthy woman.'

'I will go back to an income of one thousand pounds a year, for life,' Clemence said concisely. Her head was clear now. She had one chance—by a miracle that dreadful nightmare had given her this opportunity.

'One thousand? Surely your uncle cannot have squandered your inheritance? The lawyers will get it back for you.'

'They will get it back and they will invest it in the trust fund Mr Wallingford has set up for me. There will be money to invest in the business, maintain the properties, make sure all the staff are kept on. I will have my allowance.'

'And the rest?' Nathan's blue eyes were dark under frowning brows.

'In trust for my children, should I have any, and some lucky young Ravenhurst cousins if I do not. It had become apparent to me,' Clemence continued as Nathan appeared to be struck dumb, 'that my money might be putting off honest men and could attract fortune hunters.'

'Why one thousand pounds?' he asked. There was, surely, a faint relaxing of that frown?

'I asked Captain Melville how much a captain in the navy might hope to be paid and then I doubled it because I thought, from what he said, that even the most indolent or unlucky might expect that much prize money in a year.'

'A captain in the navy,' he echoed. The frown had gone. The corners of his eyes were beginning to crinkle.

'Such as yourself.' A tiny, warm flame of hope was beginning to fan itself into flickering life inside her.

'Oh, dear. I am afraid, my clever Clemence, that you have miscalculated.' The flame went out with a sizzle. 'You will keep this confidential at the moment, but I will return to sea as a vice-commodore.'

'A promotion? To vice-commodore? Nathan!' And somehow she was in his arms, her own tight around his neck, and they were no longer sitting up, but were full length on the bed. 'That is wonderful!'

'I am moderately pleased,' he agreed with a grin.

'You can support a wife possessing moderate means herself, in that case?'

'Is that a proposal, Miss Ravenhurst?'

'It most certainly is, Vice-Commodore Stanier.'

He rolled on to his back, taking her with him to lie cradled against his shoulder. 'I had become so used to the idea that I could not, must not, wed you that it seems almost impossible. I am not sure I believe it now. Clemence, you are *certain* you do not want the life the Ravenhursts can give you here?'

'Certain. Now, say *yes*,' she prompted, wriggling up on her elbows so she could look into his face.

'Yes, Miss Ravenhurst. I am honoured to accept your very flattering proposal of marriage.'

'Oh.' She dropped her head so her face was buried in the soft blue silk over his right breast. 'Oh, thank goodness.' The relief rolled over her in waves as she lay there, absorbing the warmth and strength of his body.

'Might I hope for a kiss?' Nathan asked.

Suddenly very shy she mumbled, 'Yes.' And found herself rolling again, this time on to her back.

Nathan leaned on one elbow and looked down at her. 'I have dreamed of this moment. I love you very much, Clemence. I realised it as I was denying it to your aunt, knowing you were listening. It was the hardest thing I have done, crushing that feeling just as I became aware of it, knowing I was wounding you as I did so.'

'Kiss it better.' She looked up at him, awed and a little

anxious. He was very close and very big and all hers. All hers. 'I love you, too.'

She had thought, when she had dreamt of this moment, that his kiss would be familiar. But it was not like the times before when their lips had met. It was not the sudden flare of physical attraction, the heat of temper or the deliberate incitement that those kisses had been.

Nathan's mouth on hers was sure, firm, very gentle. And it was quite evident that this was a beginning, a claiming, that she was now his and he would take what she could offer him, lead her, teach her until what she could offer and ask went far beyond her imagination and experience now.

Her lips parted for him and he took possession of the heat and the soft intimacy of her mouth with lips and teeth and tongue until she was moaning and writhing against him, her fingers tight on his shoulders, her body arching, seeking. His hands stayed still, cupping her shoulders, his body held away from hers, his control absolute until he finally broke the kiss, leaving her gasping. And she saw the heat and the desire in his face.

'Clemence,' he said huskily, running his hand down the curve of her cheek. 'My beautiful Clemence.' As he sat up and looked down at the bed, his expression changed to one of rueful amusement.

Clemence sat up, too. 'Oh, my goodness. This bed looks as though we've been making love on it for hours. Did I really do that in my nightmare?'

Nathan nodded. 'I'll help you straighten it. You can't sleep on such rumpled sheets.'

'I don't want to sleep at all,' she murmured, sliding her hand into the front of his robe.

'Clemence, I am trying to be a gentleman.' His breath caught as her exploring fingertips slid over his nipple.

'No one is going to believe that who sees this bed,' she pointed out, fascinated by the effect on his breathing of running her nails down his ribs and towards his stomach. She found his navel and twirled a finger into it and he groaned.

'*Clemence!* Will you make an honest man of me very soon if I let you seduce me?'

'Just as soon as it can be arranged,' Clemence promised, attacking the sash. It was not very tightly tied and he did not appear to be wearing anything under it. Suddenly diffident, she drew her hand back.

'Sure?' She nodded. 'Scared?'

'No. Shy.' She could feel her smile wobbling, just a little.

'There is no need. Just trust me. We have been naked together before—remember the forest pool.' Nathan shrugged out of the robe and it fell on to the sheets behind him like shimmering water. 'Remember the green of the trees and the cool of the water.' His hands were on her crumpled nightgown. She shifted to help him and then it was over her head and thrown to the floor and his hands were skimming down over her breasts, the curve of her waist, to come to rest on her hip.

'Remember how the water felt, Clemence,' he murmured, bending his head to her as his hands stroked. With a shiver she curled against him, partly to hide herself from his hot blue eyes, partly to touch as much of him as she could. He was aroused; she could feel him pressed hot and hard against her belly. Instinctively she moved against him and was rewarded by the way his hands stilled, tightening around her.

Nathan eased her on to her back, firmly moving her hands away when she tried to cover herself, smiling at her until she smiled back, reassured. She began to relax. This was not frightening at all, this was— 'Nathan!' she gasped as his fingers slid into the hidden folds her hands had been shielding just a moment ago, folds that she was startled to realise were wet, hot and, 'Oh, oh, Nathan…'

'Are you sure?' he murmured, shifting his body over hers.

'Sure?' His hand was still *there*, making it almost impossible to think and then he slid one finger inside and she arched up against his palm, gasping.

'Yes, yes, I'm sure. Oh, Nathan, please….' Her body seemed to know what to do, her legs opening to cradle him. Then she felt the pressure and was not so certain.

'Look at me,' he said softly as she tensed. 'Look into my eyes, Clemence. We are going on this journey together. I have you safe.'

'Safe?' She found she could smile, her eyes widening as he rocked against her, filled her, and, just when she thought this was impossible, completed her with a thrust that took her through a flash of pain into the blissful realisation that they were one.

His face went out of focus and then came back. He was watching her, his eyes dark, his face taut with strain. 'Sweetheart? Did I hurt you?'

'Mmm.' She nodded. 'It didn't matter. Oh, I do love you.' She wriggled, trying to get used to the feeling and fascinated to discover the effect that had on Nathan. She had muscles inside as well, she realised, experimenting, and watching his jaw clench and his eyelids become heavy.

'Clemence, my love. If you do that I am going to have to move.' She did it again and he smiled and moved and she forgot everything, lost everything, in this new power driving through her.

She shifted and found she could match the rhythm, watched his face with a kind of awe as he took them deeper and deeper into whirlpool of sensation and then realised that her body was straining towards something, tightening around him, and she was gasping, desperate for something she didn't know, couldn't name and his hand slid between them again and touched her, *perfectly*, and there should have been rockets and cannons and fireworks to go with the stars and the swirling blackness, but there was Nathan's voice, joined with hers and a slow, slow tumble into peace.

'I love you.'

'I love you, too.' Clemence, wrapped in Nathan's silk robe, snuggled closer against his body, letting her fingers explore up and down his ribs.

'What a good thing you had that nightmare.' He was playing with her curls, the brush of his fingers sending delicious shivers down her spine. 'But I thought you said you had it when I wasn't around.'

'It was Street, I think. I had to speak to him and Eliza just before I went to bed and for some reason he wouldn't stop talking about the incident.'

'Last night? Why did you have to talk to them then?'

'Aunt Amelia had spoken to Street about marrying Eliza and—'

'Urgh!' Nathan sat up abruptly and clutched for his ankle. 'That damned dog has just licked me.' Clemence sat up, too. There was One-Eye, tongue lolling, watching them from beside the bed. 'How did that get in here?'

'He must have been with Eliza.'

'No.' Nathan shook his head. 'He sleeps in Street's room. Which means that either she heard you crying out from there, which is impossible, or both she and Street were down here. Which means they knew you were going to dream.'

'And she fetched you, which is a scandalous thing to do.'

'And it is very odd,' Nathan added grimly, 'but those loud cries did not attract the attention of a single one of the ladies sleeping nearby. The Ravenhursts, my love, have been plotting.'

'Dinner last night—Jessica deliberately made it informal. And Theo and Elinor and Sebastian made sure you knew I was going back to Jamaica. Aunt Amelia stopped me talking to Street about his intentions and said she would do it—she must have told him to remind me so vividly that I dreamed!'

Clemence stared at him, appalled. 'Nathan, I am so sorry—my dreadful family.' His mouth was twitching. 'You aren't angry?'

'Angry? Tomorrow I am going to kiss every one of your damned Ravenhursts, Lord Sebastian and the duchess included. They nearly tore us apart, simply by existing, now they've brought us together. And now, my love, I intend to kiss you and spend the next hour making sure you forget which continent you are on, let alone that you have a legion of interfering cousins.'

'Again?' Clemence gasped, as his hands on her body became deliciously wicked.

'And again and again and again for the rest of our lives, my love. One thing you learn as a naval officer is to take every opportunity when on leave.' His voice became muffled as he slid down, trailing kisses over the curve of her hip bone.

'Oh, yes, my love. Please, every opportunity…' And Clemence closed her eyes and surrendered to Nathan and to love.

* * * * *

Afterword

In 1817, when this book is set, the heyday of the Caribbean buccaneers was long since over. But there still remained a dangerous number of pirates, freebooters and the maritime equivalent of footpads to harass the rich trade of the islands, and the government invested considerable resources on suppressing their activities. Red Matthew McTiernan and his crew are a composite of some of these unromantic and dangerous characters.

The book I found most useful in researching THE PIRATICAL MISS RAVENHURST was *Lady Nugent's Journal of Her Residence in Jamaica from 1801 to 1805* (Institute of Jamaica 4th ed. 1966), and I have followed Lady Nugent's return voyage on *HMS Theseus* for *Orion's* route and timings almost exactly.

The fan that Nathan finds in Weymouth and gives to Clemence is real, and I found it in a country auction when I was already writing the book. It seemed such a spooky coincidence that not only was I writing about a heroine called Clemence, but that the virtues of the man destined for her on the fan so exactly matched Nathan's, that I could not resist including it.

I am indebted to Historical Romance author Joanna Maitland for the translation of the difficult eighteenth-century French verses.

The dance *La Pistole*—speed-dating for the *ton* as it struck me at the time—I learned at the Victoria & Albert Museum's wonderful Regency Evening in June 2007.

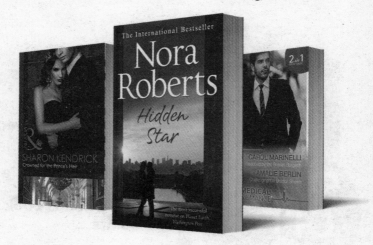